# THE FORCE
# OF DESTINY

## PHILIP DE VILLARS

PublishAmerica
Baltimore

ISBN: 978-1-60749-871-1 (softcover)
ISBN: 978-1-61582-270-6 (hardcover)
PUBLISHED BY PUBLISHAMERICA, LLLP
www.publishamerica.com
Baltimore

Printed in the United States of America

To Kay
who actually read
it

Thiel.

# PROLOGUE

The fall of 1959 was beautiful in Vienna, and the two young men were in a merry mood. The Augustinerkeller was known for its excellent grilled chicken, and the beer that had accompanied—and followed—it contributed to their good spirits. They were both students at the University of Vienna. The taller of the two, Count Giovanni Palmieri, was a handsome Italian with fine features and dark, sleek black hair that betrayed his Neapolitan and Spanish ancestry. His close friend, Philip Markham, whose rugged features and shock of unruly hair had captivated more than one lady in the city of music, was from England. He was the grandson of the Marquis of Derwent, whose title he would one day inherit.

In addition to their aristocratic birth and rather tepid Catholicism, the two friends had one other thing in common. Both of them were in love with women below their class whom their parents disapproved of. In Philip's case it was a pretty blond English girl called Jane, whom he had met in his final year at Manchester University. He corresponded with her daily and refused to be drawn into any adventures in Vienna despite many opportunities.

These opportunities were less now that Giovanni had renounced his unending pursuit of female conquests after meeting Luisa. She was German and worked for Lufthansa at Schwechat airport in Vienna. She was fair, very pretty and had a wonderful disposition. She was no great intellect and had a limited taste for the cultural delights of the Austrian capital, but she had ignited a passion in Giovanni. His eyes glistened when he talked of her candid smile, the softness of her long, blond hair and her unsuccessful attempts to imitate the German of the Viennese. But, as he sadly confided to his friend, there was no way his father, a typically bigoted and class-conscious Palmieri, would ever consent to the marriage.

"I'll marry her anyway," Giovanni insisted, banging rather too hard on the table to the annoyance of a Viennese family nearby.

"Well, I intend to marry Jane, too," Philip replied supportively.

Giovanni looked hard at his friend. "You know, Philip," he said, "we've been friends now for two years and we've had a lot of fun together. Why don't we swear an oath to marry a child from your family to one of mine? That way, we can unite the two families."

It was a quite irrational proposition for even in the late fifties marriages were no longer arranged between parents. But the beer—or perhaps the schnaps that was following it—swept away such an objection and Philip agreed enthusiastically. He picked up a knife and pricked his finger. Giovanni did likewise, and the oath was sealed in blood. It occurred to neither of them in their euphoric state that there was something, if not blasphemous, at least profane about their proceeding.

———

Giovanni was only too right about his father. He would have nothing to do with a Protestant commoner as a daughter-in-law and threatened to cut Giovanni off if he married Luisa. Her conversion to Catholicism changed nothing. Soon after, his father was diagnosed with cancer of the pancreas and died within two months. Giovanni was entertaining friends with Luisa when his mother called to tell him of his father's death. He attended the funeral but refused to participate in the family reception afterwards as Luisa was not invited. In fact, Giovanni was relieved by his father's death. Now that he was free to act as he wished, he announced to his indignant family that he intended to marry Luisa as soon as the period of mourning for his father was over.

Fate was to decide otherwise. On November 1, 1961, he and Luisa went off on a motorcycle trip in the hills around Florence. They stopped for lunch at a little restaurant, where Giovanni drank too much. He was driving his motorcycle very fast, with Luisa perched on the back, when he collided with a car that had failed to respect a stop sign. Luisa was killed on the spot, and Giovanni was taken with severe injuries to the Careggi hospital in Florence. As he lay there for months grieving over his loss, he was beset by remorse for the irresponsible conduct that had caused Luisa's death and, seeing his mother's sorrow, by guilt at his callous reaction to his father's death.

This was Giovanni's Garden of Gethsemane, but out of this mental agony came a spiritual awakening. A priest visited him almost every day, and their discussions helped Giovanni regain some serenity. With Luisa dead, his former life held no attraction for him and gradually, as he recuperated from his terrible injuries at the family's country home in Emilia Romagna, the resolution to become a priest took shape within his mind. In July 1963, he entered the *Athenaeum Pontificium Regina Apostolorum* in Rome to study for the priesthood and renounced his title.

Deprived of his own children, Giovanni developed a close relationship with the children of his sister Caterina, who had married Count Paolo della Chiesa, a member of the prestigious black nobility of Rome. Giovanni liked his brother-in-law. He was easy-going, devoid of any snobbishness and universally respected at the university and clinic where he worked, respectively, as a professor and surgeon. Caterina, however, had never forgiven him for moving the family to Florence from Rome and her closed circle of aristocratic friends.

Giovanni wondered whatever reason could have impelled Paolo to marry such a woman. They had almost nothing in common. Paolo was erudite with a broad knowledge of Italian culture, whereas Caterina liked only opera and even there he suspected that his sister was more interested in showing herself at the opera house than appreciating the music. She didn't even care much for art despite studying art history for a year and a half at Rome University. He concluded that it must have been physical attraction. Caterina had been and still was a very striking woman with dark, almost dusky features that betrayed her Neapolitan descent. They were, however, perhaps a little too angular, like those of her Spanish mother. Indeed, Caterina looked more Spanish than Italian.

The younger daughter, Carla, had inherited her mother's rather severe looks as well as her Palmieri disposition. The elder daughter, Antonietta, took after her father both in temperament and looks. She was more volatile than Paolo but she had his wit and charm, and her regular features were softened by his Italian physiognomy into a face of sensual and dazzling beauty, framed by long, dark hair that usually fell unfettered around her shoulders or was swept to one side across her full and shapely bosom.

———

Philip Markham fared better, at least in a worldly way. He married Jane in 1961 and pursued a career in the family bank, the Carlisle and District. He succeeded his father as 11th Marquis of Derwent in 1969 and in 1973 joined the Heath Government. After the defeat of the Conservatives in the 1974 election, he returned to the family bank and served as its Chairman from 1980 until his retirement in 1998 at the age of sixty. He was succeeded by his pompous but capable son, Charles.

7

There were three other children. The two girls, Louise and Marie, were quintessentially English with a greater interest in horses than men, although they both eventually married. It was only in his younger son, James, that Philip could recognize himself. He had inherited the same unruly hair and rugged features as well as Philip's facility with languages. Unlike the three others, he'd spent most summers in his youth at his French grandmother's villa in Bandol and spoke fluent French. He'd also profited from Philip's business association with the Spanish Marqués de Vincente to spend a year in Spain where he had become close friends with Vincente's son, Rodrigo. Their friendship reminded Philip of his times in Vienna with Giovanni.

James was now teaching at university in Canada, having done his Ph.D in law at the European University in Florence where he'd become fluent in Italian. Philip had always thought that, if any of his offspring were to fulfill the oath he and Giovanni had sworn so many years ago in the Augustinerkeller, it was James. But it mattered little now as Giovanni had taken holy orders and was presently Cardinal-Archbishop of Florence. It didn't occur to Philip that Giovanni was not the only Palmieri and that the force of destiny was not so easily thwarted.

# PART ONE

Sunday, June 24 to Friday, October 26, 2001

# CHAPTER 1

## Sunday, June 24, 2001

Antonietta slipped out of bed and walked towards the door of the bedroom. She could feel Giacomo's eyes following her and sensed the desire her naked body was arousing in him. She entered the bathroom. In the mirror she saw Giacomo follow her and watched him place his hands over her opulent breasts and fondle them. She felt him hard against the rounded flesh of her buttocks and let him take her. Gazing at herself having sex, her nipples hardened and she became excited. But there was little emotion in her physical pleasure. She had never been in love with Giacomo and the relationship now palled on her. It was a typical end to her affairs with men, and it disturbed her. When it was over, Antonietta returned to the bedroom and dressed.

"You're going to Mass, I suppose?" Giacomo commented, unable to hide his displeasure.

"Yes, Giacomo, I'm a practicing Catholic and I go to Mass," she replied, "whether you like it or not."

In the early days of their relationship, Antonietta had tried to understand Giacomo's radical views and even sympathized with some of them, but now she was tired of playing along. So she gave him a quick kiss and made to leave.

"See you this afternoon at the *Calcio* tournament[1]," she called over her shoulder. "Don't be late."

Antonietta shut the door of the apartment building behind her and started on the long walk to her apartment. The streets of Florence were basking in the hot June sun. In the distance over the railway tracks rose the imposing Fortezza di Basso. It was a monumental complex that had been constructed in the sixteenth century to protect the city, but it had never been attacked. Now it was the main exhibition center in Florence, and a modern pavilion, which Antonietta detested, had been built in the center of the great square inside the former fortress.

Today was the feast day of San Giovanni, the patron saint of Florence, and Antonietta felt a thrill of anticipation at the full schedule ahead of her. After Mass, there would be lunch with her family and then an afternoon with Giacomo watching their team from Santa Maria Novella play Santo Spirito in the final of the *Calcio* competition. Around six o'clock, she would attend the reception at the Archbishop's Palace and, finally, in the evening she would meet friends to watch the traditional firework display from the Piazzale Michelangelo on the other side of the Arno.

But Antonietta was not entirely happy. She was ashamed that she hadn't yet found the courage to end her relationship with Giacomo. It was easy to tell herself that she didn't want to spoil the day's festivities, or that she didn't want to hurt him. In truth, her inaction came from more selfish reasons. She no longer felt the strong physical attraction for Giacomo she'd experienced at the start of their relationship, but he still tended to her sexual needs. This was important for Antonietta.

By now, she'd reached her apartment between the Hotel Goldoni and the Piazza of the same name. She noticed two men, older but still attractive, in a Mercedes convertible staring at her. Yes, I'm beautiful, she thought, and I can have any man I want. But what's the use when it always ends like this? She made the firm resolution to break with Giacomo the following Wednesday. There was no point in ruining today's celebrations, and she was busy at work on Monday and Tuesday helping to put the finishing touches to a new multilingual dictionary. This would also give her time to decide how to do it.

Once in her apartment, Antonietta turned on the answering machine. There were a number of calls, including one from her mother. She would have to think of a story to justify her absence from the apartment that night. Her mother didn't approve of her "sleeping around," as she put it. She began to feel regret at agreeing to meet the family, particularly as her younger brother, Giovanni, would be there with his new wife, a stuck-up nonentity who never let you forget that she was the daughter of the Marquis di Manasca-Torelli. However, she would be glad to see her father, and he would make up for the others.

Although she was often infuriated by her mother, Antonietta had to admit that she wasn't entirely wrong in her criticism of her daughter's lifestyle. Her life was aimless. There seemed to be no meaning to anything she did. She had taken a joint degree in Italian and Economics at the University of Florence, but she didn't really know why. Luckily, it had enabled her to find a job at the prestigious Crusca Academy[2], but she no longer had any desire to continue working there. She would be twenty-four in two weeks time and had no idea what she wanted to do. That's why she'd followed a girlfriend's advice and decided to continue her studies in Quebec. Ironically, the Duke of Messina, a family friend and Antonietta's godfather, had just been appointed Italian Ambassador to Canada.

It was in her personal life that Antonietta most felt the lack of meaning. Only once had she thought herself to be in love, and she had been betrayed. She'd met Mario, two years her senior, shortly after starting her studies at the university. It was her first sexual experience with a man and, although it was disappointing, she'd fallen in love with the dark, tall law student. Then, the following April, friends told her that Mario was boasting to all and sundry that he'd bedded a countess. Antonietta was revolted and immediately ended the relationship, resolving never to mix out of her class again.

The result was her affair with Alessandro Ottoreschi, the oldest son of Marquis Ottoreschi. For nearly a year, the young aristocrats had roamed the nightclubs, roared around Tuscany in a Lamborghini and made love amid bottles of champagne. Then, one rainy March day, Antonietta realized that Alessandro and his lifestyle didn't fulfill her. She was bored, and she left him. After that, she'd flitted from man to man, but none of them had been able to satisfy the complex yearning within her. Worse still, none had bestowed on her the same exquisite sexual pleasure she'd experienced at school with Dana. That was even more disturbing.

Beset by these depressing thoughts, Antonietta finished dressing for Mass. She replaced the string and deeply-cut bra with more decent lingerie, and the tight jeans and tea-shirt with an elegant blouse and jacket. She wore a skirt rather than pants, which she felt were too masculine. She left her apartment and walked slowly along the Via della Vigna Nuova and the Via dei Tornabuoni, looking at the shops and their elegant wares. Some were open and fleecing unsuspecting tourists. Few Florentines would be shopping this day. Finally, she reached the Piazza del Duomo, where she met her family at the steps of the Basilica di Santa Maria del Fiore.

Her mother asked her where she'd been the previous evening. Antonietta lied and said she'd gone to the cinema. Renata smirked and asked which film she'd seen. Antonietta hesitated, trying desperately to remember what films were playing in Florence. She was rescued by her father, who ushered them all up the steps into the Basilica.

"She was with that Communist last night," Renata whispered to Giovanni.

Antonietta genuflected before the altar and knelt down in her pew to say a prayer. The rest of her family did the same, but her mother and Renata quickly crossed themselves and started looking around to see who they knew in the congregation. Antonietta remained an unusually long time on her knees. She desperately needed some direction, some meaning to her life, and she prayed for help to find it. Her father, who was seated next to her, gave her a look of concern.

"Are you alright, Antonietta?" he asked. Antonietta was amused. "You're not used to seeing me pray?"

"Well, not quite so long," he admitted. "I was praying for my knight in shining armor," she told him. Her father looked relieved. "Not Giacomo, then?" "No, Father, not Giacomo."

After Mass, the family congregated outside the Basilica and made their way down to Paolo's favorite restaurant in the historic city. It served Tuscan fare. Once they'd finished ordering, Giovanni complained that they always went to Italian restaurants.

"What do you expect," Antonietta observed sarcastically. "We're in Italy."

Renata came to her husband's aid. "There are other types of restaurants in Florence as well, Antonietta. There's a lovely French restaurant in the Via Romana."

"I prefer Italian food," Antonietta replied. "It's lighter and more natural than all those heavy French sauces. I also prefer Italian wines."

"How can you talk such nonsense," said Giovanni in his best pompous manner. "Nothing compares with a good Bordeaux or a good Burgundy."

"Just because we don't classify our vineyards or list our "grand crus" like the French doesn't mean our wines are inferior," Antonietta retorted.

Giovanni was about to respond but stopped on a look from his father.

"What's on at the opera?" Paolo asked, changing the subject of the conversation.

"*Adriana Lecouvreur*!" Caterina expostulated. "It only has one tune, and the heroine's immoral."

Paolo burst out laughing. "My darling," he said, putting an arm around his indignant wife, "if we took all the immoral heroines out of opera, there wouldn't be many left."

Mollified by her husband's gesture of affection, Caterina let herself be teased, and the rest of the meal passed off civilly. Once Paolo had finished his expresso, he left for the hospital to visit his patients. Giovanni and Renata left shortly afterwards. They kissed Caterina warmly and Antonietta somewhat frostily. Antonietta was preparing to leave as well when her mother said that she wanted to talk to her.

Antonietta sighed, trying to hide her irritation. "Mother, must we have this discussion yet again? I'm old enough to decide how to lead my life."

"Antonietta, I know you think it's none of my business, but the way you live your life affects the way people think of our whole family. When they see you always with a different man and, apart from Alessandro Ottoreschi, none from our class, they judge all of us badly. Remember that you are a Countess della Chiesa[3]."

"I'm not always with a different man," Antonietta protested. "I've been with Giacomo since last October."

"Do you think that helps?" Caterina's voice trembled with scorn. "Why can't you be more like Carla? At least she knows what's expected of her."

"What's that, Mother?" Antonietta tried not to sound insolent.

"She keeps to her own class and married young, instead of meandering promiscuously through life without any purpose like you're doing at present, and in poor company at that. Do you realize how scandalized people were that she married first even though she's the younger daughter?"

"I don't see anything commendable in giving up university to marry on your nineteenth birthday."

"Perhaps *you* don't, but that's what well brought-up aristocratic girls do. Look at Renata. She was only twenty when she married Giovanni."

Antonietta was tempted to make an unflattering comment about her sister-in-law but stopped herself. Silence was the best way to deal with her mother when she was in one of these moods. Any riposte would only infuriate her all the more.

"If only you'd gone to the Sacred Heart in Rome, like Carla and Renata, instead of that convent in England. It was your uncle's silly idea. Ever since he was Papal Nuncio there, he's been besotted by the English. Goodness knows why. It's all very well for Giovanni to go on about his English Catholic friend, Philip Something or Other, but it's still a Protestant country and they think differently from us. They don't have the same moral sense."

This was the first time Antonietta had heard mention of Giovanni's English Catholic friend. She wondered who he was but suppressed her curiosity. It was better to let her mother finish or she would be late for the *Calcio*. Little did she realize how much grief she would have saved herself, had she asked about Philip Markham.

"Look at the way you dress," her mother went on. "I mean, today you're respectable, but otherwise those tight jeans and blouses you wear are indecent. They're provocative, and vulgar too."

Caterina finished her coffee and stood up to go. "I want you to talk to your Uncle Giovanni," she told Antonietta. "Perhaps you'll listen to him."

"As you wish." Antonietta liked her uncle, and she wasn't averse to seeking the Cardinal's counsel. Her life indeed lacked purpose, and she was tired of the void she never managed to fill.

"Good. He'll see you after the reception at the Archbishop's Palace, around eight."

They parted, and Antonietta hurried off to meet Giacomo and watch the final game of the *Calcio*.

———

Many thousands of kilometers away, in Quebec, the Markham family was preparing to go to Mass at the church in the nearby town of Saint-Sauveur.

"Mommy, I'm hungry," complained Peter, the Markham's nine year-old son.

"So am I," his six year-old sister chimed in.

Their mother was unmoved. "You can eat after Mass. You know we fast before taking communion."

The children both made a face and looked to their father for support.

"I don't see the point, Veronica, of making Susanna fast. She's not even going to take communion."

Veronica looked sternly at her husband. "James," she replied, "it's good for her to prepare herself for when she does take communion."

James let the matter drop. He found his wife's insistence on fasting before taking communion quite absurd as the Church no longer required it. It was just another of her religious excesses. He went upstairs to shave and dress.

"James, hurry up or we'll be late," he heard his wife say as she mounted the stairs. There was plenty of time, but Veronica lived in constant fear of being late for Mass. Irritated, James decided to have a little revenge.

"Did I ever tell you the joke about Marie-Chantal and Gérard?" he asked.

Veronica frowned. "I hope it's not one that Bill Leaman told you. If so, I don't want to hear it."

"No, I heard it years ago from my French grandmother." This was a lie, but it was the only way to get Veronica' attention. His wife put on a long-suffering look, and James embarked on his joke.

"Marie-Chantal and Gérard are getting ready to go to Mass, like us, and he asks her to give him a blowjob. Marie-Chantal looks at him in horror and exclaims, 'But Gérard, you know I always fast before taking communion'."

Veronica was predictably outraged, as James had intended. "That's absolutely disgusting, James, and typically French."

You didn't always find it disgusting, James thought with regret. Veronica's taste for sex, and in particular for any but the most conventional practices, had waned after their marriage as she became increasingly religious. Their sexual relations, which in any case were very occasional, had now ceased altogether. If James had insisted, no doubt Veronica would have accommodated him, but the idea of making love to a reluctant woman was repugnant to him. So, he contented himself with extra-marital flings with willing South American girls on his frequent trips to the southern hemisphere.

The family set off and was soon ensconced in the church. It was a typical Quebec small-town church, large and imposing but almost empty. Few French Quebeckers now had any time for the Catholic religion. James sometimes wondered whether the priest did either, given the speed with which he hurried through Mass. It normally took him just under thirty minutes, which James found quite sufficient. Unfortunately, Veronica insisted on saying a few supplementary prayers after Mass to compensate.

Paying scant attention to the liturgy, James reflected on his life. On the whole, he was satisfied with his choice of career. Initially, he'd intended to join the family bank, but after finishing his doctorate in European Union Law, he'd decided to give academia a try. He enjoyed the freedom it gave him and, although he didn't particularly enjoy the teaching, he found legal research interesting and had acquired an international reputation as an expert on the institutional law of the European Union. He was now a full professor[4] at the National Institute for International Studies, which was situated in the charming town of Saint-Sauveur in Quebec, and he had just become Head of the Law and International Relations Section[5]

17

His decision to come to Canada had been vigorously opposed by his mother. Despite her modest origins, Lady Derwent[6] was very conscious of her position. "You won't even be able to use your title in Canada," she'd grumbled. "They'll just call you Mr. Markham." This was irrelevant for James as the only time he used his title was to get into fully-booked restaurants. Most restaurateurs in England couldn't resist having a lord[7] at one of their tables. By contrast, his father had approved his choice.

James' thoughts returned to the Institute. He was worried about the present Rector. Harold Winstone had come from the Department of Foreign Affairs three years ago to take over from Tom Buchanan, the colorful American who had built up the Institute from an inauspicious beginning into an internationally renowned college. In James' view, it was a bad appointment. The Rector had the final say in hiring new professors and almost complete discretion over the Institute's finances. In both areas, James felt that Winstone had made serious mistakes.

James was wrenched from his introspection by a fierce whisper from his wife. "James, you're not paying attention to Mass. That's a dreadful example for the children."

James looked up at the altar and saw to his surprise that the priest had finished his homily and was starting on the prayer that led up to the consecration. Suppressing a sigh, he knelt down to follow the liturgy, but his adopted piety was disturbed by his daughter tugging at his arm. He turned and saw her conniving grin.

"Behave yourself, you little heathen," he whispered. "Mommy thinks you're the heathen," she whispered back. Veronica gave both of them a baleful look and they returned to their devotions.

Thank God for the children, James thought. He was very fond of them and infinitely relieved that neither showed any inclination to emulate their mother's excessive piety. They, rather than Catholic conviction, were the primary reason why he stayed in such a sterile marriage.

———

Antonietta arrived late, and somewhat out of breath, at her uncle's reception. The *Calcio* game had lasted longer than anticipated, and afterwards she and Giacomo had joined their friends for a celebratory drink. Their team, Santa Maria Novella, had won the tournament. She was a little tipsy and hoped it didn't show.

Her uncle, the Cardinal-Archbishop, greeted her at the foot of the imposing circular staircase that led up to the large, ornate reception room on the second floor[8]. His formal attire contrasted sharply with his ever youthful looks. True, the sleek dark hair of his youth was thinner now and streaked with grey, but his face was little marked by his sixty-three years and, with finely chiseled features, he was still a handsome man. He exuded gravity in his cardinal's robes, but as he smiled at his niece, his eyes twinkling with gentle irony, Antonietta could feel the human warmth beneath the façade.

"I want a talk with you after the reception, young lady," he told her with mock severity. As it was a public occasion, she kissed his episcopal ring.

"Yes, Mother told me." She gave her uncle a radiant smile and whispered, "I'm afraid I'm a little tipsy."

Her uncle chuckled. "Does that mean Santa Maria Novella won?"

Antonietta nodded in reply and made her way upstairs to the reception. Her parents were already there and she joined them. Her father offered to fetch her a glass of champagne. Antonietta refused. She didn't particularly like champagne and anyway she'd drunk enough with her friends.

"Look, Antonietta." Her mother pointed towards a group of young men talking and laughing in the middle of the room. "There's Count Guardini's son and the nephew of the Marquis di Lescia. Why don't you go and talk to them?"

"Are you trying to marry me off again, Mother?"

"No, not at all," her mother protested without much conviction. "I just like to see you mixing with young people from your own class."

Antonietta decided to be cooperative. She was not ready for another pointless confrontation with her mother, so she wandered off and joined the young men. Rodolfo Guardini greeted her with a broad smile.

"Your team won, I hear. Why aren't you celebrating?"

"I've already celebrated enough," Antonietta replied. "If I have another drink, I'll probably disgrace myself."

"I'd like to see that," remarked Fabio di Lescia, and the assembled group of young men laughed uproariously. Antonietta walked away in disgust and stumbled upon her brother, Giovanni, and his wife. Things were going from bad to worse, she thought to herself.

"How was the tournament?" her brother asked.

Antonietta knew Giovanni had no interest in the *Calcio* and replied simply that her team had won. The conversation dragged on for a few more minutes before Giovanni and Renata moved on to mingle with other guests. Her sister-in-law hadn't said a single word to her. At least she could pretend not to dislike me, Antonietta thought sadly. If it weren't for the meeting with her uncle, she would have left the reception.

"Antonietta!" She turned round to see the Duke of Messina beaming at her. "I hear you're going to study in Canada?"

"Yes, but my mother thinks it's a crazy idea."

"Not at all. Canada is a marvelous country. I hope you'll come and visit me in Ottawa."

"Tell me about Quebec," Antonietta asked.

The Duke obliged. He was enthusiastic as he talked about Montreal, the largest French-speaking city outside France, the capital, Quebec City, with its historic buildings and quaint, narrow streets, and the beauty of the Gaspésie. When she told him that she would be in the Laurentians, his eyes lit up.

"Beautiful area. The best food you'll find outside of Italy," he exclaimed, "There's a little town called Saint-Sauveur that has a whole street full of excellent restaurants."

"Better than Paris, Don Alfredo?" Antonietta asked pointedly.

The Duke smiled. "If I remember our discussion about French cuisine, that's a loaded question. So, I'll let you be your own judge."

Antonietta explained that she was going to the National Institute of International Studies, which was located right in Saint-Sauveur. She intended to take some international finance and economics courses and perhaps a course on the European Union.

"I wouldn't mind trying for a diplomatic career once I'm finished," she told the Duke.

"That's a splendid idea. Putting your beauty at the service of your country. You can count on my help."

Antonietta couldn't have known the bitter irony of the Duke's last remark. He would indeed help her, but it was help that would usher in the darkest period of her life.

The guests began to leave. Cardinal Palmieri came up to his niece and invited her into his private quarters on the second floor. "This is your mother's idea," he told her, motioning Antonietta to sit down, "I don't particularly like playing the family priest, as you well know."

He walked over to a small fridge and took out a bottle of Soave Bolla. He poured a glass for each of them. The sight of her uncle in his cardinal's robes acting as barman caused Antonietta to burst out laughing. He didn't share her amusement.

"Even Princes of the Church have a right to enjoy the good things of life," he said with an air of reproach, "and that includes drinking a glass of chilled Italian white wine."

"I agree, Uncle, but you must admit that it's an unusual sight to see a cardinal pouring out drinks."

They toasted each other and chatted idly for a while. Giovanni was in no hurry to bring up the subject of Antonietta's lifestyle, but after two glasses of Soave Bolla, Antonietta protested that if they didn't have their serious talk soon, she wouldn't be in a fit state. Reluctantly, her uncle agreed. He asked her if there was a reason why she couldn't establish a lasting relationship with a man. Antonietta blushed.

"No, I'm not referring to that episode at the boarding school in England," the Cardinal assured her hurriedly. "I'm sure that has nothing to do with it." Sensing his niece's disarray, Giovanni put his arm around her. "Have you never felt real passion?" he asked.

"What is real passion?"

"An overwhelming attraction to another person that is at once physical and emotional and which impels you to surrender yourself completely to that person."

"And love?

"The more serene happiness of wanting to be with someone and care for that person."

"Does one lead to the other?" There was a plaintive note in Antonietta's voice.

"Ideally, yes," her uncle replied, "although in Romeo and Juliet, Shakespeare tells us that the greater the passion, the more likely it is to exhaust itself. 'Love moderately' was the priest's advice to the young couple."

"Do you agree with him, Uncle?"

"There's some truth in what he says," the Cardinal replied, "but you don't really have a choice. If you're smitten by a real passion, it's almost impossible to resist."

Antonietta was surprised by her uncle's candor. She couldn't resist teasing him. "Those are hardly the words one expects to hear from the Cardinal-

Archbishop of Florence. Mother would be shocked!"

Giovanni laughed. "Perhaps, but don't forget that before I became a priest, I was a young man who enjoyed life to the full."

Antonietta looked at him with curiosity for she'd heard rumors about her uncle's passionate love affair in his youth with a German girl. However, the Cardinal was not prepared to divulge more. "We're not here to discuss my youthful ways but your's," he reminded her. "That is, if you want to discuss them with me."

Antonietta thought for a moment. She was reluctant to talk about her personal life, even with an uncle she adored, but she felt the need to tell someone about the emptiness within her.

"You asked me whether I've ever felt real passion. The answer is not in the way you describe it. I feel attraction to a man, but it's purely physical. Every time I hope the relationship will lead to some emotional involvement, but it never does. The physical passion eventually exhausts itself, and there's nothing left but a terrible void. It's very depressing, and it worries me."

"So you've never been in love?"

"Once I thought I was in love, but I was betrayed."

Antonietta recounted her experience with Mario.

"The result was I took up with the son of Marquis Ottoreschi, Alessandro, but that didn't work either. It was a meaningless relationship, pure self-indulgence all the way. They're all like that, the men of my class. So when Alessandro asked me to marry him, I refused. Mother has never forgiven me."

Antonietta turned her eyes, full of melancholy, on her uncle. "What am I to do?" she asked.

"Well, first of all, there's no need for you to feel depressed. You know, you can't force emotional attachment, and if you haven't experienced it yet, it's because you haven't met the right man."

"It's taking a long time," Antonietta complained.

"There's a reason for that. Many people fool themselves that they have an emotional attachment to another person when in reality it's just physical infatuation. Look at all those Hollywood film stars. They divorce, remarry, divorce again with depressing regularity, and each time they fool themselves into believing that they've found true love. Your character is too forthright to deceive yourself in this way, and you should be grateful for that. It will save you from making a serious mistake that, as a Catholic, you wouldn't be able to remedy."

"Secondly, Antonietta," her uncle continued, "you're still young. There's plenty of time for you to meet a man to whom you're both physically and emotionally attracted."

"Mother doesn't think so. She thinks I should have married at nineteen like Carla."

"Rushing into marriage is not a solution for you. Carla's a different person. She finds her fulfillment in being a Roman aristocrat. I doubt whether there's real passion between her and Filiberto, or indeed between Giovanni and Renata. You have a passionate nature, and an aristocratic marriage by itself wouldn't fulfill you."

Antonietta took comfort from her uncle's words, but she still wanted his advice on her immediate plans.

"You've made a good decision to leave Italy for a while," he told her, "and Canada is an excellent choice. You'll meet a different kind of person, encounter different attitudes. It'll be a refreshing experience that will do you a lot of good. How long are you going for?"

"Two years. One year to do the courses and one year to complete the Master's thesis."

"Well, don't come back to Italy too often, forget your life here and, whatever you do, keep your background a secret. No-one needs to know you're a countess. Canadians probably wouldn't care one way or another, but don't take chances."

Her uncle stood up. "Now, young lady, you must leave me to my devotions. It's time for vespers."

Antonietta kissed her uncle and prepared to leave.

"Are you going to watch the firework display?" the Cardinal asked.

"Yes, but it's not until eleven. I've got plenty of time."

Antonietta turned towards the door, but her uncle called her back. "Don't tell your mother about our conversation. I don't think it's quite what she had in mind."

Antonietta laughed. "Don't worry, I won't," she replied.

Antonietta made her way down the baroque stairway and, gazing upon the austere faces of her uncle's predecessors, realized how different he was from them. It suddenly occurred to her that he was more like a della Chiesa than a Palmieri. Yet, despite the comfort she'd drawn from his words, nothing had changed in her life.

Would it ever? she asked herself despondently.

# CHAPTER 2
## Friday, June 29, 2001

James herded his two children into the Mercedes station wagon and stowed their equipment in the back. It was the last day of school, and both were going to play soccer. They waved goodbye to Veronica and proceeded in the direction of St. Jérôme towards the children's school. It was a beautiful day, but during the southward drive the scenery was not particularly impressive. Prévost was the real beginning of the Laurentians, and from there northwards up to Saint-Sauveur and beyond, the colorful forests and towering hills always impressed James with their commanding beauty.

Having settled his two children, James drove towards Saint-Sauveur and the Institute. It was an important day as there was a meeting of the Faculty Promotion Committee to consider Len Flint's application to become a full professor. It was an early application, and a refusal to grant it would mean that the candidate couldn't apply again before three more academic years had elapsed. Effectively, this meant Flint would have to wait another four years.

Len Flint was an amiable but mediocre academic whom the newly-appointed Senior Dean, Roy Arbuthnot, had taken under his wing. Arbuthnot was a dour Presbyterian Scot whom James distrusted. He was popularly referred to as "HB." James' friend and colleague, Bill Leaman, maintained that the initials stood for "Hard Balls," but James believed it was because Arbuthnot was as thick-skinned as the lead in pencils. Whatever the origin of his nickname, HB was unscrupulous and manipulative. In addition to being Senior Dean, he'd also managed to get himself appointed Chair of the Ethics Committee, which dealt with cases of improper behavior involving faculty members.

James had problems with Flint's application. The scholarship offered in its support was meager and had only appeared in second-rate journals. True, the outside referees were unanimous in their positive evaluation of Flint's work, but all were former classmates of Arbuthnot from NUC, where he'd obtained his doctorate. Unfortunately for HB, James had obtained two references from world-renowned professors at the Harvard School of Business demolishing Flint's submissions. As Head of Section, he had the right to appeal to outside referees to complete the application although this was rarely done.

The worst problem, however, was the veracity of the application. James had compared both the co-authored articles and the supposedly sole-authored papers with some of Arbuthnot's work, and he'd observed that the turn of phrase in all three was identical. James suspected that Flint had written little by himself. This type of academic fraud was becoming quite widespread, and one leading law journal, the *European Observer,* now employed a stylistic expert to vet submissions for this vice. James had sent Flint's and a couple of Arbuthnot's papers to the expert and he had confirmed James' suspicions.

In reality, however, Flint's promotion was a sideshow compared to the real issue at stake. HB was determined to assert his power, and what better way than to demonstrate to all and sundry that he could obtain promotion to full professor for whomever he wished. This would give him a chance to garner the support he needed to dominate the Institute and its weak, inept Rector. James was determined to prevent this.

It wouldn't be easy. The committee was likely to look favorably on the application. Arbuthnot would obviously support it, Hamid Khan was obliged to do so as the Head of the Finance, Economics and Business Section to which Flint belonged. The member appointed by Winstone, Georges Campeau from the Languages and Culture Section, was a friend of Flint's. Pierre Forget, the Section Head of LAC, might be persuaded and the member elected by the faculty, Saleema Nadjani, was a brilliant and ambitious young accounting professor from Tunisia who had little time for mediocrity. So, the best scenario was three votes against, including his own, which left Winstone as Chair with a casting vote. By convention, the Rector normally supported the Section Head, and the mere inadequacy of the application would not be enough to persuade him to do otherwise.

So, James was obliged to go one step further and make the charge of academic fraud. But how much would the opinion of an expert working for a British law journal count against the protestations of innocence from a senior member of the faculty? Even to suggest such fraud in open committee might seem outrageous and earn James the censure of many of his colleagues and

HB their sympathy. The result would be exactly the opposite of what James intended. But, at the same time, he was convinced that only the fear of an academic scandal would move Winstone to abandon Arbuthnot's protégé.

James thought for a few minutes and then decided to talk to the Rector alone before the meeting. If he could frighten him into at least abstaining, the application could be denied on a three-to-three split.

Winstone was not pleased to see him. "Isn't this a little irregular?" he said stiffly, "canvassing the Chair of a meeting just before it starts."

James met and held the Rector's cold stare. It was essential to convey an air of confidence and resolve. "I think not, under the circumstances," he replied. "I believe that a decision in favor of Len could lead to an academic scandal."

"What do you mean?" the Rector asked. He was clearly nervous.

"I don't believe that Len had any significant part in writing the papers he's submitted in support of his application."

James continued to look fixedly at Winstone, but the Rector's initial nervousness was giving way to anger. "Whatever makes you say something so preposterous?" he said, raising his voice almost to a shout.

"I've compared the co-authored papers, the papers Flint supposedly wrote himself and some of Roy's own work, and it's clear that they're all written by the same person. You can be sure it's not Flint."

"Listen, James," Winstone replied. The tone was calmer but hostile. "I think you're overreaching yourself. How dare you presume to cast doubts on a colleague's honesty."

"It's not just my opinion." James maintained a look of steely resolve, but inwardly he was dismayed by Winstone's resilience. "I have a report from a stylistic expert who works for a top law journal."

James handed the report to Winstone, who perused it briefly. His reaction was not encouraging. "You have the audacity to send work done by your colleagues to some British so-called expert and expect me to join in your little war against Roy Arbuthnot. I want you out of my office immediately."

This was the crucial instant. James had gone too far to back down but not far enough to attain his goal. He made his last play.

"You're the Rector and responsible for what goes on here. If you read the papers, you will see that I'm right. If you refuse to do your duty, I'll have no alternative, *if Flint is promoted,* but to send the papers in question and the report to the Quebec Ministry of Education."

Winstone's anger evaporated. "You wouldn't do that," he gasped.

James had won. "I'll see you in the meeting," he said curtly and left the Rector's office.

———

That same day, Antonietta ended her relationship with Giacomo. He was hurt and bitter.

"You're just a little snob," he shouted, "What you really mean is that the son of a cobbler isn't good enough for a high and mighty countess."

"That's not true, that's not what I think," Antonietta protested. "If you'd listen instead of shouting, the problem is…"

Giacomo was in no mood to listen. "You and your fascist aristocratic friends, you think you're above everyone just because some whore in the past slept with a Pope and got her family a title."

The allusion to Valeria della Chiesa and the origin of her family's title infuriated Antonietta. She was no longer prepared to spare Giacomo's feelings. "Alright, if that's what you want me to say, it's true. We come from two different worlds with different values and ideas, and we could never have overcome those differences."

"Hour's is a world of undeserved privilege. You're parasites who live well on the backs of the people, to whom you feed religion to keep them quiet. You have no values other than self-indulgence, arrogance and hypocrisy."

"That's ridiculous, one-sided nonsense," Antonietta replied acidly. "Your view of the people is as idealized as your idea of the aristocracy is a caricature. Your people, as you insist on calling them, are no more perfect or imperfect than we are."

"At least they're not decadent and egoistical monsters."

"Oh really." Antonietta's voice dripped with sarcasm. "Decadence and egoism are a matter of opportunity, my dear Giacomo. Look at your beloved Communist countries. Immediately the heroic people took over from their aristocratic or bourgeois predecessors, the first thing they did was to establish their own privileged class, which was as decadent and egoistical as any of us. The only difference is that in our countries most people live decently. Your Communist aristocrats reduced everyone to poverty. So keep your stupid ideological tripe to yourself."

Giacomo was silent in the face of Antonietta's angry outburst. He knew it was finished between them, but he couldn't resist one last jibe. "Well, I hope you enjoyed your little fling with someone from the working class."

Antonietta turned to leave but looked back at Giacomo, her eyes dimmed by sadness. "However unrealistic, I wanted it to work out, Giacomo. That's the truth, even if you don't believe me."

Giacomo made no reply and Antonietta left. It was a dreary day. The beautiful weather that had blessed the Feast of San Giovanni had turned to rain, and it was unseasonably cold. Antonietta had left work early for her unhappy meeting with Giacomo, and now she wondered what she would do with the rest of the afternoon. She wandered back to her apartment along the route she'd always taken during the eight months of her relationship with Giacomo. She looked up at the Fortezza di Basso looming before her. Perhaps it was the gloomy weather, but now she agreed with her mother that it was an eyesore. Even the streets seemed dank and devoid of life. She was glad to be leaving Florence. The city now oppressed her.

Antonietta reached her apartment but the prospect of sitting alone with only her regrets for company was too depressing. So, she decided to cheer herself up by going on a spending spree among the boutiques of Santa Maria Novella. In any case, she needed new clothes for Canada. She made for Armani on the Via dei Tornabuoni. A saleswoman approached and insisted on her inspecting the whole new collection, but there was nothing she liked.

"Perhaps something a little less expensive," the woman suggested with a smirk.

Antonietta caught the insinuation and was about to put the woman in her place when the manageress came over. She was a confidante of Antonietta's mother.

"Can I be of assistance?" she asked Antonietta.

"I was suggesting to the young lady that perhaps she might like to see our less expensive offerings," the saleswoman interjected in the same insolent tone.

The manageress gave her employee a dismissive look. "I don't think money is a problem for the Countess," she remarked tartly.

The saleswoman turned white, realizing her blunder and fearing for her employment.

"If you want something more trendy, Countess, you should try the Emporium Armani," the manageress told Antonietta.

She followed this advice and made her way along the Via Strozzi to the square of the same name and entered the Emporium. There she found a classic but low-cut evening gown with slits up the side that exposed the thighs. She took it to a young sales clerk and asked to try it on. The girl indicated the changing room and, to Antonietta's discomfiture, followed her. Rather self-consciously, Antonietta stripped down to her extremely skimpy underwear. The young girl gasped.

"What's the matter," Antonietta asked tersely, irritated but also troubled by the girl's reaction.

"I apologize, Signora," the girl stammered, "It's just that…that you're so beautiful."

Antonietta looked at the girl suspiciously, but she saw only innocent admiration. Quickly she changed her tone. "Thank you, Signorina," she said with a smile.

She put on the dress and looked at herself in the mirror. It was perfect: classic and yet provocatively sexy.

"There's a longer mirror outside," the girl said, her eyes fixed on Antonietta in wonder.

Antonietta followed her out of the changing room. A middle-aged man, who was with his young mistress, stared at her. The woman noticed and glanced at Antonietta with rancor. "Look at me, Giorgio," she told her lover. With noticeable reluctance, the man took his eyes off Antonietta.

"Why don't you try the red one," the salesgirl suggested to Antonietta.

Antonietta laughed. "Isn't that a bit too much," she said. "I'd look like a whore."

But the very idea appealed to her. She returned to the changing room, this time alone, and put on the red dress. The effect was electric, but Antonietta was not completely satisfied. She needed a new bra that would lift up her breasts and flaunt them as befitted such a dress. She changed back, took the two dresses and paid for them. The young girl, still overcome by Antonietta's beauty, made a mess of wrapping them. She apologized profusely.

"It doesn't matter," Antonietta said with a smile, giving the girl a five thousand lira tip.

She left the Emporium and strolled towards the Piazza della Repubblica, where she purchased a newspaper from a kiosk and sat down in a cafe to read it. The waiter came and offered a cup of coffee. Antonietta didn't share the

Italian mania for drinking coffee at all times of the day and ordered a glass of red wine instead. The waiter brought it with an air of disapproval.

After Antonietta left the café, she made her way to her favorite shop for lingerie, Intissimi. She picked out two bra's that would lift up her breasts and barely cover her nipples, a couple of thongs and variously colored strings. She preferred a string to a thong as the feel of it between her thighs was more sensual, but it was also less comfortable. She took this collection of erotic lingerie to the nearest sales clerk, who was in early middle age and attractive. The woman gave Antonietta a sultry look and undressed her with her eyes.

"Why don't you try on the bra's?" she asked, staring shamelessly at Antonietta's voluptuous bosom, "I think they may be too small."

There was no mistaking the real intention behind the woman's honeyed words, but they caught Antonietta off guard. Despite herself, there was a moment of temptation and then revulsion at the way the woman was leering at her.

"No, thank you," she replied. "I like them a size too small."

The woman shrugged and took an inordinate time to process the bill. Antonietta was desperate to leave the shop and nearly departed without her purchases. It took considerable effort to wait patiently while her libidinous admirer placed the lingerie in a box.

"Enjoy your purchase," the woman said with a seductive tone in her voice when she finally handed over the box.

Without replying, Antonietta grasped it and fled from the store. She'd intended to go on to the Piazza del Duomo to buy some shoes at Marco Candido, but the episode with the lesbian shop assistant was too disturbing. The fact that she had momentarily been tempted by the woman's veiled invitation raised her fears about her own sexuality. It was all the worse now that she'd just registered yet another failure in her relations with men. So, she cut through to the Piazza Santa Maria Novella and the Dominican Basilica of the same name. She lit a candle, knelt in a side chapel dedicated to Our Lady and recited the *Memorare*[9]. She prayed that she would meet a man who would fill the void in her life and still her fears.

———

Winstone called the meeting of FPC to order and the deliberations began with Hamid extolling the collegial virtues of Len Flint, his devoted service to the FEB Section and, almost as an afterthought, his academic record. He was followed by Arbuthnot, who placed particular emphasis on Flint's scholarship and the excellent references it had obtained. Neither Hamid nor HB mentioned the negative reports from Harvard. This was a clever strategy as it made it more difficult for James to bring them up. Happily for James, the third speaker, Georges Campeau, attacked him over the reports.

"Just because you have a few friends in Harvard doesn't mean we have to swallow what they say," he said, wagging his finger at James.

Campeau's stupidity gave James the perfect opportunity to introduce the reports. He seized the occasion.

"Firstly, Georges," he replied with mock collegiality, "these people are not my friends. I don't know them, but, as they're widely recognized experts in the field of business strategy, I assume Roy does."

James looked at Arbuthnot, who unwillingly nodded his assent.

"Secondly," he went on in the same friendly tone, "I'm not asking you to swallow anything. It merely seemed to me that the referees chosen by Len were, how shall I put it, a little inadequate. After all, one of them isn't even a full professor, and two of the others haven't published anything for ages. So, I thought that this committee should have the benefit of some other opinions. It's up to you to decide what weight to give them."

"Perhaps, James," said Hamid, looking very uncomfortable, "but it's not very collegial to question a Section Head's list of referees."

"It was absolutely necessary," Saleema Nadjani interjected. "The referees in the application were second-rate. We should be grateful to Professor Markham for providing us with better ones."

Saleema's aggressive tone took everyone by surprise, including James, but her own excellent academic reputation spoke in her favor and prompted Pierre Forget to come on side, albeit with more diplomacy.

"I agree that the supplementary references are important," he said, "and certainly they're very categorical. Even without doubting the credibility of Len's own references, which Hamid accepted." Pierre turned towards Hamid. "I don't doubt them, Hamid, but these additional references raise enough doubts to warrant refusing the application."

Winstone, who had been silent until now, asked if there were any more comments to be made. None were forthcoming, and he asked for a vote. As expected, the committee split with James, Saleema and Pierre voting to reject and Hamid, HB and Campeau voting to accept the application. Arbuthnot looked expectantly at Winstone, who was squirming in his chair.

"You have the casting vote, Harold," HB purred confidently.

James gave Winstone a warning look. Don't you dare play me false, you bastard, it said. There was a short silence. Finally, Winstone, looking as if he were about to throw up, gave his reluctant verdict.

"I think there are enough doubts, as Pierre has said, surrounding this application to warrant me abstaining," he said.

"This means the application's refused!" Arbuthnot shouted in disbelief. "How can you do that, Harold?"

HB was beside himself. Winstone, looking iller by the moment, muttered something inaudible and rushed from the room. Arbuthnot glared at James. "Markham, this is your doing, but it's not the end of the matter," he said, his voice vibrating with hatred.

"Yes, it is," Saleema put in firmly. "At least for three years."

"Thank you for your support, Saleema," James told her after Arbuthnot had stalked off to give his protégé the bad news.

"It's not a question of supporting you," she replied, clearly remembering their last rather acrimonious discussion about her religion. "It's a question of maintaining standards."

"Quite so, Saleema," James agreed, "but thanks anyway."

He gave her a roguish smile, which caused Saleema to blush. James chased away an inappropriate thought and left the room to return to his office. He passed Len Flint, who was looking very hurt, and HB, who didn't bother to hide his venom.

"A good day's work, eh, Markham," he hissed in his Scottish brogue.

James took no notice, but Arbuthnot would be avenged, and in a way that would bring James to the brink of insanity.

# CHAPTER 3

## Sunday, August 19 to Wednesday, August 22, 2001

Twenty hours after saying goodbye to her father at the airport in Florence, Antonietta landed in Montreal. It was four-thirty in the afternoon on a hot, muggy day. She presented her Italian passport and study permit to the immigration official, who, taken aback by Antonietta's beauty, just stared at her.

"Is there a problem?" she asked in French.

The immigration officer collected himself and beamed at her. "No, Mademoiselle. Welcome to Quebec."

"Also to Canada, right?" Antonietta countered.

"Of course," the officer replied indifferently.

It was a strange introduction to the country.

She took a taxi to Sherbrooke Street and the Hotel Versailles. She unpacked as she would probably be staying for at least a week before she could find an apartment and furnish it. It was well after eight when she wandered outside into the humid heat of a Montreal summer evening. The Duke of Messina had recommended her to walk along Ste.Catherine Street with its bistros and outdoor cafés. She stopped at a terrace bar, ordered a glass of wine and asked for the menu.

She was soon aware of the stares of the men around her. She dreaded the moment when one of them would accost her. She cursed her beauty, which seemed to bring her only problems and scant happiness. Soon enough, a young man with ridiculous rings in his ears sat down opposite her.

"You look like a stranger here," he remarked. "Where are you from?"

"Leave me alone," Antonietta replied, surprised by her own rudeness. The young man shrugged and went back to his friends.

Antonietta asked herself why she'd been so rude. Was it the stupid rings, the use of the familiar "tu"[10]or simply the tiredness and irritation of a long and tedious voyage. She left the terrace-bar without waiting for the wine. She returned to the hotel and sat alone and depressed in her room. What on earth had possessed her to come to this God-forsaken country? She thought of calling her parents, but it was the early morning hours in Italy and, in any case, a conversation with her mother was about the last thing she needed. Tears welled up in her eyes and it was only with much effort that she fought them back. She fell asleep.

Antonietta awoke in the same despondent mood as the night before. She called her parents, but unfortunately only her mother was at home. The conversation was difficult as her mother was not all sympathetic. This lack of comprehension compounded Antonietta's own doubts and unhappiness. After lying disconsolately in bed for a while, she decided it was time to pull herself together. She showered, made herself up, put on a fashionable but not too sexy summer dress and left to find a café for her morning coffee.

It was a beautiful sunny day and, although it was early, there were already many people bustling about or seated in the terraces having breakfast. It felt almost like Italy, and Antonietta's spirits began to revive. If she by any chance were to meet the young man from the previous evening, she would apologize, She really had behaved badly. As it was, she quickly came upon a café called Chez Luigi and entered. Immediately she felt at home listening to the Italian chatter of four older men sitting at one of the tables. She sat down near an open window so she could watch the people go by. One of the men got up and came over to her.

"What would you like?" he asked gruffly in English. He was short and grey-haired with a swarthy complexion. Antonietta guessed he was from Sicily or Calabria.

"I want an *espresso macchiato*," she replied in Italian.

The man gave her a wide smile and his manner changed. "Straightaway, Signorina."

The coffee arrived and the man, who turned out to be Luigi, asked Antonietta how long she'd been in Montreal. She explained that she'd arrived the evening before and was still getting used to being away from home.

"Don't worry, Signorina," he told her. "A beautiful woman like you will soon have lots of friends."

Seeing that she was not convinced, he went on to extol the glories of living in Canada. "It's an easy place to live. Easier than Italy. People are nice here, they let you do what you want. They don't interfere. The Frenchies are a pain trying to force us to speak French, but we play the game and everyone's happy."

She stayed over an hour talking to Luigi, who explained the rudiments of living in Quebec and how to get around Montreal. She told him that she was going to study at an institute in Saint-Sauveur.

"My son lives near there. He's a Volkswagen dealer in St. Jérôme and lives in Ste. Anne des Lacs," Luigi exclaimed. He must have noticed a look of distrust enter Antonietta's expressive eyes for he added hurriedly. "With his wife and five children."

Reassured, Antonietta let Luigi make an arrangement for his son, Carlo, to come and pick her up at the hotel the next day and drive her to St. Jérôme to choose a car.

"You should visit Ste. Anne des Lacs, too," he told her. "It's near Saint-Sauveur and very pretty. I'm sure you'd like living there."

After three coffees and a number of Italian pastries, all of which Luigi insisted on paying for, Antonietta decided to walk to Old Montreal. It would be a long haul, but after all the pastries she needed some exercise. She wanted to visit the Notre Dame Basilica, which was supposed to be a marvel of neo-gothic architecture with an interior modeled on the luminous Sainte-Chapelle in Paris. She was not disappointed, although it was more the ornamentation of the Basilica that was neo-gothic; the structure and form were more classical.

Antonietta came out of the Basilica into the bright sunshine. It was past noon and extremely hot. Across the street was a small restaurant that tempted her, but Luigi had told her to eat at one of the open-air cafes in the Place Jacques Cartier. So, she made her way to the square.

The east and west sides of the square were lined with restaurants. They were all teeming with people but she managed to find an empty table at one of them. The food was disappointing, the wine acceptable and the price astronomical. It was a typical tourist trap, but Antonietta didn't mind. The waiter was friendly without being all over her, and no young men with rings in their ears accosted her. She was allowed to eat her lunch in peace, observe the people walking past and gaze at the impressive St. Lawrence River in the distance to the south of the square. The price didn't bother her although, when she came to pay the bill, she couldn't help thinking it was a good thing that her family owned the Banca Regionale, which was one of Italy's most successful banks. At least I can be rich even if I can't be fulfilled, she thought.

After lunch, she walked along the quays bordering the river. They were rather uninteresting and so she turned back toward the Bonsecours Market. It was equally uninteresting, and so she just ambled through the streets of the old city. It was quaint but compared poorly with the boutiques and cafes of Florence. Most of the shops seemed to be stocked exclusively with jerseys, baseball caps and other touristic mementoes. After an hour or so she was bored and hailed a taxi. She was far too tired to contemplate walking back to the hotel.

Antonietta went back to Luigi's for supper and spent the evening chattering with some of the regulars in Italian. It was well after midnight when she finally sank down into her bed. Nevertheless, she had difficulty falling asleep. Her naked body tossed and turned in the bed. I could use Giacomo now, she confessed to herself.

———

The Chilean Airlines flight taxied to its allotted bay at Arturo Merino Benitez airport in Santiago de Chile. "Thank God," Bill Leaman muttered. He stood up and gathered his and James' briefcases from the overhead bin. He prepared himself for a long wait. To his surprise, the plane emptied very quickly.

"Chilean efficiency," James commented, well aware of his friend's low opinion of Latin Americans.

The immigration and customs formalities were dispatched with equal efficiency, and James and Bill were soon getting into a taxi outside the airport. The driver proceeded first southwards along the Vespucci ring road. At the junction with route 65, which to the left leads to the coast, he turned right towards Santiago's main street, Avenida Bernardo O'Higgins. It was early afternoon, but there were few cars on the road.

"They must all be having lunch," Bill remarked.

"It's a public holiday," James informed him. "The Feast of the Assumption."

"What the hell's that?" Bill asked.

Aware of his friend's religious skepticism, James answered Bill's question with as non-committal an explanation as possible of the assumption of the Virgin into Heaven. Even so, Bill was incredulous.

"You mean to say the old bird just floated up, like a balloon?"

James couldn't help laughing. "That's not exactly the way I learned it at catechism, but you've got the essential idea."

"Amazing," Bill concluded with mock admiration. "Tell me, do you believe in that crap?"

"I believe in its symbolic importance," James replied enigmatically.

Bill was really none the wiser with this response, but he didn't persist. Although James was his closest friend, he never felt he knew the man completely. James kept much to himself. Just how religious was he, and was there a secret life that enabled him to support his arid marriage? These were questions Bill often asked himself.

At the Hotel Bristol they were checked in by an effeminate young man. "We should've brought tin plates with us," Bill whispered loudly as they made for the elevator. James wilted with embarrassment. "Perhaps you could say it a little louder, then the whole hotel could hear," he grumbled. Bill opened his mouth but luckily for James the elevator door opened and he was able to push Bill inside. His friend remained, however, impenitent and James was glad to escape from his scurrilous comments into the solitude of the hotel room.

After a shower and shave, the two met in the bar for a couple of scotches before a late lunch. The restaurant in the Hotel Bristol has five stars and boasts an excellent array of Chilean and international dishes. Bill gazed disconsolately at the first page of the menu.

"Do they have anything edible?" he asked plaintively.

"The international dishes are on the next page," James replied. "You can probably find a steak."

James himself ordered Antarctic krill as an entrée and golden king klip filet with sea algae for the main course.

"I'm not sure I even want to watch you eat that stuff," Bill complained.

He ordered a steak for himself with a Caesar salad as his entrée. James asked for a bottle of Carmenere[11], which was so enjoyable that they had a second bottle for their dessert, after which they both slept until evening.

It was already dark when they awoke. To clear their heads, they decided to walk to a small restaurant that James knew. For the first time Bill noticed the name of the avenue on which their hotel was located.

"How come it's named after an Irishman," he asked.

"O'Higgins played a major role in liberating Chile," James replied.

Bill burst out laughing. "It must be the only country in the world to be liberated by an Irishman. God damn it, the Irish can't even liberate themselves."

"His father was Irish, but he was born in Peru."

"What happened to him?"

"He was President of Chile from 1817 to 1823, and then he was deposed. The Church and the landowners didn't like him. He went back to Peru and died there in 1842."

By now they'd reached the restaurant. James ordered a dish called *Charquican*, which consists of ground meat cooked with garlic, onions, potatoes and pumpkin, but Bill stuck to steak.

———

Antonietta harbored serious misgivings about going with a complete stranger. She wondered whether she'd end up in some Middle Eastern harem. However, when Carlo arrived to collect her at the hotel, her fears dissipated for he could only be a car salesman. He was balding, overweight and voluble.

They had some difficult communicating at first. Unlike his father, Carlo spoke pure Calabrian as he'd lived in Italy for ten years with his grandparents after the premature death of his mother. Worse still, when Antonietta didn't understand his Italian, he would switch into the rustic Quebecois French he'd picked up from his wife, which she could understand even less. Eventually they agreed to speak English, which worked for both of them even though at times Carlo had trouble with Antonietta's British accent.

She'd been wrong about Carlo. He might look like a shyster but he seemed genuine enough. There was no point in spending a lot of money on a new car, he told her, when she was only staying for two years. A used car that was still under warranty carried no more risk than a new one and was much less expensive. Alternatively he could offer her a brand new Jetta that had been used as a demonstration model. The price was very reasonable and Antonietta decided to buy it.

Carlo took her to Saint-Sauveur to open a bank account. Antonietta was becoming enthusiastic about her new abode. "It's so pretty," she enthused, "and there are so many restaurants." This reminded her of what the Duke of Messina had told her about Saint-Sauveur. When Carlo agreed to let her have the car right away upon the payment of a small deposit while she waited for funds to arrive from Italy, she seized upon the opportunity to invite him to lunch at one of the town's Italian restaurants.

After lunch, Carlo took Antonietta to visit Ste. Anne des Lacs, which she found quite attractive. It was difficult to find accommodation in Saint-Sauveur, Carlo told her, and Ste. Anne was right close by. He introduced her to his wife, who suggested that Antonietta inspect a furnished cottage near the entrance to the village that belonged to a friend of her's who was looking for a new tenant. They met the lady, who was actually from Montreal and spoke, thankfully for Antonietta, a French she could understand.

The cottage was set back from the road and surrounded by trees. It was perhaps a little isolated, but there were two other houses at some distance on either side. Inside, there were two rooms that could serve as a bedroom and study, respectively, a small living room and a large kitchen in which you could eat. The bathroom was small but modern. There was even a laundry room with a washer and dryer. The cottage was furnished simply but adequately. Antonietta was charmed by the place. There were a few pieces of furniture she would have to buy but that was all. She agreed on the spot to take the cottage, wrote a check on her new account for two months rent and arranged to move in the following Monday.

It was quite late when she arrived back at the hotel in her newly purchased Jetta, which she had some difficulty parking. She showered, changed her clothes and went off to Luigi's to eat and recount her day. Luigi beamed when she told him that not only had she bought a car from his son but she had also rented a cottage in Ste. Anne des Lacs as well.

"You'll love it there," he told her.

It was true that she would spend times of utter bliss in that cottage before leaving it with her heart breaking.

———

After finishing their business at the University of Santiago, Bill and James arrived in Buenos Aires late on Wednesday afternoon. James bought a voucher for a taxi from the central stand at Ezeiza international airport and soon he and Bill were headed eastwards towards the city of Buenos Aires. They passed a sign to Boulogne-sur-mer.

"What the hell's that for?" Bill asked in surprise. "I thought Boulogne-sur-mer was in France."

"It *is* in France," James replied, "but it's also a district of Buenos Aires."

Bill shook his head in incomprehension. "Why on earth did they choose the name of an obscure French town?"

"Because the liberator of Argentina, General San Martín, died in exile in Boulogne."

"Not a very grateful lot, these Latin Americans," Bill remarked sourly. "They exile all their liberators."

The taxi reached the city limits and proceeded down the Avenida 9 de Julio, the widest in the world, before turning right to take them to the Hotel Plaza San Martín. They made their way to the reception desk and stood in line. The receptionist, who was busy with another couple, was an extremely pretty blond.

"Shit, I'd like to roger that one," Bill whispered loudly to James, who looked at him aghast. "If you insist on being a vulgar American, couldn't you at least be a *quiet* vulgar American." Bill laughed. "She probably doesn't even speak English," he said with assurance.

The girl was certainly very attractive. The women of Buenos Aires were known for their beauty but, generally, it tended to be a diaphanous beauty. They were too slim for James' taste. This girl was different. Her figure was trim but full, and her sumptuous breasts were barely contained by her blouse. She was a picture of voluptuous lubricity.

The girl handed her clients their room key and turned towards Bill, who addressed her in the execrable Spanish he'd picked up in Texas.

"What is your name, Sir," she asked in English with only a slight accent.

Bill reddened slightly and replied "Leaman."

"Roger Leaman?" she asked innocently.

James could barely contain his mirth, but Bill was not amused. "No, *Bill* Leaman," he replied.

The girl checked him in, took an imprint of his credit card and handed him the room keycard. "Have an enjoyable stay," she said with a slight smirk. Bill slunk away without even waiting for James. The girl turned towards James.

"My name is Markham, James Markham," he told her in Spanish, emphasizing slightly the "James."

The girl looked up at him with clear blue eyes that betrayed a faint amusement. "Do you have a reservation?" she asked, using Spanish in her turn.

"Yes, it was made from Canada, at the same time as Dr. Leaman's," James replied, feeling that he owed it to Bill to raise his profile a little by emphasizing the doctoral title. However, the girl was too intrigued by James' faultless

Spanish to pay any attention to Bill's academic credentials.

"How come you speak Castilian[12] so well?" she asked, pronouncing her words with the typical slur of the inhabitants of Buenos Aires.

"I've spent much time in Spain," James explained, aware of the growing attraction between the two of them, "but I'm British."

He handed over his British passport. The girl's attitude changed immediately. The blue eyes showed no emotion, but the tone became curt, even hostile.

"I believe you let the British into Argentina," James said with a grin in an effort to lighten the atmosphere.

"Unlike you," she answered. "Argentineans are not welcome in the Malvinas."

James was annoyed. Good God, he thought, the war's been over for years, and they're still sore about it. "Well, we didn't invade you, perhaps that's the difference," he snapped, taking back his passport with a gesture which indicated that for him the conversation was over.

"You did, twice," the girl countered, turning the full force of her beautiful eyes upon James.

"We did?" This was the first James had heard of these invasions, and he didn't know whether to believe her. "What happened?" he asked nevertheless.

"We beat you both times[13]," was the proud answer.

"Then it was about time you let us win one," James rejoined.

The blue eyes lost their serenity. "War is not a game," the girl told him. "Many people died."

James' irritation vanished. There was a sadness about this comment that made him suspect she was not a stranger to one of these deaths. He wanted to apologize but couldn't think of suitable words. The girl handed back his credit card and told him the number of the room.

James was about to enter the elevator when he heard the girl call his name. He turned round and found her standing before him, the keycard to his room in her hand.

"I forgot to give you this," she said but made no effort to hand it to him.

For a brief moment they just gazed at each other. Finally, James found the words he wanted. "I'm sorry for what I said. You're right, war is not a game."

"No, it's I who should apologize," the girl replied. She smiled at him. "It's not very professional to insult the guests."

James couldn't resist the beautiful blue eyes any longer. "When do you finish work?" he asked

"At eleven," she replied as if she'd been expecting the question.

"Well, I thought I might have a drink in La Barra. [14] Why don't you join me after work?"

"Perhaps," she answered.

"Well, perhaps you'll give me my keycard." Now it was James' turn to smile. "And tell me your name."

"Carolina," she said, giving him the card.

"Then, see you later, Carolina."

She didn't respond but simply turned and walked back to the reception desk. It was no matter. James already knew the response.

———

Antonietta was enjoying her new car. On Wednesday, she visited some of the little towns dotted around the Laurentians. In the evening, when the torrid summer heat cooled, she walked around Montreal. She liked its mixture of the old and new worlds. She still had an omnipresent feeling of emptiness but she was no longer unhappy. Any nostalgia she felt for Italy was easily cured by the good-humored banter at Luigi's café.

———

After unpacking and taking a quick shower, James and Bill met in the lobby and set out for a small restaurant that James knew on Suipacha street. Bill looked in awe at the menu, which consisted entirely of beef dishes. At last, this was real food. He ordered beef empanadas as an entrée and grilled steak as a main course. James followed suit but had a tussle with the waiter, who insisted on bringing them the house wine. James sent it back and made the waiter go down to the cellar and find a bottle of Susana Balbo.

"You're just a wine snob," Bill remarked with an amused grin.

"Perhaps, but the grape they use in Argentina is Malbec, and unless it's mixed with another grape, preferably Cabernet Sauvignon, it's tannic and unpleasant. I've had their house wine, and even you wouldn't like it. But the Susana Balbo is excellent. It has about fifteen percent Cabernet."

The waiter arrived with the bottle, and Bill was forced to admit it was a good-tasting wine. "I hope they've got a few more bottles," he remarked.

"I'm too tired to drink much," said James, thinking of the luscious blond that awaited him in La Barra.

"Hopefully not too tired for a visit to the bar across the road. It's full of women."

"They're hookers, Bill," James warned, but this didn't daunt Bill.

"So what? They can't be that expensive, and I brought some condoms with me."

James sighed. He knew that Bill had been looking forward to his first night in Buenos Aires, but it was already ten-thirty and by the time they'd paid and got back to the hotel, it would be past eleven.

"Tomorrow, Bill, I promise, but tonight I'm too tired."

They returned to the hotel and Bill retreated in bad humor to his room. Once James was sure that his friend was out of the way, he left the hotel and walked to La Barra. A few minutes later, Carolina arrived.

# CHAPTER 4

## Thursday, August 23 to Friday, August 31, 2001

Antonietta was visiting the campus of NIIS. Its location was perfect, high in the hills above Saint-Sauveur, but the buildings were nondescript. Typical 70's architecture, functional but uninspiring. The main buildings were arranged around a quadrangle. Antonietta noticed that they were all connected by walkways. Must be the Canadian winter, she thought grimly. In the middle of the quadrangle was a large ornate fountain, which looked rather out of place. Three further buildings clustered around the Administration building to the south. They were obviously newer editions and were built in a quasi-alpine style that didn't marry at all with the plainness of the original buildings. They were all connected to the Administration building by walkways and housed, respectively, the Students Union on the west, some large lecture halls in the middle and the library on the east. Further yet to the south was the parking lot where Antonietta had left her car, and down the hill were the student residences.

She made for the Administration building. It was there she had her appointment with Dr. Bromhoeffer, who was the Dean of Admissions and Student Affairs. They discussed the courses she would take. The Dean encouraged her to take the course on the European Union. It was an undergraduate course, but she was allowed to take one such course.

"If you want to enter the Italian diplomatic service, it will stand you in good stead," the Dean said. "Dr. Markham is an exceptionally good professor," she added, giving Antonietta a strange look.

———

Bill awoke early after his disappointing evening. He took a shower and tried to call James, but he couldn't make head nor tail out of the phone system. So he walked down to James' room and knocked on the door. After an interval, James emerged, swathed in a bath towel.

"What about breakfast?" Bill asked.

"Go on ahead," James replied. "I've still got to shower and deal with a few things."

It was clear to Bill that James didn't particularly want to come down for breakfast, although he had no idea why. If this meant he was going to spend the morning alone, he might as well visit the city. Brushing past James before he could be stopped, he went to pick up the book on Buenos Aires that was lying on the table. Carolina gasped but didn't have enough time to cover herself before Bill caught sight of her naked body. He bowed slightly and excused himself. He took the book and made for the door.

"Too tired to go a whorehouse," he murmured on passing James. "You lying bastard."

"I'll see you around noon in the bar," James replied, hurrying Bill out of the room.

He returned to the bed and lifted up the sheet to reveal Carolina's voluptuous curves.

"He wanted to go to a whorehouse?" she asked. "You too?"

James kissed Carolina on the mouth and caressed her breasts. "I had no need of a whorehouse," he replied. When he reached her sex, it was moist with desire.

"Well, tell your friend that the girls in the Recoleta are better looking than those on Suipacha," she said, squirming under his touch.

"How do you know?"

"Because, when I need some extra money, I go to the Recoleta."

"You're a hooker?" James was astonished at the girl's candor.

She laughed, her blue eyes betraying no emotion. "Only occasionally, and certainly not at this moment." Carolina kissed James and pushed him down on the bed. She ran her tongue along his body and excited him before turning over onto her back to receive him.

———

After leaving the Institute, Antonietta drove to Quebec City. Next week she would be arranging her cottage and buying whatever bits and pieces she needed, and the week after that she would have to register for her courses, buy materials and attend an orientation course. So she'd decided to spoil herself and stay this weekend at the Chateau Frontenac in Quebec City. It stood majestically on a buff overlooking the St. Lawrence River in the heart of the city. She arrived around eight o' clock in the evening and dined alone in Le Bistro. She went to bed quite early, but it was a while before she fell asleep. This can't go on, she told herself, I need some sex.

———

"You're a hypocritical, lying, selfish son of a bitch," Bill expostulated when James turned up in the hotel bar. "So, the perfect Catholic husband spends his time screwing receptionists in South America."

"I admit I was selfish, and I did lie," James replied with a grin. "But *I'm* not the hypocrite. Are you telling me you would've passed up a chance with Carolina?"

"Okay, fair enough," Bill agreed. "But you're still a hypocrite. Just how many of these Latins have you screwed?"

"Enough." James didn't even bother to feign remorse.

"Good God, Markham, you're a fucking profligate."

"How else do you think I manage with a wife who's well on her way to sainthood? Better a few rolls in the sack down here than a divorce."

"Why on earth did you marry Veronica?"

"I had this Spanish girlfriend in Italy," James explained, not really wanting to go into details. "When she dumped me, Veronica was there to pick up the pieces."

Bill was puzzled. "But you knew Veronica from before, didn't you?"

"Yes. During my first two years at university, I was in love with a girl called Mary. I thought she was in love with me until I found a postcard she was sending to a friend. She wrote that I was a bit of a bore but she couldn't pass up on becoming Lady Markham. Veronica was the daughter of a viscount and knew my family. She was a sort of refuge."

"Is that why you're so touchy about your title?"

"Partly. I don't like being courted for my title, but, in any case, it has no significance in Canada."

Bill could sense a certain bitterness in James. It was time to change the subject. "Well, I hope tonight's on. It's time *I* got a roll in the sack down here."

James ordered Bill another Scotch to cheer him up. "We'll visit the Recoleta this afternoon, stay for dinner and then I'll take you to La Ronda. Evidently, that's where the prettiest girls are."

"What's the Recoleta?" Bill asked.

"It's one of the most exclusive districts of Buenos Aires," James explained.

"There's a cemetery where all the famous people of Argentina are buried, and it has some of the best restaurants and the most famous café in Buenos Aires. It's called La Biela, and that's where I'm meeting Carolina after I've got you settled with some lusty hooker."

Bill slapped James on the back. "That's more like it, Jimmy."

———

The following day, Antonietta toured Quebec City on foot. She visited the Plains of Abraham where the British had defeated the French and taken control of Canada. Then she wandered through the narrow, quaint streets down to the old port. The St. Lawrence River was so immense that it seemed like the ocean. Only the smell was missing. She walked around the market before going to a restaurant she'd been recommended. She ate a hearty bistro-type meal, which she washed down with an excellent Chianti Classico. The waiter was obviously intrigued by this beautiful woman who ordered a whole bottle for herself. He asked where she came from, and they chatted for a few minutes. Antonietta's French was improving quickly.

A little tipsy, Antonietta took a taxi back to the Chateau Frontenac. In truth, she was bored with her own company. However interesting Quebec City may be, she had no more stomach for wandering around alone. She stripped off her clothes and lay down on the bed, naked. She would have given anything to have an attractive man next to her. But there was no point in dwelling on her sexual frustration, so she took a shower and settled down to read some poems by Leopardi. [15]She admired his purity of style and classic forms, which encapsulated a romantic nostalgia for the unobtainable that so often gripped her.

By the time she'd finished reading, Antonietta was thoroughly depressed. She slipped into a troubled sleep and awoke around seven thirty. She showered, yet again, put on her make-up, chose the sexy black dress and lingerie she'd bought in Florence and went down for an evening meal in the plush Le Champlain restaurant. It was part of the hotel and overlooked the St. Lawrence River. The staff were dressed in seventeenth century costumes and looked faintly comical.

A young man showed her to a table by the window. "You have a lovely view from here, Mademoiselle," he told her.

Antonietta sat down and looked across at the next table. A man, she guessed in his mid forties, was also dining alone. He was very handsome and elegant. From his brief exchange with the unctuous waiter, Antonietta concluded that he was French.

She ate self-consciously and drank sparingly. She desperately wanted the man to talk to her. In fact, she wanted to be in his bed. The meal seemed to last an eternity, but still the man, who had long since finished his meal and was nursing a cognac, didn't say anything to her. The one time I want to be irresistible, Antonietta said to herself forlornly, I come across this man. Perhaps he was gay? But he didn't look gay. Antonietta finished her expresso and was on the point of leaving the table to go back to the cold solitude of her room when the man finally addressed her.

"Mademoiselle, would you like to take an after-dinner drink with me?"

Desperately trying to hide her relief and enthusiasm, Antonietta acquiesced. The man introduced himself as "Philippe," so Antonietta also used only her first name. This suited her as what she wanted was a night of anonymous sex, not a relationship. They talked about Quebec City, Canada, France and Italy. Philippe showed a surprising familiarity with Italy. As he charmed her, Antonietta's prejudices against the French began to evaporate, and her desire for him became almost unbearable.

"What are you doing in Quebec City?" she asked, ordering her third cognac.

"I'm attending a conference of surgeons," he replied.

Antonietta gave an involuntary gasp. Did this man know her father? Philippe noticed her reaction and gave a short laugh. "You don't like surgeons?" Antonietta searched for a convenient lie. "You don't look like a surgeon," she replied lamely.

It was clear that Philippe didn't believe the answer, but he said nothing. They talked about her plans for a diplomatic career and the Institute in Saint-Sauveur. Antonietta motioned to the waiter.

"Please don't have another cognac." Philippe placed his hand on Antonietta's, which made her shiver. "I want to seduce you, but not after another cognac."

Antonietta felt insulted. "You don't want to make love to a drunk woman?" she asked icily.

"I don't think there's a man on earth who wouldn't want to make love to you, drunk or not," Philippe replied with a smile that completely disarmed Antonietta. "No, it's an old-fashioned question of honor. I like to think of myself as a gentleman, and I want you to know what you're doing."

Antonietta waved the waiter away. She leaned over the table towards Philippe in such a way as to expose the lubricious splendor of her breasts. They were already hardening with the anticipation of pleasure.

"Finish your drink," she said. "A gentleman shouldn't keep a lady waiting."

———

Bill and James were seated in the Cumaná in the Recoleta waiting for their *cazuelas*, the Argentinean beef stew for which the restaurant is famous. It had been a frustrating Saturday at the University of Buenos Aires, and they were in a mood to forget it with a good meal and plenty of Susana Balbo.

"They may be charming at UBA, but once you've cleared up one obstacle, the buggers come up with another, "James complained.

"Look on the bright side, Jimmy," Bill replied cheerfully. "It gives you a reason to come back and roger Carolina."

"Which reminds me, Bill," James ventured, anticipating his friend's displeasure. "I must be back at the hotel by midnight."

Fortunately, Bill had had his fill of Buenos Aires' nightlife and was more envious than anything else. They tucked into the *cazuelas* and ordered a couple of bottles of Susana Balbo. Bill wanted to order a third bottle, but James demurred.

"No, it's not just because of Carolina," he protested, noting his friend's disappointment. "We've got a helluva journey in front of us tomorrow. We leave Buenos Aires at eleven forty and have to spend seven hours at the airport in São Paolo. We won't be back in Montreal until Monday morning."

"Well, don't over-exert yourself tonight," Bill grumbled.

They left the restaurant and returned to the hotel where Carolina was already awaiting James in his room. "You're late," she said without reproach. "It was lucky I had a master key, otherwise someone might have wondered what I was doing on this floor."

James took her into his arms and gazed into the bright blue eyes. "I'll make up for it," he promised, deciding on the spot to take a hotel room at the airport in Sao Paolo in order to recover from what would doubtless be an exhausting night.

———

Antonietta stretched as she awoke. After a night of sex she was spared her recent feelings of frustration, but she was still not completely satisfied. Philippe had proved to be a very conventional lover, and Antonietta craved more dissolute gratification. She looked over at the firm, nude body next to her and resolved to indulge herself. She stroked Philippe's face and kissed him until he stirred. Once he was awake, she ran her tongue down his torso towards his sex. She brushed her nipples along the shaft and took it into her mouth, applying herself until Philippe took his pleasure. She then moved her damp lips up over his belly and stomach and, when she reached his face, dangled her fulsome breasts before him and obliged him to perform oral sex on her. Arching her back, she reached her climax but remained on Philippe's mouth to enjoy the soft spasms of her remaining lust.

Finally sated, Antonietta regained her own room. I hope no-one saw me, she thought as she looked at her disheveled appearance in the mirror. There was no doubting how she'd spent the night. She showered, did her hair, put on some make-up and walked down to breakfast, a little embarrassed at meeting the stranger upon whom she had just forced herself with such immodesty.

Philippe was also looking embarrassed. "I think perhaps I should introduce myself properly," he said awkwardly.

Antonietta laughed, her eyes twinkling with malicious amusement. "You think it's more important to introduce yourself before breakfast than before spending the night with me?" she asked.

Philippe ignored her mockery. "My full name is Philippe de Pothiers," he announced. "To be exact, it's Count Philippe de Pothiers." Antonietta's eyes widened in surprise but, before she could react, the Count switched into Italian. "And, if I'm not mistaken, you are the Countess Antonietta della Chiesa."

Antonietta was dumbstruck. She wasn't sure what astounded her more, the fact he knew who she was or his faultless Italian. "How did you find out?" she stammered in Italian.

"Our rather over-observant waiter asked me if he should lay a place for Miss della Chiesa. After that it was simple deduction. You come from Florence and you reacted strangely when I told you I was a surgeon. You had to be Count Paolo della Chiesa's daughter."

"And the Italian?"

"My mother's Italian. She's the sister of Angelina Farnese."

Antonietta gasped. The Farnese's were an old Italian family that had ruled Parma for almost two hundred years and furnished the wife of King Philip V of Spain. Princess Angelina had been widowed young and had never remarried. She was an imposing fixture in Florentine society and a close friend of her uncle, the Cardinal. And this man was her nephew!

"We might have met," said Antonietta once she'd recovered her composure. "I don't think so," Philippe replied. "You're not easy to forget." He looked at Antonietta with some unease, "If we ever do meet..." Antonietta interrupted him before he could finish the sentence."My lips are sealed," she said with a grin. Philippe looked very relieved.

After breakfast they attended Mass, on which Antonietta insisted much to Philippe's amusement, and then walked around the city. They lunched in the terrace of one of the restaurants opposite the Chateau Frontenac. They ate lightly, and Antonietta, contrary to her custom, drank only mineral water. She had to drive back to Ste. Anne des Lacs that afternoon. As they were parting after lunch, Philippe put his arms on Antonietta's shoulders in a fatherly way.

"Don't take it amiss, but there's something I must say to you, Antonietta. You shouldn't be here like this, having an adventure with a married man. You should be with your husband or your boy-friend. It's against nature for a woman of your rare beauty to be gallivanting around aimlessly on your own."

On the way back to Ste. Anne, Antonietta reflected on her experience with Philippe de Pothiers. He was charming, good-looking but a rather pedestrian lover. Nevertheless, she would gladly have consented to become his mistress. After all, there were frequent direct flights between Montreal and Paris.

Then she recalled his last words to her. He was right. Her life was aimless and becoming the mistress of a married man who lived thousands of kilometers away was hardly a solution. The euphoria of her sexual pleasure and the agreeable feelings evoked by Philippe's company evaporated, and the old demons came back. Fighting the onset of depression as she drove along the highway between Quebec City and Montreal, she couldn't have known that in a week's time all this would be irretrievably consigned to the past.

———

James arrived back home on Monday to be told by Veronica that the Rector wanted to see him the next day. He wondered why. It was unlikely to hear about his trip to South America. Winstone was not interested in the international program and, if he ever had his way, it would probably be axed. That would also be a way of getting rid of Tom Buchanan, who had stayed on in the Institute as Dean of International Relations. He was a constant reminder to Winstone, and others, of the Rector's inadequacy. The message from

Eleanor to Veronica announcing the meeting had given no clues as to its purpose.

After his exhausting journey, James had been greeted by a display of discreet affection from his wife, who hastened to tell him that she and the children were going to England for ten days at the end of October. They would spend the first few days with James' parents in Derwent and then go for a retreat at the convent where her mother was now a nun. James was not at all dismayed at the prospect, but he felt sorry for the children. A week in a religious retreat was hardly their idea of fall break.

The next day he arrived at the Rectorate and was greeted warmly by Eleanor Leatherbarrow.

"What's this all about, Eleanor," he asked.

"I don't know," she replied and then, dropping her voice to a whisper, added. "I think Arbuthnot has something to do with it. The Rector asked me to call your home after his meeting with Roy on Friday. So be careful."

After waiting a few minutes—Winstone always made people wait, doubtless it made him feel important—James was called into Rector's office.

"James, a nasty affair has blown up," he said, adopting a collegial tone. "I need your help to deal with it."

James was suspicious. It was most unlike Winstone to want his help, particularly after the business with Len Flint.

"It appears," the Rector went on, "that a member of faculty may have had an affair with a student while she was in his class. As you know, this is a dismissible offence. He's to be brought before the Ethics Committee, and I want you to defend him."

James immediately saw the trap to discredit him and remove a possible threat to Winstone and Arbuthnot. If he won, some people would think he was just protecting a colleague from his just deserts, and if he lost, he would forfeit some of his credibility among those faculty members who saw him as an alternative to the present regime.

"Who is the professor?"

"Elliot Hunt."

Now he understood. Hunt was a brilliant young professor who had joined the Institute two years ago. He was in the same Section as Arbuthnot and made no secret of the low esteem in which he held HB. He was a threat and Arbuthnot clearly wanted to be rid of him. James was sure these were trumped-up charges for that purpose. This decided him to take the case.

"The hearing's scheduled for Friday, November 9th," Winstone told him with an air of relief that didn't escape James. "That will give you time to prepare the defense. That is, if there is one."

"Even in the Ethics Committee, a person is presumed innocent, I believe, until proven guilty," James observed coldly, taking the file from Winstone. He left the office without exchanging any further words with the Rector.

James returned to his office to go through the file. He noted the names of all the students who had testified against Hunt and went to see Ilse Bromhoeffer. He wasn't sure exactly how much he was permitted to tell the She-Wolf, as Bill rather unkindly called her, so he just asked to see the marks for Hunt's class.

Ilse was suspicious. "You're the second person to ask me that. Why do you want to see them?"

James ignored Ilse's question. "Was the other person Roy Arbuthnot?" Ilse nodded. "Did he tell you why?" Ilse nodded again."Well, I've been asked to defend Hunt, that's why *I* need to see the marks."

"Of course, but you'll have to consult them here," Ilse said in a friendly tone.

It took James little time to confirm his suspicions. All eight students, including the girl's former boyfriend, Doefman, who had instigated the charge against Hunt, had either failed Hunt's course or received a conditional pass. He pointed this out to Ilse. She agreed that it seemed more than just a coincidence.

"Do you think it's a put-up job?"

James was taken aback by Ilse's frankness. "I don't know," he replied, not wishing to go off half-cock, "but I'm damn well going to find out. I need the phone numbers of all the students in the class, including the girl's."

"Her name is Annya Nowak," Ilse informed him as she handed over the numbers. "Be careful of Doefman. He's a nasty piece of work."

So is HB, James thought grimly. He went back to his office and called Elliot Hunt. He was away until Thursday, and so James left a message arranging to meet him on Friday morning.

———

For Antonietta, it was a busy week. She had moved into the cottage on Monday and spent the week buying some extra furniture and other little things, such as a casserole for cooking pasta, a spiked saucer for crushing garlic and a hooked serving spoon. In fact, she'd bought too much, but shopping gave her an excuse to go to Montreal and enjoy the warm familiarity of Luigi's café. This helped her combat the depression that had descended upon her since her trip to Quebec City.

———

Hunt seemed surprised by James' visit.

"Have you any idea why I might be here?" James asked him, scrutinizing the man's reaction. Hunt's face was untroubled. He certainly didn't seem like someone with a guilty conscience.

"I haven't a clue," he replied breezily.

James explained about the complaint and the decision to bring the matter before the Ethics Committee. Hunt was extremely angry.

"What the fuck's going on," he demanded to know. "First, I never had any relationship with Annya before the end of term, not even a platonic one. And how come I wasn't informed that I'm to be brought before the Ethics Committee? That would seem to be the least I could expect."

"I'm informing you now, but I agree it's a cockeyed way of doing things."

"So you're one of the hatchet men?" The hostility in Hunt's voice was unmistakable.

"No, quite the opposite. I've been appointed to defend you."

"Appointed to defend me!" Hunt roared. "You mean I don't get to choose my own advocate?"

"The policy in the Institute is to choose the defender, that way he has more credibility. It prevents people getting their friends to defend them, which normally backfires."

Hunt was silent. He just glared at James.

"You have the right to refuse the Institute's choice," James added in an effort to placate him.

James could see that Hunt was of two minds. He had no reason to distrust him, but the arbitrary nature of the procedure clearly offended his American sense of civil rights.

"Why don't we discuss the case, and then you can make your mind up," he suggested.

Hunt agreed and proceeded to tell his side of the story. Yes, Annya had been in his class and from the instant he first saw her, he'd fallen head over heels in love with her. However, he'd never said anything to her. Their only conversations had been strictly about the course.

"Did you know she was in love with you too?

"Well, there are ways of showing what you feel without actually saying it. We both knew we were attracted to each other. Unfortunately for us, so did Doefman, who was jealous and kept pestering her about me."

"How do you know that?"

"We talked afterwards, you know," Hunt replied.

"Yes, of course," James agreed, feeling a little foolish. "Go on."

Hunt explained how Annya had become so exasperated with Doefman that she'd dumped him three quarters the way through class. "Looking back on it, it was a dumb thing to do. Doefman thought it was because of me, so that's why he's concocted this whole story."

"The problem is that it was indeed because of you," James observed. "This became clear once Annya started going out with you." He paused before changing the topic. "Tell me about Doefman and his record in class."

"He's an example of the worst type of student. Not as bright as he thinks and a lot to say in class. Most of it was useless babble to impress the others, particularly Annya. Then when he gets poor marks, he can't understand it and always contests them. Thinks it's the professor's fault."

"There's a lot of students like that," said James. "What about his final term paper?"

"It was not one of the worst, but lousy nevertheless. I gave it 40%, but really he deserved to fail."

"Why didn't you fail him?"

"The guy's an asshole, but he'd just lost his girlfriend, so I didn't want to rub salt into the wound."

"Also, you knew he'd soon find out that you two were together

"Yes," Hunt admitted. "I hadn't yet talked to Annya, but I was pretty sure how things were going to turn out."

James was pleased with the answer. Hunt's version was plausible and everything he knew about Doefman told in Hunt's favor. But there was still the issue of the re-evaluation of the term paper. He showed Hunt Professor Hill's assessment, in which he gave Doefman 60%.

"Graeme Hill!" Hunt exclaimed without bothering to read the assessment, "He's useless. He hasn't published a thing since he got tenure, and what he did before that was pretty awful. Arbuthnot picked him because they were both students at NUC."

Hunt's words removed the last doubt in James' mind. Arbuthnot had pulled the same trick in the Len Flint case, seeking references from his former classmates at NUC.

"Well, Elliot, it's up to you whether you want me to defend you," he said, "but I can tell you that I believe you."

"Thanks, James." Hunt stood up and shook James by the hand. "I'd be honored to have you defend me."

They agreed that James would send Doefman's paper to a certain Professor Burstein for another assessment in order to counter Graeme Hill's. James turned to leave but one last question occurred to him.

"Perhaps it's just idle curiosity, but how did you and Annya finally hook up?"

"I wandered around the campus until I bumped into her," Hunt replied.

It was an answer that would haunt James.

# CHAPTER 5
## Sunday, September 2, 2001

The day arrived to find Antonietta still sleepy after an evening on her own with too much wine and James making coffee for himself and Veronica. Later, the lovers would wonder that no premonitory signs had forewarned them of what was to happen that day. For it was so inexplicable, so overwhelming, that nature could not have remained indifferent. Yet, that Sunday dawned like any other day. It was perhaps unseasonably warm for the beginning of September and the sun created a luminosity unusual for the time of year, but this was hardly enough to prepare them for the onslaught of a passion so infinite that they would be unable to live without it.

Apart from the meeting with Elliott Hunt, it had been a very boring week for James. Bill was off in Vancouver visiting his errant wife; his Polish friend, Piotr Lesnik, was in his home country; and Danny Redfern, who was the Dean of Administration, had been tied up with preparations for the beginning of the new academic year. To top it off, today was very much the normal dismal Sunday routine. James bore the whole recurring scenario with a resignation born of the prospect of a game of tennis with Danny that afternoon.

They arrived in Saint-Sauveur from Prévost in good time for the eleven o'clock Mass. James parked in the little car park just north of the church and the family walked down to Main Street. They turned right towards the church. As they entered, James noticed a young woman walking down the aisle ahead of them, her long dark hair falling loosely around her shoulders. He hoped she wouldn't turn round. So often, a woman attractive from the back would spoil everything by turning round and exhibiting a plain or ugly face. He watched the woman genuflect before the altar and take her seat to the side in front of them.

He forgot the long dark hair as Mass started. It was not because of his devotions. His thoughts were on the upcoming tussle with HB over Elliot Hunt. He chased them away with recollections of the enjoyable time in Buenos Aires with Carolina. As always, Veronica noticed his lack of attention to Mass and chastised him. He made a half-hearted attempt to follow the priest's sermon, which was something about the fall being a time to cogitate on one's conduct during the preceding year. Why the fall? James asked himself, quite mystified.

The priest went quickly through the remaining liturgy and James was soon in line to take communion. Further on was the woman with the long, dark hair. She took the bread but refused the wine. As she turned to walk away, James caught a glimpse of her soft features. She must be very pretty, he thought. It's a pity she hadn't turned round.

He was already captivated by her. She turned into the aisle that led to her pew and had no reason to glance back at the altar. But she did, and looked straight at James. A shock went through his entire body and his eyes locked on to her's. He had never in his whole life beheld such incandescent beauty. He caught the shimmer of her dark eyes, the soft contours of her lips around her slightly opened mouth, the perfect harmony of her features, and the luxurious dark hair that cascaded down past her sumptuous breasts.

But it was not lust that gripped him. It was wonder and an overpowering desire to run across and take her into his arms. Out of the blue, he found himself submerged by an uncontrollable passion that made him tremble. The lady alongside looked at him in concern and asked if he was alright. James managed to mumble some answer without taking his eyes off the young woman. A slight push from behind told him that he was holding up the line. With an enormous effort, he wrenched his eyes away from this vision of sublime beauty and arrived to receive communion from the priest. He was so distraught that, instead of holding out his hand, he opened his mouth to receive it in the old way.

James was thoroughly shaken and knelt down to collect himself. This was senseless, incredible. How could he feel such passion for a woman he'd only seen for a few seconds? This could only happen in books. It happened to poor old Tristan, but at least he could blame it on a love potion.[16]

You're crazy, he told himself, you're a married man, you've two children, and you're in church. And she's a perfect stranger! Yet, he couldn't resist glancing over at her. Luckily Veronica was deep in her prayers, so she didn't notice. The woman, she must be in her early twenties, he decided, turned to look at him again. Their eyes met once more, and James knew that the passion was mutual. Afraid he would lose control, he averted his eyes.

"I want to leave," Susanna complained. "Why does Mommy pray so much?"

His daughter's complaint brought James back to reality, and he realized that most people had left the church. The young woman was still there, and he was drawn ever more irresistibly to her. He knew he had to leave before he did something irrevocable. He needed to get away and reason with himself.

"Come on, Veronica," he said, "I think you've said enough to God. Don't be too greedy. Let other people have a chat with Him, too."

Susanna giggled, and Veronica threw her husband one of her Victorian looks. She was not amused.

While Veronica was preparing to leave, the young woman hurried past them. Veronica commented on James staring at her. Before he could stop himself, he admitted that she fascinated him. Veronica was aghast at such thoughts in church. Thank God for your excessive piety, James thought, any other wife would have been jealous.

———

On Saturday, Antonietta had been alone arranging the cottage and she was glad to go out to Mass this Sunday. She arrived early at Saint-Sauveur and took an expresso on the terrace of a café opposite the church called La Brûlerie. It was a warm, luminous day, and Antonietta was determined to take advantage of it.

When it was time for Mass, she walked to the church. She crossed herself with holy water from the font at the entrance of the church and walked down the aisle. She entered a row of pews to the left of the center aisle, knelt down and murmured a quick prayer to the Virgin. The church filled up and Mass started. She had difficulty following the priest who spoke very quickly with a thick Quebec accent. She understood even less of the sermon, which had something to do with fall and one's conduct throughout the year. Why the fall? she thought.

Soon it was time to take communion. She was used to men staring at her, and this had given her a sixth sense. So when she turned away from the altar, she was aware of James' gaze upon her. Normally, this would have irritated her, but, still adrift in a new country, it was a comfort. She reached the left aisle that led to her pew but couldn't resist looking back at the queue of communicants in search of her admirer. That's when she saw James. Their eyes met and, in that instant, her life changed for ever.

PHILIP DE VILLARS

Antonietta was electrified by the feelings evoked in her by this unknown man, and she caught her breath in shock. She realized immediately that this was the passion of which her uncle had talked, and she stared in stupefaction at James, devouring him with her eyes. She was possessed by an overwhelming desire to run over and throw herself into his arms. She wanted desperately to give herself to him, body and soul.

Suddenly, to her dismay, he turned away. A discreet cough from the lady behind made her realize that, like herself, he'd been holding up the people in his line. Comforted, she returned to her pew and rested her bowed head on her hands, as if in prayer, pondering the enormity of what was happening to her. She felt elation at finding at last the man to fill her emptiness and relief that she was, after all, a normal woman.

Unlike James who, with what Antonietta would later call his cold English reason, couldn't accept what had happened to him, Antonietta found it quite natural that the passion she had longed and prayed for would descend upon her like this, unannounced, unexpected, with a total stranger in the most unlikely of venues. Instinctively, she knew that passion was irrational, that it could never be cultivated out of a friendship or even with a lover. If it was not there at the moment you saw the person for the first time, however briefly, it never would be. But who was he? He was taller than most French Canadians. In fact, he looked British, with his thick unruly hair and nonchalant elegance. He was good-looking in a very masculine way far removed from the prettiness of Mario or the delicate features of Alessandro. He reminded her a little of Giacomo, except that his face expressed a calm strength lacking in her former lover.

If he was British, what was he doing at Mass? Despite her four years at a convent school in England, Antonietta persisted in regarding the British as a Protestant race. Intrigued and impelled by a desire to set her eyes upon the man again, she turned round and sought him out. She found him, and once again their eyes met and betrayed their passion for each other. Then she saw the two handsome young children on either side of him and the blond woman next to the boy, deep in prayer. The horrid truth hit her. The man was married!

Antonietta's world of a few delicious moments collapsed. She felt incomprehension, followed by despondency and finally by anger. She looked at the crucifix above the altar and muttered an imprecation in Italian. The woman next to her gave her an odd look. Incapable of sorting out the powerful emotions that were in conflict within her, Antonietta stood up in a daze and, hardly aware of what she was doing, walked down the center aisle towards the man and his family. She couldn't bring herself to look at them and hurried past. Fighting back tears of distress and anger, she made for her car. She opened the door and threw herself down in the driver's seat and put her head in her hands.

It was all too cruel. How, after all her prayers, could God have played such a trick on her? She knew, in the depths of her being, that this was the only man for her, but he was married. And Antonietta was too Catholic, too attached to her family, to contemplate marriage outside the Church. Nor could she ever just become his mistress. Once she surrendered to this passion, she knew that she would forever be its prisoner.

She looked up and saw that the family had left the church. The wife was walking on ahead. She was a handsome, blond woman who held herself very erect, but there was a cheerlessness about her. She reminded Antonietta of the mothers of some of her English classmates. The boy was chatting animatedly with his father and the young daughter, who was a much a prettier version of her mother, was tugging at his arm. Antonietta noted with unhappy satisfaction that the man was adrift in his own thoughts and paying scant attention to his children. She hoped he was going through what she was. That would be some consolation.

Antonietta gasped and tried to make herself as inconspicuous as possible, for the man had crossed the road with his daughter and was coming straight at her, followed by his wife and son. They were obviously going for brunch at the Brûlerie. Her heart pounded, and in an instinctive but quite irrational gesture, she opened the back passenger window.

"Daddy, I want pancakes," she heard the girl say in English with a Canadian accent. "What are you going to have?"

"A treble Scotch," her father replied with a little grin at his daughter. The girl giggled.

Antonietta lay back in her seat with her eyes closed. She couldn't bear to have the man in her sight any more, the longing was too painful. Anyway, the three words she'd overheard, and the way he'd said them, told her all she wanted to know. He was indeed British and he had their dry, self-ironical sense of humor, which Antonietta had never quite understood. She knew that she was the reason for the treble Scotch. Mind you, he was out of luck as the Brûlerie didn't serve alcohol, but he was certainly aware of that. For

Antonietta, his reply was an admission of the turmoil she was causing him, and this fed her passion. Tearing herself away from the nearness of the man who had captured her soul, she drove off to her lonely cottage.

———

James was desperately trying to behave normally. The family had ordered their various dishes, and now there would be the long wait for them to arrive. The slowness of the service always irritated James, but today it was excruciating. All he wanted was to be alone.

"When we've finished breakfast, I must go and do some work at the office," he told his wife.

"I thought you were playing tennis with Danny," Veronica replied. From her skeptical tone it was clear she had taken the tennis game to be another pretext for a drinking bout.

James had forgotten about the game, and he didn't feel capable of playing. All he could think about was the woman in church, the soft perfection of her features, her free-flowing long black hair, the voluptuous promise beneath the modest summer dress, and the dark expressive eyes. He was sure she was European, possibly French or more likely Italian. Suddenly, it occurred to him that she could be one of the Institute's foreign students. He groaned inwardly. A fling with girls like Carolina far from home was one thing, but this woman was something else. She was dangerous.

"Daddy, aren't you going to eat?" Susanna asked with her normal wide-eyed innocence. James hadn't even noticed the food arriving. He ate without pleasure, and eventually Veronica commented on his strange mood.

"The beginning of term always depresses me," he explained without conviction, but the answer seemed to satisfy Veronica.

The family got up from the table, James paid, and he drove them to Prévost where he phoned Danny to cancel the game. James suspected Danny was relieved for he sounded a little the worse for wear. Finally, around three o' clock, he was at last alone in his office. It was then he realized the full extent of the passion that had burst upon him.

He'd felt lust for Leonore, in the first days desire and affection for Veronica, and he'd enjoyed Carolina more than he would care to admit, but nothing in his previous experience with women had prepared him for the devastating force of his feelings for this unknown beauty. Yet it was not her beauty alone, there was something indefinable about her that possessed him.

He'd come to collect himself, to find a way back to sanity and reason, but most of the two hours in the office was spent bewitched by her. Nevertheless, when he left, he resolved to do his best to put this madness behind him.

He was still thinking about her when he lay in bed next to Veronica. "I love you," he whispered to the image that haunted him. "Yes, but it's time to sleep," Veronica said firmly, taking the words for herself. James grimaced, partly because he'd nearly betrayed himself and partly out of irritation with his wife. You're going to be a lot of help, he thought, so let's just hope I never see that woman again.

———

Antonietta spent the rest of Sunday between heaven and hell. In an ever-recurring cycle she would immerse herself in her passion, imagining their first meeting, the first words, the first kiss, until reality tugged her back to the horrible truth that her romantic imaginings were a chimera. The man was married, with two children, and he was a Catholic to boot. Yet, no sooner had she set herself against the seductive fantasy of her passion than it seized control of her again, and she was soon lost once more in blissful daydreams.

After sitting around in the cottage for a few hours, alternately moping and indulging herself in the thrill of being in love at last, Antonietta realized that she was extremely hungry. She thought of driving to Montreal to eat at Luigi's place, but she'd drunk too much wine and in any case she had a vague recollection of Luigi telling her that he closed on Sundays after summer's end. So she set out to make a pasta sauce. Despite the conflict that was tearing her apart, she couldn't help laughing when she realized that, inadvertently, she had cooked a *putanesca*[17] sauce. Perhaps someone up there was trying to tell her something!

She felt better after a good meal. She comforted herself with the knowledge that she was quite normal after all. She wasn't incapable of passion, and she wasn't a suppressed lesbian either. As she lay in bed late that evening, half asleep, with her arms wrapped around a pillow, she murmured words that for the first time had real meaning for her: I love you.

# CHAPTER 6
## Monday, September 3 to Sunday, September 9, 2001

Antonietta slammed on the brakes to avoid rear-ending a car that was halted at the stop sign on entering Saint-Sauveur. Her thoughts had been elsewhere. Indeed, ever since she'd got up that morning, they had constantly dwelled on the man she'd seen in church. The night's intermittent sleep hadn't calmed the storm of feelings he'd released within her.

Upon arriving at the Institute, Antonietta saw with dismay the lines of students outside the Lecture Hall building registering for their courses. She'd been through this unpleasant process enough times in Italy to know what a frustrating time awaited her. Here it was even worse as you had to line up separately for each course. However, once in line, she let herself sink into reveries of amorous bliss. After all, she told herself, unless she fell prey to the temptation of returning for Mass at Saint-Sauveur, she was unlikely to see the man again, and so what was the harm of indulging herself in a little bittersweet happiness.

She finally made the end of one line and registered for international economics from a professor called Leaman. She then joined what seemed an even longer line for her European course. She was surprised how young the students were and then remembered that it was an undergraduate course. By now, she'd tired of torturing herself with dreams of the impossible and fought to stifle the passion that was gnawing at her.

She looked around and noticed behind her in the queue a tall, blond girl. She was very attractive but her manner was cold and unresponsive. She caught her eyes briefly and was struck by their icy grayish blue color. She stood out by her elegance. The other students were dressed in the normal drab student uniform of blue jeans and T-shirts with silly inscriptions on them, but the girl was wearing a skirt and a well-tailored and obviously very expensive jacket over a silk white blouse. She wore her blond hair down to the nape of her neck in a stylish cut. Despite her apparent frostiness, Antonietta was drawn to her.

———

James was sat in his office trying to put the finishing touches to his notes for the class on the EU. It was his only class this term, and the plan this day had been to start preparing next term's lectures on international trade and perhaps make some progress on his latest article. As it was, the plan was going completely awry. He was too obsessed by yesterday's sublime vision to concentrate on his work.

Who was she? Would he ever see her again? Worse than these recurring questions was the longing for her that consumed him. It was madness, downright madness, he told himself repeatedly but to absolutely no effect. He couldn't wrench the image of her flawless beauty from his mind.

James was startled out of his trance by the telephone ringing. It was Carlos Guarnieri from the University of Buenos Aires with some questions on course equivalencies for exchange students. James noted Carlos' suggestions, agreed to take part in a conference on European Union law some time in December at the University of Buenos Aires and afterwards walked through the quadrangle to the Administration building to discuss the matter of equivalencies with Ilse, relieved to be shut of his own company.

———

Antonietta was happy to be leaving Saint-Sauveur behind as she sped down the motorway to Montreal. Every step she took in that town was filled with the apprehension and hope of coming across *that man*. She felt emotionally drained and looked forward to the comforting ambiance of Luigi's café.

It was late afternoon when she arrived. Scorning the obligatory expresso, she drank wine. By the time she'd finished her supper around eight, she was rather drunk. Fearing the inner turmoil that would invade her once she was on her own again in the solitude of the cottage, she gladly accepted Luigi's invitation to stay at his apartment. "You're not in a fit state to drive," he told her sternly.

"What's happening, Antonietta?" Luigi asked once they were settled in his living room. He looked at her with paternal disapproval as she poured herself another grappa. "Getting drunk isn't going to solve your problem."

Whether it was the alcohol, or the exhaustion of the roller-coaster of emotions gripping her, or just the kindly presence of the older man, Antonietta burst out crying. Luigi put his arm round her. "Talk to me," he said, and out it all came: the aimlessness of her life in Italy, the yearning for fulfillment and the man at Mass who seemed to be her salvation.

"Then what are crying about, you silly girl?"

Antonietta turned her dark expressive eyes on Luigi, and he could feel her distress through them. "He's married," she said desolately.

Luigi looked at her thoughtfully and asked whether the man was happily married. Antonietta was perplexed by the question. "I haven't a clue," she replied. "Why is that important? If he's married, he's married, whether he's happy with his wife or not."

"It's one thing to ruin an unhappy marriage," Luigi replied, "but quite another to ruin a happy marriage, particularly when there are two children involved."

Now it was Antonietta's turn to be thoughtful. She conjured up the picture of the family walking to the Brûlerie, the man walking with his daughter and son and his wife, the cheerless blond, going on ahead. "No," she told Luigi. "I don't think he's happily married." For a brief instant, she found some consolation in this reflection as if it excused her sinful dreams of adulterous bliss. But she knew this was not so.

"I don't intend to return to the church in Saint-Sauveur," she declared firmly. "That way I won't see him again, so I won't be tempted."

When Antonietta was finally lying in bed, she realized that her head was spinning. I really must cut down on my drinking, she resolved. To reward herself for this virtuous decision, she allowed herself to sink into rapturous dreams where she was making love to the stranger whom she desired with an all-consuming passion.

———

Life was not improving for James. Not only was he beset by yearning for the unknown beauty from Mass, he was now also despondent. He wanted to see her again, he had to see her again, but he knew that he shouldn't. Quite incapable of anything constructive, he set off through the walkway that led to the FEB building to pester Bill, who had returned from Vancouver the previous evening.

"Jimmy, I'd love to get pissed with you," his friend told him, "but, first of all, ten in the morning is a bit early even for me, and in any case I've got to prepare the orientation seminar for foreign students this afternoon."

James' disappointment was palpable and so Bill tried to console him. "You should come. It'd be better than disrupting everybody around here like you did yesterday, according to Danny and Piotr. You never know, perhaps there'll be some good talent there."

James suddenly had a strange presentiment. He was sure that the young woman was European, possibly Italian, and she could conceivably be one of the foreign students at the seminar. He was tempted to accede to Bill's suggestion but checked himself. The last thing he wanted was to come face to face with her in front of a gathering of students and faculty. He didn't trust himself. Better to get a grip and do some work. He left Bill's office and made his way dutifully back to the solitude of his own.

———

Antonietta liked Bill Leaman. He had a freshness and a down-to-earth approach that set him apart from the pompous professors she'd known in Italy. He was still a good-looking man, but his lifestyle was clearly beginning to take its toll. She liked that too. People who insisted on doing everything in moderation were so tedious. After he'd finished explaining about the academic program at the Institute, he was followed by the tall blond girl Antonietta had noticed when registering.

Antonietta was struck again by the girl's attractiveness as well as her coldness. She listened to the mellifluous voice detailing the various campus facilities and nearby bars and restaurants. "One other important matter," she said in conclusion. "The Students Union puts out a survey of the professors with a brief biography and a student evaluation." To Antonietta's surprise, the girl gave Bill a puckish grin and the coldness about her seemed to evaporate.

"It's all lies, that book," Bill interjected, and everyone, except the Chinese students and a very solemn German, laughed.

After the seminar. Bill stood at the door to shake hands with each student and exchange a few words. When Antonietta arrived at the door, he was so awestruck by her beauty that he became tongue-tied. So it was Antonietta who, embarrassed by Bill's silence, took the initiative of introducing herself.

"Pleased to meet you, Antonetta," Bill managed eventually, mangling her name.

She gave him a dazzling smile that left him quite stunned. Once the last student had left, he raced all the way to James' office where his friend was still trying desperately to write something for his article that made sense.

"Jimmy," Bill exclaimed. "I've just met the most beautiful girl I've ever seen. She's absolutely spectacular, fucking incredible."

He stared at James with a look of marvel on his face. James was taken aback both by Bill's enthusiasm and his uncommon lack of vulgarity, apart from the obligatory expletive. "I suppose you'd like to roger her," was all he could say in reply.

Bill ignored the comment. "I've never seen a more gorgeous woman," he enthused.

James' increasing astonishment at Bill's reaction to the girl began to give way to a nagging suspicion, for he too had seen a woman of incomparable beauty. Could it just be a coincidence? He felt a shiver go through his body. "What's she like?" he asked nervously.

"Long dark hair, soft features, a sensuous mouth, and unbelievable eyes."

It was not perhaps the most eloquent of descriptions, but James needed no more. Half in horror and half in exhilaration, he now realized that the unknown beauty from Mass *was* a student in the Institute. Desperately, he tried to hide his agitation from Bill. Luckily, his friend was far too obsessed by what he'd seen to notice James' reaction.

"What's more, she's in my class," he told James. "Why don't you check your class list to see if she's in your's."

"What's her name?" James asked as casually as he could.

"Something woppish," Bill replied. "Della something."

James looked through his class list and found the name *Antonietta della Chiesa.*

"Is that the name?" he asked, trying to stay calm.

"Yes, that's her," Bill replied.

Fortunately Bill had to go to a meeting and so James was left alone with his swirling emotions as it dawned on him that he would be seeing this woman every Tuesday and Thursday in class. He hadn't the slightest idea how he would cope.

He pushed away the article. There was no, absolutely no hope for any meaningful progress, so he might as well indulge himself. He accessed student records on the computer and looked up his Italian student. He felt a hollow feeling in his stomach as he put an identity to what until then had just been an image of sensual perfection. *Della Chiesa, Antonietta Maria Assunta*, he read, *born July 14, 1977 in Rome, Italy. Roman Catholic. Joint degree in Italian and Economics, University of Florence, 234 rue des Lacs, Ste.*

*Anne des Lacs, Québec.* There was no telephone number.

James stared at the screen. So this was her, the unknown beauty. He was no longer capable of stemming images of her from flooding his mind. He saw her in front of them as the family entered the church, in line to take communion, the softness of her features as she turned away from the altar. He recollected the first sight of her matchless beauty and the look she gave him after turning round furtively in her pew. He realized that she must know he was married, and he wondered, no, hoped she was suffering the same torment as himself. One thing was certain. He wouldn't go to Mass at Saint-Sauveur next Sunday.

"How about that drink, my good fellow?"

James looked up, startled, and saw Danny grinning at him from the doorway. "Right away," he replied, immensely grateful for the distraction.

———

Antonietta was bored and somewhat dismayed. She was at the reception for new students to the Institute sponsored by the Students Union. It was taking place in the same gloomy lecture hall as the seminar the previous Wednesday. Most of the students were first-year undergraduates and they ignored her. Even the new graduate students seemed to give her a wide berth. She was not used to such treatment.

Then, the German exchange student, Wilhelm, came up and engaged her in a laborious conversation. They were both in Markham's and Leaman's classes and Wilhelm had already read some of the textbooks for the two courses. Antonietta, who was too emotionally overwrought to settle down to reading about international economics or the European Union, listened politely but took nothing in. Fortunately, she was rescued by the tall blond girl before she was called upon to comment on Wilhelm's readings.

The girl introduced herself. "I'm Petra Markovic," she told Antonietta, interrupting Wilhelm, who went off in a sulk to find another victim. "I believe we're both registered in Professor Markham's course."

Antonietta was taken aback by Petra's friendliness, which seemed quite at odds with her usual manner. Then she remembered the incident at the seminar, which had revealed a sense of fun beneath the icy exterior. She was glad to talk her.

"Yes," she replied. "Tell me, what's he like?"

"I had him for international trade last year. He's well-organized, fair but distant. Very British."

"British?" exclaimed Antonietta. The man at Mass was also British!

Petra laughed at her response and the cold blue eyes softened and sparkled with amusement. "What's wrong with the British?" she asked. Antonietta sought desperately for an adequate response. "Nothing," she stammered. "You just don't expect to find British people in Quebec." It was a pretty sorry answer, and so she quickly changed the subject.

"By the way, my name's Antonietta, Antonietta della Chiesa."

The two young women shook hands.

"You certainly made quite an impression on Bill Leaman," Petra remarked. "I bet he went straight to Professor Markham to tell him about the raven-haired beauty from Italy."

Antonietta was strangely pleased by this indirect compliment, but it was curiosity about the British professor that dominated her. "Why would he go to see Professor Markham?" she asked.

Petra smirked. "They're good friends. Rumor has it that Markham, Leaman, Lesnik and Redfern are drinking buddies."

Antonietta immediately thought of the triple Scotch the man had wanted after seeing her at Mass. Could he possibly be this Markham? The thought set off the longing within her, and she was aware that she was flushing.

"Are you alright," Petra asked. There was no more trace of her coldness. It was clear that she'd taken a liking to Antonietta.

'I'm a little upset," Antonietta replied. "Until you came to talk me, everyone except that boring German ignored me." This was not, of course, the reason but it was not a complete lie either. The indifference of her fellow students had indeed hurt her.

"It's because you're too beautiful," Petra told her. "You intimidate the men and the women are jealous of you. Besides they're mostly undergraduates and younger than you. It's not much of a loss. The men are all jocks and the women mostly airheads."

Antonietta was amused by Petra's dismissive comments, but she doubted that she was being entirely truthful. "Even him?" she asked, remembering the way Petra had gazed at the captain of the football term when he'd made his presentation at the seminar.

"I hate myself for it," she admitted, "but I'm crazy about him. His name's Brett Taylor. Unfortunately, he's going out with that vulgar Quebecoise." She motioned to the dark-haired girl standing next to him. She was wearing too much makeup, skintight jeans and a halter top.

"What about him?" Antonietta was referring to the young man next to Brett Taylor.

"That's Brett Doefman. He's a nasty piece of work, and Taylor's under his influence."

"And him?" Antonietta pointed to a short, rotund man with sparse reddish hair growing unevenly on his head.

"Another nasty piece of work," Petra replied. "That's Arbuthnot, the Senior Dean. Everyone calls him HB, but no-one really knows why. Some say it stands for Hard Balls."

They both laughed.

"He's powerful and vindictive," Petra went on. "Once he tried to threaten me into testifying against a professor who's being accused of having sex with a student who was in his class."

Briefly she explained to Antonietta what she knew about the Hunt case. "I think it's a put-up job orchestrated by that shit Doefman and HB. Markham's defending him, of course."

"Why of course?" Everything about Professor Markham now seemed important to Antonietta.

"Because he and HB are sworn enemies," was Petra's answer, which for some reason pleased Antonietta.

They moved over to the table where the cheese and wine were laid out. The cheese was Dutch and German and the wine Australian and Chilean. Antonietta wrinkled up her nose in disgust. She hated Dutch cheese, which she found soapy, and she thoroughly disliked the sweet aftertaste of Australian and Chilean wine.

"Do you want to go to a good restaurant?" she asked Petra, who was laughing at the expression on Antonietta's face.

It was only five in the afternoon, but the many restaurants in Saint-Sauveur were probably already open. Petra was enthusiastic and within half an hour they were ensconced in Gio's, where Antonietta had treated Carlo to lunch.

"I'm in my fourth year, I'm twenty-one and I come from Edmonton, Alberta," Petra told Antonietta in answer to her questions. "I was born in Yugoslavia and I came to Canada when I was four."

Antonietta briefly recounted where she was born and where she'd lived before coming to Canada and then changed the subject. There was so much she didn't want to reveal, in particular the passion that was tearing her apart.

"Which courses are you taking?" she asked Petra. Petra replied and then repeated the question to Antonietta. In response to Antonietta's answer, she pulled out of her briefcase the survey on the professors. "Here," she said. "Look up your professors."

Antonietta read in alphabetical order, firstly Forget, then Leaman and finally Markham. Leaman was rated an excellent professor, Forget fair but boring. A strange nervousness gripped her when she turned to the entry on Markham. *Markham, James. Educated at Ampleforth College, Manchester University and...*

Antonietta nearly choked and stopped reading. After four years at a convent school in England, she knew that Ampleforth was a Catholic school. So he was British and Catholic! Just like the man in Church, and how many of those could there be? Now she was certain that this Professor Markham, in whose class she would be every Tuesday and Thursday, was the object of her consuming passion. She was shaken by a thrill mixed with dread. When she saw him, how would she resist him? Yet, she had to.

"Are you okay?" Antonietta's agitation was obvious to Petra.

"Yes," Antonietta replied with effort. "It's just that some good friends of mine went to the same school as Professor Markham."

Petra looked at her skeptically but didn't press the point. They left the restaurant and Antonietta drove Petra back to the student residence just below the Institute. They agreed to go to Mont Tremblant together the next day.

Once Antonietta was back at the cottage, she threw herself on to the bed. She was sure that the man in the church was James Markham, and she knew that her existence from now on in Quebec would be a torment. To see the man you long for twice every week and not be able to throw yourself into his arms but instead have to take notes from him about the European Union, how more cruel could fate be? How would *he* react? Did he already know she was in his class? She just hoped that he was going to suffer as much as her. In fact, she would make sure of it.

One thing was certain. She wouldn't go to Mass at Saint-Sauveur on Sunday.

————

After much discussion, the Markham family set out for Notre Dame Basilica in the old city of Montreal. At the same time and with the same intention, Antonietta was leaving Ste. Anne des Lacs.

Antonietta arrived first at the Basilica, which was already quite full. She found a seat at the back, which enabled her to take in all the magnificence of the building's interior. She said a brief prayer and then settled back to contemplate the beautiful stained glass windows. Something made her turn her gaze towards the entrance of the Basilica. Thunderstruck, she saw James and his family walk down the aisle, genuflect and sit a few rows in front of her.

Antonietta's immediate reaction was to get up and leave, but she couldn't. Her eyes riveted on James, the power of her passion prevented her from moving. She imagined herself in his arms, kissing him, and an irresistible force drew her towards him. Before she knew what she was doing, she found herself standing up, about to walk over to where he was seated. Horrified, she stopped herself and sat down again. The people in her row eyed her with suspicion.

Once she was seated again, Antonietta silently prayed the *Memorare* and implored the Virgin to help her control herself. Her prayer was answered for she managed to stay for the whole Mass, but the yearning for the man she strongly suspected was her professor never left her. The worst moment was when he turned round and their eyes met. Her only consolation was that it was clear from the man's expression that their feelings for each other were mutual, although this was hardly any help to either of them. She didn't take communion but instead remained seated, her head bowed in prayer so as not to see James. After an atrocious hour, the Mass ended and Antonietta left quickly, emotionally drained.

As for James, he'd felt ill at ease when the family took their seats in the Basilica. He put it down to the dreadful time he'd been through since last Sunday's fateful Mass. Nevertheless, it disturbed him, and he began to look around at the congregation to distract himself. In disbelief he found himself looking straight at Antonietta. He gasped and quickly turned back. He was white, and even Veronica, who normally had eyes only for the crucified Christ above the altar, asked him whether he was feeling ill. He was briefly tempted to tell Veronica the truth but, by a supreme effort, he mastered the violence of his desires.

"Well?" his wife insisted.

"No, I'm fine, Veronica," he muttered. "It must be Bill's Scotch. He always buys this cheap stuff."

Veronica gave her husband a look of scornful disapproval and returned to her devotions without further comment. Peter, who had seen the look between his father and Antonietta, glanced at him inquisitively but said nothing.

James steeled himself not to turn round again and masked his inner turmoil by appearing to pray. In fact, it was the vision of unparalleled beauty behind him that filled his thoughts, not the Lord or anyone else from the celestial host. He dreaded the walk back from taking communion when he couldn't fail to see her. As it was, he didn't see her face as it was covered by her hands, but the sight of her lovely black hair flowing past her shoulders was almost as unsettling. Usually, James was ready to leave immediately Mass ended, but this time he stayed put, ostensibly praying, in order to have Antonietta leave first. He felt sick to his stomach from this effort at self-control.

As the family finally left the Basilica, Veronica commented approvingly on James' newly-found religious fervor. In the distance, he saw Antonietta opening the door of her car. She looked up and their eyes met again. Both of them wanted desperately to run towards the other. As it was, they unhappily went their separate ways.

# CHAPTER 7
## Monday, September 10 to Friday, September 14, 2001

It was Monday morning and James was in his office thinking, as always, of Antonietta. It was worse now that he knew who she was, and seeing her at the Basilica had brought him almost to the point of surrender to the passion he felt for her. He longed to see her again, yet at the same time dreaded tomorrow's class. It would take a supreme act of will to behave normally, but somehow he had to find the strength to do so.

The telephone rang. It was Elliot Hunt informing him that he and Annya were back from their trip and that Annya was at home awaiting his phone call. James realized he'd put the Hunt case completely out of his mind, so bedazzled had he been by his obsession with Antonietta.

"I'll call her straight away," he promised, which he did. It was arranged that Annya would come to his office at eleven-thirty on Wednesday morning.

———

Antonietta had also come near to surrendering herself to James at the Basilica and entered Bill Leaman's Monday class in a daze. Hard as she tried, she couldn't keep her attention fixed on what the professor was saying. More important to her was the fact that Leaman was a good friend of James Markham. She imagined the two of them drinking and laughing together, then she added herself to the imagined scene with James—he'd become James now in her reveries—putting his arm around her as they left the party together. She imagined them kissing before getting into the car and returning home, *their* home.

"Miss della Chiesa!" It was Professor Leaman who was calling her. She looked up, startled. "That's the second time I've called your name," Bill remonstrated with good humor. "You were daydreaming, I believe. Lucky fellow!" The class burst out laughing and Antonietta reddened with embarrassment. As she left the class, Bill took her aside and apologized.

"I'm sorry if I embarrassed you."

Antonietta gave him a lovely smile. "It's true that I was daydreaming. It's I who should apologize," she replied.

———

James drove his children to school and then took the same road back to Prévost and on to Saint-Sauveur. It always irritated him that Veronica wouldn't take on this chore, but she insisted that driving the children interfered with her morning prayers, which had to be said at nine o'clock. James nursed his irritation. At least it distracted him from the infernal longing for Antonietta della Chiesa.

Once in his office, James looked over his notes for the day's lecture. He might as well not have bothered, for his mind was locked firmly on the prospect, both exhilarating and alarming, of seeing and, God forbid, perhaps even meeting Antonietta. That was all he could think about, at least until a devastated Bill Leaman burst into his office with news of the attacks on the Twin Towers. James looked vacantly at his friend, who was practically in tears.

"You mean, they just flew two planes into them?" he asked incredulously. Bill, unable to speak anymore, just nodded.

They went down to the Faculty Lounge in the Administration building to watch the television. For some time, as the horror unfolded in New York, James didn't think of Antonietta. Then Winstone arrived and announced with his customary pomposity that, in view of the national tragedy in the United States, classes would be canceled that day.

James' immediate reaction was relief at the postponement of his ordeal, but beneath the relief was a disappointment that bordered on despair. He had to see Antonietta again. While his colleagues continued to watch with perverse fascination the scenes of destruction and death on the television, James was lost in reverie about the enchanting and irresistible woman who had captured his soul.

During this time Antonietta was in the Students' Union with Petra looking in horror at the dreadful images from New York. "It's horrible," she cried, her eyes full of tears. "It serves them right," said Petra harshly. Antonietta was shocked. "How can you say such a thing?" she protested. Petra's eyes were icy blue. "They bombed my country, so now someone has bombed them. We're quits."

Antonietta remembered that Petra was from the Serbian part of

Yugoslavia, but nonetheless she was shocked by her thirst for vengeance and was about to stalk off when Brett Taylor entered the room and announced that classes had been canceled for the day. Immediately, the events in New York were relegated from her mind. One thought alone now dominated her. She wouldn't see him!

Forgetting her argument with Petra, indeed forgetting even her presence, Antonietta stood up. She had apprehended the class with James to the point of considering a withdrawal from the course, but now it was canceled she felt the same emptiness that had plagued her at home in Italy. She fought back her tears and was about to rush off when Petra stopped her.

"Antonietta, I apologize, what I said was insane. It was an impetuous reaction." The grayish blue eyes were misted over, and there was a pleading tone to her voice, and something else. Impetuously, Antonietta took Petra into her arms. "I'm not upset with you, Petra," she said softly and left.

Once back in the cottage, Antonietta sat down with a large glass of Scotch to take stock of her situation. So far in Quebec, she'd slept with one married man and fallen desperately in love with another. To top it off, the relationship with her new friend, Petra, was not entirely free of sexual undertones. The obvious conclusion was to pack up and return home before she did something she would really regret.

It was by now eight-thirty in the evening in Florence, and she called her parents. By a miracle, her mother was out and it was her father who answered. The mere sound of his warm voice strengthened Antonietta's resolve to return home, but when her father asked her in jest whether she was returning, she said no.

"That's a very forceful no, Antonietta," her father remarked. "You wouldn't have fallen in love, would you?"

Of course, she'd fallen in love, and at that moment she knew she couldn't leave. It was beyond her power to envisage an existence where she wouldn't see James.

"Well, I hope you'll be back in time for our wedding anniversary on December 16th," her father said.

Antonietta grimaced. It was a family tradition to gather for her parents' wedding anniversary, but family gatherings were not always a joyous occasion for her. Nevertheless, she promised her father that she would come.

———

James, Piotr and an irate Bill were engaged in a noisy conversation about the attack on the Twin Towers when Annya arrived. She was an extremely pretty blond and, at the sight of her, Bill's humor improved considerably.

"Can't blame Hunt, can you?" he commented to Piotr as they walked away. "She's a real dish."

Annya was blushing, and James realized that she'd heard Bill's remark.

"Don't worry about Professor Leaman," he told her. "He's incorrigible but quite harmless."

He motioned her to sit down. "I'd offer you a coffee, but my machine's broken down, so how about a Scotch?"

Annya looked at James in astonishment. "A Scotch?" she repeated.

"Yes, why not?" he replied flippantly, not dreaming that she would accept. It was just a ploy to make her feel at ease.

"As you say, Professor Markham, why not?"

Annya pushed back her blond hair with delightful nonchalance, and the joke was now on James. It was highly irregular to feed alcohol to students in your office, but he was hoisted by his own petard.

"Okay, you know what's going on," he said as he handed Annya the Scotch. "I'm sure they're out to get Elliott, but I need to hear from you directly that your relationship didn't start before the marks were handed in."

"No, we both knew that we'd fallen for each other, but we didn't even speak of it before the end of term. We did nothing wrong." Annya seemed almost in tears at the injustice of the accusations against them.

"I believe you, Annya," James told her with a comforting smile. "When did you finish with Doefman?"

"About two-thirds of the way through the class?"

"Was it because of Elliott?"

Annya appeared to hesitate.

"Tell the truth, it won't hurt."

"At first I was attracted to Brett because he was good-looking, assertive and popular. Later I realized he was a total jerk. He treated me like his property. It would never have lasted anyway, but once he realized I'd fallen for Elliott, he made my life a misery. I couldn't stand him any more, so I dumped him."

James was satisfied with the explanation.

"So how did you and Elliott finally get together?"

"I wandered around the Institute until I bumped into him," she replied. For some reason he couldn't fathom, this answer troubled James. But he put his unease aside and asked the final question, somewhat embarrassed.

"When did you become...intimate?"

"That afternoon."

"Good Lord!" was all the reply James could muster.

His reaction amused Annya who was still laughing when she left the office. Once she was gone, James called Doefman.

"I don't have much time. It's the beginning of term in case you hadn't noticed," he told James.

James' reply to this haughtiness was scathing. "At four on Thursday, you have no class. You will be in my office if you wish to pursue your case. I will not be at your beck and call, young man."

He hung up without waiting for a response.

———

After her class with Professor Forget ended at noon, Antonietta intended to go straight to the library. Instead she went in the opposite direction and found herself in the LIR building near James' office, where she caught a glimpse of Annya leaving. She was laughing. A sting of jealousy whipped through Antonietta. How dare he flirt with other girls! She made for the office, impelled by an irrational impulse to fling James' supposed infidelity in his face. On the way she bumped into Bill Leaman. He was surprised to see her.

"Miss della Chiesa?" he asked. "Are you on your way to see Professor Markham?"

Antonietta was thoroughly disconcerted. "No," she stammered, blushing. "I'm on my way to the library."

"Ah, I see." Bill paused. "Well, you'd better go in the opposite direction," he suggested with an amused look on his face.

"Thank you," Antonietta murmured and turned round.

She never went to the library. Sick with jealousy and longing, she went instead to the church where her ordeal had started. Gazing upon the statue of the Virgin, she prayed for strength to resist her adulterous passion.

———

Thursday arrived and with it the first class together for Antonietta and James. It was the occasion they had both desired and feared. It would no longer be at a distance, sanctified in some way by the holy place in which it took place, that their eyes would meet, but close up in the relative intimacy of a classroom. Neither knew how they would cope, both were full of apprehension but neither one nor the other would have forgone the occasion.

James entered the classroom. He always avoided looking at the students in a way that would enable him to identify individuals. He preferred them as a blur of anonymity. Today, however, his eyes danced around the class seeking Antonietta. He saw her, and his mind became a complete daze. He introduced himself almost inaudibly to the class and then announced that he would go through the class list.

Antonietta was in no better shape. Before James arrived, she felt sick to her stomach. Petra, seated next to her, remarked on how white she was.

"It must be nerves," Antonietta told her.

"You don't need to be nervous," Petra replied, "He's a good teacher and a very decent guy."

At that moment James entered the classroom and confirmed Antonietta's worst fears and fondest hopes. He *was* the man from Mass. She trembled and grasped the ridge of the desk.

James was going through the class list. "Anderson." "Present." "Aworski." "Present" and so on. All by their family name. Then "Antonietta." Antonietta couldn't answer, overcome by the emotion of hearing him pronounce her name. Petra dug her in the ribs and finally she responded, "Present."

"How come he called you by your first name?" Petra whispered.

"Perhaps he can't pronounce my last name."

"That can't be it," Petra retorted. "According to Professor Pettroni, he speaks fluent Italian."

Antonietta looked at Petra in amazement. James spoke Italian! How on earth could that be? God in Heaven, she thought, everything is conspiring against me.

James was aware that he was making a complete mess of his introductory class. Normally, he used it to put the students at ease, make a few jokes and set out the main tenets of his approach to the course. As it was, he was under the spell of hearing Antonietta's voice. He was quite unaware that he'd singled her out by using her first name. He was about to flee to the quiet of his office and digest the marvel of seeing and hearing Antonietta when he remembered his best lines.

"If you don't want to come to class, or if you're too hung over, that's fine by me. This is a university, not a bloody high school. But what we do in class is on the exam. So it's in your own interest to show up." He managed a grin and added, "Besides, I don't want to prepare all this boring stuff for nothing."

By now the students were roaring with laughter, and Antonietta was staring in wistful adoration at the man she loved.

Once the class was over, James quickly disappeared. Antonietta, at her wits' end, followed Petra out of the room. Petra's face lit up when she saw Brett Taylor waiting for them with one of his friends.

"Do you two want to come for lunch," he enquired.

All Antonietta wanted was to go home to the solitude of her own thoughts, but she could see that Petra was desperate for them to accept the invitation. She agreed all the more reluctantly as Wilhelm had ingratiated himself into the group. They made their way in glorious sunshine across the quadrangle past the incongruous fountain and between the FEB and Administration buildings to the Students Union. To Antonietta's dismay, the group made for the cafeteria where the food was abysmal and no alcohol was served. She picked up a wilted salad and a small bottle of Pellegrino water.

Meanwhile, James had regained his office. He was furious. He'd made a fool of himself in class because of that damned girl but, despite his anger, he was soon lost in reminiscences of her presence: her beauty, the sound of her voice, her very name. God, I want her, he admitted to himself and then came a sobering reflection. He was a fine person to be defending Hunt. If he didn't pull himself together, he'd end up before the Ethics Committee himself. The vision of a triumphant and vindictive HB lording it over him strengthened his determination to fight the foolish passion that was threatening to destroy both his marriage and his career. He called Claudio Pettroni for a game of squash. He didn't particularly like the game, but at least it would take his mind off Antonietta.

———

Lunch was as excruciating as Antonietta had feared. Brett and his friend kept talking about James' weird behavior in class. Wilhelm remarked that he had found him "disappointing," which infuriated Antonietta. Pretentious ass, she felt like telling him.

"It was probably just a hangover," concluded Brett with a chuckle. "He and his friends are big drinkers. He'll be okay the next class."

During the whole conversation, Petra observed how much the conversation troubled Antonietta. Finally, she couldn't resist asking the question that had plagued her ever since James had called Antonietta by her first name. "Have you met Professor Markham somewhere before, Antonietta?"

"No, never," Antonietta assured her.

There was no doubting the honesty is her expressive eyes, but Petra was perspicacious enough to catch the longing in them as well. She couldn't understand how it had come about, but her new friend seemed to have fallen head over heels in love with James Markham.

A group of students from their class with James arrived at the next table. They began to talk about his strange behavior as well. Antonietta could bear it no longer and left. Once she arrived home, she collapsed on the sofa, overwrought, in tears. She wanted him, she wanted him so badly that it was physically painful. She had trouble breathing.

More out of despair than a desire for a drink, she opened a bottle of wine and poured herself a glass. She picked up the registration package from the Institute and flipped through the notes on the professors until she came to the only one that mattered to her. Now she read that James had done his doctorate at the European University Institute in Florence between 1988 and 1991. So, for three years they had lived in the same city, walked the same streets, perhaps even attended Mass in the same church! It was incredible, she could hardly believe it. What would have happened if he'd seen her?

Antonietta was suddenly beset by the dreadful idea that James might have glanced at the young teenager she was then without interest. After all, he must have frequented women of his own age. She was overcome by a jealousy as powerful as it was irrational. She finished the bottle of wine without enjoyment and fell asleep on the sofa.

---

Doefman entered James' office with an arrogant swagger and sat down without being invited. James looked at him searchingly and said nothing. After a little while, Doefman's confidence seemed to wane. He crossed his legs nervously.

"You have made a very serious allegation against Professor Hunt, Mr Doefman," James said finally. There was a hint of menace in his voice as he added, "You'd better be able to back it up."

Doefman might have been nervous, but he was not intimidated by James. "Hunt deserves to be fired," he spat out. "He did everything he could to make me seem like an idiot in class, just so he could steal my girlfriend. I'm a good student and that son of a bitch kept putting me down just to impress Annya."

"I think we can do without the bad language, Mr. Doefman," James remonstrated before going on with deliberate brutality. "I understand from Miss Nowak that she ended her relationship with you quite simply because she couldn't, as she put it, stand you any more."

Doefman blanched but refused to budge. "That's not true," he objected. "If it hadn't been for that Hunt, she'd never have left me."

James realized that his attempts to intimidate Doefman were not succeeding. So he changed tactics.

"I notice that the students who, apart from yourself, testify to having seen Professor Hunt and Miss Nowak together are students who received a poor mark in the course."

"So?"

Despite the haughty tone, James sensed that Doefman was on the defensive. He pressed home the advantage. "So, it could be argued that they are no more impartial observers of what happened than yourself, and no more credible."

Doefman was clearly taken aback by James' tack and remained silent.

"In addition," James continued, "I should like to point out that seeing two people together doesn't necessarily mean they're having an intimate relationship."

"I have witnesses who saw them kissing," Doefman retorted defiantly. "The reason why these witnesses are students who got poor marks is because they didn't have anything to lose by helping me. The others didn't want to make waves."

Doefman was regaining his confidence, and James saw no further possibility of shaking his story. Perhaps he would have better luck with the other alleged witnesses. All he needed was for one to break down and confess that he or she had lied, and this should discredit the whole case against Hunt.

———

Petra was with Antonietta in the Students Union trying to persuade her to attend the reception for foreign students. "It should be enjoyable," she told her. "Besides," she added with a wicked grin, "you can teach Professor Markham how to pronounce your family name."

That was the whole point, Antonietta wanted to cry out, *he'll* be there!

However much she longed to see and talk to him, she dreaded not being able to control herself. But, maintaining her composure with great effort, she went along with her friend's banter.

"Do come," Petra insisted, and Antonietta agreed. It would give her a chance to see whether James was going through the same anguish as herself, although exactly how this was going to help her was not at all clear. In fact, nothing was any longer clear for Antonietta, buffeted unmercifully between her passion and her resolve to resist it.

———

James had finished giving Ilse the names of the students he wanted to see in connection with the Hunt case. She agreed to have her secretary set up the meetings, which was a great relief. However, this also meant that he was back in his office with nothing else to do but work on his article. Try as he might to interest himself in the intricacies of the European Union, Antonietta constantly returned to haunt him. He found himself imagining that he was kissing her, telling her that he loved her, listening to her own protestations of love. God, you're a soppy sentimentalist, he told himself, putting an abrupt end to these seductive fantasies.

"James, don't forget the reception for the foreign students in half an hour."

It was Bill Leaman. Realizing that Antonietta would doubtless be present, James demurred, pretexting the article he was writing.

"You have to come," Bill replied. "You're the Assistant Dean of International Affairs, and Tom can't make it."

James reluctantly agreed to attend, but it was a reluctance tinged with barely suppressed excitement. He tried working for a few more minutes on his article and then left the office and made his way to the Lecture Hall building. Halfway across the quadrangle, he stopped. Of course he was desperate to see Antonietta, but it was sheer folly to go to the reception. Nevertheless, he carried on, as he knew he would.

He saw her at once. She was, thankfully, at the other end of the large room, talking with Petra Markovic, who seemed to have become her friend. They made a stunning couple: the dark-haired Antonietta with her incomparable beauty that smoldered with lubricious sensuality and the blond Petra, whose classic good looks hinted, despite their chilliness, at an innate eroticism. James could see the attraction between the two girls and felt uneasy.

It was Petra who saw James arrive in the room. "Look," she whispered to

Antonietta, "Professor Markham has arrived." Antonietta willed herself to keep calm and refused to turn round. "Well, he had to come, didn't he?" she replied as indifferently as she could. "After all, he's Assistant Dean of International Relations."

"Oh, my God," Petra exclaimed. "He's been nabbed by Wilhelm." Petra giggled and Antonietta, despite the conflicting emotions of dread and longing that swirled within her, couldn't help following suit.

"Miss della Chiesa, please come with me."

It was Professor Leaman. Before Antonietta could object, he took her by the arm and led her towards James. "It's time you met Professor Markham," he told her firmly. Antonietta's stomach gave way and she arrived before James trembling like a leaf.

"James, may I introduce the lovely Antonetta della Chiesa," Bill announced, still mangling Antonietta's name.

James and Antonietta were forced to look straight at each other. James felt his resistance drain away with every second he gazed into Antonietta's dark, glittering eyes. There was no mistaking the passion they expressed.

"Pleased to meet you," he said and abruptly left the room.

Bill stared after him, shocked by his apparent rudeness. "I apologize," he told Antonietta. "He's not normally such an asshole."

He couldn't have known that Antonietta, who with difficulty had restrained herself from collapsing into James' arms, was both relieved and elated by his departure. It had averted a potential scandal and at the same time shown her that he was undergoing the same ordeal as herself. Life would be a torment for Antonietta at the Institute, but so would it be for the man she loved. That was a consolation. More than that, in the midst of her anguish, it brought her a measure of contentment.

"It's not important," she assured Bill.

She stayed a little longer at the reception but, with James' departure and Petra flirting outrageously with Brett Taylor, there was nothing to keep her there. So she left.

———

Bill was highly indignant. "Markham, you're an asshole. I introduce you to the most divine girl we've ever had in this Institute, and you're rude to her. Do you have some explanation?"

James had been expecting Bill to come to his office and remonstrate with him over the episode at the reception, but he hadn't been able to decide whether to tell him the truth or not. On the one hand, it would be a relief to share his torment with a close friend, but he was afraid to appear a lovesick fool.

"Well, are you going to tell me?" Bill insisted.

James sighed and looked warily across his desk at Bill. He caressed the afternoon stubble on his chin. He sighed again. It was time to confess. "I'll tell you if you promise not to make fun of me. It's bad enough as it is without me becoming a laughing stock for my friends."

Bill agreed, and James began his tale. He told Bill about the first time he'd seen Antonietta at Mass, the intensity of the feelings she'd evoked in him, his irresistible longing for her, the second sight of her in the Basilica, the mess he'd made of his introductory class because of her, and the fateful meeting that afternoon when he'd nearly lost control of himself.

"I'm at my wits' end, Bill," he admitted. "You can't imagine how desperately I want her. This whole business is just crazy"

There was a short silence while Bill reflected upon what James had told him. He had no desire to mock his friend. "It's not that crazy, James," he said. "She's unbelievably beautiful and sexy as a goddess. If I wasn't so besotted by that errant wife of mine, I'd probably have fallen in love with her myself."

James was silent, lost in his own thoughts.

"Your problem's worse than you think," Bill went on. "She's nuts about you, too."

"I know," said James, "but how come you do?"

"Well, our delightful Antonetta has been in a complete daze since the beginning of term. Once you left, she didn't even bother to stay at the reception. What's more, I caught her this week on her way to your office. When I challenged her, she turned all red and told me she was going to the library. She's not a very good liar."

"When did you see her?"

"Wednesday, the day you interviewed Annya."

This news took James completely by surprise. So Antonietta had already known who he was even before their class. But why was she coming to see him? Surely, it wasn't…?

"What are you going to do?" Bill asked with a trace of impatience, interrupting his friend's train of thought.

"What *can* I do? If ever I give in to this…" James hesitated before continuing, "this passion, it'll be for ever, and it'll destroy both my marriage and my career. After all, Bill, I *am* married, and she *is* a student in my class."

Bill was unimpressed. "That's not it at all, James, and you know it. Your marriage is a sham and as long as you're very discreet, you can get away with sleeping with her. No, you're afraid of losing control of your life, To put it bluntly, Jimmy, she scares the shit out of you."

Bill was partly right. James knew that once he gave in to the lure of Antonietta, she would possess him completely.

"I'm going to say a few rosaries with Veronica," he said morosely, "Perhaps the Lord will help me."

"Jimmy, you can say all the mumbo-jumbo Papist prayers you like, but you two are going to end up together." Bill stood up and made to leave the office. "Mark my words," was his parting shot.

James reflected on Bill's words. It was true that his marriage was an empty shell, but there were the children and also the distress that a divorce would cause Veronica. Perhaps he could have Antonietta as his mistress? However, despite Bill's sanguinity, James was sure that sooner or later there would be a scandal, and this would cost him both his marriage and his career. In any case, his passion for Antonietta was like an alcoholic's craving for booze. Once he gave into it, he would be its slave. No, it was divorce and re-marriage or nothing at all, and he didn't want the emotional chaos such a scenario would provoke.

A foreboding descended upon James. He was resolved to combat the passion that threatened such havoc in his life, but where would he find the strength to deal with the constant presence of the woman he desired with such unyielding force?

# CHAPTER 8

## Monday, September 17 to Saturday, September 29, 2001

The next Monday, James met two of the students who had testified against Hunt and two others that had not. It was a disappointing experience. The two hostile witnesses stuck to their story that they'd seen Hunt and Annya kissing, although the number of times varied between once and four times. It was clear to James that they were lying, but he couldn't shake them. The other two students, who had received good marks in the course, said they'd seen nothing, which, apart from adding weight to James's contention that Hunt was a victim of students out for revenge, didn't prove anything tangible.

So Tuesday came and the second class together for James and Antonietta. That morning Antonietta rose early to wash her hair and prepare herself. She wore a tight blouse unbuttoned low enough to afford a glimpse of her breasts, which were barely contained by her tiny bra. The blouse was tucked into a short, tight skirt that showed off her shapely, sunburned legs to perfection. Her long dark hair flowed down to her shoulders over the elegant Versace jacket she left undone so that the view afforded by her blouse was not obstructed. She put on a tasteful but tantalizing amount of glossy lipstick and mascara. She would make James suffer as much she would from their class together.

Petra looked at her in amazement when she walked into class. "You look incredible," she exclaimed. "Is that for Professor Markham?"

Antonietta was saved from having to reply by James' entry into the classroom. She could feel herself tense up while she waited for him to see her. Their eyes met briefly and she was gratified by James' grimace. This time, she would make sure to walk right past him at the end of class before he could rush off.

The effect on James of Antonietta's appearance was in fact more devastating than she realized. Try as he might, he couldn't prevent his eyes constantly straying in her direction and devouring her shameless lubricity. It eclipsed all thoughts of the European Union, and the lecture was a disaster. When it ended, a number of students came up with questions in order to make sense out of the chaos of James' presentation. One of them, an arrogant young man by the name of Ken Wrangel, was extremely argumentative. Just at that moment, Antonietta walked past them and James forgot completely what Wrangel had asked him. He gave some evasive answer and Wrangel stalked off in disgust.

Immediately after the class, James drove to Ste. Agathe des Monts and sat by the lake. What was he going to do? What did Antonietta's appearance mean? Was it just her way of dressing? After all, she *was* Italian. It was known that French women bought clothes that were one size too small for them, perhaps Italian women bought them two sizes too small? James couldn't suppress the impression that she was taunting him. He swore he wouldn't give in, and in the next class, by God, he'd control himself. After all, he was British, well at least three quarters British. He put his passing weakness down to the genes he'd inherited from his French grandmother.

———

James' newly-found determination to put the emotional turmoil of the last weeks behind him brought a certain peace of mind that enabled him to pursue his task as Hunt's defender with more success than heretofore. He interviewed the remaining five students who had testified against Hunt. One of these was Brett Taylor, and James had heard from Bill that he was a nice lad who'd unfortunately fallen under Doefman's influence. James interviewed him alone.

"If I'm not mistaken, Mr. Taylor, Professor Hunt's course was the first you failed. Is that so?" James asked pleasantly.

Brett Taylor agreed.

"Well, do you think that's sufficient reason for wanting to destroy his career?'

The change in tone was brutal, and Taylor turned white."That's not it at all, Professor Markham," he mumbled.

"Then what is it?" James asked.

He was impressed by Taylor's politeness, which contrasted sharply with the arrogance of Doefman and his other cronies. Bill had been right. Here was the weak point.

"He stole Brett Doefman's girlfriend," Taylor replied. It sounded very much like a pat answer.

"Not according to her, and don't you think that she's in a better position to know than you?"

Taylor was silent for a few moments. Then he spoke very quietly and with little assurance. "I saw them walking hand in hand in the quadrangle."

"Oh, come on, Brett," James said scathingly. "Even if they *were* lovers, do you honestly expect me to believe they would hold hands in the middle of the bloody Institute?"

"It's the truth," Taylor insisted. He was red in the face and clearly uncomfortable.

"It's not, and you know it," James told him. He then added in a friendlier tone, "You're a nice kid, Brett, but you've let yourself be talked into participating in a very nasty and immoral machination to destroy an innocent man's career. Think about it, and call me any time you feel like it."

Brett Taylor said nothing more and walked slowly out of the office, leaving James feeling a little more optimistic about Hunt's chances. It was possible that Brett would crack and two of the other students seemed less dogmatic than their written testimonies suggested. If the captain of the football team deserted Doefman, these two might well follow.

The phone rang. It was Ilse wanting to see him. He made his way down to her office.

"What's up, Ilse?" he asked.

"Sit down, James." Ilse's manner was collegial but she seemed embarrassed.

"James," she continued, "you've always been one of our best professors, and the students have fought to get into your class. Yet, as of today, I have six students who want to withdraw from it. Whatever is going on?"

James didn't answer immediately, but he respected Ilse and so he answered truthfully but vaguely. "I've a little problem, Ilse, but I think I'm dealing with it. I hope the lectures will improve."

Ilse looked at him keenly. "It wouldn't be because of a certain young lady in that class, would it?

"How, in God's name, do you know?" James stared at Ilse in amazement.

"It's very strange," she replied. "When I recommended your course to her, I had a premonition. I hope I wasn't right."

"Well, Ilse," James replied. "She does have a nasty habit of putting me off my stroke."

Ilse gave a faint smile. "Don't put your career in danger, James. That would be a criminal waste, however beautiful she is. Remember Tristan and Isolde. They both died."

"That's very comforting, Ilse," James replied wryly. "Thanks for the warning. I'll make sure to heed it."

———

Brett Taylor was again waiting for Petra after their Thursday class. He was with some friends, and they wanted to go for lunch. There was no way Antonietta was going to eat the awful food in the cafeteria and wash it down with water or weak coffee. So, she agreed to accompany them on condition they went to the student bar. They started off and were joined by the omnipresent Wilhelm, who appeared happier with the day's class.

She soon regretted her decision. Brett and the two British students, Malcolm and Simon, went on about James again, his first chaotic lecture, his alleged drinking habits and his reputation as a decent guy. There was obviously something about him that fascinated the students.

"Mind you," Brett commented. "It's not much fun being cross-examined by him." Petra shot him an icy glare. "Is that to do with the Hunt case?' she asked. In reply Brett muttered something incomprehensible. Sensing the awkwardness of the situation, Simon brought the conversation back to James. "What's his wife like?" he asked.

Petra glanced at Antonietta and answered quickly, "Insipid." Unfortunately, her attempt to shield Antonietta from a topic that she knew would upset her was torpedoed by Brett.

"It shouldn't bother him. Rumor has it that he's got a mistress in Argentina," he announced.

Luckily, Antonietta was looking down at the time and no-one saw the tears well up in her eyes. She quickly got up and, mumbling an apology, rushed to the washroom where she threw up. She was beginning to hate James Markham. He was nothing but a selfish brute who enjoyed tormenting women. She didn't return to the bar, and Petra was left to explain her flight as best she could.

Antonietta drove back to the cottage, her view of the road almost obscured by the tears that filled her eyes and ran down her cheeks. Once she arrived, she ripped off her provocative clothing and changed into a pair of jeans and a blouse that she buttoned up to the very top. She felt betrayed, and an excruciating misery descended upon her.

What exactly had she expected? That James would stop the lecture and sweep her off her feet.? Is that what she really wanted, to be enslaved in a passion that meant a rupture with her family and excommunication from the Church? She threw herself down on the bed, feeling cheap and immoral. It still hurt terribly, that mistress in Argentina, but it was better than surrender to a passion that menaced everything she held dear. If only she didn't want him so badly.

There was a knock on the door. Intrigued, Antonietta wiped the tears from her face and went to open it. It was Petra.

"How did you get here?" Antonietta asked in surprise.

"I took a taxi," Petra replied. "We need to talk."

"What about?"

"James Markham."

Antonietta gave a start. "How did you guess?" she asked in a tremulous voice.

Petra sat down on the sofa, where she was joined by Antonietta. "It didn't take genius, Antonietta. I began to suspect when you overreacted to his biography. I hadn't a clue why, but it was strange. In class, you're constantly on tenterhooks and you spend all your time trying to catch his eye and then avoiding it. The notes you take don't make any sense. To cap it all, the last two classes you've gone out of your way to dress in the most outrageously sexy and provocative fashion."

"Did I look like a whore?" Antonietta asked shamefaced.

"No, Antonietta." Petra put her arm around her friend's shoulders. "You were magnificent. He must be really British not to have cracked."

"Petra, I don't want him to crack. I'm a Catholic and he's married. We can only ever be lovers."

"Well, what's wrong with that?"

"Petra," replied Antonietta, her eyes gleaming with intense emotion, "if ever I kissed him, let him into my bed, I would be his forever. That would be no better than him divorcing his wife and marrying me."

"Then why did you dress the way you did?"

"To make him suffer like I'm suffering. But it didn't work. He didn't even notice me today. He was probably thinking of his Argentinean mistress."

Antonietta could no longer control her sobs. Petra comforted her, took her face and wiped away the tears. "Antonietta, there is no Argentinean mistress."

The grief in Antonietta's eyes vanished. "But, Brett…"

"Brett was exaggerating. Bill Leaman told me that James Markham had a good time in Buenos Aires. I told Brett, and he made a mountain out of a molehill."

Tears of relief streamed down Antonietta's cheeks.

"So what are you going to do? It's quite clear to me that James Markham's as crazy about you as you are about him."

Antonietta's brief feeling of relief was swamped anew by the anguish of her predicament. "What I want is him, for ever. I want to be his wife, bear his children, spend my life with him, *that's* what I want," she said, the emotion choking her voice. "But I can't. So, I'm going to do nothing. Nothing, nothing…" Her voice trailed off.

"I don't believe you." Petra gave Antonietta a long, hard look. "If it's real passion you feel for him, and I think it is, you can't beat it. Eventually you'll give in."

Petra's words echoed those of her uncle, and Antonietta found a strange solace in them. They did nothing to solve her dilemma, but they restored her spirits and she invited Petra to eat at the little French restaurant in Prévost on the road to Saint-Sauveur. They had an excellent meal, albeit preposterously expensive, and Antonietta was happy to forget her own troubles by listening to Petra's tale of amorous woe.

"I know Brett likes me," she recounted, "but he seems incapable of shaking off that Françoise. Who knows? She and Doefman are off to Ottawa for a debate next Wednesday and Thursday. Perhaps something will happen then."

Antonietta paid for the meal and drove Petra to the student residence.

"Your family is wealthy, isn't it?" Petra remarked as she got out of the car. Antonietta nodded reluctantly. They were straying into dangerous territory. "I don't believe your uncle's a simple priest," her friend added. "Please, Petra, let's not go there," Antonietta implored.

Petra made no answer but kissed Antonietta softly on the lips. "Dress more modestly for class, Antonietta. If you feel you can't go through with it, it's unfair to tempt him." With that she vanished into the residence.

The pleasure of her kiss lent yet another layer to Antonietta's problems.

———

The following Wednesday was a black day for James and Elliot. The Rector's office had sent them both a formal notification of the composition of the Ethics Committee that would consider the accusations against Hunt. Apart from HB and Ilse Bromhoeffer, who were *ex officio* members, there was Fred Gowling from FEB, a protégé of HB's, who was appointed by Hamid Khan, Ed Williams from James' own Section, the Rector's appointee, whom he had hired for the LIR Section without consulting anyone, and Claudio Pettroni from LAC, who had been chosen by lot. Apart from Pettroni and Ilse, who would be fair, Gowling was closely linked to Arbuthnot and would doubtless follow his lead and Williams' association with Winstone augured badly.

"We've got two definitely against us but probably three, and two we can perhaps convince of your innocence," James told Elliot grimly. "Unless we have what we're looking for from Burstein and hopefully a breakthrough with the students testifying against you, it doesn't look good."

Hunt left James' office decidedly shaken.

―――――

The Thursday class passed badly for both James and Antonietta. She was consumed by longing for him, and her attempts to take notes ended, as always, in dismal failure. The doleful expression in her eyes communicated itself to James, who gave yet another unimpressive lecture. The class ended again with a group of confused students swarming around him with questions.

Antonietta followed Petra out of the class, but she was in no mood for lunch. Instead she returned to the solitude of the cottage where she listened to songs of Laura Pausini[18] and wept.

―――――

Shit, shit and shit again. James looked in disbelief at Burstein's reassessment of Doefman's paper, which had arrived that Friday morning. Hunt had given him 40% and James hoped to see an even lower mark from Burstein, but instead he'd given the paper 60%. This was lower than the 65% given by Graeme Hill, but it would not serve to exonerate Hunt. He couldn't use it. He had little difficulty imagining the hay that HB and his friends would make of it. They were stuck with Hill's reassessment.

James put his head in his hands. His whole defense of Hunt had been based on two key points: that the students who testified against him had received low marks and were out for revenge, and that Hunt had been fair in his marking of Doefman's paper. The second line of defense was now blown apart, and it was open to HB and his acolytes to use Hill's reassessment as evidence of bias in Hunt's evaluation of Doefman's paper. This would probably enable them to persuade a majority on the Committee to accept the testimonies that Hunt had infringed the ethics code of the Institute. It was not entirely logical but it was enough to cost Hunt his career. He had little faith in an appeal to the courts.

James called Hunt to come and review Burstein's reassessment. His colleague was clearly shocked by the mark assigned to the paper and very quickly found a number of points that Burstein had approved but which he maintained were wrong.

"That may be so," said James, "but we can't use this reassessment. Why the hell did you choose Burstein?"

"He's the authority in the US on labor relations, but I didn't realize how parochial he is. I guess he just knows about the US, not Europe."

"Why didn't he tell us that?"

"He's an academic. He thinks he knows it all," was Hunt's sardonic reply.

James put his arm round his colleague. "Elliot, we're now stuck with Hill's reassessment, which means we're probably fucked. As you're a religious man, I advise you to pray. Because, my dear Elliot, we need a miracle."

Once Hunt had left, James picked out an article he'd written on occupational health law in the European Union. It was part of a series edited by a Professor Ewart van Wezel of the Erasmus University in Rotterdam. He looked up the university on the internet and noted van Wezel's email address. He wrote him a short email merely asking him to comment on Doefman's paper, which he scanned and then enclosed as an attachment. European professors were an arrogant bunch and he probably wouldn't reply, but it was worth a try.

———

With one suffering from unrequited love and the other fighting a passion that devoured her, Petra and Antonietta decided to go shopping for clothes in Montreal. "Ugly women cry," Petra told her friend. "Pretty women spend money."

So, here they were buying clothes that Petra could ill afford and Antonietta didn't need. It was a lot of fun and certainly helped take their minds off their unhappy love lives.

"Come with me. I'm going to try on those jeans. They're really sexy," Petra exclaimed.

"You'll never get in them," Antonietta objected.

Petra was insistent and once in the cubicle stripped off the jeans she was wearing and the string underneath. Antonietta was fascinated by her nudity.

"Do you shave there?" she asked.

Petra laughed. "No, it's just been used a lot."

"Petra!" Antonietta was shocked but couldn't help laughing.

"No, actually, I have it waxed. They call it "un bikini intégral" in Quebec. You don't do that?"

Antonietta didn't really want to answer, but Petra pressed her. "No, in Italy women don't do that," she admitted.

"Well, you should. It improves the sensations."

Against her will, Antonietta let herself be dragged to a beauty salon. It was a very intimate and embarrassing experience, but the feel of the string afterwards on her naked flesh was highly erotic.

They arrived back at Antonietta's cottage strangely exhilarated. They opened a bottle of wine and drank it and then another. They talked and drank into the early hours, mostly about their unhappy personal situations. Petra was particularly upset because she'd hoped against hope that Brett would profit from Françoise's absence in Ottawa to make a move. It hadn't happened. By the time they'd finished the last bottle of wine, an excellent Chianti Classico that neither was in a fit state to appreciate, they were both very drunk.

"I can't drive you back home," Antonietta slurred. "So why don't you stay here. I'll sleep on the couch."

Petra walked unsteadily to the bedroom and looked in. "Nonsense, this bed's big enough for two," she said.

They undressed down to their bra and string and climbed into bed. Antonietta lay down but she normally slept naked and the bra bothered her. Without thinking, she sat up and took it off. Petra stared at her bare breasts and very gently began to caress them. It took Antonietta a few seconds to realize what was happening, but this was time enough for her to become too aroused by Petra's delicate touch to protest.

Petra undid her own bra. Her breasts were smaller than Antonietta's, but they were shapely and inviting. Images of Dana came back to Antonietta, and memories of the pleasure that the older girl had given her. She didn't resist when Petra pushed her down on the bed. Exhausted emotionally by the heartache and yearning of the past weeks, Antonietta abandoned herself to her friend's lust.

Antonietta's body tensed as Petra slowly pulled down her string. Involuntarily she opened her thighs to receive Petra'a tongue on her newly denuded sex and gasped when she felt it. Petra caressed and played lasciviously with her, and soon Antonietta was aware of nothing but her mounting desire. She let herself be turned onto her stomach and moaned blissfully at the smoothness of Petra's pert breasts brushing against her buttocks. Petra opened them up and ran her tongue and then her fingers along the crack between them. Antonietta cried out and begged for release. Petra obliged by using her tongue in a most shameless way while her fingers brought Antonietta, with tantalizing softness, to a violent climax. Still not finished, she turned Antonietta over and drained the remnants of her sexual desire.

"Now it's my turn," Petra announced.

She lay down beside Antonietta, her lips glistening with her friend's wetness. Antonietta came on top of her and kissed and fondled her tight breasts, luxuriating in the softness of the skin and the hardness of the nipples on the palms of her hands. She ran her tongue down the golden smoothness of Petra's body until she reached her sex, where she quickly, almost impatiently, slipped off the string that was covering it. She marveled at the discrepancy between the cold splendor of the young woman she had first glimpsed at registration and the twisting, naked girl lying before her with her thighs wide open, desperate for pleasure. Antonietta titillated Petra until her thighs were drenched from sexual excitement.

"I want it like you," she whispered hoarsely.

Antonietta turned Petra onto her stomach and ran her nipples, still taut with lust, over her girlfriend's trim buttocks. She administered the same dissolute pleasure with her tongue that she had enjoyed and, using the fingers of both hands, brought Petra to a paroxysm that convulsed her whole body.

———

Antonietta woke first and one glance at the naked Petra lying on her stomach next to her in bed recalled their night of sex. She jumped out of bed and rushed to put on a bathrobe.

"Oh, my God," she exclaimed out loud.

She could hardly believe what she'd done but, despite the drunkenness, the recollection was only too vivid. How, after all these years, could she have allowed herself to do this again with a girl. In a daze, she wandered into the kitchen, mechanically ground some coffee and prepared two expressos.

Embarrassed and repelled by her own perverted sexuality, she woke Petra up.

"Petra, have some coffee."

Petra opened her eyes and smiled prettily at Antonietta. "Do you realize we're lovers," she said, turning over and exhibiting her breasts and sex quite brazenly to her distraught friend.

"No, we're *not*," Antonietta cried. "We were drunk and it just happened."

"We were also very horny," Petra observed with the same wanton smile. "We both enjoyed it, so don't pretend otherwise. Why don't you come back to bed. I wouldn't mind doing it again now we're sober."

"Petra!" Antonietta stood up and walked away from the bed in horror. "We're going to get dressed and we're going to have breakfast at the Brûlerie," she said firmly.

After breakfast Antonietta drove Petra to the student residence. "I've got two papers to write, so we'll see each other on Tuesday," she told Antonietta. "By that time our hormones should have settled down." Antonietta's eyes clouded over. "I hope we'll still be friends, Petra. You're the only friend I have here."

Petra lent over and kissed her on the cheek. "Don't worry, Antonietta. Of course we're still be friends." She got out of the car but poked her head back in. "You were a great lay. Best I've ever had." She grinned and walked off, leaving Antonietta completely mortified.

Antonietta returned to the cottage. She was still in a state of shock over her lapse, which Petra's crude comment made seem even more blameworthy. It brought back all her old demons, but she was comforted by the ache she felt when she thought of James. She sought for some excuse for the unnatural delights of the previous night. Perhaps Petra was right. This sort of thing happened occasionally between women. In any case, she told herself, she deserved some respite from the agony she was going through. In the end, she managed to convince herself that it was all James' fault. If she didn't love him so much, she'd have found some man to relieve her sexual frustrations.

# CHAPTER 9

## Tuesday, October 2 to Friday, October 19, 2001

It was time again for James' class, but this time Antonietta was more apprehensive about finding Petra after their intimacies of Friday night. As it happened, Petra was all smiles when they met in class. "Oh boy," she told Antonietta. "Have I got some news for you. I'll treat you to lunch."

Once they were ensconced in the restaurant, Petra took a deep breath and began her tale of joy. "You know that Doefman and Françoise were at that debate in Ottawa?" Antonietta nodded. "Well, they went to bed together!"

Antonietta looked at Petra in disbelief. "But Doefman's supposed to be Brett's best friend!"

"No longer," Petra replied with grim satisfaction. "On Friday, Françoise told Brett what had happened. That night he called me but, as I told him, I was in bed with you."

Antonietta gasped in horror. "You said *that*! How could you?"

Petra drew Antonietta to her and kissed her demurely on the cheek. "No, of course, I didn't, you silly goose."

"So what's happened since then?" Antonietta asked, greatly relieved despite her indignation at being compared to a bird.

"We've spent all the time in bed," Petra replied.

Antonietta felt a stab of jealousy but she quickly recovered. "I'm so happy for you, Petra," she said. "At least one of us has found happiness."

"Tonight," Petra went on, "Brett, me and some others are meeting Bill Leaman for a drink at the students' bar. You must come."

Antonietta had no real desire to be a witness to Petra's and Brett's newly found happiness. It was partly jealousy, but above all their happiness highlighted her own misery. However, Bill Leaman would be there and he was, if student gossip were to be believed, James' closest friend. So desperate was her longing for James that even a surrogate was better than a night alone with her sad fantasies in the cottage. She accepted.

Antonietta made her way despondently back home and made a half-hearted attempt to study. She was glad when it was time to leave for the bar, but she had no idea how to dress. On the one hand, she wanted Bill to go back to James with tales of her sexy appearance, but then again she didn't want to appear a whore. You could never be sure with Anglo-Saxons. Her Latin temperament revolted. To hell with it, she thought, they can think what they like! It was cold and wet, and so she put on a clinging sweater and skintight jeans.

She was the last to arrive. Professor Leaman was already in an expansive mood. Petra and Brett was interlaced together and Simon and Wilhelm were engaged in an acrimonious dispute about the 1966 World Cup Final, in which England had beaten Germany due to a disputed goal.

Bill Leaman gleamed with delight at seeing her. He made a few totally inappropriate comments, which amused Antonietta. She hated people who weighed every word and always said the right thing. Suddenly, he became serious and bent over to whisper in Antonietta's ear.

"Are they together?" he asked, pointing to Petra and Brett Taylor.

Antonietta nodded. "Françoise cheated on him with Doefman, so he's jumped on the occasion to leave her for Petra," she explained.

Bill looked thoughtful and, after a few more mouthfuls of beer, was about to leave when Brett leaned over the table with a question.

"Tell me, Professor Leaman," he said uncertainly. "Is it true that Professor Markham has a mistress in Buenos Aires?"

Petra shot him a poisonous look, but Brett was too far into his cups to notice. Bill blinked drunkenly. Forgetting Antonietta's presence, he answered the question. "I wouldn't say a mistress, but I think he and Carolina had a good time together, if that's what you mean."

"That happened a long time ago," Petra observed quickly, aware of Antonietta's acute distress. Her hostile manner made Bill realize his lack of tact. "Yes," he agreed, anxious to make amends, "It was in August. He's not been back since."

Soon after that he left and, once in his car, called James. "Hello, Jimmy," he drawled. "I've just spent the evening with Antonetta."

There was silence at the other end of the phone. "Is that all you're calling about," James eventually replied.

"No, you ungrateful son of a bitch, I'm calling to tell you that you may have a break in the Hunt case." Bill could hear James catch his breath. "Petra Markovic, you know who she is?" he asked.

"Of course, she's Vice-President of the Students Union."

"Well," Bill went on, "she's now going out with Brett Taylor."

"So?"

"So, there's been a big bust-up between Doefman and Taylor. It seems Doefman fucked Taylor's girlfriend, and that's why he's now with Markovic."

"Will he testify against Doefman?" James asked.

"Leave it to me," Bill replied. "I'll go through Markovic."

James put the phone down. At last there was a glimmer of hope for Elliot Hunt. He felt immensely relieved. He didn't particularly like the man, and he couldn't help feeling that this antipathy accounted in some measure for his lack of success in making any headway against Hunt's accusers. He was also very envious. While he was grounded in the austerity of his house, Bill was talking, and laughing no doubt, with the woman he loved.

Antonietta didn't remain very long after Bill's departure. The sight of Petra and Brett evoked the hopelessness of her own passion, and now her jealousy had a name to feed on, Carolina. Her mind dulled by pain, she returned to the cottage.

———

The following three weeks were unbearable for Antonietta. At the beginning, the novelty of being in love had given a bitter sweetness to her sufferings, and then had come the excitement of seeing James in class and the malevolent joy of stoking his passion for her. Now these consolations had palled, and there was only hopeless longing and jealousy. Petra was completely caught up in her new love affair and had little time to spare for her. Antonietta didn't really mind. Although she was genuinely pleased for Petra, the contrast between her own misery and Petra's happiness was too excruciating. Even her visits to Luigi brought scant relief from her emotional agony.

Unable to concentrate on any work, Antonietta passed her lonely days drinking too much and listening to Laura Pausini. As she played *In assenza di te*$^{MBOL42\backslash f"Symbol"\backslash s1219}$ for the umpteenth time, she went listlessly through her notes from Professor Forget's class. She threw them down in despair. The paper on Canadian confederation due on Friday was beyond her present capabilities.

The next week she was summoned to Dr. Bromhoeffer's office. "It appears that you haven't handed in a paper for Professor Forget," Ilse said not unkindly. "Is there a reason for that?"

Of course there was a reason, but Antonietta could hardly tell Dr. Bromhoeffer that she was prey to a hopeless passion for James Markham that completely paralyzed her. She turned red. "I haven't done Professor Leaman's paper either," she said glumly.

Ilse stared at the young woman, whose anguish was only too obvious to her. "Antonietta, I'm not blind. I'm quite aware of what's distressing you. May I make a suggestion?" Antonietta nodded, although she was not sure she wanted hear it. "Why don't you return to Italy? Your time here is doing you absolutely no good.

"I can't!" Antonietta almost shouted.

"You can't or you don't want to?"

Antonietta was silent. What could she say? She didn't want to admit the truth to a colleague of James, but to lie was pointless.

"Do you think you could finish the paper by next Monday?' Ilse asked, diplomatically changing the subject. Glad of the chance to end this embarrassing interview, Antonietta nodded. "Good," said Ilse. "I'll think up some excuse for Professor Forget."

Antonietta stammered out her thanks and fled from the office.

———

"Daddy, I feel awful."

James immediately saw the opportunity this presented. It was Sunday and the family was preparing for Mass. A sick child meant he could stay at home, as Veronica wouldn't miss Mass even if her offspring were about to expire. James felt Peter's forehead. It was a little warm.

"Veronica," he called. "Peter's ill. He's got a temperature, and he feels like throwing up."

Actually Peter had said nothing about throwing up, but it seemed a nice touch. Veronica came downstairs and eyed her son with suspicion.

"Are you sure you're not just saying that, Peter?"

James came to his son's rescue with a thermometer. "Thirty-eight point six," he pronounced. "No, I'm afraid he's got to stay home."

"Well, you'll have to stay with him," Veronica said crossly. "I'm not missing Mass because of a little fever."

"Was it really so high, my temperature?" Peter asked his father once Veronica and Susanna were safely out of the house.

"Shame on you, Peter. As if I would lie to your mother!"

James' broad grin confirmed his son's suspicion that this was exactly what he'd done. It was a lie that would set in motion the denouement that James and Antonietta so feared and yet pined for.

––––

The evening at Luigi's conversing with him and his Italian friends alleviated Antonietta's misery without curing it. Now, on a dull Sunday morning, she was driving back to Saint-Sauveur. Originally, she had intended to hear Mass at the Basilica in old Montreal, but she was drawn, against her will, to the church where it had all started. She knew that it would solve nothing, indeed it would make everything worse, but she had an irresistible desire to set her eyes on James.

She arrived at the church just as Mass was starting. It was only partly full and she had no difficulty finding a seat. She searched in vain for James. Then, to the right near the front, she recognized James' daughter. She was turning round to survey the congregation, obviously bored with the liturgy, until her mother muttered something to her and the young girl returned with noticeable reluctance to her devotions. Antonietta realized with dismay that James was not with them. She moved down the church to a pew across from the two Markhams. She fastened Veronica in her sight. She was not unattractive with her golden blond hair that Antonietta hated so much, but her features, naturally pleasant, had a pinched aspect. She was, as Antonietta had noticed when she first saw her, cheerless.

Yet this was the woman James slept with, made love to, had children with, lived with. A furious jealousy seized hold of Antonietta. Why did this insipid, cold English woman have a right to the joys that were denied her? What merit had she to enjoy the man who was her's by right of love? Watching Veronica cross herself and gaze in wonder at the altar, Antonietta revolted against all she believed in. Life was unfair, God was deaf, the Virgin a hypocrite. She felt more and more nauseous as the jealous anger built up inside her. Finally, she rushed out of the church and threw up on the porch. A few passers-by below on Main Street gave her strange looks. Overcome by embarrassment, Antonietta made for her car and returned home.

As she sat down in the cottage with yet another glass of wine, it was clear to her that she couldn't go on. What was the point of staying to suffer this torture? At least in Italy she had her friends, here she had only Petra and that friendship had a perverse side. She resolved to return to Italy at the end of the semester, without asking herself why not straightaway. For, like an alcoholic who vows to give up drinking on a morrow that never comes, Antonietta could only envisage leaving at a time that hadn't yet arrived. She skipped her classes on Monday and traveled to Montreal to book her flight for December 14 This way she fulfilled the promise to her father to attend her parents' wedding anniversary on the 16.

———

Bill Leaman had finally arranged the meeting between James and Petra Markovic. It took place in his office.

"Miss Markovic," James began. He felt ill at ease. Having to ask a favor from a student, and particularly one as delicate as this one, was embarrassing. But it had to be done if Hunt's career was to be salvaged.

"As you may possibly know, I'm representing Professor Hunt before the Ethics Committee. He is accused of…" James sought for the appropriate euphemism, "having a too close relationship with a female student in his class."

"I know about it," Petra said.

James found her poise unsettling and wasn't quite sure how to go on. Bill came to the rescue.

"The point is, Petra, Professor Markham thinks that the students testifying against Hunt have been put up to it by Doefman, including your boyfriend, Brett Taylor. Brett's captain of the football team and if we can get him to confess the truth, we're sure some of the others would follow suit."

"You want me to persuade him to confess?"

Bill and James nodded. Petra was silent for a few seconds.

"I'd like to help, as I don't believe it either, but there's a problem. If Brett confesses that he lied, he's likely to be thrown out of the Institute."

"I understand your concern, Miss Markovic," James replied, his formality contrasting sharply with Bill's casual manner. "What I should like is for Brett to swear an affidavit, which I could then use to persuade some of the others to retract and do likewise. I promise not to make the affidavits public without their consent."

"Then what use are they?" Petra asked, fixing James with her cool, grayish-blue eyes. God, she's intimidating, he thought. "I'd rather not say," he replied. "I'm afraid you'll just have to trust me."

Petra wavered. James Markham was held in high esteem by the students, except perhaps those who were suffering through his present class, and this was due in no small measure to his reputation for being fair and straightforward. She decided to trust him.

"Okay, I'll do it," she said.

"Thank you, Miss Markovic," James replied, suppressing his amusement. Any other girl would have said she would try, but this one clearly intended to be obeyed! She was bloody attractive, but James didn't envy Brett Taylor.

"Here is my home number." He handed Petra a card. "Call me there if I'm not at the Institute."

———

It was the afternoon but Antonietta had only just left her bed. She had a hangover and felt sick and utterly dejected. She'd booked her ticket for Italy but hadn't been able to face attending classes. She was too devastated by the prospect of leaving Quebec and James. There was a knock on the door. She opened it and saw Petra standing before her.

Petra stared at Antonietta in horror. She was hardly recognizable. Her face was puffy, her normally shimmering eyes were dull and expressionless, and the lovely long dark hair lay lank and unkempt around her shoulders. She stood unsteadily in the doorway, dressed only in a bathrobe despite the advanced hour.

Petra threw her arms around her friend. "Good God, Antonietta. You look awful!" She led her to the sofa and they sat down together.

"I *feel* awful," Antonietta replied. "But I'm glad to see you."

Petra surveyed the scene of desolation around her. Books and papers littered the table, empty bottles of wine and whisky were strewn around, CDs and their boxes as well as empty and half-empty glasses were all over the place, an elegant jacket and skirt lay untidily on the floor, but there were no dirty dishes. "When did you last eat?" she asked peremptorily.

Antonietta answered with a shrug. Petra noticed an airline ticket on the coffee table. She picked it up.

"Are you going home for Christmas?" she asked.

"I'm going home for good," Antonietta replied, her voice choking with emotion.

"Then why did you buy a return ticket?"

"Because here I didn't have the courage to buy a one-way ticket, but once I'm back in Italy away from him, I'll find the strength not to come back."

Petra shook her head in disbelief. She pointed to the table. "Is that Leaman's overdue paper?"

"No, it's Forget's, but I don't care. I'm leaving the Institute anyway."

Antonietta's face was a picture of misery. It was difficult to visualize this dejected and broken young woman as the glowing beauty Petra had noticed at registration. She was shocked and saddened, but she was also extremely relieved to have come. Antonietta desperately needed help or she would break down completely.

"You go and take a shower, put on some make-up and dress as sexily as only you know how," Petra ordered. "I'll clear up this mess."

Antonietta went off obediently into the bathroom.

God, how much has she drunk, Petra asked herself in dismay as she collected the bottles and glasses. While she was bringing some semblance of order to the cottage, she made her plans for Antonietta. They would have breakfast at the little café in Prevost, then she would help Antonietta finish her essay for Professor Forget. It would probably take most of the day. Tomorrow she'd see Bill Leaman. He owed her a favor. They had to get Antonietta together with James Markham before she destroyed herself. The best way was to hold the party for the foreign students at Markham's house instead of Leaman's and then make sure they were left alone together when it was over.

Antonietta came out of the bathroom, dressed in a towel with her long wet hair now glistening with restored health. She grinned coquettishly at Petra. "Temptress," protested Petra, but she was happy to see Antonietta feeling better.

She sat down at the table and looked over Antonietta's notes for her essay on confederation while her friend dried her hair and made herself up in the bedroom. When Antonietta came back to the living room, the transformation was complete. She was wearing a low-cut sweater that showed off the swelling curves of her breasts and a short skirt.

They had breakfast, after which they spent the day working on the essay, interspersed with pasta cooked by Antonietta. Petra forbade her any wine until the essay was finished, and Antonietta submitted herself humbly to Petra's discipline. Once the term paper was finished, they celebrated with some wine. It was late, but Petra refused Antonietta's offer to drive her home.

"You're tired, and I'm not leaving you on your own. I want to make sure you're in class tomorrow," she said.

Antonietta laid her head on Petra's shoulder. "You saved my life, Petra. I was in complete despair." She recounted the scene in the church, her return home, the drinking binge, the purchase of the tickets to Italy, her feelings of sheer hopelessness, and the drinking again.

Petra's face was solemn. "Promise me you'll pull yourself together, Antonietta. I don't want anything bad to happen to you." She was near to tears and Antonietta couldn't resist kissing her. "This time I'm sleeping on the sofa," Petra declared. "I don't trust myself in bed with you, and now I've Brett to think about."

Antonietta stood up. "That's a pity," she said and went off alone into the bedroom.

_____

After his meeting with Petra, Bill went immediately to talk to James, who was very pleased to see him.

"Time for a liquid lunch, Bill?" he asked with evident desire.

"A good idea," Bill replied.

He'd get James feeling nice and mellow with a few Scotches inside him, and then he'd spring his request, get James to agree and then quickly inform everyone so that he couldn't change his mind. Bill had even worked out how to get James and Antonietta alone together at the end of the party. It required some help from Danny and Piotr, which was another hurdle to cross but, above all, they had to make sure that Antonietta came to the party. This was Petra's job. She would play on Antonietta's irrational jealousy of Annya Nowak.

"Good God, Bill, you must be crazy," James protested in reply to Bill's request for a change of venue. "I'm not having that woman in my house."

"Look, Jimmy." Bill was all sweet reasonableness. "There are more foreign students this year, and your house is bigger than mine. What's more, the weather's so cold that it'll probably snow, and unless they've cleared the road, it's a difficult drive up to my place. In any case, you know she won't come."

A couple of whiskies later James had agreed. Bill rushed off to make the necessary arrangements, while James returned to his office. What had he done to deserve this, he asked himself. His life hadn't been a barrel of laughs before Antonietta, but at least he'd come to terms with it and it had its compensations.

The guys, the trips abroad, uncomplicated girls like Carolina. And now? James groaned inwardly as he sat down in a vain attempt to advance his article. A single thought kept disturbing him. What if she did come?

# CHAPTER 10
## Friday, October 26, 2001

Antonietta was resolved not to go to the party at James Markham's house even though—or perhaps because—Petra had assured her that his wife and children were away in England. That, at any rate, was her firm intention when she arose that morning.

After Forget's class, she went to the library and attempted to immerse herself in Canadian history in order to chase away thoughts of James and the temptation of the party. After a dispiriting hour or two leafing aimlessly though some books, she returned to the cottage and treated herself to *vitello alla marsala*. She was determined to spend the rest of the day and the evening on her own but quite unusually, particularly for these days, she drank only one small glass of white wine at lunch.

At six-thirty, she found herself in the shower, and half-an-hour afterwards she was putting on lingerie that was blatantly erotic. She dressed in a bra that lifted up but barely contained her breasts and a tiny string that left her buttocks completely nude. She went to the bathroom where the light was brighter in order to make herself up. In the full-length mirror on the bathroom door, she observed with satisfaction the rampant lubricity of her underwear. She put her hair into a chignon, which emphasized her statuesque bearing. Finally, she slid on the shameless red dress she'd bought at the Emporium in the Via Strozzi. It exposed not only the enticing cleft between her breasts but also the smooth skin of her sunburned thighs. Despite the cold weather, she kept her legs bare. Her high heels came from Marco Candido.

It was only when she was on her way out of the door of the cottage that Antonietta fully realized what she was doing. She wasn't going to the party, she reminded herself, and hesitated. But by now she was all dressed up and it seemed silly to stay at home. Besides, she rationalized, it would be rude not to go. Already the other students thought she was stuck up. Anyway, she wouldn't stay long.

Petra had insisted on giving Antonietta directions to James' house despite her repeated assertions that she wouldn't attend the party, and she was now following them with her stomach churning over. When she reached the small commercial center at the entrance to Prévost, she was trembling so hard that she had to pull in. It was madness to go to James' house, she told herself. How would she react to being in the place where he lived with his wife and children? Would he speak to her and, if so, would she be able to control herself? The only sensible course of action was to turn back, but the thought of Annya Nowak flirting with James decided her to continue. Making every effort to control the emotions that were threatening to submerge her, Antonietta drove on to James' house.

She descended from the car and walked unsteadily to the front door. She tried to lift her arm to ring the bell, but she was paralyzed by a mixture of apprehension and excitement. Luckily, Bill had been looking out for her and opened the door.

"Ah, Antonetta," he exclaimed, "I'm so glad you could make it." It was a heartfelt greeting as he'd been worried right up until this moment that she wouldn't come. "Let me take your coat."

Bill had to suppress a gasp when he saw how Antonietta was dressed. He had never seen a more voluptuous apparition. With some difficulty, he stopped himself from staring at the sight of the uplifted and barely covered bosom offered by Antonietta's deep décolleté. The delicate outline of mascara accentuated her dark expressive eyes and her sensuous lips glistened with glossy, pale pink lipstick. The hair was done in a chignon and the classic elegance of her provocative red dress complemented a ravishing ensemble of tasteful but overpowering sensuality.

"Let me introduce you to our host. Perhaps this time he'll be a little more polite," Bill suggested.

"Please don't disturb him on my account," Antonietta replied, trying to head off the moment she dreaded.

Bill was not, however, to be dissuaded, and he escorted her over to James, who was talking with Wilhelm and Petra. Petra broke off from the conversation and came towards Antonietta to embrace her. "You came after all," she said. "I'm so glad."

Sandwiched between Petra and Bill, Antonietta trembled as she waited for James to finish his interminable conversation with Wilhelm. Finally, Bill interrupted the earnest German.

"James, you've met Antonietta della Chiesa before," he said, pronouncing her name correctly for once. "Perhaps this time, you'll be a bit more polite."

Oh God, so she *has* come! James was hit by an empty feeling in his stomach. Praying for strength, he turned round to face Antonietta. What he saw was a woman even more captivating than the image he'd gleaned from his stolen glances at her. Awkward, nervous, trying to avoid her eyes, he was nonetheless forced to talk to her.

"Professor Leaman tells me I was very rude to you, Miss della Chiesa," he said so quickly that the words tumbled over each other. "I assure you that it wasn't meant that way. And I hope, err, I hope you're enjoying yourself here."

Prodded by Petra, Antonietta replied in a quavering voice. "I never thought anything of it," she stammered. "Thank you."

No-one, including Antonietta, had the slightest idea why she was thanking James. She lifted up her face and they looked at each other with longing in their eyes. Realizing the danger, Bill acted quickly to prevent a premature explosion of passion from ruining his carefully laid plans for the end of the evening.

"Come on Antonietta, let's get you something to drink."

Antonietta followed Bill to the bar in a state of shock. Petra had been detained by Wilhelm, so she was deprived of her friend's support. Thankfully, the two other professors who were reputed to be close friends of James were there to entertain her.

"Tell us about Florence, young lady. They say it's a lovely place, that they do."

Antonietta was amused by Danny's thick Irish accent, which she suspected was exaggerated for her benefit. She was glad to play the game. After a while they were joined by Petra and so, their job done, Danny and Piotr mingled with the other students.

"I don't see Annya," Antonietta said to Petra, who had the decency to blush. "She's not coming, is she?" Petra shook her head. "It was just a ploy to get me here, wasn't it?" Antonietta tried to sound cross.

"Yes," Petra replied, "and it worked."

"No it didn't because I'm leaving soon."

Antonietta sounded very firm but nevertheless let herself be led over to a group of students that included Simon, the British student. They were joined by Brett. The wine flowed and there was much laughter, but Antonietta had the sensation of being a spectator of her physical self among this circle of students in James' living room. She listened to her words as though they were being spoken by another person. She kept hearing herself say that she was leaving soon, but she never made any move to go.

It was ten o'clock and people began to leave. Antonietta looked round for Petra, but she had disappeared with Brett. Simon and the two other students in their group were also making for the hallway. She had no excuse to stay any longer. She was about to put down her wine-glass when Professors Leaman and Redfern arrived with a full bottle of wine.

"I was just leaving," she protested weakly, letting Bill fill up her glass.

"Nonsense, the night is but young," Danny told her.

"The best time at a party is the end when all the boring people have left," Bill added.

Bill and Danny inveigled Antonietta into a long conversation about Italy. Suddenly she realized they were the only persons left. She could hear James taking leave of the last students. She was between dread and anticipation.

"Come on Danny, let's go and put some music on."

Bill pulled at Danny's elbow and they both disappeared. Antonietta waited for the two men to return, but instead it was James who entered the room. He looked at Antonietta in blank amazement.

"You're still here!" he exclaimed, and then immediately corrected himself. "Sorry, that sounds awful. It's just that everyone else has left."

"I'm waiting for Professor Leaman and Professor Redfern," Antonietta replied timidly. "They just went to put on some music."

James realized what was happening. His friends, with Bill no doubt in charge, had engineered this moment of intimacy between himself and Antonietta. He looked at the luscious young woman standing with her wine-glass in *his* living room and wondered what on earth he was going to do.

"Bill and Danny have left," he said tonelessly.

"Well, then I'd better leave too," Antonietta replied.

James could have said yes, bundled her out of the house and spent the next few hours between relief and regret, but he couldn't bring himself to do it.

"No, you're not," he said gruffly, restraining himself from taking the trembling Antonietta into his arms. "I'll join you with a Scotch while you finish your wine."

He walked over to the impromptu bar and swore. "Those blackguards have drunk all my Scotch."

"I think there's another bottle in the kitchen," Antonietta murmured, desperate now to prolong their encounter.

"Well, let's go into the kitchen," James proposed, still avoiding the beautiful dark eyes that would be his downfall.

Antonietta stood watching James pour out a glass of whisky, or rather she listened to him for he had his back to her. She waited for him to turn round. Surely he would put an end to this awful charade. Surely now he would take her into his arms.

James still had some will to resist. For weeks he had fought this passion, this irrational, overwhelming passion. He'd wanted to protect his marriage and his integrity. Now he was alone with Antonietta and one word, one gesture would suffice to bring her into his arms and into his bed. If he turned round, he was lost. He turned round.

They looked at each other, not furtively like all the times before, but unabashedly, without averting their gaze. James saw before him a young woman of incomparable beauty, elegantly sensual, her eyes aglow with passion for him. He was overcome with desire for her.

As for Antonietta, she felt faint. How many times had she conjured up this scene only to deny to herself that it could ever happen. Yet now it was happening. She was so lost in the wonder of the moment that she let slip her wine-glass. It crashed to the floor. Instinctively, she bent to pick up the pieces of broken glass.

"No, Antonietta, don't!" James yelled, but it was too late. She had cut herself and blood was oozing from the small wound on her finger. James took her hand and led her to the sink, where he put the bleeding finger under the cold water tap.

"I'll get something to bandage it," he told her.

Antonietta stared absently at her finger. She felt no pain and saw no blood. All she knew was that James had called out her name, touched her, taken her hand. She waited in a daze for him to return. He came back with a band-aid and gently wrapped it around the finger. When he'd finished, he continued to hold her hand. Antonietta could bear it no longer. She looked up at James with eyes full of longing and desire.

"I can't take it anymore," she said in Italian, laying her head on James' shoulder. James lifted up Antonietta's face and his fragile resolve melted before her dazzling beauty and the shimmer of her eyes. "Nor can I," he whispered in the same language, as if afraid of the words.

Their mouths moved slowly and irresistibly together. It was a long, intense kiss into which they poured all the yearning and heartache of the past two months. It was as if time were standing still. For both of them their kiss seemed to last an eternity. With their lips joined, their tongues intertwined, their bodies clasped tightly together, they had become as one in a world beyond space and time. Nothing else existed. Their lives before no longer had any meaning for either of them.

James gently broke off their embrace and took Antonietta by the hand. He led her, without a word, upstairs to the bedchamber where they would consummate their passion. When they reached the top of the stairs, James felt Antonietta squeeze his hand. He turned round and she drew him close to her. "Hold me," she beseeched. "Hold me tight."

James felt her body trembling. "What's the matter?" he asked.

Antonietta lifted up her head and James saw tears clouding the shine of her eyes. "I'm afraid," she answered. "I'm terribly afraid."

James' eyes widened with surprise. "But why?"

"I'm afraid that tomorrow you'll have regrets and send me away." Antonietta gave James a look of utter desolation. "I couldn't bear that."

James pulled Antonietta's face towards him and kissed her. "I love you," he told her, "from the depth of my heart and from the profoundest recesses of my being. My love for you is indelible. I will never send you away because I'll never again be able to live without you."

Antonietta kissed James rapturously. "I love you with infinite passion," she declared in her turn, her whole countenance glistening with ardor. "The moment I first saw you in church, like Isolde, I lost myself in you."

When they reached the conjugal bedroom, Antonietta shook her head. "No, not in there. Not where you've made love to your wife."

"That was a very long time ago," James assured her, ushering her instead into the guest bedroom, which was bathed in moonlight.

Antonietta moved towards the window and stood in the light. The anguish, the tears and the trembling were gone, and the self-assured young lady who deftly undid her chignon and let her long black hair flow down and partly cover her décolleté was unrecognizable from the emotionally distraught woman of a few minutes ago. She kicked off her shoes with a happy frivolity and slipped down the straps of her dress. It fell to the floor and she stood there, dressed only in the skimpiest bra and a tiny string. It was a sight of such unbridled sensuality that James caught his breath in awe.

With a slight smile on her face that recalled the Mona Lisa, Antonietta picked up her dress and turned to walk towards the armchair where she was going to place it. James stared in admiration at her firm and perfectly rounded buttocks, left completely nude by the string. "Good God," he murmured.

Antonietta was facing him again now, and her hands moved behind her back to undo her bra.

"No, stay like that," James ordered.

He stared at her as she stood, practically naked, in the moonlight and then walked slowly over to her.

"Do I please you, Professor?" she enquired playfully.

"Never before have I beheld such perfect beauty," James replied, taking Antonietta into his arms. His hands moved down the smooth skin of her back to her buttocks. He felt her tense up as he caressed them.

Antonietta took off her bra and threw it carelessly to one side of the room. James hardened with lust before the overpowering lubricity of Antonietta's bare breasts. They were full but firm and perfectly shaped. Hesitantly, scarcely aware of what he was doing, he passed his hands over the silken, taut skin. He felt Antonietta shudder and her nipples become erect under his touch. She pushed his arms gently aside and pressed her body against his, offering her mouth for a long and ardent kiss. Her flesh was hot with desire.

"Make love to me" she whispered. "Right now."

She began to unbutton James' shirt. "Such haste," he teased her.

"You've tortured me long enough, Professor Markham," she countered, the languor in her eyes giving way to a mischievous glint. "It's time for you to make amends."

Antonietta pulled out the shirt from James' pants and made him take it off. They walked over to the bed and James sat on it. Antonietta knelt down in front of him. She took off his shoes and socks. The spectacle of this woman he had desired for so long all but naked before him, undressing him, inflamed James.

She undid his belt and slid off his pants. James could hardly believe what was happening when she took down his briefs and began to fondle him. She placed his shaft between her lush breasts and stroked it softly with her fingers. Then, taking it into her hand, she ran her erect nipples along it. James was already beside himself with ecstasy when she took him into her mouth. He wanted to stop her so that he could feel himself within her, but he was helpless as Antonietta, her beautiful face covered by the long, dark hair that fell over James' belly, fellated him to an ejaculation of a violence he'd never experienced before. She looked up, her lips wet from his effluent, and it was a vision of such erotic splendor that James felt his virility stir anew. Antonietta moved her lips up his body and kissed him.

He placed her on the bed beside him and kneaded her sumptuous breasts before teasing the nipples with his tongue, which he moved slowly down to her string. She opened her legs and he ran his hands between her damp thighs. He could feel her impatience but first he caressed the golden tanned skin of her legs. "Please," she pleaded, and at last he drew down the string to expose her denuded sex.

He pleasured her with an intrusive expertise that had her twisting and moaning in rapture. Never before had she tasted such sexual delight with a man. She was torn between a craving for pleasure in the Sapphic manner and a longing to feel the man she loved within her body. She could feel the moisture of her lust begin to trickle down her thighs.

Aroused by the odor of Antonietta's sexuality, James hardened. Once he felt that her climax was near, he penetrated her. When Antonietta felt him enter, her body exploded and she could hear herself scream. The climax was so brutal that, involuntarily, she dug her nails into James' back. She squeezed her lover within her to bring him to his culmination and, when she felt James' warmth inundate her, she was submerged by a feeling of utter bliss. Their mouths met, and their tongues furrowed deep into the caverns that had given them both so much pleasure.

"I hurt you," Antonietta exclaimed when finally James turned away and she noticed his back. "I've never ever done that before. I'm sorry."

James turned back and kissed her. "Don't be sorry. I'm no masochist, but to know the pain came from you…" He stopped, not knowing quite how to continue.

Antonietta came on top of him and their kisses gained in intensity and they made love again. This time, after descending to use her mouth, Antonietta mounted James and they took their pleasure together with the alluring sight of Antonietta's breasts heaving before James' eyes, inviting him to enjoy them. Still they were not satisfied, and it was the early hours before their pent-up passion for each other was sated and the longing that had tormented them was stilled.

"James, tell me again that you love me." Antonietta entreated as they lay together intertwined.

"Say that again," he replied.

"Tell me again…"

"No, say my name again."

Antonietta threw herself on James and repeated his name amidst countless kisses.

"Do you remember the first time I said your name?" he asked her.

"Oh, that awful first class. I nearly died when you came in. When you called me Antonietta, I almost fainted."

"And now?"

"I can survive any class with you now, Professor Markham, because I'm your mistress."

James looked worried. "You're a practicing Catholic. Being the mistress of a married man doesn't bother you?"

"Do I have a choice?" she responded. "Did I ever have a choice?"

There was a brief silence before James answered. "No, no more than me. It was always inevitable although we fooled ourselves otherwise." He kissed Antonietta's upturned mouth, but this didn't remove his concern. "But are you happy?" he asked. Antonietta smiled at his disquietude and brushed her lips against his chest. "Ecstatically happy, my love, and after all I've been through, I deserve it."

Suddenly, Antonietta propped herself up like an inquisitor and looked fixedly at her lover. "James, I want a truthful answer from you."

James was taken aback by the abrupt change of mood. "Of course," he said with a trace of nervousness.

"Actually there are two questions," she went on. "Why was Annya Nowak laughing with you in your office? Secondly, do you have an Argentinean mistress called Carolina? And," she added for good measure, "is she blond?"

James burst out laughing and tried to kiss Antonietta.

"No," she told him. "Kisses are fine, but first I want the truth."

"Alright," he conceded, having stolen a kiss. "Which fantasy shall we begin with?"

"Annya," Antonietta replied, "and she's not a fantasy. She's here and she left your office laughing, so you must have enjoyed your time together."

James was completely at a loss for he had more or less forgotten the whole incident with Annya. "I saw her because I'm defending a professor against allegations of sexual impropriety, and she's the girl in question." he explained. "I have no idea why she was laughing." Then, he added flippantly. "Perhaps it was the whisky I gave her."

"Whisky!" Antonietta's eyes blazed with jealous anger. "You gave her *whisky*!"

"Well, I didn't have any coffee," James replied, uncomfortably aware of the inadequacy of his response. However, he wasn't prepared for the ferocity of Antonietta's reaction. She picked up a pillow and rained blows down on his head. "I hate you," she cried. "Faithless man!"

After the surprise at being attacked out of the blue by a pillow, James began to enjoy the sight of Antonietta's gorgeous breasts swaying in front of his eyes and her mouth pursed in indignant wrath. She was the irresistible image of sexual jealousy. After warding off several blows, he finally took hold of her hands and forced her down on the bed. He pressed his mouth against her's and her resistance quickly crumbled. She pleaded with him to enter her. As they both reached their climax, James felt the sharp pain of Antonietta scratching the wound on his back.

"You little vixen," he scolded.

"That was for the whisky," she answered without any remorse.

Sated once more, they lay next to each other.

"How did you know she was coming out of my office? You didn't know who I was at that time."

"Yes I did," Antonietta contradicted with a smirk. "After I saw you that Sunday at Mass, I went back to the car. I realized you were married and I was in despair. Then suddenly I saw you walking with your daughter towards me. I don't know why, but I lowered the back window and I heard you tell your daughter that you wanted a treble Scotch."

"You heard that?" James was astonished. "You were right there near us?" Antonietta nodded and went on with her narrative.

"So I knew that the man who had inspired such passion in me was British, from his accent, Catholic, because he'd taken communion, and he liked to drink. The day of the foreign students' seminar I met Petra. She told me you were British and that you drank a lot with your friends."

"Bloody cheek," James remarked.

Antonietta grinned at him and gave him a kiss. "The truth often hurts," she said, ducking under his threatening arm. "Then at lunch she gave me that thing on the professors to read. I saw you went to Ampleforth, and so you were British, you liked drinking and you were Catholic. It had to be you."

"How did you know Ampleforth was a Catholic school?

"I spent four years at a convent school in England."

Antonietta sensed danger. She remembered her uncle's advice not to divulge her background. She reverted quickly to the topic of Annya Nowak.

"So when I saw Annya coming out of your office, I was going to march in and tax you with inconstancy. Then I bumped into Professor Leaman."

"Yes, he told me. I wish he hadn't stopped you. It would have saved us weeks of torment."

"No, James." Antonietta's expressive eyes suddenly became very serious. "I know that what we're doing is a sin. Now at least I can tell myself that I fought against my passion for you until it was beyond my power to resist any longer. It makes the guilt easier to bear."

"I suppose you're right," James agreed without much conviction. "But why this jealousy about Annya? She's happily shacked up with Elliot Hunt."

"Petra told me they were having problems and that she would be after you at the party."

"She told you that, and it made you jealous?" Antonietta nodded. "So that's why you came to the party, because you were jealous of Annya?" Antonietta nodded again. James took her warm, nude body in his arms.

"My darling," he said with an amused smile. "We are the innocent victims of a Machiavellian plot hatched by your friend Petra and my friend Bill. He got me to host the party and she made sure you would come. And here we are, irrevocably together."

"Do you regret it?" Antonietta asked, her eyes misting over.

James gazed upon her exquisite face, put his hands around it and drew her towards him. "From the first instant I saw you in church, I've loved you in a way I never conceived possible," he said slowly and deliberately. "I tried to deny it to myself, to fight it, but in the end I no longer had the strength. I never will have."

Antonietta avoided James' embrace. "Did you say the same to your Argentinean mistress?" she asked, her eyes all at once burning with suspicion.

Without waiting for her to take hold of her favorite weapon, James pinned Antonietta down on the bed. "What's this nonsense about an Argentinean mistress," he asked.

"I believe her name is Carolina."

"Did Bill tell you about her?" Antonietta nodded.

"God, he annoys me so much when he blabs to the students."

James' words infuriated Antonietta, who wriggled out from his grasp and sat up glaring at him. "Oh, so now I'm just another student, am I? Well, go back to your Carolina!"

Antonietta was about to get off the bed, but James pulled her back. "You're not going anywhere, Antonietta, and you're going to listen to me." Antonietta let herself be pushed down on the bed, a trifle too easily in her mind, but she was relieved that James had held her back.

"I met Carolina in August, before I first saw you. She was the receptionist at the hotel Bill and I stayed at in Buenos Aires."

"Did you go to bed with her?"

James saw the resentment in Antonietta's in her eyes, but there was little point in lying. "Yes."

"Was she blond?"

"Yes."

"With blue eyes?"

"Yes."

Antonietta looked at James dolefully. "You prefer blue-eyed blonds, don't you. Admit it. Like Annya, and your wife, and that Carolina." Tears welled up in eyes that gazed in sorrow at him.

James couldn't believe what he was hearing. How could this woman, this flawless beauty for whom he would gladly sacrifice his marriage and his career, how could she be reduced to tears of jealousy over a girl he hardly knew, a wife he'd never loved and a woman of passing pleasure in a far-away land.

"Listen to me, Antonietta," he said, keeping her pinned down on the bed. "No woman could match your beauty and no other woman has ever or could ever inspire in me the intense passion I feel for you."

Antonietta let James kiss her, but between kisses she made him promise never to go to Argentina, or indeed anywhere, without her. James agreed readily. They made love a final time.

So began their few months of happiness together.

# PART TWO

Saturday, October 27, 2001, to Saturday, May, 4 2002

# CHAPTER 11

## Saturday, October 27 to Monday, October 29, 2001

James awoke to find his face covered by a woman's long, black hair. At first he was puzzled, and then he remembered. It wasn't a dream, it had really happened. That scene in the kitchen when the last shreds of his resistance had succumbed, their first kiss, Antonietta's fears and their passionate declarations of love, the sensual perfection of Antonietta's nude body, their unbridled love-making, Antonietta's fierce jealousy.

He disengaged himself and contemplated her beauty. She looked even lovelier this morning, sleeping with a contented look on her face. He touched her breasts and ran his fingers lightly down the soft skin to her sex, which was still damp from the night's pleasures. He felt a fierce desire but stopped himself from waking her. He made do with admiring her lubricious nakedness. After a few minutes, he went quietly downstairs to make coffee.

Antonietta awoke after James had left. She felt strange. The pain of longing that usually accompanied every awakening was absent, and where was she? She looked around the room. Relief and happiness flooded her senses. She had surrendered at last, and the torment was over. She turned over and saw with horror the empty place next to her. In a panic she called out James' name.

"I'm here," he replied, entering the bedroom with two small cups of expresso. He noticed the alarm in Antonietta's eyes. "What's the matter?" He quickly put down the two cups and took his new mistress in his arms.

"Never, never, *never* get up without waking me first," she cried. "I thought you'd left me!"

James shook his head. "What am I going to do with you? After all the times last night I told you that I loved you, that I couldn't live without you, you *still* persist in believing I would leave you?"

"Promise you'll wake me first next time," Antonietta insisted.

Forgetting the coffees, James laid her down on the bed, took off his dressing gown and made love to her.

---

"No regrets?" James asked, stroking Antonietta's moist and satisfied body.

"Regrets?" she replied. There was a slight tone of irony, even bitterness, in her voice. "Regret at not waking up every day aching for you, at not going to the Institute with that horrible mix of dread and hope that I might meet you, regret at suffering through the torture of your classes, regret at the loneliness and despair of sitting in the cottage drinking too much and listening endlessly to Laura Pausini." Antonietta paused. "No, I've no regrets, none at all."

James was taken aback by Antonietta's forcefulness. "Was it that bad?" he asked.

"Yes," she replied and shuddered at the memory of it. "The worst time was the last three weeks."

She told him about seeing Veronica in church and her near breakdown afterwards. "Without Petra, I'm not sure what I would have done." She looked at James with anguish. He absorbed the tears that were beginning to flow down her cheeks.

"All that is over, my love," he told her gently. "There'll be no more despair and loneliness, and perhaps at last I can start to do some work and give decent lectures."

"Did I stop you?" Antonietta asked gleefully.

"You know damn well you did. All I could do was think of you, want you and tell myself constantly that I couldn't have you."

James tested his coffee. "It's cold," he declared. "I'll go downstairs and make two fresh cups."

"I'm coming with you," Antonietta declared. "I'm not letting you out of my sight."

James handed her one of Veronica's dressing gowns but she refused it. Instead she used a large towel. James stared at her. She was absolutely gorgeous with her hair disheveled, her lips slightly swollen from their acts of love and a soft, languorous look in her eyes. He resisted the temptation to take her right back to bed, and they made their way downstairs hand in hand.

While James was grinding some fresh coffee, Antonietta wandered off into the family room to look at James' collection of CDs. She returned, holding one triumphantly in her hand.

"Laura Pausini!" she exclaimed. "Did you listen to her, too?"

"Of course," James replied, keeping an eye on the coffee pouring into the two expresso cups. He picked them up and took them into the family room. Antonietta preceded him and put on the CD. Then she sat down next to James and eyed him with timidity.

"What's the matter, Antonietta?" he asked.

Hesitantly, Antonietta brought up the subject of his marriage. "I know it's indelicate, but I think I have a right to know," she said.

James drew her to him, kissed her, undid the towel and laid her across his thighs. He caressed her breasts and belly lightly while he explained his relationship with his wife.

"Promise me you'll never make love to her again," Antonietta implored. "I couldn't bear the thought of you with another woman."

James bent down and kissed her. "I promise."

Antonietta put her arm around James' head and held his face close to her's. Her eyes had a melancholy about them. "What happens when she comes back?" she enquired, not really wanting to hear the answer.

James stroked Antonietta's hair in a comforting gesture. "We shall be together more than you would imagine, and until then I'm going to live with you."

Antonietta sat up, threw her arms around James and kissed him in a torrent of passion.

"Does that arrangement suit you, Signorina?"

"It's the most wonderful present you could give me," she replied.

In her fervor, Antonietta had wrenched open James' dressing gown and the sensation of her splendid breasts against his chest inflamed his desire for her.

"Let's go back to bed," he whispered between their kisses.

"Yes, but first, James, you must shave or my thighs are going to be very sore."

James grinned. "That sounds like an indecent invitation."

"Nothing's indecent between us, James," Antonietta answered with a candor that enchanted James.

They made their way up the stairs, James still in his bathrobe, Antonietta completely naked. Once they were in the bedroom, Antonietta slipped off James' gown and drew him to her. He was seduced by her nudity, but Antonietta stopped him from kissing her. Her eyes were full of doubt and worry.

"Is this really happening?" she asked. "Are you sure this isn't a dream?" James took her hand, turned slightly and placed it on his back. "I think this proves it's not a dream," he told her.

Antonietta kissed the deep scratch she'd given him. "Does it hurt?"

"Yes, particularly as you scratched it again."

Antonietta came round and kissed James on the mouth. "What do I have to do to earn your forgiveness?" she cajoled.

James lay down on the bed with a wicked grin, and Antonietta did his bidding. When she'd finished, he satisfied her in similar fashion.

"You like it that way, don't you?" he remarked after her violent climax.

"Yes," she said, "except you forgot to shave and now I'm really sore."

"Serves you right for the scratch," James replied.

———

It was nearly three in the afternoon when they finally arrived at Antonietta's cottage. There was a message on the answering machine from Petra.

"Antonietta, I've been calling you all day, so I guess things worked out with James Markham. I'm so glad for you. Tell him I need to see him as I've finally got Brett to admit he lied about Hunt and Annya. Bye."

If Antonietta had turned the machine off straightaway, she would have spared herself a dreadful moment, but she left it on long enough to catch Petra's final comment.

"By the way, I hope he satisfied you in bed as well as I did."

Antonietta felt the blood rush to her head and her stomach give way. Oh, Petra, how could you, she thought. For a brief instant she stood there, convinced that her happiness was in ruins. Shame and despair wracked her and tears welled up in her eyes. She was beginning to tremble when she felt James' arms engulf her and his kiss upon her neck. She didn't dare turn round to look him in the face.

"Come," he whispered.

"Where?" she asked almost inaudibly.

"Into the bedroom. Where else?"

James led a blushing Antonietta into the bedroom. "Undress," he told her.

Obediently, her eyes avoiding his, Antonietta slipped off the long, red dress she had donned for the party, unhooked her bra, which fell to the ground, exposing her breasts, and removed her string. She stood there quite naked, her face bowed. She was acutely embarrassed.

"Lie down on the bed," James ordered.

Too ashamed and sexually excited to argue, Antonietta obeyed again. James undressed with such agonizing slowness that Antonietta became wet with anticipation. At last, he was naked and came on top of her.

"I'll not be bested by Petra Markovic," he declared with a sly grin. Antonietta started to protest, but James cut her off with a fierce kiss that left her panting. He toyed unmercifully with her sex and, once she was engorged with desire, turned her over and caressed and kneaded her buttocks. He ran his tongue and fingers between them, reducing her to a frenzy. He ignored her groans and pleas and continued to tantalize her. It was only when she was incoherent with lust that he finally took pity on her. Without removing his tongue from between her buttocks, he used his fingers on either hand to penetrate and massage her. Soon, Antonietta's body could take no more and convulsed in spasms of such intensity that at first they were painful for her. She felt herself drowning in a sea of voluptuousness and didn't even hear the screams that James was wrenching from her. Once the aftershocks of her volcanic climax had subsided, she felt James enter her where no man had dared before. She wanted to stop him, but she was paralysed by the perverse delight it gave her. The discomfort only served to increase the pleasure.

When it was all over, Antonietta remained on her stomach. James kissed her in the neck and whispered, "Why don't you turn over?"

"Because I'm too ashamed," she replied. When she did turn over, James could see that she was blushing. "How did you know what Petra…" Antonietta stopped, too embarrassed to continue, and looked away.

James turned her face towards him and kissed her. "I had a Spanish girlfriend, Leonore, who was bisexual. She liked nothing better than regaling me with her lesbian infidelities."

Antonietta pulled herself away and glared at James, her exquisite eyes flashing with indignation. "Is that how you think of me?" she cried. She picked up a pillow and rained blows on James' head. Before he could react, Antonietta had him pinned him down on the bed.

"I'm *not* a lesbian, and I'm *not* bisexual," she told him vehemently. "I'm a normal woman who was seduced by an older girl at school, which, by the way, happens to a lot of girls, and I've only had that one drunken episode with Petra ever since. Besides," she added, "it was your fault."

"*My* fault?" James exclaimed in astonishment. "How do you work that one out?"

Her indignation passed, Antonietta grinned at James. She knew her explanation was quite illogical. "I had sex with Petra because I was consumed by longing for you, and I couldn't have you. So I had to do something to take my mind off you."

James caressed Antonietta's voluptuous breasts, imagining them being kissed and fondled by Petra Markovic. He felt a sharp pang of jealousy. "Your problem is that you're oversexed," he said crossly. "Promise me you won't ever do that ever again."

Antonietta looked down at James, her eyes glowing with passion. "There will never, *never* be anyone else for me," she replied with fervor. "I wish it were otherwise because you're married, but it's not."

She rolled off James and propped herself up, looking accusingly at him. "I've never let a man take me like that before," she told him, pummeling his chest gently with her fists in mock outrage. "You're a wicked man."

"You know you can be expelled for striking a professor," James riposted.

Antonietta smiled prettily at him. "And *you* can be dismissed for sleeping with a student in your class"

James laughed. "*Touché*," he said, but then became more serious. "Which means that we must be very discreet, at least until the end of the academic year when I intend to marry you."

Antonietta gasped. "James, you can't marry me, you're already married."

"I'll get divorced. I don't want you as my mistress whom I have to hide, I want you as my wife, I want everyone to know you're mine."

"I *am* your's, whether people know it or not." Antonietta's eyes dimmed. "I can't marry you. I come from a very Catholic family, and I'm a practicing Catholic myself. I could never contemplate marrying outside the Church." Tears began to trickle down her cheeks.

"So you can envisage leaving me at some stage?" James' tone was almost savage.

"No, never," she replied with feeling.

"You can't seriously want to be my mistress all your life?"

"No."

"Well, you either have to marry me, be my mistress or leave me. Which is it to be?"

James was aware he was tormenting Antonietta, but the thought of losing her was too intolerable to bear.

"Please, James, let's just love each other," she pleaded. "I'm here for two years. A lot can happen in two years."

James looked down at her. "I ask one thing. Don't do an Elena Muti on me."

"Elena Muti?" Antonietta asked, quite perplexed. "Who's she?"

"Shame on you, you have a degree in Italian literature and you don't know who Elena Muti is?"

"That's your fault too," Antonietta replied. "You put me in such a state that I can't think of anything but you."

"You're a liar, but the loveliest liar I've ever known."

James kissed her and Elena Muti was forgotten as Antonietta returned his kiss and they made love again, this time more conventionally. When their amorous frolics were over, Antonietta suddenly exclaimed, "Sperelli! She was Sperelli's mistress in *Il Piacere!*[20]"

"That's right," James replied, "She almost destroyed him by leaving without an explanation. Never do that to me, or I don't know what I'd do."

"I promise," Antonietta assured him.

It was a promise she would not keep.

———

After they had made love yet again, James asked Antonietta to call Petra. "We're running out of time," he explained. "The hearing is a week on Thursday, and I need to get some students on side."

Antonietta dialed Petra's cell. She prayed that her friend wouldn't say anything that would cause her further embarrassment.

"Petra?"

"Antonietta! So our little plan worked. Are you two now an item?"

"Yes, he's here next to me in the cottage."

At least Petra was forewarned. "Did you get my message?" she asked.

"Yes," Antonietta replied. "We both heard *all* of it."

She heard Petra catch her breath. "Oh, my God, I'm so sorry, Antonietta. I hope it didn't ruin everything."

Antonietta gave James a sidelong glance. "Actually, it all worked out for the best. He was even better than you."

There was a brief silence. "I'm jealous," Petra said quietly. It was time to change the subject.

"James says you can meet him with Brett whenever you wish on Monday."

"Oh, so it's *James* now, is it?" Petra couldn't resist teasing her friend.

"It's a bit silly to call him Professor Markham when we've spent the last twenty-four hours making love," Antonietta countered.

"*All* the time?" Petra was impressed.

"Well, perhaps not *all* of it," Antonietta conceded.

It was agreed that Petra and Brett would meet James in his office the next day at ten o'clock.

———

It was Sunday evening and James' Mercedes pulled up outside Danny's house. All three of James' friends were curious to see the new couple together. Antonietta entered the room first, having taken off her coat in the hall. She was wearing a tight-fitting green dress that gave more than just a hint of the voluptuous body beneath it. Her hair was swept to one side of her face and flowed down over her fulsome bosom. The earring on her exposed ear glittered with reflected light. But what struck all three of the men was not Antonietta's elegance and beauty but the radiance she exuded. Particularly for Bill, who knew her better than the other two, the difference between this poised young woman whose eyes shone with happiness and the anguished, distracted student in his class was startling.

James came in and, smiling at Antonietta, put his arm around her. The tense moroseness of the past weeks was gone. Looking at the pair, any misgivings Bill might have had about bringing them together evaporated before their obvious delight in each other. Nevertheless, he couldn't resist a provocative jibe.

"You're late," he announced, "I suppose you were screwing?"

James was about to give a curt reply, but Antonietta forestalled him. "It's my fault, Professor Leaman," she said. "You see, I'm oversexed."

There was a brief silence. James was aghast at Antonietta's frankness and the others were completely taken aback. It was Danny who reacted first. "She got you there, Bill," he exclaimed, roaring with laughter. "That'll teach you to try and embarrass her."

"An excellent answer, Antonietta," Bill admitted. "Come and sit here." He pointed to the chair next to where James had taken a seat.

"No, I prefer it here," Antonietta replied, sitting down on the floor in front of James. She leaned her head against his knee and he stroked her hair and kissed on the head. They were gestures of such naturalness that none of the other three, even Bill who hated public displays of affection, felt the temptation to mock. The passion uniting the two lovers was so palpable that it inspired respect.

Once James and Antonietta had been accommodated with their drinks, a Scotch for James and a glass of Sauvignon Blanc for Antonietta, Piotr surveyed them with an air of concern. "Who else knows about you two?" he asked

Before either James or Antonietta could answer, Bill interjected. "Does the She-Wolf know?"

Antonietta was puzzled. "Who's the She-Wolf?" she asked.

James laughed. "A few years back, Bill saw a film that he considers a masterpiece of European culture. It was called *Ilse, the She-Wolf of the SS*. As Bromhoeffer's first name is Ilse, he couldn't resist it."

"She's also German," Bill put in with a smirk of satisfaction.

James ignored Bill's latest sally. "To answer your question, Piotr." he said, "apart from you three, the only person who knows for sure is Petra Markovic. Ilse Bromhoeffer knows that we were attracted to each other, but no more."

"Attraction is hardly the word I'd use," Antonietta commented reproachfully.

James smiled at her. "It's a British understatement."

Antonietta shook her head. "We were consumed by longing for each other is what you should have said," she insisted.

James stroked her hair apologetically. "Actually, Ilse wanted me to persuade you to go back to Italy."

Antonietta laughed. "She tried to persuade me too. She said my time here was doing me absolutely no good. So, I bought a ticket for Italy."

"You did *what!*"

"It's a return ticket for the Christmas holidays," she explained to her irate lover, "but you only have to say the word, and I won't go."

Immensely relieved, James was magnanimous. "No, you should be with your family over Christmas," he conceded. Then, ashamed of his display of jealousy, he abruptly changed the subject.

"I'm seeing Petra Markovic and Brett Taylor tomorrow morning at ten," he informed the others. "Evidently, Taylor's prepared to admit that he was put up to accusing Hunt by Doefman."

Bill whistled. "Good for Markovic, she's come up trumps."

"How are you going to handle it, James?" Danny enquired. "If Taylor admits he lied, he could get thrown out of the Institute. He might be prepared to admit it to you, but I doubt if he'll do so publicly."

"Yes, I know that," James replied. "What I intend to do is to have him sign an affidavit saying that Doefman put him and the others up to accusing Hunt wrongly. I'll promise not to make it public without his consent, but I'll use it to try and turn some of the others. If I can get at least two of them to sign similar affidavits, I'll go to HB and hopefully bluff him into dropping the case."

"That means you have to make the affidavits public," objected Piotr.

"No," said James with a Machiavellian smile. "All I need to do is get HB to *think* that I'm going to make them public. As I said, I have to bluff him."

Antonietta, who'd been listening proudly to James outline his strategy, suddenly remembered something. "Petra told me that he tried to threaten her into testifying against Hunt," she announced.

"Who?" James asked.

"That HB person," she replied.

Bill whooped with joy. "I think we've got him, Jimmy!" He patted Antonietta on the back "You're not just a pretty face after all, Antonietta," he told her.

"That confirms my suspicions," James said. "It'll help in the game of bluff. However, I still need those other affidavits. I think I know which students may come over, but I'll check with Petra and Taylor tomorrow."

The evening passed pleasantly enough but James and Antonietta were anxious to be alone together. Around eleven, James rose from his seat.

"Come on, Antonietta, time to go," he told her.

Antonietta gladly followed him, put on her coat and left Danny's house with James' arm around her. At the end of the driveway, there was a street lamp and the two turned to look at each other. Antonietta inveigled her hand into James' pocket and drew out the car keys before he could stop her. She held them up with a victorious gleam in her eyes.

"What are you doing with those?" James demanded to know.

"I'm going to drive because you've had too much to drink." she replied and walked towards the car. She stopped at the driver's door and looked back at James.

"In the first class I had with Bill, I daydreamed about coming with you to one of your evenings. I imagined leaving the house with your arm around me and then driving back to our house. I can hardly believe this dream has come true."

––––––

Antonietta found it strange to be driving to the Institute without the usual foreboding and longing. She could still feel James' kisses on her lips and his caresses on the intimacies of her body. He'd brought her an expresso in bed, and in their subsequent lovemaking they'd lost a sense of time. As a result, she was going to be late for Bill's class, but she couldn't care less. She smiled contentedly at the thought of James still in the cottage.

James arrived at his office just before ten. Petra and Brett were waiting for him outside. Petra was clearly embarrassed, as well she might be in James' view, and Brett looked downright scared.

"Sorry, I'm late," he said cheerfully and opened the office door. He ushered in the nervous couple.

James decided to come straight to the point. "This is an unpleasant business, and I appreciate your help." He smiled at Brett. "What I want is to have the case closed without anyone, including you Brett, getting hurt. This is how I intend to do it."

He outlined his plan with a confidence he didn't entirely feel, emphasizing what he knew was essential for Brett. "I won't make public either of your affidavits without your permission."

Brett stared silently at his feet, but Petra had no qualms. "You can use mine how you like. It's the truth and just shows HB for the shit he is," she told James.

She had overcome her discomfiture at meeting the man whose girlfriend she'd bedded and was treating James more like a friend than one of her professors. James, on the other hand, couldn't suppress his jealousy of this beautiful young woman who had bedded Antonietta. Brett continued to stare at his feet.

"I recommend you strongly to make the affidavit," James said sternly, "if you want to live with yourself and keep respect."

He didn't mention Petra but the allusion was obvious. Brett looked up at his girlfriend. She kissed him and whispered in a cajoling voice, "Please, Brett, do it for us." After some more reflection, Brett shook himself out of his torpor.

"Alright, Professor Markham, I'll do it."

Petra rewarded him with a delightful smile, but James had the feeling that she was prouder of her victory than Brett's return to honesty.

James drove them both to his friend, François, who was a notary and had been told to stand by to take the affidavits before there was a change of mind. James had Brett recount how Doefman had put him up to lying about Annya and Hunt and insisted that he also mention HB's inducements aimed at encouraging him and the other students to give this testimony, as well as his implied threat to Petra. Petra also swore an affidavit that HB had threatened her with not graduating if she didn't testify against Hunt.

James read through the two affidavits. "Excellent," he told them, "but I need at least two other affidavits like Brett's. Who do you suggest I should try?"

Both Petra and Brett concurred that Ben Toll and Michèle Letellier were the least committed to Doefman. These were the same two students James had found more malleable. He returned to his office and called them on their cell phones. Somewhat nervously, they agreed to meet him at nine the following morning.

———

James was alone in the cottage. It felt strange to be in Antonietta's abode, waiting for her. With almost adolescent joy, he heard her car pull up. The door opened and Antonietta threw herself into his arms.

"I was so afraid you wouldn't be here," she told him feverishly.

"I was afraid you'd never arrive," James replied.

"What are those pieces of string?" Antonietta asked, her eyes widening with surprise.

"I'm going to punish you for your infidelity with Petra," James explained. "I'm going to tie you to the four posts of the bed and submit you to sexual torment."

Antonietta looked at James with a mixture of alarm and curiosity. "Are you being serious?"

"Completely," he replied. "Get undressed."

Antonietta opened her mouth to protest, but James shut it with a kiss. "It's not really punishment," he said, "because at the end, you will experience an orgasm of such unparalleled violence that you might even faint. It's called *la petite mort*."

Antonietta submitted to her punishment. Once he had secured her legs and arms, James proceeded to stimulate her with a softness of touch that at first brought her little excitement. But as he continued, her body began to react. It was never enough to bring her to a climax but it constantly increased her sexual tension. She implored him to satisfy her, but instead he continued to arouse her until her whole body became taut with lust. It has to end, she told herself, but it went on and on. Eventually she lost consciousness of where she was, aware only of the burning desire between her thighs that infused her whole being. She didn't even hear her groans and incoherent pleas. With an expertise that surprised even himself, James brought her slowly but deliberately to her culmination. Antonietta gave a deafening scream and then went limp. She had fainted, but her body still reacted as James depleted the residue of her desire.

Antoniett regained consciousness with James looking down on her. "Are you alright," he enquired anxiously, untying her.

Antonietta smiled wanly. "As well as one can be after *la petite mort.*"

"So you've done this before?" James couldn't conceal his jealousy.

"No, James," she replied. "I've never done this before. I've never done a lot of things before."

"I thought nothing was indecent between us?"

"I said that as a good Catholic girl before I knew how dissolute you were," she told her lover. Suddenly, her eyes misted over and she became serious. "Do you still love me even though I let you do all these things to me?"

James took Antonietta into his arms. "You know very well that I love you. I love you more with every passing moment."

Now it was Antonietta's turn to dally with James, and she did so with a skill that left him exhausted and speechless. Once he'd recovered, James poured out two glasses of whisky.

"Why do you have to have to spend so long in Italy," he asked, sitting down next to Antonietta on the sofa.

"What's the point of me coming back any earlier," she pointed out with a trace of resentment. "You'll be busy with your family over Christmas and the New Year."

"Perhaps, but it's a long time to be separated from you." James' obvious dismay at her long absence comforted Antonietta. "Will you meet me on January 4th in Montreal?" she asked. "No, I'll come to Toronto to meet you and we'll spend the night there."

Antonietta's eyes glowed with delight.

# CHAPTER 12

## Tuesday, October 30 to Friday, November 2, 2001

The next day James kissed Antonietta and left the cottage to drive to the Institute. It was going to be another sunny day. In fact, ever since Antonietta and he had come together, the gloomy overcast skies of the previous two weeks had dispersed. It was as if nature itself were rejoicing in their fulfillment. Some of the trees on either side of the highway still had their leavers and the dramatic colors of red, yellow and amber combined with the brilliant azure sky to create a picture of imposing beauty.

James forced himself to think of his imminent meeting with Ben Toll and Michèle Letellier. He'd decided on a different strategy from the one he'd employed with Taylor and Petra. Instead of putting the two at ease, he would play on their nervousness. So, once they were ensconced in his office, he let them sit in tense silence while he slowly took Brett Taylor's affidavit out of his briefcase.

"Like you, Brett Taylor testified to seeing Annya Nowak in a compromising position with Professor Hunt before the end of term," he began gravely. Then, after pausing for the right dramatic effect, he added, "Unlike you, he has now seen the error of his ways."

James watched the two students look at each other. He suspected that they regretted their role in the duplicitous scheme hatched by Doefman and were looking for a way out. The resentment of receiving poor marks in Hunt's course had probably worn off, and with it their desire for revenge.

"Brett has admitted that he lied and that he was put up to it by Brett Doefman and encouraged by Professor Arbuthnot," he told them. "This is his affidavit." He held it up. Now came the crucial moment when he would succeed or not in bringing the two onside.

"The effect of this affidavit is twofold," he went on. "Firstly, I know it's the truth, as you do, and it casts considerable doubt on the other testimonies against

Professor Hunt, particularly coming from as respected a student as the captain of the football team. Secondly, it gives us an excellent basis for appealing any decision against Professor Hunt by the Ethics Committee to a court of law."

The two students were by now quite ashen.

"Are you aware of the implications for you of an appeal to a court of law?" James asked. The two shook their heads, both looking downright frightened. "It means that you will be called upon to give evidence. Unlike in the Ethics Committee, you will have to do so under oath. If you lie, you commit perjury, which is an offence that is punishable by a mandatory prison term."

"We didn't really want to do it,' Michèle Letellier burst out. "Brett was so upset and we were angry with Hunt. No-one liked him and he's a very hard marker. Then Professor Arbuthnot made it seem that we were doing the right thing. So we thought it might be true. After all, Ben knows Annya from Edmonton, and she's a flirt."

"I'm not blaming you," James said, handing Michèle a kleenex. Now it was time for the carrot. "In fact, I want to help you both."

The two students looked expectantly at James.

"What I want is to have the matter closed before it even comes before the Ethics Committee. That way you don't have to lie, nor do you have to tell the truth, which could result in your being expelled from the Institute."

"But how?" Ben Toll asked.

Any pretence that they had told the truth was now completely abandoned. James gave them the two affidavits to read.

"It's true Arbuthnot threatened Petra," Ben remarked. "I remember the icy stare she gave him. She's the only one of us who had any sense."

"Well, there's still time for you. Will you swear a similar affidavit? I promise not to make it public without your consent, and I'm sure that will not be necessary."

"What good are the affidavits if you don't use them?" asked Michèle. James smiled. "I didn't say I wasn't going to use them, Miss Letellier, I merely said I wasn't going to make them public."

The two students looked at each other again. Michèle was still hesitant, but Ben suddenly sported a broad grin. He had a very good idea of exactly what purpose the affidavits would serve. He agreed readily for both of them.

They drove to François' office, where everything went smoothly and quickly, and by a quarter to eleven, James was back in his office. He called to see whether Antonietta had left the cottage. She was still there.

"I fell asleep," she explained, "so I'll be late for class."

"Well, don't bother coming," James told her.

"I wouldn't miss it for the world," she answered.

Before leaving for class, James checked his emails. Much to his surprise, there was one from Professor van Wezel. To his even greater surprise, and horror, van Wezel had given Doefman's paper 70% with the comment that, despite one or two inaccuracies, it presented a fair assessment of European labor law. James forwarded the email to Elliot Hunt with the cryptic remark "I don't think I'll be using this." It was a remark that would have significant repercussions in the future.

James entered the classroom with his old self-confidence. He caught Petra looking at him, probably wondering where Antonietta was. He smiled at her and made a gesture to indicate that her friend had overslept. It was rather imprudent, but luckily no-one understood except Petra. After about ten minutes, Antonietta arrived.

It was the first decent lecture James had yet delivered, but Antonietta found herself daydreaming about the marvelous days she'd just spent and took little in. They had agreed she would go to lunch with her friends to alleviate any suspicions that might arise. James would use the time to do some work on his article. They would meet back at the cottage around two.

----

Lunch was enjoyable and highly amusing, particularly for Petra and Antonietta. Speculation was rife as to James' sudden resurrection as a good teacher. The general consensus was very near the truth. "He must be getting laid," Brett Taylor suggested, and all agreed with him.

"I wonder who it is?" Petra couldn't resist testing the waters.

"I know who it is," Simon replied without looking at anyone in particular. Petra took fright and quickly changed the subject.

As they were leaving, Simon took Antonietta aside. "Be careful, old sport," he told her. "You're never sure who you can trust in this place."

"Can I trust you?" she asked. "Of course," he replied with a grin. "I'm British, and we Brits stick together. My lips are sealed."

----

James returned to his office after class. He was relieved to have given a decent lecture at long last, but he longed to be back in the cottage with

Antonietta. He regretted her going for lunch with her friends. He thought of making an appointment to see HB but it was lunch time and neither he nor his equally unpleasant secretary would be available. So, he turned without enthusiasm to his article. At first it was hard going, but then the ideas began to come. Suddenly he noticed that it was already a quarter past two. He jotted down some more ideas and prepared to leave. There was knock on the office door. It was Annya Nowak.

"I hope I'm not disturbing you, Professor Markham," she said, turning the full force of her pretty smile on James. "I have two questions I wanted to ask you."

The first question concerned the hearing against Hunt.

"Annya," said James, using the girl's first name without thinking. "You must know all I've told Elliot, and there's nothing more I can add."

James had decided not to inform Hunt about the affidavits and how he planned to use them. It was a delicate matter, and he neither wanted to give Hunt false hope nor divulge his plan before the time for its execution. Annya accepted his answer without demurring, which suggested to James that at least this question had little import for her. He waited for the second one.

"I'm in your international trade course next term," she explained, "and I want to know whether there are any legal prerequisites to take the course. I'm worried about being out of my depth."

Annya might talk about her worry but the smile that played about her lips and the sparkle in her clear blue eyes belied it. In any case, the prerequisites for every course were stated in the Institute's syllabus. James pointed this out and added that he was sure she wouldn't be out of her depth.

The phone rang. It was Antonietta, who was very upset. "James, what are you doing? It's twenty to three and you're still in the office. You were supposed to be home at two." James' heart sank. He had been so fascinated by Annya's performance that he hadn't realized the time passing.

"I'm sorry," he said. "I got tied up. I'm leaving immediately."

Antonietta hung up without replying. James turned round and saw Annya staring at him. The amused glint in her eyes had disappeared. "I'm sorry I made you late," she said coldly. "Thank you for your time."

James drove to Ste. Anne des Lacs with foreboding. Not only was he late, but part of the reason for this was Annya Nowak. He knew Antonietta's capacity for violent and irrational jealousy, and so he prepared himself for a difficult reception.

Antonietta met him at the door. She had obviously been crying, and she was overwrought. She pummeled his chest. "Why, why?" she cried. With effort, James finally got her into his arms and held her trembling body close to his. Once she'd calmed down, he sat her down on the sofa next to him. He took her face in his hands, drew it towards him and kissed her.

"Antonietta, I hate myself for being late. I got caught up in my article. I'm sorry, I really am."

Antonietta looked at him with tear-filled eyes. "What's more," she told him dolefully, "you were distant on the phone."

James had intended to tell Antonietta about Annya, but he realized that it would be courting disaster in her present state. Instead, he let their kisses become more and more passionate amidst fervent declarations of love. As they lay together after having made love, Antonietta made James promise he would never be late again. Remembering his own disarray while waiting for her to arrive at the cottage, he readily agreed. But something in the tone of his voice disturbed Antonietta. "What's the matter, James," she asked fearfully.

Knowing what she was probably thinking, he reassured her. "Antonietta, it's true that something is bugging me, but compared to my love for you, it's irrelevant." He took her into his arms and kissed her all over her body until she begged him to take her again, which he did in a less conventional way. "You're impossible," she murmured contentedly, nestling against him afterwards.

"So, James," Antonietta asked, propping herself up with an inquisitorial air, which was her normal way of questioning him after making love, "What's bugging you?"

James pushed her back down on the bed. This way he could better control any outbreak of jealousy.

"Now, I'm telling you this firstly because I don't want any lies or concealment between us, and secondly because it's part of what disturbs me." James drew a breath and plunged in, hoping for the best. "I was about to leave at about two fifteen when Annya Nowak came to see me." Antonietta glared at James and tried to wriggle free. "Now listen to me. I wouldn't be telling you this if there was any need for you to be jealous. When will you finally understand that there is no-one, *no-one*, who can ever mean anything to me but you?"

Antonietta was only half convinced. "It doesn't change the fact that you were dallying with her in your office while I was waiting here in despair for you," she retorted.

"I wasn't dallying with her," James protested. "Now will you listen to what is bugging me or not?"

Antonietta cocked her head to one side. "Only if you promise to throw her out of your office the next time she appears." Relieved that the storm had passed, James promised.

"She came ostensibly to ask about progress in the case, which she knows anyway from Hunt, and then she asked a totally unnecessary question about prerequisites for my trade course next term. All this raises the inevitable question. If she flirts with me like this, perhaps she did the same with Hunt? What's more, one of the students I saw today knows her from Edmonton and says she is indeed a flirt."

"Of course she is, and she'd better keep her hands off you," Antonietta said grimly. Thinking of Annya, she tried to stop James kissing her but surrendered quite quickly.

"There are other things that trouble me as well. I sent Doefman's paper to a professor in Holland and he gave it 70% against 40% from Hunt. He intimated it wasn't a bad paper at all. Then there's a strange thing that may just be a coincidence." James paused and Antonietta looked at him expectantly. "When I asked Hunt how he and Annya had gotten together, he replied that he'd wandered around the Institute until he bumped into her."

"Well, that seems quite logical," commented Antonietta.

"Yes, but when I asked Annya the same question, I got exactly the same reply, as if they'd rehearsed it together."

"So what does this all mean, James? That Annya and Hunt are lying, and the others are telling the truth?"

"I can't really believe that. After all, we know Brett Taylor and the two today lied. They've even taken affidavits to that effect."

Antonietta's eyes glowed with pride. "You got them to sign affidavits?"

"Yes, I browbeat the poor couple, but I'll see they won't get into trouble." James let Antonietta kiss him passionately. "I have a funny feeling about this whole business, but not enough to give up on Hunt. I have no proof he's lying and plenty of proof the others are."

"When are you seeing HB?" There was anxiety in Antonietta's voice.

"Probably Thursday or Friday." James stroked Antonietta's hair. "Don't worry, my love, he won't eat me."

"No, but he'll want to get even."

James could feel her anxiety and brusquely changed the conservation. "I want to meet that Italian godfather of your's," he said.

They dressed and set off for Montreal. Within an hour, they were seated in Luigi's café. He had no need to ask who James was. Antonietta's happy serenity and the adoration with which her eyes fastened upon her companion told the whole story.

———

Antonietta was in the process of browning some sausage meat for a *risotto*. She felt an inner peace that had always eluded her. It was not just the fulfillment of the all-consuming passion that had wracked her ever since that fateful Mass at Saint-Sauveur. Before James, she had constantly worried about her inability to establish a meaningful relationship with a man, even fearing that the affair with Dana at boarding school had sown the seeds of perversion within her. Certainly, until James, she'd never experienced the same sexual fulfillment with men that she had with Dana or even Petra. James was able to exorcise these demons. He satisfied her sexual needs beyond her wildest imaginings, combining seamlessly the conventional techniques of heterosexual love-making with the erotic and intrusive intimacies of Sapphism. He alone understood that she required both.

The doorbell rang. Intrigued, Antonietta opened the door and found Bill Leaman standing there with a sheaf of papers in his hand.

"I've come to talk to James about my tenure application but I hope I'm early enough for supper," he said with a broad grin.

"I'm just making a *risotto*," Antonietta replied, "There should be enough for three."

"What's *risotto*?" Bill asked suspiciously.

"It's arborio rice cooked in olive oil with some onion into which you pour a bouillon until it's all absorbed. It's a creamy rice dish. Today we're eating it with sausage meat and wild mushrooms," Antonietta explained, returning to the stove.

"Where's James?"

"He's at the Institute. He'll be back soon."

Bill poured himself a large Scotch and eyed Antonietta suspiciously. "Do you ration poor old James?" he asked.

"Yes."

Bill sighed. "Why is it that women always try to stop men drinking?"

Antonietta scattered some parsley into the sausage meat and put it aside. She turned round and looked at Bill, her eyes twinkling with amusement. "For two reasons," she replied. "Firstly, we don't want to become widows and secondly, it's not very gratifying to have sex with a drunken man."

Bill grunted and sipped his Scotch. He watched Antonietta pour some rice into a casserole. He was struck again by the sharp contrast between the Antonietta of a week ago and the carefree, happy woman cooking for James.

"When are you two getting married?" he asked.

Antonietta finished pouring a small amount of bouillon into the rice and salted and peppered it. She lowered the flame and left the casserole uncovered. She placed some butter in a small frying pan, waited for it to melt and put in wild mushrooms together with some salt, pepper and nutmeg. Only then did she turn to face Bill.

"I don't like to think about it, Bill," she told him, her eyes losing their lustrous shine. "It would mean a break with my family and my religion, and I'm terrified that James would hold it against me if he lost the children as a result of the divorce."

"But you can't go on forever like this," Bill objected.

"We're in love, we're happy and there's no rush," Antonietta replied.

"I just hope nothing untoward happens."

"Why should it?" Antonietta asked nervously, but before Bill could answer, James arrived. He kissed Antonietta and greeted Bill.

"Come and eat," Antonietta called, placing a Caesar salad in a bowl on the table. "James, open a bottle of wine."

Her imperious tone amused James, who went off and chose a bottle of Valpolicella, a pleasant fruity wine of no great distinction that should appeal to Bill.

They discussed Bill's tenure, which he insisted on seeking despite James' misgivings. Then Bill announced that Carol was coming on Wednesday for a few days. "For me it's make or break. I don't want to go on like this," he informed them. James suspected it was his own idyll with Antonietta that had precipitated this decisiveness.

"Don't do anything rash, Bill," he warned.

"Rash!" Bill was beside himself. "I've been waiting five years for her to come and live with me. I don't think I'm being rash."

They finished the meal, Bill and James had two Scotches and then Bill, assuming that his friends wished to be alone, got up to leave. "When are you seeing HB about Hunt?" he asked James as he put on his overcoat.

"Friday at eleven."

"Well, may the force be with you."

"Thanks, I shall need it," James replied grimly.

After Bill had left, Antonietta sat James down on the sofa and fretted. "Why is it always you who has to do the dirty work?"

"I was appointed by the Rector to defend Hunt, so I have no choice."

This reply didn't convince Antonietta. "You go out of your way to do battle against HB and I know you. If they deny Bill his tenure, you'll be at the forefront of the fight. Why, James? These are horrible people, they'll stop at nothing."

James took Antonietta in his arms and kissed her. "Don't worry, my darling, they don't know about us and it seems I'm the only the senior faculty member who has the stomach to fight HB. Perhaps it's pride, perhaps a sense of justice, I don't know. I just hate his kind. Corrupt, hypocritical, ambitious to the point of megalomania, without humanity. A typical bloody Presbyterian."

Antonietta couldn't resist teasing James. "That's the Catholic in you talking," she told him with an indulgent smile. "I'm sure not all Presbyterians are like that."

"Leave me my prejudices," James retorted. "Anyone can be tolerant, but it takes character to be prejudiced."

Antonietta burst out laughing. She stood up and stripped off her clothes. "You talk too much," she told her lover. "How about some decadence?"

He took her on the sofa and let himself be pleasured by her. Many times. It was after midnight when they finally went to bed. Suddenly, Antonietta remembered her take-home exam for James' European course.

"It's due tomorrow, James," she cried, "and if I don't hand it in, people will talk."

James grinned at her. "Get the laptop and we'll do it in bed."

———

"Senior Dean, Professor Markham is here to see you," HB's secretary announced with fitting solemnity.

Arbuthnot stood up and frowned at his colleague. "So, Markham," he hissed, "You've come to plead for your client, I see."

James said nothing. He just glared at HB, who winced at the hatred and contempt in his eyes.

"Well?" HB asked with a nervousness that he couldn't quite master despite himself.

"Why don't you sit down?" James said. His manner was cold and disdainful. "I have something for you to read."

Arbuthnot slumped into his chair. This was not the way he'd imagined the interview. He'd seen himself as the grand inquisitor receiving Markham as a supplicant humiliating his pride before his, Arbuthnot's, authority. Instead it was he who was cringing before the implacable expression on James' face.

James threw the four affidavits on HB's desk. "Read them," he ordered. "Read them *very* carefully." Arbuthnot made a dismissive gesture. "Read them, Arbuthnot," James repeated in the same icy tone of command. "Read and be damned. Or don't read them and be doubly damned."

It was supreme bluff for James knew that these affidavits amounted to little. He couldn't use them, and if HB didn't panic, Hunt was in serious trouble. James watched HB read the affidavits. Never for one second did he relax his stern demeanor. Once HB had finished reading, James made his play. Everything depended on it.

"You will see, Arbuthnot," he said with calm hostility, "that not only have the students lied, but you, a professor, you, the head of the Ethics Committee, have actually encouraged them to lie and even threatened the Vice-President of the Students' Association with reprisals if she didn't lie for you."

James eyed Arbuthnot, who was staring in disbelief at the affidavits. Suddenly, in an onset of fury, he ripped them up and grinned savagely at James. "So where are your precious affidavits now?" he asked with a maniacal laugh.

"You disappoint me, Arbuthnot," James said scornfully. "You're stupid enough to believe those were the originals?"

He held up the originals of the affidavits. Arbuthnot made a move to grab them but James slapped him in the face with his hand. His signet ring left an ugly red mark on Arbuthnot's skin. James lifted his hand a second time and Arbuthnot cowed before it. James dropped his hand and addressed Arbuthnot with brutal severity.

"These affidavits will destroy you, and all those who've aided and abetted you. They will have you unseated and hauled before your own committee to be disciplined and dismissed for abuse of power, lying to your colleagues and bringing the Institute into disrepute."

Arbuthnot stared at James, his mouth open, without saying a word. He appeared to be in a daze and for one moment James thought he was going to faint. It was time for the final bluff.

"I don't give a shit about you, Arbuthnot. In fact, I'd love to see you dismissed and discredited, but for the sake of the Institute's good name, I'm proposing a deal to you."

HB didn't react. He obviously couldn't bring himself to utter the words that would signal another defeat at Markham's hands. James made his crucial pitch.

"You have the right as Chair of the Ethics Committee to drop the case against Hunt. Do that and I won't make the affidavits public."

"But the members of the committee can appeal to the Governing Council against my decision to drop," Arbuthnot cried.

James realized to his great relief that he'd won. "Then stop them," he snapped. "They're your creatures, so make them obey you." He turned to go but added before he left. "Next Friday, I will destroy you unless you do as I say. *Drop the case.*"

———

Antonietta had the impression that Forget's class would never end. She was on tenterhooks, wondering what had transpired between James and HB. A dreadful foreboding gripped her that this day would sound the death knell of her happiness, and she longed to drown her worries in James' arms and the comfort of his kisses.

Finally, the class ended and Antonietta rushed to the car park. She drove quickly through Saint-Sauveur, nearly killing an old woman who was crossing the road with maddening slowness at one of the crosswalks. Never had the short journey to Ste.-Anne-des-Lacs seemed so long or the countryside so unwelcoming in its winter austerity. With a sigh of relief she saw James' Mercedes parked in front of the cottage and skidded to a halt beside it. She raced to the door, flung it open and threw herself at James who had just risen at the sound of her arrival. After asking about Arbuthnot, she implored him to make love to her.

"Take me in any way you wish," she told him. "Just make me forget my fears."

After they'd made love, Antonietta asked James whether he'd told Hunt. "No," he replied. "Until HB actually drops the case, I haven't won." He started to get up to fetch himself a drink.

"You're not going anywhere," Antonietta said fiercely. "I haven't finished with you yet." She kissed him passionately. His lips were still damp from her own wetness, and this aroused her all the more. She ran her tongue down his body and took him between her breasts. James was helpless before the sight of Antonietta's nakedness, the sensual feel of the taut skin of her breasts surrounding his sex and the expertise of her caressing fingers. Once she had dealt with him, she moved up his body, drying herself on the hair of his chest. Her nipples betrayed her renascent desire and James took hold of her and placed her perfunctorily on all fours.

"This is the only way to keep you quiescent," he declared, running his hands over Antonietta's buttocks.

"Satyr," she whispered, but there no reproach in her voice. She willingly let him service her in the most dissolute way with tongue and fingers and then indecently satisfy his lust for her. As always the discomfort excited her. When she'd stopped moaning, James put his hands around her breasts from behind and brushed them along the still erect nipples.

"Can I have my drink now?" he asked, kissing her in the neck.

Antonietta turned round and gave him a dazzling smile. "Yes, I think we're finally done."

# CHAPTER 13

## Saturday, November 3 to Wednesday, November 21, 2001

The tears didn't start on Saturday, but the lustrous shine in Antonietta's eyes was dimmed by sadness. When they made love, she clung to James as though he were about to disappear. He ran his lips down her body, but she pulled him back towards her. "Kiss me," she said, and from the tone of her voice James could sense her distress. He kissed her, lay down next to her and placed her head on his shoulder. "It's not going to be as bad as you think. We'll be together every afternoon, and I'll try and get away in the evenings as often as possible."

"What about your research?" Antonietta enquired with a smile.

"To hell with my research. Do you think I'd be able to concentrate on the bloody European Union knowing you're on your own in this cottage?"

Antonietta propped herself up and looked anxiously at James. "Promise me you won't make love to your wife?" James nodded his acquiescence. He gazed into Antonietta's eyes. "Remember that this situation is your doing. You only have to say one word, and we can be together."

There was a silence before Antonietta answered. "I will marry you, James," she said, "but let me decide when and how. I prefer to suffer loneliness and sadness than do anything that could endanger our love."

"I don't see how anything could," James countered sharply.

"The divorce will be messy. There are children involved, there's your career, not to mention my religious scruples and your wife's. Our families will not approve, your children will not approve, people here will suspect—rightfully—that we broke the rules. We've only been together a week, without doubt the most wonderful week of my life, but I don't want to face the trauma of your divorce before our relationship has stood the test of time."

"How can you be so reasonable?" James asked petulantly. "All I can think of is how much I love you and how much I want to be with you."

Antonietta smiled. "My darling, I may be a volatile Latin," she said, stroking James' face, "but I'm also a woman, and women are more patient and far-sighted than men. You see only the present and the desires that momentarily dominate you; we are more concerned with the future, with what is permanent. I want my future to be with you, and I'm not going to do anything rash which could prejudice that."

James rose from the bed and walked over to his jacket. He pulled out two tickets.

"On December 7th we're going to the opera to see *Adriana Lecouvreur,*" he informed Antonietta. "I'll tell Veronica that I have a conference and we'll stay in Montreal until Sunday. Do you think we can do that without putting our relationship in danger?"

Antonietta jumped out of bed and threw her arms around James. Ignoring the ironical look on his face, she kissed him passionately and dragged him back to the bed. Their cares about the future were submerged in the joys of the present.

Late that afternoon, they drove to Montreal and attended Mass at the Basilica. Afterwards they went to a chic restaurant in the old port that specialized in French cuisine. "It'll make a change from Italian," James told Antonietta, who launched into her normal diatribe on the superiority of Italian food and Italian wines over their French rivals. However, she was graceful enough to admit that the escargots and the rack of lamb that followed them were delicious.

Immediately they arrived back at the cottage, Antonietta made for the bedroom. She whipped off her clothes and undressed James. She pressed her naked body against his. "Satisfy me as only you can," she beseeched him. "Make me forget that it's our last night together."

James gazed into her iridescent eyes. "It's not our last night together," he said. "There will never be a last night for us."

———

Inexorably, the time came for James to leave for the airport. As he was opening the door of the cottage, Antonietta appeared in the living room. She was wearing the same bra and string she'd worn on their first night together. Her lips gleamed sensuously with glossy lipstick. James gazed at her, quite captivated. Slowly she slid off her bra and string and walked towards James with a wanton expression on her face. "Don't you want me?" she asked.

It was too much for James. "Temptress," he exclaimed, taking his luscious mistress into his arms.

It was five-thirty before James arrived at Dorval[21] airport. Luckily, the plane was late and the passengers were only just going through customs. It was strange to see his wife walking towards him, blissfully unaware of the tremendous change in his life. She kissed him perfunctorily on the cheek and apologized for their lateness.

"You know Air Canada, James," she said. "I sometimes think they're late on purpose to discourage people from traveling with them. I always have the impression the flight attendants think of us as nuisances."

James laughed. Their dislike of Canada's national airline was one of the few things he and his wife had in common. He kissed his two children. Peter tensed up as normal. He found men kissing each other to be a silly and embarrassing French habit. Susanna, on the other hand, gave her father a big hug.

"Well, did you have a good time?" he asked his offspring.

It was Veronica who answered. "It was an excellent retreat," she enthused. "The priest who ran it was a Jesuit, very erudite and convincing. He said that Peter might have a vocation."

Peter made a grimace. "What's a vocation?" asked Susanna. "It means you don't marry and wear silly clothes," her brother replied. Veronica looked predictably aghast but James was highly amused.

"Really, James," his wife chided. "You're no support for me at all." With that, she stalked off towards the exit. James and the children followed, Susanna holding on to her father's hand and looking up at him in adoration.

Nothing had changed in the Markham household, and yet everything had changed.

———

Antonietta was desperate to see James. She paid little attention in her two classes and rushed home immediately after Forget's class where, to her immense joy, she found James already there. She collapsed into his arms.

"I love you," he said, wiping away the tears and kissing her tenderly.

Antonietta's expressive eyes implored him. "Tell me you didn't make love to her," she pleaded, incapable of masking the jealousy that was tormenting her. James shook his head. "Swear it," Antonietta insisted. James smiled at her persistence. "I swear it, my love."

They kissed again, more passionately. "Make love to me, James," Antonietta whispered. "Make love to me in the most licentious way possible." They made for the bedroom. On the way, Antonietta stopped to take the cord out of the kitchen drawer.

It was nearly four in the afternoon by the time they'd slaked their desires. James looked down at the dark beauty nestled against him. She turned her face up towards him. Her features were softened by the contentment wrought by her sexual indulgence and her eyes were shining with delight.

James sighed. "The problem is, Antonietta, you look so lovely after we've made love, that I always want to start all over again."

"Then why don't you?"

"Because, my darling, I have to pick up the kids in half an hour."

The mention of James' children brought Antonietta back to the harsh reality of their situation. She quickly changed the conversation. "What's happening with HB?" she asked.

James, sensing her distress, kissed her before answering. "As yet, nothing," he replied. "If he drops the case, we'll have to invite Hunt to the celebration."

Antonietta sat upright and glared at James. "*Without* Annya," she said fiercely.

"That's impossible," James objected.

"If you really loved me, it wouldn't be impossible," Antonietta countered, getting up from the bed. She put on a bathrobe and stalked off into the bathroom. James followed. She pushed away his hands as he tried to wind them around her breasts, but she couldn't avoid his kiss on her neck.

"I won't invite either of them," he murmured.

Antonietta swiveled round and fixed James with a penetrating stare. "Promise?" Without answering, James deftly slipped off her bathrobe and held her naked body close to his. "Promise?" she repeated. "I promise," he replied.

———

It was Wednesday morning and Antonietta was sat in Bill's class. She was calmed by the fact that James had spent the two previous afternoons and evenings at the cottage. His plan had been to work in the evenings at the Institute to make up for his afternoons with Antonietta, but it had proved impossible for him to pass by Ste. Anne without calling on her. Once there, it was equally impossible for him to leave. When he did leave, there were always tears from Antonietta, who would be left lonely and despondent.

When she returned home this day after her classes, there was no James at the cottage to greet her. She sat down on the sofa feeling empty and downcast There must be some explanation for his lateness, she told herself, but she had to struggle to hold back her tears.

James finally arrived around one thirty. Antonietta pushed him away and heaped reproaches upon him for his lateness. He backed her up against the wall and forced her to kiss him. She surrendered grudgingly but soon broke away. "Where were you?" she asked, unable to hide her suspicions. Always in the back of her mind was the image of the blond Annya. James laughed. He knew exactly what Antonietta was thinking and was tempted to tease her but he abandoned the idea when he saw the anguish in her eyes.

"I was informed just before noon that the Ethics Committee has dropped the case against Elliott Hunt," he told her.

Antonietta, forgetting her umbrage, cried out in triumph. "James, you did it, you did it! I'm so proud of you." She was about to embrace him with great passion when she noticed the strange expression on his face. "What's the matter?" she asked, "Isn't this what you wanted?"

"It's Hunt." Antonietta could sense the perplexity in James' voice. "I went to see him, and he didn't even thank me. He was really quite offish. Bloody ingrate!"

"Good, now we really don't have to invite him to the celebration," Antonietta replied, kissing her petulant lover with such ardor that Hunt's lack of gratitude was forgotten. She made James sit on the sofa while she slowly stripped in front of him. Once she was completely naked, she undressed James and ran her hardened breasts down his body before pleasuring him with her mouth. Then she made him follow her into the bedroom. She lay down on the bed in shameless abandon, her legs suggestively apart. "My turn," she told her lover.

They were, as always, late for the celebration at Bill's place. Carol was there, but the atmosphere between her and Bill seemed tense. Piotr, who hated dissension because he had so much of it at home, was looking glum. Danny was making an effort to enliven everybody, but he was already a little drunk.

"My God, what a gloomy lot you all are!" James exclaimed as he entered the living room. "This is supposed to be a celebration, for Christ's sake!"

James' good cheer and Antonietta's radiance succeeded where Danny's drunken efforts had failed. Piotr brightened up, Danny relaxed and seemed to become more sober, and Carol was too intrigued by James' new mistress to pursue her disagreement with Bill. She and Antonietta went off into the kitchen to make supper.

"My God, Itie and Chink food," groaned Bill. "Why don't we men go off to MacDonalds?"

"Don't be so crass, Bill," James scolded.

Bill was about to reply, but James cut him off by describing his strange meeting with Hunt.

"Perhaps that means he *was* lying," suggested Piotr.

"No, if he'd been lying, he should be even more grateful," James replied. "I think he's just a shit."

The men continued to drink and complain about the Institute until Carol and Antonietta arrived with the food. Antonietta had cooked a traditional *bolonese* and Carol sautéed beef with vegetables and sweet and sour pork. The meal was served with penne and rice cooked with chicken and eggs. Despite Bill's misgivings, he had to admit the food was delicious. As they sat around afterwards sipping the Courvoisier James had purchased for the occasion, Danny sprung his news on them.

"Ceara's coming for Christmas," he announced, his voice choking. He probably would have started to weep, were it not for the explosion of joy that greeted his announcement. All of them knew how much he'd missed his daughter. He hadn't seen her for two years. Carol and Antonietta kissed him and the men slapped him on the back. Danny filled his glass up and sat back in his chair, tearfully happy.

―――――

Bill dropped Carol off at the airport in Montreal. He fetched her bags from the trunk and deposited them in front of her. Without saying a word, he got back into the car and drove off to Antonietta's cottage. It was Saturday afternoon, and he was certain he would find James there.

It was James who came to the door, which Bill found incautious. "I could have been anybody," he told his friend, "You really should be more discreet." James just laughed but Antonietta, who had heard Bill's comment, was worried. "He's right, James," she said with a shudder.

James ushered Bill into the living room. He noticed that his friend was pale and upset. "What's the matter?" he asked. Bill sat down on the sofa, his head between his hands. "It's all over," he said dismally. "We're getting divorced."

While James looked on, not knowing quite what to say, Antonietta sat down next to Bill and put her arm around him.

"I'm sorry, Bill, I really am." Bill glanced up gratefully at Antonietta's sympathetic face. "But it's not the end of the world," she went on. "You couldn't continue as you were, and now you can get on with your life." Bill nodded. "You can even start flirting openly with Petra," she told him with a mischievous smile. Bill smiled back.

"You're a lucky guy, Jimmy," he said with feeling. "She's not only beautiful but adorable with it."

"There's only one way to deal with the blues, my friend," James told Bill as he handed him a glass of whisky. "That's to get thoroughly pissed."

After a few whiskies, Bill cheered up. "How do you manage to get away from home so often?" he asked James.

"Because of my overdue paper," James replied. "At least, that's what I tell Veronica."

"Veronica's going to smell a rat one of these days. Either you two behave with more circumspection or, James, you leave Veronica and marry Antonietta. If you two go on like this, you're asking for trouble."

Bill's words made an impression on Antonietta. After he left, she summoned up the courage to tell James that they should see each other less. Reluctantly, James agreed. "I suppose I'd better spend some evenings at home," he conceded. When he left Antonietta around six, she had difficulty containing her emotions. As she listened to him drive away, a feeling of emptiness and desolation descended upon her. She opened a bottle of Chianti and then another. It was a lonely, pitiless evening.

———

The pressure of work, and the need to forestall Veronica's suspicions, finally persuaded James to work on his article at home. It was a hard decision. He missed the woman he loved with such boundless passion, and he was conscious of the grief his evening's absences caused her. His only consolation was the hope that Antonietta's distress would hasten her decision to marry him.

Thursday arrived and, as James entered the classroom, he glanced quickly in Antonietta's direction and then began the lecture. He had overcome the incoherence of the beginning of term, but his lectures still lacked their normal sparkle. Unfairly, he held the students partly responsible for his predicament, and every class was an effort. Today was no exception, and it was without enthusiasm that he acknowledged Wrangel's hand. Another self-opinionated question, he thought, trying to hide his irritation.

The question was interminable and, after a while, James lost the thread of Wrangel's discourse, if indeed there was one. When finally the student had finished, he didn't have the slightest idea what he'd been talking about. Without any intention of humiliating him, he asked Wrangel to repeat his question. The class thought James was deliberately putting the young man down and roared with laughter. Wrangel glowered at James.

That day, James stayed with Antonietta until late in the evening. He was aware that he'd humiliated Wrangel. It had been unintentional but he hadn't been able to bring himself to apologize.

"You should have, James," Antonietta told him, "I don't like having enemies around us. We're at risk and it only takes one person to see us."

"The Lord will protect us," James replied facetiously.

Antonietta rebuked him. "Don't blaspheme." She tried to repel his renewed advances but soon succumbed. However, she made him shave before he made love to her.

––––

The next day, Antonietta had lunch alone with Petra. They talked, as always, about their love lives. Petra was still madly in love with Brett, but she admitted that he was a jock. "He's got a great cock, but a small brain," she told her friend, who, despite her discomfort with Petra's vulgarity, couldn't help laughing. "And you? When are you going to make *the* decision?"

"Not yet, I need to be sure our relationship can stand the strain of the divorce," Antonietta replied.

"Well, be careful," Petra warned. "James has made an enemy of Wrangel, and he's a friend of Annya, who's jealous of you. That's a dangerous combination."

Antonietta repeated Petra's warning to James, who didn't take it seriously. Bill also warned them at their Sunday get-together. "You two are so besotted with each other, even a blind man could see it! You're courting danger. For Christ's sake, get married."

Antonietta became very afraid. She made James leave early and spend the rest of the evening with her in the cottage. She made love to him with a frenzy that worried him.

"What's the matter, Antonietta?" he asked.

Antonietta sat up, her eyes full of sorrow. "We mustn't see each other again," she said. "Someone's bound to realize what's going on, and it'll ruin your career."

With that, she collapsed sobbing on the bed. James drew her to him. He was tempted to tell her that he didn't need his academic job, that he was a shareholder in the family bank and that he wasn't going to let anyone come between him, Lord Markham, and the woman he loved. Instead, he just comforted Antonietta and, when she stopped weeping, declared that hell could freeze over before he would consent not to see her again.

Antonietta came on top of him and devoured him with kisses. "I couldn't leave you," she cried. "I couldn't live without you."

"Anyway, you can't leave me," James told her. "We're going to *Adriana Lecouvreur* on December 7th, and the next day we leave for Mexico."

"*Mexico*!ì Antonietta looked at James in joyful astonishment. "You're taking me to *Mexico*?"

"Yes, we leave the day after the opera."

"How long are we going for?" All sorrow was now banished, and Antonietta's eyes sparkled with happiness.

"Five days. Remember that you leave for Italy on the 14th."

Antonietta's eyes dimmed fleetingly but she chased away the specter of their separation. "All I want to think about is that we shall be together all day and all night for a whole week."

———

James was going over the notes for his class when the phone rang. It was Carlos Guarnieri from the University of Buenos Aires to tell him that the conference on the European Union, at which James had promised to give a paper, would be held from December 17 to 19. James immediately realized the impossible situation he was in. He couldn't refuse without causing offense to Guarnieri and ruining the Institute's relationship with UBA. Yet if he agreed to go, he risked incurring Antonietta's jealous wrath. After all, he'd promised never to go anywhere, *particularly* not to Argentina, without her. He tried to play for time.

"I must check with the Institute to make sure there's nothing on that week," he obfuscated.

Guarnieri was not to be put off. "James, we're counting on you. You've got to come."

Feeling slightly sick to his stomach, James agreed.

———

They'd been back in the cottage for over two hours before James summoned up the courage to tell Antonietta about the conference in Buenos Aires. Her reaction was worse than he'd feared. She jumped out of bed, put on her dressing gown and glared at him.

"You promised *not* to go to Argentina without me," she cried, her voice quivering with jealous rage. "You promised me. If you break that promise, I never want to see you again. *Never.*"

"Antonietta," James pleaded, "I have no choice. I agreed to this before we knew each other. I can't go back on it without ruining the Institute's relationship with the University of Buenos Aires."

"*I don't care about the University of Buenos Aires,*" Antonietta screamed, tears streaming down her face. "You tell me now that you're not going, or you leave and never come back."

"Postpone your flight to Italy and come with me," James suggested.

"No, I can't. I have to be in Italy for my parents' wedding anniversary. I promised and *I keep my promises.*"

Antonietta threw James his clothes. He was angered by her unreasonableness, so he dressed silently and walked out of the cottage. He couldn't bring himself to leave. He walked back, but Antonietta had locked the door. He called her name but there was no answer. After a frustrating few minutes, he drove off.

Inside the cottage, Antonietta had thrown herself on to the sofa. It cost her an enormous effort not to respond to James. She knew she was being unreasonable, but the image of James with Carolina stoked a furious jealousy within her that she was unable to control. Torn between a desperate need for the man she loved and anger at his inconstancy, she drank herself into a stupor.

———

James dropped off the children for school and drove to Ste. Anne on the off-chance that Antonietta had decided not to attend her class with Bill. The previous evening had been one of the worst he'd ever spent, followed by a sleepless night. He was desperate to see Antonietta and tell her that he wouldn't be going to Argentina. However, when he arrived at the cottage, the Jetta was gone.

He passed by Bill's class on the way to his office. He saw Antonietta in the back row. Her face was drawn, and he hoped it was because she too had spent a sleepless night. He reached his office and went morosely through the day's mail. He was soon lost in thoughts of Antonietta, but a knock on the door brought him out of his sad reverie. It was Annya Nowak. He stood up to greet her and then sat on his desk. Annya remained standing.

"I just wanted to thank you for helping out Elliot," she explained. Her hair, which framed her oval face with perfect symmetry, seemed even blonder than usual and accentuated the deep blue of her eyes. She was wearing a blouse that was unbuttoned enough to reveal the cleavage between her breasts. Despite himself, James was drawn by her seductive allure. He returned her smile.

"He told me it was Arbuthnot's decision to drop the case," Annya went on. She gave James a penetrating look. "Is that the whole story?"

James was in a quandary. He understood now why Hunt had seemed so ungrateful and why Arbuthnot was in such high spirits. Yet, the only way to remedy the situation was to divulge the existence of the affidavits. He couldn't do that without putting the students at risk.

"I had a conversation with Professor Arbuthnot," he told Annya. "I think he realized it would do him no good to pursue the matter."

"Really?" Annya's eyes danced flirtatiously, inviting James to dally with her. They were very close to each other. At that moment the door of James' office opened and Antonietta walked in. She took one look at Annya and James together and stopped dead, her eyes blazing with rage.

"*Spergiurato!*" she spat at James and marched out.

James was devastated. He couldn't have imagined a worse scenario for their first meeting since yesterday's row. He hurried Annya out of the office, muttered some excuse and rushed off after Antonietta. He caught up with her in the parking lot. She was almost hysterical and pushed him away.

"Go back to your blond Annya," she shouted. "Leave me alone. I hate you, I hate you!"

Before James could get hold of her, she was in the car. He had to jump backwards as she reversed out of the parking space. She drove off quickly, much too quickly. James was gripped by despair and fear. Despair that he'd lost Antonietta, fear that she would have an accident. He walked to his car and went off after the woman he loved.

James drove through Saint-Sauveur with a hollow feeling in his stomach. His body trembled as he turned off the highway towards Ste. Anne. To his relief, Antonietta's Jetta was in front of the cottage, She was still in it. He pulled up beside her. They both got out of their cars and Antonietta threw herself, sobbing, into James' arms.

"Forgive me, forgive me," she implored between their kisses.

"There's nothing to forgive," he replied, stroking her long dark hair, "I love you, and I'm not going to Argentina."

Antonietta laid her head on James' shoulder. "I love you, and you must go to Argentina." She glanced up at him, her eyes glistening with joy through her tears. "But I'm glad you said you wouldn't go."

James stroked her cheek. "A promise is a promise, isn't it?" He was answered by a kiss of such passion that it left him in a daze. Antonietta laughed at his stunned expression, put her arm in his and walked him into the cottage.

Wrangel, who had followed James to Ste. Anne, watched them go. The images in his camera would be his revenge for the humiliation Markham had inflicted on him in class.

Blissfully unaware that they had been spied upon, James and Antonietta were frantically making up for the torment they'd been through. Suddenly, Antonietta broke off their love-making.

"What was she doing in your office?" she demanded to know. James explained. "That's not why she came to see you," Antonietta declared flatly. "You know that." It was true, James admitted. "I don't want you talking to her ever again," Antonietta ordered. Instead of replying, James began to play with her nipples. This always stimulated her libido and, thankfully for James, she forgot about Annya.

It was after a late lunch that they finally discussed Argentina. "I promised not to go, and I'll keep that promise," James told Antonietta. She shook her head. "No, you have to go, I realize that, but you must swear not to see Carolina." She took out her Roman missel and opened it at a reading from the Gospels. She made James swear on it, but this didn't calm her jealousy.

"I shall go through hell while you're there," she said forlornly.

"I shall go through hell the whole time you're away in Italy," James responded.

# CHAPTER 14
## Thursday, November 22, 2001, to Thursday, January 4, 2002

Despite their passionate reconciliation, both James and Antonietta remained unsettled. For all the promises James had made, Antonietta couldn't overcome the fear that one day he would leave her as he had after their quarrel. James himself was beset by guilt for having driven off, abandoning Antonietta to her despair. They sought comfort in unremitting bouts of frenzied love-making. James came to the cottage every afternoon and most evenings, despite Veronica's complaints. Luckily her suspicions were still directed at James' supposed drinking, but the lovers realized that sooner or later she would sense the truth.

The strain of their situation began to show. At their Sunday get-together at Danny's that weekend, Bill remarked that they both seemed pale and tense. "You can't go on like this," he declared. "Either you split up, or you get married." Antonietta shot Bill a look of sheer horror. "How can you even *think* of us splitting up. It would kill me," she cried, pressing herself against James.

Bill regretted the clumsiness of his remark. "I didn't mean it," he told an ashen Antonietta, "I'm just trying to make you two face up to reality."

Later in the car, James tried again to persuade Antonietta to marry him. "Wait until I come back from Italy," she pleaded. "We'll talk about it then."

This eternal procrastination aggravated James, who began to wonder whether Antonietta would ever agree. He was in a somber mood when he arrived home. The house was in darkness and he sat in the living room, sipping a Scotch. Perhaps they should split up. But the very thought made him feel sick to his stomach.

———

Their day of deliverance finally arrived. Term was over and they were driving down to Montreal. They arrived at *Le Reine Elizabeth* about five and immediately went to their room. Within no time, Antonietta was naked and lying on the bed, waiting impatiently for her lover. "Men wear too many clothes," she complained. For some reason, this comment made James extremely jealous. "I don't like you talking about men in general," he said huffily.

Antonietta sat up and pulled him, half undressed, down on to the bed. She removed the rest of his clothes with an expertise that only served to increase James' jealousy. She came on top of him, dangling her succulent breasts provocatively before his eyes. He grasped them, turned her over on her back and devoured their delicious softness with his mouth. Antonietta squealed with delight and pushed James down her body.

"Don't you want me to shave first," he asked.

"No, I want to feel your tongue right there, right now," she replied with unconcealed lust.

They made love with a dissolute abandon that had deserted them in the oppressive days leading up to their departure. All their problems dissipated in the silken sheets of the hotel bed. The Institute, Veronica, the constant need to hide and lie belonged to another world far away from the splendor of their room overlooking the Place Ville Marie. Afterwards, they took a shower together and then Antonietta sent James down to the bar in his tuxedo while she prepared herself.

When Antonietta appeared about three quarters of an hour later, there seemed to emanate a collective gasp from the customers of the bar. She was wearing the black dress she'd bought at the Emporium in the Via Strozzi. It was identical to the red dress she'd worn to such devastating effect at James' party. The black color accentuated the timeless classicism of her beauty, while the deep slits exposing her legs almost up to her thighs and the tight décolleté that only partly covered her opulent bosom revealed her unbridled sensuality. She had done her hair in a chignon and was wearing diamond earrings and a diamond necklace.

"They're not real," she whispered to James, who was staring at her in speechless admiration. Her eyes glittered radiantly beneath the mascara and the glossy pink of her lips tempted James to a kiss. Antonietta evaded him. "You'll ruin my make-up," she said with a laugh. They had a drink and, the evening being unusually warm for so late in the year, walked to the opera house.

It had been their intention to dine in a restaurant after the opera, but

Antonietta wanted only to be alone with James in their room. They ordered a bottle of Barolo and some sandwiches, which were left untouched while they made love. They had them in the early hours and then fell asleep in each other's arms.

A few hours later, they were drowsily preparing themselves to go the airport. Antonietta was wearing a pair of very tight jeans and a sweater that seemed to be at least two sizes too small for her. With her lovely face still softened by the afterglow of their night of sex, she was a picture of blatant lubricity.

"How am I supposed to keep my hands off you," James groaned. Antonietta gave him a delightful smile. "You're not," she said, walking up and pressing herself against him.

They nearly missed their plane.

———

They arrived in Guadalajara a little after four in the afternoon. They took a taxi and drove half an hour from the airport to the historic center of the city where their hotel was situated. They showered and dressed. For once, Antonietta didn't insist on James making love to her straightaway. She was too curious to see the city, so James took her up to the panoramic terrace on the roof of the hotel. She gazed in wonder at the architectural wonders of Guadalajara: the Cathedral, the Teatro Degollado, the Government Palace, and the other imposing buildings that clustered around the squares of the historic city.

"So, this is what it'll be like when we're married," James remarked with a sly grin

"What do you mean?"

"Less sex and more sightseeing."

Antonietta downed the rest of her red wine, a Mexican one that was surprisingly good, and stood up. "I'll make you eat those words," she declared. "Literally?" James enquired, and they both had a fit of giggles that greatly amused some Americans at the next table.

"Like to laugh, these Mexicanos, don't they?" one of them observed in a loud voice.

"Ignorant people," Antonietta fumed. "They can't even tell the difference between Italian and Spanish. "

They made love in countless ways on the large bed in their spacious suite.

Their troubles seemed even further away than in Montreal, and they kissed and caressed each other without any inhibition. Antonietta made no effort to stifle the screams of ecstasy that James' expertise wrung from her, and she rendered him measure for measure. Despite the air-conditioning, they were both bathed in perspiration when finally their bodies could take no more pleasure.

——

Later, during the agony of her separation from James, Antonietta would look back on her days with him in Mexico as the happiest of her life. That Sunday morning, they woke up in each other's arms and made love lazily. They had time for a quick expresso before making their way across the Plaza de Armas to the Cathedral for Mass. Afterwards they had lunch and went on a horse-drawn tour of the old city.

That afternoon Antonietta gave herself to James with the same abandon as the previous day. The pleasure they took together seemed never-ending, at least until Antonietta's other appetite took over.

"James," she whispered after yet another devouring kiss. "I've got to eat something."

"And I need a drink," her lover replied.

——

His business at the University of Guadalajara concluded, James picked up a rental car and they drove to the coast. On the way they passed some eerie mud flats and crossed a long bridge that seemed to carve the mountains in two. They had lunch in the picturesque colonial city of Colima, which is dominated by a threatening volcano that occasionally belches black smoke. Between Colima and Manzanillo, where they were headed, they drove past a coconut forest. The tall trees, with their rather obscene clusters of nuts, swayed in the light breeze. Antonietta giggled at the sight and nestled up to James. "Wait till we get to the hotel," he said, "otherwise we'll have an accident." Antonietta paid no attention and continued to play with him.

They finally arrived at *Las Hadas.* The beach of the resort stretches out to a cove that is sheltered from the turbulence of the Pacific Ocean. Behind it rise majestically the brilliant white buildings of the hotel and the surrounding apartments with their minarets and domes. They look down over marbled arcades of cobblestone paths interspersed with little squares, fountains and tropical flowers.

"It's like something out of a thousand and one nights," Antonietta exclaimed. She slipped off her shoes and ran over the hot sand to the sea. She dipped her feet into the calm and inviting water. James watched her, marveling at the difference between the blithe young woman playing in the sea and the tense and fearful Antonietta of a few days ago.

Their room contained the same Moorish motifs with arches and a marble floor. It looked over the complex and beyond to the sea. Antonietta could hardly tear her eyes away from the exotic beauty of the scene: the dazzling white of the buildings, the pale yellow of the sand glistening in the heat, the turquoise of the sea and the azure blue of the sky. James came up behind her and squeezed her in his arms.

"Happy?" he asked.

Antonietta sighed. "I could stay here all my life," she replied.

The twenty-four hours they spent at *Las Hadas* passed like a dream for Antonietta. They lay on the sand, basking in the Mexican sun, they swam languidly in the warm sea, frequently they would return to the room to gratify their hot, lustful bodies and when they were hungry, they would walk along the beach to the restaurant and eat fresh seafood to the sound of waves lapping gently against its façade. When they were forced to leave in order to return to Guadalajara, it was like being turned out of the Garden of Eden.

Antonietta made James promise to bring her back one day. "Otherwise, I won't leave," she told him.

"Let's not" was his laconic reply.

For James, it was another Antonietta he experienced in *Las Hadas*. The sun and magic of Mexico stripped away the veneer of fear and guilt and revealed her natural carefree high spirits. Her beauty glowed in its natural setting, and her body responded to the slightest touch. She had the intense sensuality of the dark women of the south. For James the temptation to linger, perhaps to stay for ever was strong, but he knew he had to resist it. His children and Antonietta's religious scruples still stood in their way, however happy they might feel at this moment. It would be a long road yet before they could live openly together, somewhere on the Mediterranean where the sea and the sand and the sun would complement and succor the infinity of their passion.

---

The day of Antonietta's departure for Italy inevitably arrived, and she awoke with a sick feeling in her stomach. It was only three weeks, but her need for James was such that she was unable to conceive of life without him. On the rare days she didn't see him, she was reduced to misery. How would she cope with three weeks? She was tempted to cancel her flight, but she felt bound by the promise to attend her parents' anniversary. Besides, she told herself without much conviction, it would be nice to see her friends again.

James had slept little, torn between sweet images of the blissful time in Mexico and dread of the separation from Antonietta. He had difficulty believing it could really happen. Yet the fateful day had dawned and soon he would be taking her to the airport.

The drive to the airport and the brief wait before Antonietta left to go through security were excruciating for both of them. Finally, they could stand it no longer. It would be better to get the parting over and done with. Antonietta stood up and, fighting back tears, made James promise again and again to think of her every second of the day.

"Please, please, no Carolina or Annya," she begged.

James promised. "I'll meet you in Toronto on January 4th and we'll spend the night in a hotel there," he told her.

After one final passionate kiss, Antonietta tore herself away and hurried off, not daring to look back. James watched her go through security and disappear. A terrible feeling of emptiness came over him as he walked towards the parking lot.

———

No member of Antonietta's family was there to greet her on her arrival in Florence. What a fine beginning for my holiday, she thought despondently She was making for the taxi stand when she encountered the family's faithful old retainer, Tonio. Well, at least they hadn't completely forgotten about her.

"How is our little Countess?" Tonio asked with a broad smile. All the servants were very fond of Antonietta. She kissed him affectionately on both cheeks.

"I'm well, thank you Tonio," she replied untruthfully. In fact, she'd spent the whole journey fighting a voracious jealousy. At times she had more or less persuaded herself that James would leave her for Carolina or at least take the Argentinean to his bed. At other times she'd managed to console herself that, if he loved her as much as she loved him, he would remain faithful to her. However, even this consolation had not overcome her feeling of emptiness.

It was strange to be back in Florence. The sights were familiar but

Antonietta felt like a foreigner. Her heart and her existence were elsewhere. Tonio, who was used to Antonietta's vivacious high spirits, interpreted her silence as disappointment that only a servant had come to meet her.

"The Countess della Chiesa and the Count Giovanni with his wife are in Rome with the Countess Carla," Tonio explained, "and the Count della Chiesa is still in Perugia at a conference."

Antonietta smiled. All the della Chiesa children had known Tonio since they were born, and her father was only eight when her grandfather had first taken Tonio into the family's service. Yet, he always showed this old-fashioned deference to all of them.

"I hope they'll be back tomorrow," Antonietta remarked.

"They are coming back this evening, Countess."

Once she'd unpacked, Antonietta dialed James' cell number. There was no answer. She made the same call about ten times before eventually he answered. Antonietta heaped reproaches on him.

"Where were you? I was going out of my mind."

"My darling, how could I know when you were going to call?"

"You should have been waiting."

James ignored the rebuke "I love you, and I miss you. I didn't sleep all night."

"Well, I hope you didn't. To think of you sound asleep when I was tortured by fear and jealousy would be too much."

They talked for half an hour. Antonietta made James promise again and again not to see Carolina. Far from comforting her, the telephone call brought home the distance separating them. Suddenly, their love seemed brittle and endangered. Damn that university in Buenos Aires. Why did they have to pick a time when she was away in Italy to invite James?

Feeling alone and dejected, Antonietta remained in her room until her mother arrived with Giovanni and Renata. They were obviously pleased to see her, which brought some solace. Then, her father arrived. He embraced her warmly. Despite the dark thoughts oppressing her, Antonietta enjoyed the meal and the excellent Italian wines her father served in her honor.

———

James was glad to be at the conference. Meeting colleagues, listening to tedious papers and giving one himself provided a welcome diversion from his yearning for Antonietta. Moreover, the conference proved quite interesting.

James gave his paper on the institutional failings of the European Union and the shortcomings of the Treaty of Nice. One of the American professors gave a windy discourse on the federal nature of the EU, with which James disagreed and said so quite forcibly. After a pleasant lunch of excellent Argentinean *bife* accompanied by a drinkable Malbec, the conference resumed on the topic of trade relations. A very serious Mexican professor gave a dry but discerning analysis of the economic agreement between Mexico and the EU, for which James acted as moderator.

The day ended at five. Carlos drove James back to his hotel and invited him to dinner that evening. He accepted with alacrity as the prospect of being on his own with only a frantic desire for Antonietta as company was not appealing. They agreed to meet at eight. In the mean time, James showered and waited for Antonietta's call, which came at precisely six o'clock. She plied him with questions about his day, and then came the inevitable "Did you see her?"

James could tell that Antonietta was distraught. He told her that he hadn't seen Carolina, he promised not to see her and he repeated again and again all she meant to him and the infinite depth of his love for her. They talked for about half an hour, but the distance, their pent-up emotions and jealousies and the impersonal nature of the communication left them both frustrated. After promising for the umpteenth time not to see Carolina, James rang off. He felt despondent. The carefree days in Mexico seemed far, far away. Not caring for the solitude of his own company, he went down to wait for Carlos in the bar.

———

Antonietta felt equally downcast after their phone call. Hearing James so far away exacerbated her fears. She was obsessed by the idea of Carolina. She hadn't been planning to attend the Lescia's Christmas party, but now she decided to go. At least it would take her mind off James. She put on a long dark brown dress that showed off her voluptuous figure without being openly erotic. It was cut low enough to suggest a hint of cleavage but no more. She wore her hair down and put on just sufficient make-up to accentuate the brilliance of her eyes and the soft curves of her mouth. Even her mother congratulated her. "You look extremely lovely," she told her.

Everyone else at the party was dressed with equal elegance. Unfortunately, this didn't overcome Antonietta's regret at coming for she was stuck with Fabio di Lescia and Rodolfo Guardini and their circle of aristocratic friends. They might constitute the cream of Florentine society in her mother's eyes, but she found them insufferably arrogant and boring. She was on the point of leaving to call James when she was accosted by a blond woman who was probably in her late thirties. Her classic beauty was only rivaled by the eroticism of her attire. Her slinky white dress was open down to the waist. It afforded a tantalizing glimpse of her voluptuous breasts and showed off her golden bronzed skin. She wore a diamond in her navel. Two slits up each side of the dress exposed her thighs. The striking blond hair was done up in a chignon. She gazed languidly at Antonietta with hazel-colored eyes.

"Countess," she purred. "I've been wanting to meet you. I am the Marquesa de Avila y de la Torre."

"I've just come back from Canada," Antonietta stammered, mesmerized by the Marquesa's raw sensuality.

The Marquesa smiled. It was a licentious, enticing smile. "Let's hope you're here to stay."

Antonietta tore herself out of her trance. "I can't place your accent, Marquesa," she said. "You're not Spanish, are you?"

The Marquesa smiled again and moved her tongue suggestively along her upper lip. "I was born in Czechoslovakia, but my late husband was Spanish, so that makes me Spanish too," she replied, seeming to caress the words as she spoke them.

Antonietta's mother suddenly appeared. She didn't acknowledge the Marquesa, which surprised Antonietta. "Come, Antonietta, your father wishes to talk to you." With that, she hauled her daughter away. As soon as they had rejoined her father and Giovanni with Renata, her mother lectured her.

"Don't talk to that woman," she told Antonietta. "She has a very bad reputation."

"But she's a Spanish Marquesa," Antonietta objected. "I thought you wanted me to mix with people of my class."

"She may be a Marquesa," her mother replied scornfully, "but only because she married a man forty years older than herself. People even say that he met her in a brothel."

"You should watch out," her brother interjected. "People also say she has a weakness for beautiful young women."

Caterina was horrified. "Giovanni, don't mention such things. Look how you've shocked Antonietta."

It was not shock that Antonietta was feeling. Giovanni's remark disturbed her for a quite different reason. She knew now why the Marquesa had sought her out and she was horrified to have fallen under the woman's spell. It brought back all her old doubts. She resolved to give the seductive Marquesa a very wide berth. Nevertheless, when she left the party, she couldn't resist a furtive glance in her direction.

———

It was a pleasant, warm summer evening in Buenos Aires, so James decided to walk to the Hotel Plaza San Martín where the conference dinner was being held. Why on earth did they have to choose the hotel where Carolina worked? he asked himself. He arrived with some misgivings. Across the entrance hall, he saw a pretty blond girl at the reception desk dealing with a client. It was Carolina.

The sight of Carolina gave James quite a jolt. She looked as serene as he remembered her. He couldn't resist a feeling of jealousy as he watched her smile at the young man who was checking in. He was tempted to walk across and interrupt them but stopped himself. Instead, he waited until Carolina was occupied with her back to him and snuck past into the banquet room. However, he couldn't resist another look towards the reception desk on his way out of the hotel after the banquet. Carolina was no longer there. He wondered what she was doing and was tempted to visit La Barra in the hope of meeting her there. Appalled with himself, he turned resolutely in the direction of his hotel. Thank goodness he was leaving Buenos Aires tomorrow.

———

Antonietta could hardly believe she was on a plane for Canada and that in a little over ten hours she would be making love to James. The last few nights had been very trying for she'd been consumed by desire for her lover.

Yet, despite her lust for James and the enormous relief that their separation was ending, Antonietta was no nearer to making the crucial decision. There had been sporadic incidences of friction, but her whole family without exception had been delighted to have her back. The time in Rome with Carla and Filiberto had been surprisingly enjoyable, perhaps due to the arrival of their new baby and the enlivening presence of her older brother, Paolo, and his girlfriend, Monica.

The religious ceremonies over Christmas had also played their part by strengthening her Catholic faith, in particular the solemn Tridentine High Mass celebrated by her uncle on Christmas Eve with its imposing ritual and transcendent music. So, the idea of a breach with her family and her religion in order to marry a divorced man was even more difficult to envisage than before she returned home for the holidays. Yet it was impossible for her to renounce James. Her passion for him dominated her to the exclusion of all else.

———

While Antonietta was counting the seconds to her arrival in Toronto, James was driving to Trudeau Airport to catch the midday flight to Lester Pearson. He'd begun to think this moment would never come, but soon he would be holding Antonietta's nude body in his arms. The intensity of his desire for her made him feel slightly queasy. He'd never experienced a more difficult time than this separation from Antonietta. It had brought home to him, if ever this were necessary, the depth of his feelings for her. Yet, there were so many obstacles to their life together. Besotted with Antonietta, James had tended over the last months to neglect his children, but he'd spent much time with them during the holidays and they had returned to their former closeness. The idea of abandoning them was now more problematic. Yet the only feasible alternative, giving up Antonietta, was beyond his comprehension.

———

James ran towards Antonietta as she emerged from customs. She dropped her suitcases and threw herself into his arms.

"It was horrible," she choked. "At times I thought I'd die."

James looked at her fixedly. "It was the worst time of my life. You're never going away again."

Antonietta's answer was another passionate kiss and they made for the taxis. Within an hour they were in their room. Very quickly their love-making gained in passion and audacity. James pulled out some cord from his overcoat.

"Just in case you didn't behave in Florence," he explained.

Antonietta turned away so that James couldn't see her blushing. Thinking of the lure of the Marquesa, she let him tie her legs and arms to the four posts of the bed. He tantalized her unmercifully. Every time her groans started on a crescendo that indicated she was moving towards her climax, he would stop and kiss her lips and caress her breasts. She pleaded with him until she was no longer capable of coherent speech. When her body finally exploded, she felt herself plunged into a sea of voluptuous pain followed by endless spasms of utter ecstasy. Her whole body was bathed in perspiration and she panted from sexual exhaustion. James undid her and took her body, still trembling from the cataclysm of her orgasm, into his arms. He fondled her breasts, played with her nipples and caressed her hair. She turned her face up towards him for a kiss. "I love you," she said.

It was a while before Antonietta recovered, but when she did, she took hold of the cord to tie James up and used her nipples in a way that aroused him unmercifully. She took him between her breasts and ran a finger gently up and down his shaft. He had sworn to himself that he wouldn't beg for mercy, but when she used the tip of her tongue with infinite softness, he couldn't bear it any more and begged her to finish him. Antonietta shook her head. She kept James in an agony of suspense until she eventually used her mouth to satiate him. He had the impression of drowning her.

"What happened in Florence?" James suddenly asked, surprised by his own suspicions.

"You tell me first about Buenos Aires," Antonietta countered, her hands tightening themselves around James' body.

"Nothing *happened*. It's just that the bloody people organizing the conference had the bright idea of having the banquet in the hotel where Carolina works."

"You saw her?" Antonietta buried her face against James. She didn't want to see the expression of guilt on his face that would plunge her into misery, but he made her look at him.

"It was inevitable," he said, looking directly at her and hoping that his face wouldn't divulge the whole truth. "I had to pass through the reception hall, and she was at the desk. I made sure she didn't see me. I had no contact with her, I swear that to you."

"Were you attracted to her?" The question gave Antonietta away. The shock on James' face covered any hint that he was lying when he said no.

"Who were you attracted to?" he asked.

Antonietta had no escape. She recounted the episode with the Marquesa at the party. "It was a passing fascination," she insisted. "I would never have done anything."

James was staring at her with a strange expression on his face. She didn't know whether he was angry or hurt or what. "I love you, James," she went on, her voice breaking with emotion. "Please say you forgive me, *please*." Tears welled up in her eyes, and she was thankful for them. Perhaps they would bring her James' forgiveness. Suddenly, to her immense relief, James smiled.

"Was Dana blond?" he asked.

Antonietta was taken aback by the question. "Yes, but why do you ask?"

"Because so is Petra and so probably was the Marquesa. It's not *you* who should be jealous of blue-eyed blonds, it's *me*. I'm going to have to keep you away from them."

James expected Antonietta to be indignant, which always rendered her even more desirable, but instead she gave him the most promiscuous smile. "So is Carolina, so perhaps you could introduce me to her," she suggested.

"Antonietta!" James was beside himself, and Antonietta burst out laughing. "Serves you right for teasing me," she said, kissing him. "Really, you needn't worry James. If I really were bisexual, I would've had more than one brief encounter since Dana."

James wasn't convinced. What Antonietta didn't know was that he'd met the Marquesa nearly ten years ago in Spain on the occasion of a dinner given by his friend Rodrigo's father, the Marqués de San Vincente, in honor of the sixty-fifth birthday of the Marqués de Avila y de la Torre. He had been accompanied by his young wife, and James had been awed by her voluptuous blond looks and the crude sensuality she exuded. Knowing Antonietta's highly charged sexuality, he wasn't surprised that she'd been attracted to her and probably, despite her denials, tempted by the sexual delights offered by the Marquesa. He felt a sting of jealousy but comforted himself with the hope that Antonietta's love for him was powerful enough to resist the temptation of lesbian pleasure.

# CHAPTER 15

## Monday, January 7 to Friday, February 8, 2002

Bill arrived at James' office in a state of high agitation. His friend was on the phone to Antonietta, and from the general drift of the conversation Bill gathered that he was trying to calm her down.

"I can hardly throw her of my class," James was telling Antonietta. "Try to be reasonable." The conversation seemed to end in a stalemate.

"Problems?" Bill asked with a slight smirk.

"It's all very well for you to smirk," James replied crossly. "I love that woman, but she drives me crazy with her jealousy of Annya Nowak."

"Well, she has a point. That girl's always looking at you as if she'd jump into the sack at the first opportunity."

James grunted. "Perhaps, but she's in my international trade class at eleven, and there's nothing I can do about it. Antonietta refuses to see that."

"Jimmy." There was an urgency in Bill's voice as he came to the reason for his visit. "Winstone's set my tenure hearing for April 12[h] and the election of the faculty representative for Feburary 6th."

"That seems fine."

"Yes, but the bastards have set this coming Friday as the deadline for candidates to declare themselves. That doesn't leave us much time to find someone on my side who could be elected."

"Which is exactly why they've set such a short period. I'm sure Winstone didn't think of it. This smells of HB."

They agreed to a council of war that night at Bill's.

———

James made sure to leave immediately after his class. He saw Annya coming towards him but managed to avoid her. In fact, he arrived at the cottage before Antonietta. This mollified his volatile mistress somewhat, but she still demanded to know what Annya had been wearing, whether she'd smiled at

173

him or approached him at the end of the class.

James took Antonietta into his arms. "Listen, Antonietta," he said, trying to sound firm. "I don't want to go through this scene every Monday, Wednesday and Friday. Annya's in my class. If she wants to speak to me, I can't refuse and if she wants to smile at me, I can hardly slap the smile off her face. You know how much I love you, you've had enough proof of that, so stop being jealous of Annya."

"Promise to come back here *immediately* after the class," Antonietta insisted, turning dark, mournful eyes upon James.

He couldn't resist kissing her but still held out. "There's more than Annya in the class. I can't just rush off every time."

Antonietta pouted. She was using all her wiles, which were all the more effective as her sweater had a plunging neckline that gave James more than a glimpse of the erotic delights awaiting him once the matter was settled. He surrendered.

"Alright, I'll tell them that I have an appointment at noon and can't stay for their questions. They can email me or come and see me in my office." Antonietta's eyes sparkled in triumph, but she wasn't finished yet. "Except Annya," she declared, "she can limit herself to emails."

———

Despite the seriousness of the occasion, Bill couldn't resist teasing James when he arrived that evening. "What price was peace?" he asked, assuming from Antonietta's radiance that she'd been pacified.

"I'm not allowed to stay after class in case Annya talks to me," James replied shamefacedly.

"You're a weakling, Markham," Bill told him.

"Oh yes? You try and deal with Antonietta when she's in a jealous mood." He nodded in her direction where she was chatting with Danny's new girlfriend, Bernadette, and his daughter. "Particularly when she's wearing that sweater."

Bill laughed and slapped James on the back. "You have a point, Jimmy."

While the women talked among themselves, the men discussed the election of the faculty representative. It was agreed that a candidacy of any one of them would be counter-productive. Because of their closeness to Bill, they were unlikely to be elected and, even if elected, not very credible on the tenure committee. What they needed was a full professor whom they could trust.

After much discussion, it was agreed that James would ask Christine Desmoulins to stand. She had impeccable academic credentials and James felt, as her Chair, that they could trust her.

"I know she dislikes HB," he told the others.

"Why do *you* have to ask her?" Antonietta had joined the men.

"Because he speaks that froggy language, and that'll make her melt," explained Bill.

Antonietta's eyes blazed.

"Antonietta, she's forty-five and not particularly attractive as well as being married with four kids," James made clear very quickly. Antonietta nestled against him. "Good," she whispered.

The women joined the men, and the rest of the evening passed off pleasantly enough. Around eleven James drove Antonietta back to the cottage. Despite the late hour, she begged him to stay and make love to her. As they lay together afterwards, she asked him when they could next get away.

"I have a meeting in Montreal on Tuesday, February 5th," he replied. "You can come with me and we'll spend the night there." Antonietta was overjoyed. "What's more," James went on, assuming that this piece of information would also please Antonietta, "the Italian Ambassador is coming to the Institute in May."

"What for?" Antonietta asked edgily. They were again entering dangerous territory.

"To preside over a ceremony making us a repositary for all EU documents. It'll be a godsent for my research."

"That's marvelous." Antonietta tried to sound enthusiastic but she had turned white. The last thing she wanted was to come face to face with the Duke of Messina. She didn't care about revealing who she was to James— this had to happen anyway—but she was concerned about the tale Messina would recount back in Italy. He was too perceptive not to guess the truth about her and James and too austerely Catholic to accept it, particularly as it concerned his goddaughter. Luckily, James was too immersed in covering her with kisses to notice her reaction. She stopped him when he reached her belly.

"If you descend any further, you'll have to stay another hour," she told him.

It was already past one o'clock and, with regret, James left. Neither of them had yet brought up the subject of their marriage, and each thought it was the fault of the other.

———

The next morning James went to see Christine Desmoulins before his class at eleven. At first she was unwilling to stand, using as a pretext the book she was editing on international organizations.

"Christine, it won't take up hardly any time," James argued. "We need you. You have credibility and you can be relied on to stand up to HB."

"You think he's out to get Bill Leaman?" Christine asked, at last showing some interest.

"Absolutely. He wants to get Bill as a means of avenging himself on me for his defeat over Flint's full professorship."

"And Hunt?" Christine queried with a smile.

"What do you mean?"

"Come on, James, you're not having me believe that Arbuthnot dropped the case against Hunt out of the goodness of his heart. I don't know what you did, but you did something to make him drop it. I'm sure of that."

"Perhaps," James agreed. It was comforting to think that at least someone had seen through HB's apparent generosity of spirit even if that idiot Hunt was taken in. "Christine, we really need you on that committee."

Christine gazed thoughtfully into space before answering. "Alright, James, I'll do it. I don't particularly like Bill Leaman, but I like HB even less."

James thanked her effusively.

———

By Friday's deadline, there were three candidates for the election as faculty representative on Bill's tenure committee: Christine, Larry Flint, who'd obviously been put up to it by HB, and Brian Wilkins, a full professor from LAC. James and Piotr talked of canvassing for Christine, but Danny dissuaded them.

Antonietta and James didn't stay long at Danny's. Bill insisted on repeating his admonition for them to be more discreet and James could see that this upset Antonietta. On the way home, she was very quiet. James stayed with her in the cottage.

"We're going have to make a decision soon, Antonietta," he said.

"It's not *a* decision, it's *the* decision," she replied heatedly. "Unless you're planning on leaving me."

James didn't bother to answer. Instead he almost dragged Antonietta into the bedroom. "I'll show you what I'm planning on doing," he said as he undid her blouse. She let him undress her completely. He caressed her breasts, her stomach, her belly, between her thighs. He made her turn over, stroked her buttocks and ran his hand between them. Antonietta found something peculiarly erotic about being touched so intimately by her lover who was fully dressed. Eventually, she couldn't bear it any longer. She rolled over and undid James' belt. Without undressing him any further, she dispatched him with her mouth. He did the same with her.

———

The campaign for faculty representative on Bill's tenure committee started in earnest right away on the following Monday. All of HB's gang, led by Gowling and Williams, who had finally shown his true colors, were seen canvassing for Larry Flint. This alarmed Bill and Piotr, who insisted that they should also start campaigning for Christine, despite Danny's strictures. James was more sanguine. "You can't turn a donkey into a purebred," he told them. "No-one except HB's diehard cronies are going to vote for Flint in preference to Christine or Wilkins."

The meeting with Piotr and Bill meant that James didn't arrive back at the cottage until one o'clock. He was met by a distraught Antonietta.

"You've been talking to her, haven't you," she accused him.

James didn't reply. He just caught hold of Antonietta and pinned her against the wall. "I was talking with Bill and Piotr. The HB gang are already canvassing for Flint, so they wanted us to do the same for Christine. I said it wasn't a good idea."

Mollified, Antonietta let James kiss her and lead her into the bedroom. After they'd made love, he took her face between his hands and smothered it in kisses. "I'm going to make love to you all afternoon," he said and kissed her again.

"You can't" she replied sadly. "I have a lecture with Professor Wong at three on Asian history and culture."

Antonietta was late for her class.

———

"I can't understand what HB's up to," James was saying. "There's three weeks to the election and yet they're campaigning like it's this week. That goes against the elementary rule of campaigning. You start gently and gain momentum, otherwise you peak too early."

"Perhaps they figure that they need time to convince people," Bill suggested. "After all, Flint's a pretty weak candidate. God knows why they chose him."

"Perhaps," James said, "but by being so aggressive, they're making sure that everyone sees him as HB's candidate, which I can't understand either. At the most, Arbuthnot's only got seven committed supporters in the faculty. A lot of other colleagues may fear him but this doesn't mean they're going to vote for his candidate in a secret ballot."

"I think I know what they're up to," said Danny. "By ostentatiously campaigning hard for Flint, HB hopes to push us into doing the same for Christine. That way, he and his supporters can paint Christine as our candidate, which, of course, she is. Most of the faculty are neutral between us and them, so I bet you that a week or so before the election, HB's lot will dump Flint and try to persuade our colleagues to vote for a neutral candidate as a compromise choice. That way they hope to get Brian Wilkins elected over Christine. Flint is just HB's stalking horse."

"That supposes he can rely on Wilkins," Piotr objected.

Antonietta had been listening closely to the discussion. She asked Bill if he had a copy of the survey of professors.

"Why?" Bill asked in surprise.

"Just give it to me," she told him. "You'll see." While the others continued to talk about the campaign, Antonietta looked through the survey.

"Eureka!" she cried, startling her male companions. "Williams and Wilkins both went to UBC."

"So what?" Bill was skeptical. "They weren't there together. Wilkins is much older than Williams."

Antonietta gave Bill a look of triumph. "Agreed, but they were in the same fraternity, Alpha, Beta, Zeta."

Danny, all smiles, congratulated Antonietta. "You're a genius, my lovely lady. That clinches it. Now we know that Wilkins is HB's real candidate." He pointed a finger at the others. "No canvassing for Christine, or we fall into HB's trap."

———

The next Friday, the inevitable happened. True to his promise to Antonietta, James had rushed from his class and was putting away his notes before leaving for the cottage when there was a knock on his office door. It was Annya Nowak. She was dressed in a tight blouse and short skirt. She was tanned from her skiing holiday. She'd let her blond hair grow longer and it cascaded down past her shoulders. It was a most appetizing picture and James could not fail to appreciate it.

"What can I do for you, Annya?" Involuntarily James used the girl's first name again, which obviously pleased her despite his very guarded tone. She gave him a smile in which seduction mingled with malice.

"Nothing, Professor Markham," she replied with studied formality. "I've come to promise you something."

Annya's answer added astonishment to James' discomfiture. "Promise? I don't understand."

Without being asked, Annya sat down and looked up at James who was standing awkwardly by his desk. She continued in her perfectly modulated voice, stroking her hair playfully as she spoke. "You don't have to rush off after every class. I promise not to accost you."

James struggled to stop himself blushing, but the mocking smile on Annya's pretty face told him that he'd failed. He was furious with himself.

"I have no problem with you accosting me, as you put it," he countered hotly.

"I'm sure you don't," Annya replied coolly, "but perhaps someone else does."

The sheer impudence of the girl saved James. Infuriated by it, he was able to look Annya straight in the eyes.

"I don't know what you're talking about, Miss Nowak. I have these meetings in St. Jérôme at 12.30 every Monday, Wednesday and Friday, but I'm going to change the times. Hopefully, it won't be necessary for me to rush off, as you put it, starting next week."

The force of James's reply disconcerted Annya, but she gave one last parting shot.

"That's good news," she said, furrowing her brow. "You know how students like to complain." With that she left the office. James was too relieved at her departure to worry about the subtle menace in her last words.

He made for the parking lot and drove to the cottage, wondering the whole length of the journey how to tell Antonietta that Annya had come to see him. He arrived at the cottage and took a pliant Antonietta straight to bed. She reveled in the shameless intimacies with which he indulged her. As she lay cradled in his arms afterwards, James plucked up the courage to tell her of Annya's visit. To his astonishment, Antonietta just smiled up at him.

"I know she came to see you."

"How?

"I had to hand in a paper for Professor Martinez that I forgot yesterday. Afterwards, I met the two Brits, Simon and Malcolm, and we had coffee together. By the time we'd finished, it was nearly twelve, so I decided to see whether you were keeping your promise."

"So, you were spying on me?"

"Yes," Antonietta admitted. "I'm not going to apologize for it. It's your fault for making me lose all sense of dignity."

James laughed and kissed Antonietta. "Go on," he told her.

"I saw you rush out of class…" Antonietta began.

"Ah," James interrupted, "That must have made you feel very proud." There was a hint of bitterness in his voice as he thought of the conversation with Annya that had followed his abrupt departure.

"No, James." Antonietta was contrite. "I felt guilty for making you do such a silly thing."

James began to have a sense of relief. This whole business was going to be much easier than he'd feared.

"I saw Annya follow you," Antonietta went on. "She was all tarted up, short skirt, tight blouse. She's even grown her hair long like mine. I could have scratched her eyes out."

"Did she see you?"

"No. I followed her very discreetly and saw her enter your office." Antonietta glanced up at James, and he could see her eyes mist over. "I thought I was going to die. It was all I could do to stop myself barging in on you."

"Thank God, you didn't. It was bad enough as it was."

"So I gathered. When she came out of your office, she looked like thunder. I was so relieved that I started to laugh. Luckily, she was too preoccupied to notice. She stalked off, and I came home as quickly as possible to be here before you."

"Why?"

"Because I wanted to put you to the test. I didn't want you to know I'd been at the Institute. I wanted you to tell me about Annya and not because you feared I might possibly have seen her go to your office."

"And if I hadn't told you?"

"Then I wouldn't have trusted you any more."

James sighed. "Why are you so jealous of Annya Nowak?" he asked as he played with her nipples. Antonietta moaned softly before pushing James' hand away. "First, tell me what that girl wanted," she demanded.

James recounted the incident. "It was disturbing, to say the least," he concluded grimly. "She's guessed about us, she's jealous and she's capable of anything. Why she can't make do with one professor, God alone knows."

"Because, my darling, she's been in love with you ever since you were silly enough to offer her whisky. After all, she *is* Polish."

"That's a little unfair on the Poles," James chided, but he was amused by Antonietta's resentful bitchiness. "Anyway, you must relieve me of my promise. Annya was quite right. If I continue to rush off like that, there'll be complaints from the students, and that won't help us."

Antonietta's reply was to throw her naked body on top of James and kiss him with such ardor that it took his breath away. "I should never have asked you for that promise, so I'll make amends by treating you to an afternoon of the most indecent sex."

"What about your class with Professor Wong?" James asked with an amused smile.

"This afternoon I want debauchery," Antonietta replied.

She lived up to her engagement. After teasing James by running her fingers and nipples along his shaft, she made him turn over onto all fours. She caressed his buttocks with her hands and breasts and ran her nipples between them. She penetrated him with them, one by one, and followed up with her tongue. James could scarcely believe what was happening when she grasped his genitals with both hands. He came very violently.

"Now it's you who's soiled the bed," Antonietta observed with satisfaction.

James turned over and gazed at Antonietta with a bemused look on his face, but she was too sexually aroused to notice. She kissed him with complete abandon, pressing the stiff flesh of her breasts against his chest. "Take me in the same way," she whispered. Very soon her body was shuddering under James's indecent ministrations. She screamed when she reached orgasm and drenched James' hand.

"Did I shock you," she asked James afterwards.

He laughed. "A little, I must say."

"Do you think I'm a whore?" she asked.

"No, my love, but we certainly went beyond the common decencies of regular folk."

Antonietta pushed James back down on the bed and crouched over him.

She was a magnificent sight, naked, her lips slightly swollen, her eyes glistening with sated desire, her breasts still taut, her body damp from their excesses, her hair disheveled.

"I don't care about common decencies," she declared. "My whole body exists for your pleasure and the pleasure you give me. Where we touch each other and how we touch each other is our concern and no-one else's."

It was well after seven when James arrived home. He was late for supper.

"Where have you been?" Veronica asked, her voice expressing suspicion for the first time. "You don't seem to have been drinking."

"I apologize, Veronica," James replied, blanching slightly at Veronica's inquisitorial tone. "Bill's having problems with his tenure, and we met to discuss it."

"Well, perhaps in future, you could do your discussing during one of your drinking sessions instead of making us all wait for supper."

Feeling rather like a scolded schoolboy, James agreed. He was relieved that Veronica apparently believed him, but her compliance could no longer be taken for granted. This worried him.

———

The second week of campaigning saw a noticeable slackening in the promotion of Flint's candidacy. Despairing of tricking Bill's friends into an open effort on behalf of Christine Desmoulins, HB had obviously given his men orders gradually to switch their efforts to Brian Wilkins. By the end of the week, they were openly putting forward the LAC professor as a compromise choice, portraying Christine as too close to James and hence to Bill to be objective.

By Friday, Bill had become alarmed at the number of people who were being courted by HB's cronies. At the Saturday evening get-together, he was nervous and ill-tempered. It took all of Danny's Irish charm and Antonietta's radiance to restore his spirits. Even so, he couldn't resist projecting his misgivings about his own future onto James and Antonietta.

"If that Annya knows what's going on, you can bet she's told her friends, particularly that Wrangel guy, who's probably never forgiven you for humiliating him in class," he told James.

Usually James laughed off Bill's warnings, but since the episode with Annya he was worried himself although he kept his sinister thoughts hidden from his emotional Italian mistress.

"What do you expect us to do?" he asked Bill. "Break up?" There was a gasp from Antonietta. James quickly put his arm around her and drew her to him. She buried her face in his neck.

"Marry Antonietta," Bill growled. "You should leave Veronica, she should leave the Institute and the two of you should *get married.*"

On their way back to the cottage, Antonietta reproached James for what he'd said. "How could you say such a thing?" she asked, her eyes brimming with tears. James, who was looking fixedly ahead to guide the car through the blinding snow, didn't reply at first. "How? How? How?" Antonietta repeated.

James pulled into a lay-by and took his trembling mistress into his arms. He kissed her.

"I'm sorry, Antonietta. Bill irritated me, and I didn't measure my words. I should have known you'd be upset. Please forgive me." As he said the last words, he wiped away the tears that were beginning to glide down Antonietta's face. "Only if you make love to me before going to Prévost," she murmured under his kisses. Antonietta always said Prévost, never "home." For her, James' home was the cottage.

———

James was waiting in the bar at the *Le Reine Elisabeth* for Antonietta. Her entrance was even more spectacular than the last time. Her new dress was long and cream-colored. It clung to her body and exhibited a low décolleté that was accentuated by the buttons on the bodice that seemed to strain under her lavish bosom, and it was supported by two thin shoulder straps that invited to be thrust aside, letting the dress fall and revealing the full splendor of her lubricity. She was wearing her hair down, the dark cascade highlighting the clarity of her dress. Her eyes sparkled aside the tasteful mascara and the soft, inviting contours of her lips glistened beneath the glossy pale-red lipstick. A short beige jacket of classical cut enveloped her shoulders. Instead of a necklace she wore a beige choker. In her ears she wore studs of emerald, one hidden by the flow of her hair. She was a picture of such sensuous perfection that James was speechless. Even the waiters seemed paralyzed, and James was vaguely aware of a strange silence descend upon the room as if no conversation could contend with Antonietta's matchless beauty.

They took a taxi to the Place des Arts where they were to see Puccini's masterpiece, *Tosca.* It was Antonietta's favorite opera, but this time she felt an even greater intimacy with the two main characters. For her it could have been James' singing Cavaradossi's lovely aria *Recondita harmonia,* comparing his dark-haired mistress with the blond Attavanti, and she found herself in the passionate jealousy of Floria Tosca. They decided to skip the third act. Both of them found the music far below the beauty and drama of the previous two acts. Besides, Antonietta was hungry.

"All you ever think about is eating," James complained.

"That's untrue," she protested. "I think much more about sex."

Once they arrived back in the hotel room, Antonietta started to take off her dress. James stopped her. "Leave it on. I want to admire you far from the madding crowd." He turned the radio to a station playing soft music. They danced, holding each other close and kissing like two teenagers on a romantic first date.

"You're not seeing much of my dress, James," Antonietta remarked.

"That's true," he agreed, stepping back to take in the whole picture. Her hair was now a little disheveled and the lipstick had disappeared, leaving behind the faintest touch of gloss. James sighed. It was too much, particularly as Antonietta was slowly beginning to strip. Once she was fully naked, she made James lie on the bed while she undressed him. She took him into her mouth but stopped before his climax.

"I want you in me," she told him. "I want to feel your warmth within me. I want to be as one with you."

She lay down and James came on top of her. Their kisses gained in intensity as their excitement mounted and finally reached its apogee. They lay together afterwards until Antonietta fell asleep. James gazed at her. He could never live without her, he had to marry her, but whenever he reached this conclusion, as he did most days, the image of his two children, particularly his daughter, came to mind. He suspected that Antonietta went through the same vicious circle with her love for him forever at odds with her religious faith and her family ties. Since Christmas, they had only mentioned their marriage in passing, but sooner or later they would have to face reality.

———

They arrived late afternoon at Bill's to find out about the result of the election for the faculty representative. Bill's expression when they arrived revealed the good tidings.

"She got 70% of the vote!" he announced. "Wilkins got 22% and that jerk Flint only got 8%. It's a triumph!"

Danny and Piotr were already present. James phoned Veronica to tell her the news and inform her that he would be celebrating with the lads. It was a very short call. The men congratulated themselves on securing Christine Desmoulins' election. Bill was euphoric, but Danny dampened his optimism.

"It's not a done thing yet, Bill," he cautioned. "You've still got HB against you, and Hamid's decision will turn on your references. Assuming that Winstone picks one of Arbuthnot's pals as his appointee, that could mean three to three if you don't have Hamid onside, and that's assuming Forget votes for you. Winstone has the casting vote and, according to custom, he votes with the Chair. Hamid's the key. If you don't have him onside, you're toast."

There was a silence, and Antonietta looked anxiously over at James. "What's the matter?" she asked.

"Danny's being a party pooper," Bill answered.

"You're right," said Danny, observing Bill's doleful expression. He poured him another Scotch. "Let's look on the bright side. At least we've got Christine to keep them honest. That's worth a lot."

The wine and whisky flowed, and it was nearly midnight when James and Antonietta arrived at the cottage. She laid her head on his shoulder.

"Are you coming in?" she asked tremulously.

"It's late," he replied. "I should go home. I'm afraid that Veronica might be waiting up for me."

Antonietta tore herself away from James and got out of the car, slamming the door behind her. He did likewise and caught up with her as she was opening the door of the cottage. He forced her to turn round and kiss him. There was a little resistance but it was soon over. When the kiss ended, Antonietta looked down to hide her tears.

"Forgive me, James. I know I'm being unreasonable, but I can't help it. Ever since I saw you in that church, I've lost all my self-control."

James put his hand under her chin and lifted up her face. He kissed the tearful eyes. "I don't want you to have any self-control," he told her softly. "I want you just the way you are."

His words brought a smile to Antonietta's mournful face. "In that case, come in and make love to me."

It was nearly four in the morning before James arrived at Prévost. Luckily, Veronica had long been asleep.

———

The euphoria of Christine's election did not last long. On Friday, a circular came round from the Rector's office giving notice that Larry Flint had been appointed to Bill's tenure committee. The atmosphere that evening at Danny's was very morose.

"I'm fucked," Bill wailed. "I'm fucked unless Winstone has the guts to vote with Hamid."

"We always knew that Winstone would appoint a crony of HB to the committee," Piotr pointed out. "All that's changed is now we have confirmation."

"You know," Danny began, looking very thoughtful. "This appointment may turn out to be HB's biggest mistake."

"It seems like a fucking clever move to me," Bill retorted. "He wants me out, and with Flint on the committee, he goddam may get his way."

"Let's hope not, Bill," said James, trying to soothe his friend. He put his arms around Antonietta who was clearly upset by the turn of the conversation. She was very fond of Bill and hated the thought of losing him.

"What are you getting at, Danny?" he asked.

"This appointment tells us three things, all of which are going to upset a lot of people who hitherto haven't paid much attention to what's going on in the Institute." Danny paused, leaving the others in anticipation of what he was going to say.

"Firstly," he went on, "It shows that Winstone cares nothing for the opinion of faculty. To appoint someone to a committee who's just been soundly rejected by his colleagues is an insult. People will take it as such."

Danny took a sip of his Scotch. "Secondly, it shows everyone that Winstone is completely dominated by HB. Otherwise he wouldn't have made such a stupid decision. Thirdly, HB has just demonstrated to everyone that he is capable of riding roughshod over faculty opinion to get his way. He's shown his true colors."

"So what's the overall effect of all this," Piotr asked. Faculty politics had never been his strong suit.

"Winstone has lost credibility and respect, and HB is seen for the ruthless bastard he is. In future years, when our champion here," Danny pointed at James, "is installed as Rector, we'll see that it was now when the uncommitted majority of our colleagues began to realize what's good for them."

"I don't want to be Rector," James said flatly. "I want to marry Antonietta and go and live somewhere on the Mediterranean."

Antonietta looked at James in amazement. "You'd leave the Institute?" she asked. "What would you do?"

James toyed briefly with the idea of telling Antonietta the truth, that he didn't need to work and that he would be much happier spending his days with her in the sunny climes of southern Europe than professing law.

"I was just dreaming," was the answer he eventually gave.

The glow in Antonietta's eyes dimmed.

# CHAPTER 16
## Friday, February 22 to Monday, March 11, 2002

Antonietta was too excited to pay much attention in Professor Forget's class. Once it ended, she was having lunch with Petra and then she and James would leave for Chile and Argentina. The last two weeks had passed very slowly, and Antonietta could hardly believe this day had finally come. There had been fewer tears than usual, but the effort had exhausted her.

She met Petra at a restaurant in Saint-Sauveur. Despite her happiness to be leaving with James, her face bore marks of fatigue that Petra noticed. "The sooner you two get married, the better for you," she remarked.

"That's what Bill is always saying," Antonietta replied. "James wants us to get together once term ends."

"And you?"

Antonietta sighed. "Sometimes I wish we could just go on like this forever. Other times, I can't stand our situation and want to get married."

Petra sensed the turmoil within Antonietta and tactfully changed the subject to her own boyfriend. They were going skiing at Mont Tremblant for reading week, but she wasn't sure how it would turn out.

"He thinks I boss him, and he's beginning to resent it," she explained.

Antonietta smiled sympathetically. "The problem is, Petra, you do boss him."

"I can't help it. He's so infuriatingly indecisive."

The conversation moved on to their classes and Antonietta's trip to South America. Then it was time to go. As she watched Petra walk away to meet Brent with an air of sadness about her, Antonietta was convinced their relationship wouldn't last. She made a mental note to tell Bill.

———

Antonietta felt an enormous sense of relief once they were airborne. There was no-one to see them, no Veronica for James to rush home to, no Institute to take away her precious time with him. She drank wine, attempted to eat the dismal Air Canada food and fell asleep, her head on James' shoulders. Promptly at midday on what was now Saturday, they arrived in Santiago de Chile and took a taxi to their hotel. To James' relief, their room was ready.

"Sightseeing can wait," he told Antonietta firmly, "I want you."

It was late in the afternoon when they left the hotel to wander around downtown Santiago. Antonietta didn't find it particularly interesting and they soon returned to the hotel. What they really wanted was to be together and make love. They spent a happy evening indulging themselves.

The next day, Sunday, they went to Mass early at the Cathedral in the Plaza de Armas and then spent the day in Valparaiso and the nearby seaside resort of Viña del Mar. By the time they were back in their hotel room, they were worn out after a long day.

"Darling, do you mind if we go straight to sleep," Antonietta asked.

"That's fine. It'll prepare us for being married."

"James, that's a horrible thing to say."

James had expected Antonietta to be indignant, but instead she was gazing at him with melancholy. He took her into his arms. "I was teasing you, Antonietta. I'm tired too."

He turned on his side, expecting Antonietta to cuddle up to him. He adored going to sleep with the feel of her breasts pressing against his back. Instead she pulled him over and came on top of him.

———

On Monday, they had breakfast at the hotel. James had arranged his meeting at the University of Chile for ten o'clock and Antonietta was booked on a bus tour of the city and the surrounding area. They were both tired after the excesses of the previous night.

"I'll have to give up work once we're married," James said with a wry smile. "I'll be too tired to get up in the mornings."

"Then perhaps we shouldn't get married," Antonietta replied, returning the smile a little too enigmatically for James. He said nothing, aware of the constant battle within his mistress between her love for him and her religion and family. Where will it all end, he wondered as he left the hotel to walk to the university.

———

Antonietta arrived back at the hotel from her tour at twelve thirty and she found James waiting for her in the lobby. She threw herself at him and, despite all her efforts, couldn't fight back her tears. James kissed her lightly on the cheeks and then more passionately on the mouth, disregarding some hotel guests who were staring at them with disapproval.

"Why the tears?" he asked. "We've only been apart for a little over two hours."

"Are you saying you didn't miss me?" Antonietta demanded, leading James to the elevator. By the time he'd restored her to a state of relative serenity, it was time to go to the airport. They checked in for the LAN flight to Buenos Aires.

———

Luckily, the man at the reception desk in the Hotel Melia recognized James and there was no blue-eyed blond in sight to arouse Antonietta's jealousy. They made love with lazy ease and then had dinner in Puerto Madero. Dressed in a light blue summer dress that clung to her body and showed off her bosom, her hair flowing casually down to her shoulders, tastefully made up, Antonietta was a picture of incandescent beauty, at once wholesome and lubricious.

After dinner, James took Antonietta to the Café Tortoni to listen to tango music. They listened and watched until the early hours, captivated by the sensuality of the dancers and the nostalgic yearning of the sound of the bandoneon. When finally they made it back to the hotel, Antonietta flung herself into their lovemaking with zest and abandon. Without any shame she indulged James with the most intimate acts and demanded the same from him. It was already light by the time they'd finally sated themselves. It seemed pointless to go to sleep, so they showered and walked along the wharves of Puerto Madero until fatigue overcame them. They returned to the hotel, had a continental breakfast of croissants and expresso coffee and went to bed.

When they awoke, it was late afternoon. They set off for the Recoleta. After their tour, James took Antonietta to a restaurant. She let him order for her. They started with the inevitable *empanadas,* followed by the restaurant's speciality, which was fresh Patagonian deer with mushroom crust and fresh cuartilo cheese. The Susana Balbo which they were served was a Riserva from 1999. At the table next to them, there was a family who were speaking both Spanish and Italian. Antonietta was almost happy. She felt at home in this Latin environment and the meal was superb, but still the jealousy gnawed at her. She couldn't resist the inevitable question.

"The answer is no," James answered. "I never came here with Carolina."

They moved to La Biela for dessert and coffee. Luckily, Antonietta didn't ask the same question. "It really *is* like being in Paris," she remarked instead. "But better as there are no French people here."

James shook his head. "You accuse me of intolerance, what about you and the French?"

Antonietta giggled. "I do it to annoy you," she replied.

It was soon time to go. At ten next morning, James was seeing Carlos Guarnieri and if he and Antonietta were going to indulge their sexual appetites in the usual fashion, it would be wise to go to bed early. They stood up and Antonietta planted a quick kiss on James lips. He led her by the hand out of the café.

As they left, a young and very pretty blond woman watched them go. Her serene features briefly lost their composure.

"Is anything wrong, Carolina?" one of her friends asked.

"No," she replied. "It's nothing, absolutely nothing."

———

Antonietta insisted on accompanying James to see Carlos Guarnieri. They arrived at the Law Faculty near the Recoleta and were shown to Carlos' office. They sat down and Carlos ordered coffee. James was amused as normally the Argentinean was very businesslike with little small talk. Yet today, he showed no haste and plied Antonietta with compliments. It was with obvious reluctance that he finally came round to business. He gave Antonietta a university newsletter to read.

"I'm sure our discussion would bore you," he told her.

Antonietta leafed absently through the newsletter. It didn't really interest her and she was about to put it down when she came to the report on the conference that James had attended. There was fulsome praise for his contribution, which filled her with pride, and at the end of the report a brief description of the banquet at the Hotel Plaza San Martín. Antonietta remembered James telling her that the banquet was held in the hotel where Carolina worked. Now she knew which one it was.

"What are you going to do for the rest of the day?" Carlos asked them.

Before James could answer, Antonietta said hurriedly. "I want to see the Plaza San Martín." She gazed innocently at James, who was looking very ill at ease.

"Ah, you want to see the monument to the Fallen of the Malvinas," Carlos observed.

"Yes, that's it," agreed Antonietta, not knowing that the monument even existed.

———

Although the monument was not the real reason for her visit to the Plaza San Martín, Antonietta was much affected by it. It brought home to her the folly and waste of war. As she read through the names, so many of them Italian in origin, she reflected on how they had died for nothing. After four years in a convent school in England, she knew the British well enough to understand that they would never give up the Malvinas. Under their deceptive air of self-deprecation, they were a proud and hard people. For the first time in her life, she was glad of the French. At least it meant that a quarter of James was Latin, and she'd deal with the other three quarters.

James tried to lead Antonietta towards Suipacha street where there was the small restaurant in which he'd dined with Bill.

"No, James," she said, pointing in the opposite direction towards the Hotel Plaza San Martín, "I want you to spoil me. I want to eat in that elegant hotel."

James was horror-struck. The last thing he wanted was for Antonietta to come face to face with Carolina, but if he demurred, she would guess the reason and he would have no peace until he took her to the hotel. So, he decided that the lesser evil was to agree. Carolina had once told him that she hated early morning shifts. Normally she worked from three to eleven, and it was now twelve thirty.

"Come on, then," he told a surprised Antonietta, who had expected him to be at best evasive.

There was no Carolina in the hotel. Antonietta scrutinized the reception desk, but the only woman in sight was a slim brunette. She excused herself once during the meal, ostensibly to go to the washroom but in reality to search again for the elusive Carolina. In vain. She fell prey to a terrible suspicion that James had contacted Carolina to forewarn her of their visit. That must be why he'd so readily agreed to have lunch here. She returned to their table.

James commented on the rather dispirited way Antonietta was eating the very excellent grilled fish they had both ordered. Her large, dark eyes were full of distrust. "Did you tell her that we were coming?" she asked.

Now James understood why Antonietta had come to the Plaza San Martín. It wasn't for the monument but to have lunch in this particular hotel. He smiled at her, and took her trembling hand.

"How did you know it was this hotel?" he asked in turn.

"I read in the newsletter Carlos gave me that the banquet was here, and I remembered you telling me it was in the hotel where Carolina worked." Antonietta didn't dare look up at James.

"And you're not enjoying your meal because you think I tipped her off that we were coming?" Antonietta nodded. "The answer is no. I've never had any contact with Carolina since that one time I was here with Bill. In any case, I had no need to tip her off as I never expected you to find out where she worked." Antonietta was suddenly all smiles. James' explanation made sense.

"Now, enjoy your meal," he told her.

"Only if you forgive me for tricking you into coming here."

James stood up and came round to Antonietta. He kissed her on the lips. "I love you," he said simply

That night, to make up for her unfounded suspicions, Antonietta made love with rare savagery. She was insatiable and left James panting with exhaustion. At the end she was seated astride him, flaunting her erogenous breasts, which were damp from the sweat and effluent of their sexual profligacy. She grinned lasciviously and began to caress them suggestively. "This way you can imagine I'm with another woman."

Caught between sexual arousal and raging jealousy, James could only groan helplessly as Antonietta rode him to yet another climax. When it was over, she bent down and kissed him.

"Would you like us to hire some girl to make it a threesome," she whispered, her eyes alight with rampant promiscuity.

James exploded. "How can you even think of anything like that?"

"It could be fun, and I know you fantasize about me with other women."

James rolled her over onto her back. "It may be my fantasy, but there's a helluva difference between fantasy and actually watching you with another woman. The mere thought of it makes me ill with jealousy."

Antonietta caught the veiled allusion to the Marquesa. She pulled James' head towards her and kissed him with passion. "I was teasing you, James. I love you entirely, exclusively, even obsessively. I could never have sex with anyone else."

In fact, she would.

———

The next day they took a plane to the seaside resort of Punta del Este in neighboring Uruguay. The drive from the airport to the hotel took them through pleasant wooded countryside. The hotel itself was located right on the beach. Antonietta gazed at the large stretches of golden sand and the sea rolling gently in from the Atlantic Ocean. A woman passed by speaking Portuguese. She was dressed in a minuscule bikini that left her buttocks completely bare.

"She must be Brazilian," James commented.

"That's the sort of bikini I'm going to buy," Antonietta told James. She noticed the look of horror on his face. "Nothing you say will persuade me otherwise."

"It's indecent," he protested.

"No, it's sexy," Antonietta retorted, grinning provocatively at her lover. "Don't you want me to be sexy?"

James groaned. "How am I supposed to lie demurely on the beach with you practically naked beside me?"

"I'll make sure you're properly satisfied before we leave the hotel room."

They checked in and Antonietta dragged James to one of the hotel's boutiques where she bought a ludicrously expensive Brazilian-style bikini. "The less material there is, the more it seems to cost," James grumbled. Nonetheless, he insisted on paying despite Antonietta's protests.

"You're going to earn it," he threatened, shaking his head at the thought of his lubricious mistress parading her nudity on the beach.

"Only if you shave first," Antonietta declared, divining what James had in mind. "Otherwise I'll have sore buttocks."

They spent the next two days sunbathing, swimming in the pristine sea, sipping a variety of alcoholic drinks from the beach bar and returning every hour or so to the hotel room. Antonietta was the picture of erotic perfection. The top of her bikini exhibited her shapely breasts more than it covered them, and the flimsy bottom exposed her well-rounded buttocks and barely covered her sex. Antonietta's brazen flaunting of her body exacerbated James' lust, while the heat of the sun combined with the scantiness of her attire to stimulate Antonietta's already strong sexual appetite.

On Saturday, they had lunch in the hotel after spending the morning on the beach. The flight to Buenos Aires only took an hour, so they were able to linger over their lunch with the marvelous spectacle of the ocean before them. They arrived in Buenos Aires with two hours to spare and went to the Air Canada lounge to wait for their flight to Toronto.

They arrived in Toronto around ten-thirty on Sunday. Antonietta spent much of the flight nestled up to James. Once in Montreal, she was fearful that he would return to Prévost immediately. From her doleful expression James guessed what she was thinking but said nothing. When, instead of continuing northwards to the Laurentians, he made for downtown Montreal, Antonietta let out a squeal of joy. They had lunch at a French restaurant on Ste. Cathérine.

Antonietta's mood became more somber as they traveled up Highway 15. The cold and snow contrasted sharply with the weather in Punta del Este and this accentuated her melancholy. When they arrived at the cottage, she begged James to stay. Although he knew that Veronica would be wondering why he was so late, he couldn't resist Antonietta's imploring eyes. He called Bill and told him that he was supposed to be at his place discussing the tenure application. Bill was to call them if Veronica phoned and he should tell her that James had just left. Around six-thirty, Bill duly called and James had to leave Antonietta in tears. At home he was met by an irate Veronica.

"Why are you so late?," she demanded.

"I was at Bill's," he replied, feeling very guilty. "We were discussing his tenure application."

"You might think a little more about your family and less about that vulgar friend of your's," Veronica declared. "I had to look after the children and missed my none prayers."

James couldn't contain his exasperation. "Is that all you think about? Your bloody prayers?" he cried.

"Don't add blasphemy to neglect of your family," she shouted back at him.

James left the room in disgust and went off to find the children.

———

The wretchedness that gripped Antonietta after James' departure was more severe than ever previously when they parted after spending time together. To console herself, she listened to her messages in the hope of a cheery welcome home from Petra. She was not disappointed, but the message that followed plunged her into the depths of apprehension and despair. It was from her mother, delivered in the best imperious Palmieri style, informing her daughter that she was arriving in Montreal at 2.15 on Saturday, March 16 for a whole week.

For Antonietta, this meant a week without James and she sank down on the sofa and wept. It was bad enough to play host to her suspicious and authoritarian mother without being deprived of the man she needed like the air she breathed. She opened one and then another bottle of wine and drank herself to sleep.

————

James drove the children to school earlier than normal on Monday morning and arrived at the cottage a little after eight-thirty. Antonietta was overjoyed to see him.

"James, thank God you're here." She flung her arms around him and devoured him with kisses. "My mother's coming for a week," she informed him. "That means I can't see you for a whole week."

James wiped away Antonietta's tears. "Nonsense," he said. "We'll take a room in a motel somewhere. We're both free on Tuesday and Thursday afternoons. You simply tell your mother you have a class, or you have to study."

Antonietta's face lit up and she smiled through her tears. She got up, took James' hand and led him into the bedroom.

————

It was Tuesday afternoon and Bill was looking for James. He was not in his office, so Bill drove immediately to Antonietta's cottage. James' car was parked in front. Bill rang the doorbell, and after a wait that strained his patience, Antonietta came to the door. She was in her dressing gown.

"James, it's Bill," she called.

James appeared, likewise attired.

"Is that all you ever do?" Bill enquired irritably. "God Almighty, it's three in the afternoon. Can't you two think of anything else but fucking your brains out?"

James was about to give a very sharp answer but desisted on a nod from Antonietta. She'd realized immediately that there was a good reason for Bill's irritability.

"Bill, what's the matter?" she asked, leading him into the living room. "May I pour you a large Scotch," she added with a comforting smile.

"Please," Bill mumbled. There was silence while he waited for the whisky. He took a large gulp. "Hamid and HB have fucked me," he explained. "They've exchanged two of my referees for two mediocre assholes, who don't know shit from shinola, and these fucking nobodies have recommended against tenure. Into the bargain, that prick Dickens says that my application is "premature." I knew I shouldn't have taken a Brit."

"Which is why you've come to seek my help, I suppose," James remarked dryly.

"Point taken, Jimmy," Bill conceded. "But I'm in deep shit. Hamid is going to recommend against, and you can be sure that Flint and HB will follow suit. Even if you, Christine and Forget vote in favor, I'm fucked because Winstone will be only too happy to follow tradition and vote with Hamid."

"It's no good moaning and regretting what we can't change," James said with a certain impatience. "We know that the changes were made by Hamid at HB's suggestion, which means that he also chose the replacements. I bet you they're fellow students from NUC."

"Even if they are, it doesn't get us anywhere," Bill objected.

"I'm not so sure," James replied. "I'm going to check up on these referees. If indeed they were at NUC and if we can find some real connection between them and HB, we can ask to have them replaced on the ground of possible bias."

"The others on the committee won't agree," Bill objected again.

"Forget might and although he's under HB's thumb, Hamid's an honest guy."

After Bill left, Antonietta felt oppressed. "It's as if we're in the lions' den, and they're waiting to pounce on us," she said, her eyes wide with apprehension. James tried to soothe her, but the prospect of her mother's visit was also depressing her and she remained downcast.

"We shall see each other anyway," James reminded her, "so take that unhappy expression off your lovely face." Antonietta responded with a weak smile and rested her head against James' shoulder. "We'll go to France for two weeks after term ends," he told her. "We'll fly to Paris, spend some time there and then drive down to Bandol."

——

It was Friday and James was sat in his office at nine o'clock waiting to meet with Christine Desmoulins. When she arrived, she was bursting with animation.

"Keighley and Mauser did their doctorates at NUC at the same time as Arbuthnot. That's obviously why he picked them. There's no other reason. Keighley's from Wickham, which is a minor business school, and Mauser isn't even a full professor. The obvious choice from Chicago would have been Broderick."

"Who is one of the referees Bill chose and who was replaced by Hamid with Mauser," James commented.

"What are you going to do?"

"I'm not sure."

In fact James had decided to go and see Tom Buchanan. Tom had contacts all over the place, and before becoming Rector of the Institute in 1986 he'd been Chair of the Economics Department at Chicago. He saw no point in burdening Christine with this information. She'd played her role, and now it was up to him.

It was past ten when Christine left. There was no time to return to the cottage, so James called Antonietta. She was disappointed but the news of some hope for Bill consoled her.

"Try to come back immediately after your class," she beseeched him. "Annya or no Annya."

James laughed. "She doesn't pay any attention to me anymore."

"I'm not surprised. You made her so mad the last time she came to your office." The satisfaction in Antonietta's voice was palpable.

———

"You certainly will *not* go and work at the Institute," Veronica was telling James very firmly. "You hardly spend any time with your family except on Sundays, and today is Sunday."

"Mommy's right," Susanna put in. "We hardly ever see you."

The combination of his wife's intransigence and his daughter's reproof convinced James that he had no alternative but to spend the day with the family. Using the pretext of checking the tire pressure, he went to the car and, with considerable trepidation, called Antonietta on his cell with the news that he would not be seeing her that day as he'd promised. Predictably, she was angry and upset.

"Well, if you don't want me, I'll call Petra," she threatened. "She's tiring of Bret, so perhaps she might like to have sex with me even if you don't."

"Antonietta, don't even *think* of doing that." Although James didn't really believe her, he was seized by a ferocious jealousy.

"I will," Antonietta replied with a coolness that exacerbated James' jealousy, "Before, I'll go to Mass at Saint-Sauveur so that you can see what you're missing."

James tried to reason with her, but Antonietta hung up. He called back, but she didn't answer. He returned to the house, obsessed by a longing for his mistress and pursued by images of Antonietta and Petra together. It was going to be a horrible day.

The family arrived at Mass. To James' relief there was no sign of Antonietta. They all knelt for the obligatory prayer. It was soon over for James and the children, but Veronica remained deep in religious fervor for a few more minutes. As a result, she didn't notice her husband turn white when a beautiful dark-haired young woman swept past them and took her place in a pew a little further down on the same side. Oh, my God, did she have to do this to me, James thought, his stomach churning under the force of his jealous passion. Antonietta turned round and their eyes met briefly. James gripped the railing of the pew in a struggle to control his emotions.

Despite her outward calm, Antonietta was faring no better. It seemed to her that every second increased her yearning to throw herself at James. The beginning of Mass brought no relief, and fearful that she would soon no longer be able to control her feelings, she fled from the church. As she passed James, she couldn't resist a quick look at him.

Veronica noticed Antonietta's precipitate departure, and she was suspicious. "Who was that dark-haired girl who rushed out of Mass?" she asked James as they left the church. "She seemed to know you."

"She's in my European class," James replied as casually as he was able, adding for no apparent reason, "She's Italian."

"She's very beautiful," Veronica remarked thoughtfully.

———

With bad grace, Veronica agreed to drive the children to school on Monday so that James could ostensibly have time to prepare his eleven o'clock lecture and attend to some administrative matters.

"I shall be late for my terce prayers," she complained.

"No you won't if you drop the kids off at eight-thirty," James replied, barely concealing his irritation.

He arrived at the cottage a little before eight and saw at once the tell-tale signs of Antonietta's distress: the empty bottles of wine and the CDs of Laura Pausini lying around without their jackets. It didn't seem she'd been with Petra. He turned on the coffee machine and made two cups of expresso. Gingerly he opened the bedroom door, still half fearing to find Antonietta with her blond girlfriend. He spilled some of the coffee and swore loudly.

"James!" Antonietta was alone and overjoyed to see him. "Put the coffee down," she ordered and threw her naked body against him. Her desire for him was so powerful that the mere caress of his hands on her breasts was sufficient to bring her close to orgasm. She pushed him down her body and within seconds of his tongue touching her intimacy, she came to her climax. She then asked James to penetrate her.

Afterwards, Antonietta nestled against James. "I knew I was being really stupid yesterday," she admitted, "but I couldn't control myself. The thought of not seeing you drove me crazy."

"We can't go on much longer like this." James said

"I know," Antonietta replied, "Let me get my mother's visit over first, and then we'll decide what we're going to do."

"You mean we have a choice?" James asked sharply.

Antonietta stroked his face. "No, my darling, we have no choice."

Later James would use the ambiguity in these words to pervert his image of Antonietta.

# CHAPTER 17

## Thursday, March 14 to Friday, April 12, 2002

James met with Tom Buchanan on Thursday, March 11. He explained the whole scenario that was taking place over Bill's tenure.

"Tom, they're out to get at me through Bill. HB sees me as an obstacle to taking over this place and if he manages to have Bill kicked out, our colleagues will understand which side their bread is buttered on."

"So what do you want from me?" Tom asked.

"A little detective work," James replied. "You know a lot of people in academia. See whether there is any way to disqualify Keighley and Mauser."

Tom reflected for a moment. "I promised myself that once my Rectorship was over, I'd give academic shenanigans a wide berth," he said.

"For Christ's sake, Tom," James pleaded. "You're our only hope. If you don't help, a good academic has his career ruined, and this place will be run by a mediocre megalomaniac. He'll destroy the Institute that you built up."

James had touched Tom's weak spot. He stood up and put his arm around James. "You're a good man, James, and Bill's lucky to have such a friend. Be patient. I'll do what I can."

Once James was gone, Tom picked up the phone and called his secretary. "Will you get me Jim Reilly, Pat. He's the Chair of Economics at Chicago."

———

Antonietta arrived late at Dorval airport on Saturday after tearing herself away from James. She felt despondent. She wouldn't be seeing him for forty-eight hours and would have to put up with her mother instead, who was waiting for her and not very pleased.

"The least I expected was to find you here to welcome me," she complained.

Antonietta kissed her mother on both cheeks. "I'm sorry, Mother," she said contritely, "I got lost."

Caterina's expression suggested strongly that she didn't believe her daughter, but she said no more. Antonietta led her to the Jetta, put her luggage in the trunk and started back to Ste. Anne. It was still snowing and seemed even colder.

"How can you survive in such a climate?" her mother asked. "In Florence, it's already spring, and here you'd think you were in the Arctic Circle."

This isn't going to be fun, Antonietta thought, observing her mother's pinched appearance. "It's not always like this," she replied. "The fall was beautiful." Caterina wasn't impressed. "Well, the climate clearly doesn't agree with you. I've never seen you looking so pale."

It's not the climate that makes me pale, Antonietta felt like replying but didn't. She was aware of her mother's penetrating stare and feared she might guess the truth.

"I hope you haven't thrown yourself at some man," her mother went on in a suspicious tone, confirming Antonietta's apprehension.

Antonietta felt the anger mount within her. For a split second she was tempted to fling the truth into her mother's disapproving face, but fortunately she resisted the impulse and let her rage subside into indignation.

"I never throw myself at men," she replied. "Men throw themselves at *me*."

"Well, I hope none have here," her mother commented acidly. "I don't want a son-on-law who's not only a commoner but a North American as well."

They arrived at the cottage. "Where are you going to sleep," her mother wanted to know. "There's only one bedroom."

"I'll sleep on the sofa."

Caterina's face froze in horror. "A Countess della Chiesa sleeping on a sofa," she cried. "Now I've seen everything."

Matters improved a little when Antonietta took her mother to eat at Gio's. She was impressed by the food, and the intimate atmosphere of the restaurant calmed the tension between the two of them. That was until Caterina brought the subject around to Gina della Chiesa. Gina was one of Antonietta's four cousins and the only one she really liked.

"You'll never guess what she's done." Her mother was beside herself. "She's married a *divorced* man, and outside the Church of course. Everyone is shocked, even Maria Luisa, who normally accepts almost anything. She won't even talk to her daughter now."

Antonietta could sense herself turning white. If her easy-going aunt, Maria

Luisa, was prepared to cut her daughter off for marrying a divorced man, how much worse would *she* fare if she married James.

"I'm glad to see you don't approve either," her mother observed with satisfaction, taking Antonietta's ashen expression for condemnation of her cousin.

Antonietta had no idea how to react. There was no point in contradicting her mother. She had to spend the next week with her, away from James, and the prospect of spending it in an argument about marrying a divorced man was horrific. She might even betray herself.

"I'm surprised Aunt Maria Luisa reacted so badly," she stammered.

"*Badly?*" her mother countered. "It's the only time I've known her behave correctly. It's inconceivable that a della Chiesa would marry a divorced man. Inconceivable."

Caterina had raised her voice, and people were beginning to look at them askance. Antonietta noticed nothing. Her mother's words were the confirmation of all she feared, that her marriage to James would be at the expense of her family ties. Her dilemma, always terrible, was now like a knife in an open wound.

Antonietta changed the conversation, asking about little Claudio. Mercifully, Caterina was only too happy to regale her errant daughter with Carla's maternal bliss. Antonietta barely listened and sipped her wine in a daze of misery. She longed to be alone, she longed for James' comforting presence, but all that awaited her was the loneliness of the sofa and her mother's ominous presence in the adjoining bedroom.

"You must be tired, Mother," she said once they'd finished their expressos. "Let's go back to the cottage and you can have an early night."

Her mother agreed and they drove to the cottage. Antonietta sat on the sofa reading listlessly while her mother prepared herself for bed. They kissed perfunctorily and Antonietta was at last alone. She lay on the sofa in the dark turning over in her mind the hopelessness of her situation. Tears rolled silently down her cheeks. Exhausted and in despair, she fell into a troubled slumber.

—

Throughout the whole time of her visit to Canada, Caterina did little but criticize everything. When she wasn't complaining, she was trying to persuade her daughter to return to Italy. Although Antonietta's patience was strained to the utmost, she bore it all with remarkable stoicism. She knew her mother and, despite her exasperation, kept her temper under control. From her earliest childhood she had been taught to respect her parents.

Worst of all, she was not able to seek much relief from her ordeal by seeing James. She'd met him in a motel on Tuesday, but their presence had evoked the motel owner's suspicions. When they left, he made a veiled allusion to professors and their female students. Regretfully, they decided to forego other such occasions. In any case, Antonietta's mother was so furious at being left alone until seven in the evening that another rendezvous was impossible. So, Antonietta was reduced to casting sorrowful eyes at James during their Thursday class together and a few surreptitious meetings in his office.

Initially, James had been more sanguine about the visit of Antonietta's mother, but the affair with Gina had shaken him. He feared it would fortify Antonietta's reticence to turn her back on her family and religion. He was preoccupied and worried, and the false gaiety of Danny's party for St. Patrick's Day did little to improve his state of mind. Besides, he felt lost without Antonietta. Bill, too, was not in the best of spirits. Only Danny's ebullience at the news that Ceara was coming for Easter and Bernadette's cheeriness saved the evening

As the week progressed, James' mood became more and more somber. The Tuesday rendezvous with Antonietta had done more to upset than soothe him. Antonietta was clearly under stress, and God alone knew what ideas her mother was putting into her head, and the motel owner's remarks were unsettling. He was quite capable of contacting the Institute. The occasional phone calls they managed normally ended with Antonietta in tears, and their clandestine meetings in his office had come to an abrupt end after Christine Desmoulins nearly caught them *in flagrante delicto*. To top it all, there was still no news from Tom Buchanan.

Finally, the day arrived for Antonietta to drive her mother to the airport, her mind entirely absorbed by the prospect of meeting James at *Le Reine Elisabeth*. Caterina, despite the snobbery that often clouded her judgment, was an acute observer, and her suspicions about her daughter's life in Quebec were strengthened by Antonietta's strange animation.

"Promise to come home soon," she told her daughter.

"When I've finished my Master's degree," Antonietta replied.

Without exchanging any more words, Caterina kissed her daughter and walked off through security. Antonietta watched her go with a mixture of relief and sadness. Her mother had many faults, but she was still her mother. She fought back tears as she watched her disappear without looking back again. She turned round and, to her inexpressible joy, found James waiting for her. She ran towards him and threw herself into his arms.

"I didn't expect to see you here," she said, breaking off from their passionate embrace. "You told me you'd meet me at the hotel."

"I couldn't wait," James told her.

Once they were in the hotel room, Antonietta quickly stripped and, pulling James onto the bed, began to undress him. To James' surprise, she seemed calm, almost serene, and there was little evidence of the anguished week she must have spent. Or had it been so anguished? As she made to pull down his briefs, James stopped her.

"Do you know why I came to meet you at the airport?" he asked.

Antonietta shrugged. "At this moment, I don't care," she replied. "I want sex."

James surrendered to her lust and they made love. Antonietta was demanding and carefree. James, though transported to ecstasy by Antonietta's body and the delights it offered, couldn't still his fears. He'd expected to find a distraught Antonietta desperate for emotional comfort, instead his mistress seemed happily consumed by her sexual appetite. When finally she lay exhausted in his arms, she asked why he'd met her at the airport.

"Because I was afraid you wouldn't come to the hotel."

Antonietta shot up and looked at James in amazement. "Why ever not?"

"I feared your mother might have persuaded you to return to Italy."

Antonietta was silent at first. Then she kissed James and looked into his eyes, her own intense and moist with emotion.

"Every night last week I spent alone on the sofa, turning over in my mind how to resolve what seemed an insoluble dilemma. Yes, I did imagine returning to Italy, giving you up, but when I did, my head began to spin, I was sick to my stomach and I felt a pain, a physical pain, in my chest. It was as if I were suffocating. Then the last night, yesterday, I imagined the opposite scenario. I imagined being married to you, having our children, living every day with you. I felt an immense happiness tinged only by sadness that my parents and my Church would have disowned me, but even this sadness contained the hope that one day my family would understand, and that God would forgive me for surrendering to a passion that I never sought but which no woman could have withstood." Antonietta paused and gazed at James. "I have made my decision, and for me there is no longer a dilemma."

They made love one more time and then discussed their immediate plans. It was agreed that, on their return from France, James would leave Veronica without telling her about Antonietta. He would take an apartment or move in with Bill. They would live together later in the summer, end of August perhaps, so that neither Veronica nor the Institute would know for certain that they had already been lovers for a long time. Their marriage would have to wait until the divorce came through, which would take at least a year. In the immediate future, Antonietta agreed that they must be discreet to avoid making Veronica suspicious.

"You should also spend more time with your children,' Antonietta suggested with reluctance. "That way, it will be more difficult for Veronica to turn them against you."

They had their Saturday lunch at Luigi's and arrived back at the cottage mid-afternoon. Despite all her good resolutions, Antonietta was loath to let James go, but she acquiesced without her usual tears and reproaches when he finally left for Prévost.

———

The next week was Holy Week and the last classes were held on Tuesday. Antonietta and James spent Thursday evening at Bill's with the others. It was not a particularly jovial occasion as the problem of Bill's tenure weighed heavily upon all of them.

"Nothing's happening," Bill complained. "Tom's come up with nothing."

"Be patient, Bill," James counseled. "I know he's working on it."

There was little else to be said, and all further attempts to cheer Bill up failed miserably. Antonietta and James took advantage of the morose ambiance to leave early. They wanted to spend what was left of the evening together because they were not going to see each other over Easter. This was a season of special devotion for Veronica, and she spent almost all her time in Church. So, James had to look after the children.

However, once Easter Sunday Mass was over, even Veronica felt she had done her duty by the Lord and His Son and, contrary to James' expectations, raised no objection when he tentatively suggested that he should go to the Institute to finalize his exam questions. She merely pointed out that if he hadn't spent so much time drinking with his friends, he would've done them already.

The exams had, of course, been prepared and handed in to Ilse long ago, but Veronica was not to know. It was to the cottage and not the Institute that James was headed.

Feeling strangely nervous, James made his way to Ste. Anne. He was relieved to see Antonietta's Jetta parked in front of the cottage and stopped the Mercedes beside it. He made for the door but, instead of opening it with his key, he knocked. Puzzled but happy to be drawn away from her studies, Antonietta answered.

She stared at James in joyous disbelief. "James," she cried, embracing him with her normal verve. Without waiting for an explanation for his unexpected apparition, she led him into the bedroom and demanded that he make love to her.

"What about your studies?" he asked jocularly.

Antonietta slid off her thong and lay down on the bed, naked, her legs apart. "Do you really care?" she asked, playing lasciviously with herself. She was a picture of such wild and dissolute sexuality that James tore his shirt in the haste to undress.

———

The following Thursday, James received the much-awaited phone call from Tom Buchanan asking him to come to his office.

"Is it good news?" he asked, unable to bear the suspense.

"Yes," Tom replied.

James walked through the quadrangle, pausing to throw a looney[22] into the fountain and make a wish.

Tom came immediately to the point. "You were right. Mauser and Keighley are indeed friends of Arbuthnot. They were in the same doctoral class together at NUC."

Tom paused. James was disappointed. "I know that already, Tom. It doesn't necessarily get us anywhere, particularly with the line-up of the committee."

A wicked grin came over Tom's face and James realized there was more to come. "Okay, Tom, you've had your fun. Now spill the beans before I throttle you."

Tom chuckled. "You never spoke to me like that when I was Rector."

"For Christ's sake, tell me what you know." James was almost out of his seat in frustrated expectation.

"OK. Jim Reilly, the Chair of Economics at Chicago, was appointed Assistant Professor by me back when I was Chair. More than that, I helped him get tenure in what was a very difficult case. So he owed me big time, and I called it in."

"I had Jim grill Kevin Mauser," he went on. "He's up for a full professorship, and after a little badgering and some none too subtle hints about needing Jim's support for his promotion, Mauser cracked and confessed all. Both he and Keighley had been put up to writing negative references by Arbuthnot. In fact, it was Arbuthnot who wrote both references."

James smiled. This was better than he'd ever dared hope.

"Jim contacted Keighley and told him of Mauser's confession. He saw immediately that the game was up and confirmed Mauser's account. In return for a promise not to make them known, the two signed statements outlining what had happened."

"But what's the use of the statements if we can't produce them for the committee," James asked in alarm.

Tom gave a self-satisfied smile. "The statements were only intended as a guarantee that the two would go through with the other part of the bargain."

"What's that?" James tried to master his exasperation. Tom pulled two letters out his desk drawer.

"These letters are addressed to Hamid Khan for you to give to him personally. They are from Keighley and Mauser announcing that they are withdrawing their references in deference to Broderick and Yankovitch, who are senior to them and more qualified to judge Bill's work."

James heaved a sigh of relief, but he was bothered by Tom's approach. "Wouldn't it have been better for them to send the letters directly to Hamid?"

"No. There is nothing to prevent Hamid ignoring these letters. More important, you'll have to convince him that the statements will be used if he doesn't replace Mauser and Keighley with Broderick and Yankovitch."

"If I don't have the statements, what's to make him believe they exist?"

Tom shook his head. "James, you're normally sharper than this. Who is Hamid going to consult on this?"

"Arbuthnot."

"Exactly, and Arbuthnot will immediately contact his two friends and find out that the statements exist. He also knows they are true."

"What if Mauser or Keighley tell him that Jim promised not to make them known?"

Tom gave his wicked grin again. "They won't. Jim's promise only holds if they keep their little gobs shut."

James returned to his office and made an appointment to see Hamid the next afternoon at four. He then went to the cottage to inform Antonietta of what had happened. She was thankful for Bill's sake, but she was troubled that James was going to be the one to tackle Hamid and Arbuthnot.

"Why is it always you who does the dirty work," she cried. "Why can't Tom go, or Christine or Danny or..."

James took his worried mistress into his arms. "This is important, my love. It's a question of Bill's whole career. Perhaps I'm fooling myself, but I think I'm the best person to deal with Hamid and HB."

Antonietta's beautiful dark eyes were full of foreboding. "Promise me this will be the last time," she implored. "We're near our goal now, and I don't want anything to come between us and the happiness that awaits us."

———

James entered Hamid's office and greeted him politely. He nodded at Arbuthnot. He'd expected to see HB there, indeed his presence was a necessary element in his strategy. He wasted no time in small talk.

"Hamid, I have two letters for you," he said very calmly. "They are from Kevin Mauser and Henry Keighley."

Hamid reacted with predictable surprise, but there was no hostility in his voice. "Why would you have them, James, and what do they say? We already have their refer..."

Arbuthnot cut Hamid off. "What game are you playing, Markham?" he asked aggressively.

James ignored Arbuthnot. "Let me answer your two questions in the opposite order, Hamid," he said in the same calm tone. "The letters say that they both wish to withdraw their references and suggest that you use Borderick and Yankovitch instead as they are more senior and more competent to assess Professor Leaman's work."

Arbuthnot exploded in rage. "You interfering, arrogant son of a bitch," he roared at James. "Just because you're a damn aristocrat, you think you can poke your nose into everything." He glared at James, expecting a riposte that didn't come. "Well, you can't" he finished rather lamely.

James continued to ignore Arbuthnot. "To answer your second question, Hamid, the reason why I am here to give them to you is that they come with an explanation."

Hamid was by now quite ashen. Even Arbuthnot was silent. It was obvious that James had information to impart that spelled trouble for them. Hamid had no idea what it was, but Arbuthnot clearly harbored a horrible suspicion.

"Both Mauser and Keighley have signed statements that they were induced to submit negative references for Bill Leaman by Professor Arbuthnot, with whom they were fellow students at NUC." James turned towards HB. "Indeed, Arbuthnot, they even claim that you wrote the references yourself."

Hamid looked at HB in horror. "Is this true, Roy?" he asked, aghast.

"Of course, it's not," HB snapped. "Markham has contrived all of this to save his friend." He made to snatch the letters from James, who fended him off.

"I had no knowledge of all this," Hamid wailed.

Arbuthnot looked at him with contempt and shook a fist at James. "I shall report you to the Board of Governors for this disreputable attempt to subvert a committee by making outrageous allegations against the Senior Dean."

"You will be making no report to the Board of Governors, Arbuthnot," James replied firmly but still without raising his voice. "The Chair of Economics at Chicago has the two statements. You can check with Mauser and Keighley."

There was a silence. Hamid was slumped in his chair and Arbuthnot was wiping the abundant perspiration from his forehead. He knew that he was beaten, beaten yet again by this insufferable, interfering Englishman.

"There are two possible outcomes to this unpleasant situation," James went on. "If you persist in using these references, the statements will be made public and you, Arbuthnot, will lose your job, and Hamid will lose all respect and credibility." He turned to Hamid. "I believe you knew nothing about Arbuthnot's machinations, but you will be perceived as weak and naïve. You'll have to resign as Chair."

"What is the other outcome?" Hamid asked timidly.

"You withdraw the references from Mauser and Keighley and replace them with references from Broderick and Yankovitch and, if they are positive, as I expect, you will support Professor Leaman's tenure. So will you, Arbuthnot."

"And the statements?" Hamid enquired tremulously.

"They won't be needed. Once Professor Leaman's tenure is confirmed, I shall instruct Jim Reilly to destroy them."

"There's no time to get new references," Arbuthnot growled in a final display of defiance.

"That's your problem—and Hamid's." James shrugged his shoulders in a gesture of disdainful indifference. "Either you get the two references from Broderick and Yankovitch, or you suffer the consequences."

Hamid nodded his agreement while Arbuthnot just stared ahead into space, as if in a catatonic trance. The battle won, James left. He went immediately back to his office and called Bill.

"Bill, I've got good news for you," he told his friend with a light heart. "They're going to replace the references from Mauser and Keighley with those from Broderick and Yankovitch. If they're positive, Hamid and Arbuthnot will support you for tenure."

There was a brief silence at the other end of the phone as Bill digested the news. "Jesus!" he exclaimed. "How the hell did you pull that off, James?"

James recounted the whole scenario, dwelling with particular glee on Arbuthnot's raging discomfiture.

"I tried to be optimistic," Bill said, his voice breaking with emotion, "but I doubted that you and Tom could pull it off. I owe you guys. You've saved my neck."

"It should never have been in danger," James replied. Then, lightening his tone, he added. "However, buy an extra large bottle of J & B for tonight, and I'll call the others."

––––––

On Saturday, Hamid called James at home. He was upset and worried.

"I knew nothing about those references," he assured James. "I've sent off requests by email and courier to Broderick and Yankovitch asking them to get their references to me by Friday morning. If they don't arrive, I'll have the meeting postponed."

"That's good, Hamid." James' tone was conciliatory. This was an opportunity to wean Hamid from Arbuthnot's sphere and perhaps make an ally of him. "I believe you didn't know about the references, but take my advice and don't let yourself be used by Arbuthnot any more. He's not a very ethical person."

"So I realize," Hamid replied.

James made his way back to the dining room where the children and Veronica were having breakfast.

"You were very late last night, James," Veronica remarked.

"Yes, I know, but we solved the tenure problem for Bill, and so we celebrated. Unfortunately a bit too much, so I stayed on at Bill's to sober up."

Veronica gave her husband a look of disgust and said no more. Unwisely, failing to detect the note of suspicion in her voice, James told her that he planned to go to the Institute that afternoon to mark some exams.

"You seem to spend a lot of time at the Institute these days, James," Veronica remarked. "I sometimes wonder why."

"There's been a lot going on recently," James replied as nonchalantly as he could. "Exams, seeing students, Bill's tenure case."

"Is that dark-haired Italian girl among the students you see," Veronica asked pointedly.

James turned to fetch himself another coffee. He'd already had more than enough but he could feel the blood drain from his face and he was afraid this would betray him.

"No," he lied.

Luckily by the time he'd finished pouring out the coffee, adding sugar and stirring it, Veronica had cleared the table and left the room. Thank God, this will soon be over, he thought as he drank the coffee without any enjoyment.

He spent that afternoon with Antonietta. He told her about Veronica's suspicions. "She even made an allusion to you," he said.

"How does she know about me?"

"She saw you look at me that time you came to Mass at Saint-Sauveur to punish me for not coming to the cottage."

Antonietta paled. "What an idiot I was."

They agreed that James would have to be home in time for supper. As he was leaving, Antonietta held on to him. "One last kiss, James," she entreated. He kissed her, long and passionately. "Remember that in a week's time we shall be on our way for two weeks in France together," he whispered.

Antonietta nodded but insisted on yet another kiss.

———

The next week passed peaceably although everyone was on tenterhooks. The meeting of FPC was scheduled for Friday, April 12, and until it had granted

Bill's tenure there was still room for doubt. The references from Broderick and Yankovitch arrived on Thursday afternoon by fax. They were extremely positive, one calling Bill's work "original, incisive and considerably above average." Hamid eventually got hold of James around seven and told him the good news.

"What did Arbuthnot say?" James asked.

"Nothing. He just glared and waved me out of his office," Hamid replied with a sigh.

———

The committee was waiting for the Rector to make his royal entry. Christine had been briefed by James and was curious to see how HB and Hamid were going to manage their volte-face. She noticed that Hamid was looking anxious. Arbuthnot's mouth twitched nervously from time to time and the red tufts of hair on his head seemed to stand out more than usual. Forget had his normal puzzled air as if not knowing why he was there at all. Flint also looked confused.

Winstone finally arrived. "Good morning, ladies and gentlemen," he intoned pompously and then corrected himself with a mirthless smile. "Or should I say, lady and gentlemen." No-one laughed and Winstone quickly called on Hamid to make his presentation.

"There has been a change in the referees," he began hesitantly. "Two of the referees, Professors Mauser and Keighley, have withdrawn their references on the grounds that they do not feel competent to judge Professor Leaman's work. They suggested that we use Professors Broderick and Yankovitch instead, as they are more senior and experts in Professor Leaman's field."

There was a stir in the committee. Winstone forsook his normal air of lordly indifference, which he meant to be impartiality, and looked questioningly at HB. Poor Forget was even more confused. Flint was staring into space.

"These two new referees have given extremely positive assessments of Professor Leaman's work," Hamid went on. "Together with Professor Khaladi, they recommend tenure without any reservations. Professor Dickens also recommends tenure although he believes it to be too early. However, there is no precedent in this Institute for treating tenure cases differently just because they're brought early. This means that there is a four to zero consensus among the referees in favor of tenure. As a result, I am changing my recommendation and urge the committee to grant tenure to Professor Leaman."

"It seems a little irregular to change the referees at this late stage," Forget objected mildly.

"Perhaps," HB interjected, "but what is important is to be completely fair, and it seems to me unfair to ruin someone's academic career on the basis of comments from referees who admit themselves that they are not competent to judge."

Forget nodded his agreement. Christine and James exchanged looks. Winstone, who had listened to the whole discussion with growing amazement, asked if there were more comments. Neither Christine nor James saw any point in adding to the consensus, Flint had been told by Arbuthnot to keep quiet and Forget found the whole business far too complicated for another submission. Winstone called for the vote. It was unanimous in favor of granting tenure.

# CHAPTER 18

## Saturday, April 13 to Saturday, May 4, 2002

James arrived at the cottage on Saturday around three to pick up Antonietta for their trip to France. She was wearing a pale green jacket with a short skirt that showed off her shapely legs. As usual, the white blouse was at least one size too small and accentuated the fullness of her bosom. Her hair flowed untamed and voluminously over her shoulders. She flicked it back and James caught sight of the emeralds in her gold earrings. Her make-up was tasteful and lightly applied.

James shook his head in wonder. "Every time I see you after a day's absence, I marvel anew at how beautiful you are." He kissed Antonietta lightly on her cheeks, not wanting to spoil the perfection of her countenance. She couldn't resist teasing him. "How very decorous, James. One would think we're already married." It was too much for James. He took his gorgeous mistress into his arms and gave vent to his ardor.

It was a pleasant flight and, unusually for Air Canada, they arrived on time early in the morning. They went quickly through immigration with their European passports and were waved through customs. James picked up the rental car and they were soon in the thick of Paris. James felt again the animation Paris always conjured up in him. It was his favorite city, but he wasn't going to confess this to his Italian mistress.

They crossed the Pont Neuf and arrived at the Hotel Esmeralda across from Notre Dame Cathedral. It was not among the finest hotels in Paris, but James had always stayed there, and he was fond of the quaint old building. Besides, it was well situated. The owner greeted James as an old friend and showed them immediately to their room. James went to the window and gazed in admiration at the lofty Gothic splendor of the cathedral. When he turned round, Antonietta was already stretched out on the bed, completely naked.

"I want sex," she declared, opening her legs.

"Shouldn't I shave first?"

"No, James, I want it *now, right now.*"

James needed no second bidding. He shed his clothes quickly and clasped hold of Antonietta's hot body. The humidity and odor of her sexuality wrought a frenzy in him. He mounted her and they took their pleasure violently together, inundating each other with the effluent of their gratified lust. But once was not enough and they continued to indulge themselves without restraint or shame. It was early afternoon by the time they'd exhausted their pursuit of pleasure. James called a taxi—he wasn't going to drive in Paris more than necessary—and they had a late lunch in a brasserie. In the evening, they dined on a bateau mouche as it slowly winded its way along the Seine.

———

The next day they set out for the South of France. Once they'd passed the town of Orange, the sky opened up into a brilliant blue. The northern clouds melted before the unseasonable warmth of the southern sun. Antonietta felt her body respond to the change in climate. She was more alive, more sensual, and a feeling of exhilaration gripped her as they neared the Mediterranean, *her* Mediterranean. All her negative feelings about the French dissolved in the brilliant colors of Provence. After passing the tollbooth at Cassis, the Mediterranean suddenly came into view and Antonietta clapped her hands for joy.

"I've missed it so much," she lamented, tears streaming down her face.

To console her, James drove to Les Lecques instead of Bandol so that they could walk along the beach. They sat in a cafe at the end of the seafront and gazed out to sea. They watched children playing on the sand and paddling in the sea. One day, their own children would be doing that in this same sea. Antonietta put an arm around James and buried her face in his neck. "Thank you," she murmured.

———

The days the couple spent in Bandol were magical for both of them. The presence of the Mediterranean, the spring warmth, the azure blue and gold colors of Provence, the budding vines, the café terraces, the walks along the beach, the romantic dinners, all this infused them with a new vigor and their love for each other blossomed as never before. They resolved to spend their life together in Italy and immerse themselves in the sensuous charms of southern Europe.

"Now, I'm here, it's difficult to believe that Canada exists," Antonietta said as they took their breakfast of croissants and expresso coffee in the little restaurant on the beach at Les Lecques.

Imperceptively, their moods began to change as the day of departure neared. Before them were difficult days, the prospect of which was only bearable because, at the end of their trials, they would be together, here on the Mediterranean. They traveled back to Paris and spent the night at the Hotel Esmeralda. The next morning, a Saturday, they made for the airport with heavy hearts.

As she sat in the plane traveling towards Montreal, Antonietta's emotions swirled between sadness at leaving the south of France, apprehension at what awaited them and fragile anticipation of the joys to come. Once they arrived at Dorval, the dreary reality of their life in Quebec came as a shock after the two weeks they'd spent happily together. A despondent silence descended upon them as they drove towards Ste. Anne. It was a dull, overcast day and as they came further north into the Laurentians, snow still lay copiously on the ground. The cottage where they had lived their illicit love affair seemed bleak and unwelcoming. An involuntary shiver of dread ran through Antonietta.

"Please stay with me," she pleaded.

James took her in his arms. "I can't," he replied. "I don't want Veronica to be suspicious. I'm going to leave her next week, and she mustn't think that it's for another woman."

"Am I just another woman?" Antonietta asked, her dark eyes glistening with sad reproach.

"No. You are the love of my life."

Antonietta consoled herself with the thought that she would see James on Monday, and soon they would be living together. Yet, despite this joyful prospect, Antonietta couldn't suppress a nagging doubt, which intensified in the loneliness of the cottage. What she was planning to do was sinful, and her doubt was fed by fear of divine retribution. Unable to bear it any longer, she went to six o'clock Mass at Saint-Sauveur. She prayed for forgiveness, imploring the Virgin to intercede for her. Slightly comforted, she returned home to find a message from James telling her that he must see her tomorrow and would call again later. The tone of his voice was urgent and worried.

A terrible foreboding gripped Antonietta. What had happened? Had Veronica found out about them? Were there some problems with his children, problems that would keep him in his marriage? The foreboding turned to panic and Antonietta paced around the living room waiting in terror for James' call. When it came, she nearly tripped over racing to take the phone.

"I've been summoned to the Rector's office at three on Monday afternoon," James told her. "Veronica says that Eleanor sounded very upset."

"Who's Eleanor?" Antonietta asked.

"The Rector's secretary."

A feeling of impending catastrophe came over Antonietta. She begged James to come round, but it was impossible. He tried to comfort her on the phone, but she was still distraught when he rang off. Unable to sleep, she drank some wine and tortured herself by playing over and over again Laura Pausini's song of painful separation, *Come se non fosse stato mai amore*[23].

———

James was in a black mood when he attended Sunday Mass with his family. He was preoccupied both by worry over the Rector's summons and dread at the difficult week that lay ahead. What on earth did Winstone want? He tried to downplay his anxiety by telling himself that it was doubtless another of HB's tricks, but he couldn't convince himself. Why would Eleanor have been so upset if it was just that? He wished himself with fervor a year hence when all these troubles would be behind him and he and Antonietta would be married.

Mistaking James' preoccupation for religious devotion, Veronica commented on his new attitude when they left the church and made for the Brûlerie to have brunch. Petra was there with Brett. James greeted her by her first name, as she did with him, which annoyed Veronica.

"You're getting very familiar with the students," she remarked.

"She's a friend of Bill's," James replied defensively.

"That's not a reason," Veronica retorted. "He's hardly a person to emulate."

Brunch proceeded with agonizing slowness. Finally, making some excuse about checking his mail and perhaps finding out what the Rector wanted, James escaped to visit Antonietta. She was in a terrible state. The Rector's summons filled her with a menacing presentiment. They made love with a frenzy, desperate to drown their fears in sexual pleasure. When it came time for James to leave, Antonietta clung to him.

"I'm so afraid," she sobbed, trying to drag James back into the cottage. With much effort, he resisted. "The last thing we need at this time is a showdown with Veronica," he told her.

Antonietta nodded, her eyes moist with fear and sadness, and, after a final passionate embrace, let him go. She was beset by oppressive anxiety. Soon that anxiety would turn to despair and misery.

———

James' apprehensions were confirmed upon being ushered into Winstone's office. Arbuthnot was there as well with a look of triumph on his face.

"Please take a seat, Professor Markham," Winstone said with great solemnity.

James did his bidding with a hollow feeling in his stomach. He suspected what was coming although he had no idea how the Rector had found out about his liaison with Antonietta. He had his answer when Winstone pulled out a collection of photos.

"Perhaps you would be good enough to explain these, Professor Markham?" he asked in the same formal tone.

James looked at the photos. He realized immediately that they'd been taken the day Antonietta had burst into his office to find him with Annya. It was the scene of their passionate reconciliation, and their embrace left little doubt as to the nature of their relationship. He remembered how Wrangel was always carrying his camera with him, so it was probably he who had taken the photos to avenge himself for his humiliation in class. There was an expectant silence as Winstone and HB waited for James' answer. He didn't oblige them.

"Well, Professor Markham?" the Rector enquired impatiently.

"What explanation do you need?" James replied with a shrug. "The photos would seem to be self-evident."

"So, you admit to an intimate relationship with a student in your class?" Arbuthnot snarled. James nodded.

Arbuthnot was clearly about to launch into some vengeful diatribe when Winstone held up his hand to stop him. He addressed James in a friendly way that seemed completely out of place.

"James," he said, "you have rendered outstanding service to the Institute as a researcher, teacher, as Assistant Dean for International Affairs and in the short time you've been Chair of your Section. I want to spare you the indignity of a disciplinary hearing before the Ethics Committee."

HB tried to interject but Winstone again stopped him.

"If you resign, there will be no hearing. This way the matter doesn't become public knowledge. I advise you to agree. Think of your wife and children."

James was stunned by Winstone's apparent generosity. Perhaps he'd misjudged the man. The Rector's next words disabused him

"Think about it, James. We will take no action until after the Italian Ambassador has come on May 9 to open the new EU library. As you arranged it, he will expect you to be there."

So that was it. The last thing Winstone wanted was a scandal that would threaten his only achievement, which, in fact, had been obtained solely because of James' reputation. But it was a fair deal. James agreed to hand in his resignation after the visit from the Italian Ambassador, effective July 1, 2002.

After leaving the Rector's office, a very shaken James went to see Antonietta, who was waiting anxiously for him. He told her what had happened. "I'm to resign after the visit from the Italian Ambassador."

Antonietta was overwhelmed by worry and grief. "Your career will be ruined," she sobbed. "What will you do? How can you get another job? No-one will hire you once this gets out." She laid her head on James' shoulder. "Arbuthnot will get his revenge even if you resign. I always knew he would."

It would have been so easy for James to tell Antonietta who he was, that he had no need of his academic job, that he had enough money from his shares in the family bank to live without working. But he didn't.

"I'll get an academic job elsewhere," he told his weeping mistress without conviction. "Perhaps in Europe. HB won't even know."

"Any place will contact the Institute," Antonietta wailed. "Winstone will tell HB and he'll make sure you get a bad reference."

Antonietta clung to the man she loved. They moved to the bedroom and, as if they sensed it was the last time, they made love with a kind of desperation. "I have to take Susanna to a concert tomorrow in Montreal," James told the distraught Antonietta. "I'll be back late. So, I'll see you on Wednesday, and I swear I'll make you forget all this."

Hiding her misery, Antonietta smiled wanly. James had enough problems without adding her anguish to them. She watched him drive off. It would be a very long time before she felt again the warmth of James' body or his kisses burning on her lips. The agony of their separation had begun.

———

Left alone in the cottage, Antonietta was tortured by guilt. If only she hadn't stayed on at that party, all this would never have happened. She became convinced that she was the cause of James' ruin, and a single idea obsessed her. She had to save James' career, but how? Should she go to the Rector and tell him that it was she who had seduced James? Or that she was not really a student in his class because she'd always been going to leave at Christmas? No, Antonietta reluctantly concluded that neither approach would work. Egged on by his rancorous Senior Dean, Winstone was only too happy to have the chance of destroying James' career. Antonietta toyed with offering herself to him but set aside the idea in disgust.

Suddenly, she remembered the EU collection being donated by the Italian Ambassador on behalf of the European Union. Don Alfredo was her godfather. Was it possible to persuade him to make the donation contingent on James' continuing presence at the Institute? Antonietta felt an immense surge of hope. She rushed off to the church in Saint-Sauveur to pray for the success of her new plan.

As she prayed, she realized with growing horror that she couldn't have it both ways. She couldn't save James and at the same time continue her adulterous relationship with him. She knew Messina. Even her mother mocked his excessive piety and straighlaced Catholicism. He would never agree to save James unless she renounced him. He took his duties as her godfather far too seriously for that. Antonietta felt giddy. Her whole being rose up against the idea of renouncing the man she loved, but it was the only way. She had gotten James into this mess, she had to get him out of it even it meant never seeing or talking to him or making love to him again. Antonietta felt a storm of tears well up, but she suppressed them. She had to act quickly, like an automaton. If she once reflected on the enormity of what she was doing, she wouldn't have the strength to carry it through. She had to leave the cottage immediately and Canada as well, once she'd seen Messina.

Antonietta returned home. No sooner had she arrived than the phone rang. Probably it was James, but with a superhuman effort that left her exhausted and grief-stricken, she didn't answer and then sat down to write the most difficult letters of her life. One was to Dean Bromhoeffer withdrawing from the Institute and another to her landlady enclosing a check for the May rent and telling her to keep the damage deposit. In addition she would leave the furniture she'd bought for the cottage.

The third letter was her greatest torment. She knew that Messina would require her to promise both to renounce James and to make sure he wouldn't seek her out. So, she had to write a letter to the man she loved with an all-consuming passion that would convince him that she didn't love him and never had. She started it many times, but every time she broke down into hysterical weeping. More out of emotional exhaustion than any rational ability to think, she penned the infamous lines:

*James, it's all over. It should never have started. I am returning to Italy. Please let me be. Antonietta.*

Then she added the cruelest words of all: *Please drop the key in the mailbox. You won't need it any more.*

She called Carlo and told him that she had to leave Canada because of family problems. She would leave the Jetta at Luigi's so he could sell it and deposit the money in her account minus whatever commission he wanted to take. Then she called Alitalia. She knew how heartbroken she would be when she left Canada and she preferred the Latin warmth of her own countrywomen to the cold efficiency of the Air Canada hostesses. She booked a flight from Toronto late afternoon on Wednesday to Florence via Milan. Finally she packed her clothes and some books and momentoes in between bouts of sobbing and throwing up. She couldn't bear to look back at the cottage when she left. Two hours later, after stopping several times to fight back thoughts of James that caused her such physical pain that she was unable to drive, she arrived at the Hotel Versailles.

Antonietta spent a sleepless and wretched night. Her sense of loss gave her the sensation that her heart was really breaking. She felt nauseous and her head throbbed. Constantly she had to fight the temptation to rush back to the cottage. At one stage she couldn't stand it any more and started to call James. It was only with the greatest effort that she stopped herself. After that, her night was a trance of misery alleviated only by the insidious consolations of the minibar. In the morning, she ordered a double expresso in her room. Trembling, she called the Italian Embassy in Ottawa. At first the receptionist was very uncooperative.

"The Ambassador do not take personal calls," she told Antonietta in poor English.

"He will take one from me," Antonietta answered imperiously in Italian. "I am the Countess Antonietta della Chiesa and he is an old friend of our family, and also my godfather."

The girl acquiesced. Antonietta wasn't half a Palmieri for nothing. Within seconds, she heard the voice of Don Alfredo.

"Antonietta!" he exclaimed. "It's lovely to hear from you."

Without divulging her reasons, Antonietta asked to see the Duke. He was only too happy to oblige and it was agreed that they would meet at the Embassy at noon. Realizing that this offered her the opportunity to leave Canada a day earlier than planned, Antonietta called Alitalia to change her flight. She knew that the longer she stayed in Canada, the less capable she would be of fighting the longing for James that was devouring her. It was not the longing of before their affair, but a painful, desolate longing for a paradise that she was about to exchange for hell.

Before leaving for the airport, Antonietta went to say goodbye to Luigi and leave her car for his son. She gave him the same family reason for her precipitate departure from Canada but, from Antonietta's demeanor and her puffy eyes, Luigi guessed the reason was more likely a problem with her Englishman. He embraced Antonietta. He had come to regard her almost as his own daughter and was very sad to see her go. He wished her well and asked her to keep in touch. Antonietta promised to do so but knew she wouldn't keep her word. She would have to put as much distance between herself and Canada as possible if she was going to keep the oath that Don Alfredo would surely require from her.

Antonietta took a taxi to the airport and boarded a plane for Ottawa. She arrived a little after eleven and took a taxi to the Italian Embassy. The Duke had clearly briefed the receptionist for she was all smiles and courtesy with Antonietta. Within minutes, Don Alfredo himself came to fetch her. They went to his office.

Antonietta recounted the whole story of her love for James, their attempts to resist the passion that had descended upon them, their surrender to it, the blissful six months they had spent as lovers, the photos and James' impending dismissal.

"Please save him, Don Alfredo," she begged. "The Rector desperately needs that European library. If you threaten to withhold it, he'll do whatever you say."

Antonietta's eyes were swimming with tears and her beautiful face was etched by grief. Messina contemplated her with compassion, but there was also a severity in his mien. Antonietta knew that what she was asking was quite irregular, and there was no reason for a man of Messina's strict morality to take pity on his adulterous goddaughter. She had to offer a sacrifice if she was to persuade him.

"If you help me, I will swear on the Holy Scriptures to renounce James Markham and never to see him again," she said unsteadily.

With that, the self-control she'd maintained with great effort gave way. She put her head in her hands and wept. Messina came round his desk and put his arm around Antonietta to comfort her. There was a short silence as the Duke reflected.

"I will help you," he said finally. "I don't particularly like that Rector. He's a weak individual and thoroughly untrustworthy. Besides, Dr. Markham *is* the reason we're putting the library there."

The Duke smiled down at the weeping Antonietta. "So no Dr. Markham, no library."

Antonietta had a momentary feeling of joy at Messina's words, but when he fetched a Bible for her to take the oath, the misery returned. She had the impression that the pages of the Book were burning her hand as she laid it on them. Trembling, she swore to renounce James, never to seek to him out and to refuse to have anything to do with him if he came to her. She was not to tell him that she had saved his career by this sacrifice.

Antonietta felt a dreadful hollowness in her stomach. She was certain that she was forswearing all happiness in this world and condemning herself to perpetual sorrow and despair. Unable to maintain any further conversation, she quickly left the Embassy but not before setting her eyes upon Messina. He flinched at the depth of the suffering that was mirrored in them.

Once outside the Embassy, Antonietta began to realize the irrevocability of her decision. She would never see James again, never hold him, never feel his kisses, never again laugh and argue with him, never make love to him. He was banished from her life. It took all her strength of character to continue. As she sat in the departure lounge at Lester Pearson Airport waiting for her flight to Milan, she was almost comatose with grief. At times she had difficulty breathing. Twice she had to rush to the washroom to throw up. She was desperately afraid of breaking down completely and fought to chase thoughts of James from her mind. The magazines she'd bought to divert herself couldn't shake the one terrible thought that obsessed her: James was lost to her forever.

After an hour and a half of torment, Antonietta finally boarded the plane for Italy. She'd wanted a seat in business class, believing this would give her greater privacy, but they were all taken. So, she took her seat in economy next to an old Italian lady. When the plane took off, she felt her heart break within her, one part of it remaining with her love and the other, broken and useless, traveling with her to Italy. Tears streamed down her face. The old lady touched her arm in a gesture of sympathy.

"You are beautiful and young," she told her. "Time will heal your sorrow." Antonietta thanked her, but she knew that time would not help. Her passion for James was too infinite ever to fade away through the passage of time.

Once the captain had turned off the seatbelt sign, one of the airhostesses, who had noticed Antonietta's heartbroken demeanor, came to offer her a seat in an empty row at the back of the plane. Antonietta looked hesitantly at the old lady, not wishing to offend her.

"Go," she said with a smile. "A good cry will do you good."

Antonietta went to the back of the plane and wept as silently as she could. The airhostess discreetly brought her a little food and some wine. Antonietta drank the wine but couldn't bring herself to eat. At times a feeling of utter despair and emptiness came over her, and she felt as if she were suffocating. The airhostess was concerned and asked whether she should enquire if there was a doctor on board. Antonietta assured her that she would be all right. The airhostess looked unconvinced.

Antonietta was exhausted by the time she arrived in Milan, which was a help. She was too tired to think. She had a coffee and some Austrian buns with butter and jam before boarding her plane for Florence. Once there, she took a taxi to her parents' villa in Fiesole. She dreaded meeting her mother but, to her relief, only Anna, the old maid who had practically brought her up, was at the home. Her mother was in Rome with Carla and the baby, and her father was at a conference somewhere. Anne didn't expect them back for another two days.

Antonietta started to climb the stairs to her bedroom when she began to sway. She would have lost her balance if Anna hadn't caught her. She turned round and threw herself into Anna's arms.

"Come, little Countess," Anna said as she led Antonietta upstairs to her old bedroom. "Have a sleep, child. You look exhausted. We'll talk when you feel better."

Feel better? As she sank down on her bed, Antonietta doubted that she would ever overcome her pain at the loss of the man she loved with all her being. Worn out by convulsive sobbing, eventually she fell asleep whispering James' name.

———

After dropping off the children at school on Wednesday, James made for the cottage. He was worried. He'd tried several times to call Antonietta, but there had never been an answer. His worry turned into terrible foreboding when he saw that Antonietta's Jetta was not parked in front of the cottage. Whatever was going on? Apprehensively, he opened the cottage door with his key and entered.

The first thing he noticed was that the picture of the Virgin, which normally hung on the wall of the living room, was missing. He began to feel even more uneasy. He went to the bedroom and stared in horror at the empty closet. "No, no!" he shouted. "No, no!"

He returned in a daze to the living room and saw an envelope on which was written his name. Trembling, already suspecting the worst, he opened the envelope and read the letter it contained.

James sank down on the sofa and stared at the letter. He read the brief, cruel message over and over again in the hope that the words would change. His body felt cold but his head was hot. He had the sensation that it was about to burst. He tried to stand up but couldn't move. He tried to collect his thoughts but couldn't think. His being was paralysed by an overwhelming sensation of utter hopelessness. It was unbelievable, it was impossible, he tried to tell himself, but the letter told him differently. The woman he loved with such infinite passion had left him. Antonietta was gone.

Unaware of time passing, James remained seated on the sofa for a long time, not moving, unable to comprehend. Why? Why? he asked himself over and over again. The pain of losing Antonietta was unbearable and he felt himself sinking into a stupor. Neither his body nor his mind could cope with the disaster that had befallen him. He had to get away from this place of memories where every item and every inch reminded him of his lost happiness.

He called Veronica and told her that something had come up, and he had to go to Montreal for some meetings. They should last a couple of days.

"That means I have to look after the children again," she complained. "You've only just come back from France."

There was a note of suspicion in Veronica's voice. Now she's suspicious, James thought bitterly, just when there's no longer any need to be. He left the cottage, put the key in the mailbox and made for Montreal. He booked into a hotel. This was where he would try to put his life back together and restore his sanity.

———

It was late evening when Antonietta awoke from a troubled sleep. With horror she realized that the events of the last days were not a nightmare but brutal reality. She had left James. She pictured him reading her letter, and the pain was so unbearable that she desperately sought escape from the image. The most sensible course of action would be to go downstairs and talk with Anna, even call some friends, but she couldn't master her tears long enough to leave the bedroom.

There was a knock on the door. It was Anna. She'd heard Antonietta crying and was bringing her hot soup. "It'll give you strength," she told the pitiful young woman and sat on the bed to make sure that Antonietta drank it. Afterwards she had Antonietta tell her the whole woeful story.

"Don't tell the family," Antonietta implored. "I'm wretched enough without having to endure my mother's censure."

"Well, child," Anna replied. "You're going to have to pull yourself together, or your tears will give you away."

Anna was right, but how could she behave normally enough not to raise her family's curiosity? All she felt capable of was lying on the bed and weeping for her lost love. That alone provided some relief, scant though it was, from her torment. Nevertheless, she promised Anna to make an effort. She would allow herself one last night of lamentation before facing up to the wretchedness of life without James.

———

After checking into the hotel, James remained seated on the bed for hours. At first, he was numb from grief and shock, but gradually a conviction began to form within his mind that he'd been played for a fool, and the grief gave way to a simmering anger. He dwelled on Antonietta's reluctance to commit herself to marrying him, her enigmatic remark in Santiago that perhaps they shouldn't get married, and her confession that she'd entertained the idea of leaving him during her mother's visit. Now it was clear to him what she'd meant when she told him once that they had no choice. She'd never intended to marry him and now that he was about to be disgraced, she'd dropped him like a hot potato. He fed on his anger, stoking it until he succeeded in perverting his image of Antonietta. Dismissing the innumerable proofs of her love for him, he told himself savagely that he shouldn't waste time regretting her. She had the morals of a whore and a bisexual one at that. She'd probably been screwing Petra all along as well as himself.

After a night spent between brief bouts of sleep and much weeping, Antonietta was woken at ten o'clock on Thursday by a very determined Anna.

"I have prepared breakfast for you, child," she said kindly but firmly. "Get dressed and come down to eat it."

"I can't" Antonietta responded, burying her head in the pillow to stiffle a new onset of sobbing.

"You must, Countess Antonietta," Anna persisted in the same no-nonsense manner. "Think of who you are, and stop behaving like a lovesick schoolgirl."

"But I *am* lovesick," Antonietta moaned.

Anna was unyielding. "Perhaps, Countess, but you have to face your parents tonight, and you'd better start pulling yourself together. Crying like a baby isn't going to bring you back to him."

Antonietta surrendered to Anna's implacable logic. She showered, made herself up, dressed and went downstairs. She drank coffee and ate voraciously, suddenly realizing that she was very hungry. After breakfast, Anna dispatched her into town to buy some groceries. The beauty of Florence lying below Fiesole and the warm Italian sun brought some comfort to the tortured young woman. By the time she returned to the villa, Antonietta had come to accept that she would have to live with the pain and misery of her new reality.

———

James remained a couple of days in Montreal until he felt able to face life again. By the time he arrived back in the Laurentians on Saturday afternoon, the passion he'd felt for Antonietta had been converted, superficially at least, into loathing and contempt. He went to see Bill to inform him of his forced resignation.

"Oh. my God!" Bill groaned in dismay. "What does Antonietta think about all this?"

"I don't want her name ever mentioned again in my presence," James declared and poured out all his venom. "For me the whore no longer exists," he concluded, but the bitterness could not completely mask his grief.

Bill eyed his friend with sympathy. "I knew there would be hell to pay if you two broke up. Now I wish I'd never got you together."

"So do I," James replied. "On the other hand, she was a good fuck," he added with an uncharacteristic vulgarity that had Bill shaking his head in disbelief.

"Vulgarity doesn't become you, James," he admonished his friend. "Whatever she's done, Antonietta doesn't deserve it. There must be an explanation for her leaving."

"The explanation is only too obvious," James responded caustically. "She doesn't want to be with a loser. But don't fret. You'll never hear me mention that damn woman's name again."

# PART THREE

Sunday, May 5, 2002, to Friday, November 21, 2003

# CHAPTER 19
## Sunday May 5 to Wednesday, June 5, 2002

Antonietta awoke to the now familiar pain of her loss. Her pillow was soaked with tears, and the bedclothes were in disarray from her frantic attempts to find relief from her suffering in sleep. Until today, she'd seen little of her family and, with great effort, had been able to hide from them the torment that was ravaging her. Her mother had remarked on her listlessness, and Antonietta's occasional and uncharacteristic bouts of irritability had angered her, but she'd put all this down to the nefarious influence of North America. A few weeks in Italy would cure her daughter.

Today, the family would attend Mass together at the Basilica. Afterwards they were to lunch with the Cardinal, who was anxious to hear about his niece's experiences in Canada and, Antonietta feared, the reason for her precipitate return to Italy. All this would be an ordeal, and she felt ill with dread. She arose from her bed and made her way into the bathroom.

"Oh, my God!" she exclaimed, looking at her shattered appearance.

Her eyes were dull and puffy, her hair dank and lifeless and her features wore the imprint of her anguish. Fighting back another onset of sobbing, she took a shower and began to recapture some semblance of her beauty. Naturally gifted in the art of female contrivance, she had within minutes masked the damage, although a knowing eye would be able to discern the sad reality behind her outward splendor. Luckily, her mother was too wrapped up in Carla's baby and Renata's pregnancy to notice, and her father was equally taken up by his new duties as President of the Association of Italian Hospital Surgeons. As for Giovanni and Renata, they were unlikely to take the trouble to penetrate the surface of her apparent normality. That just left her uncle.

———

James was not present when the Italian Ambassador arrived on Friday, May 17 at the Institute. Winstone, no doubt encouraged by HB, had obviously decided that while James' presence was necessary, there was no need to flaunt it. He would attend the ceremony when the Institute formally took possession of the European collection, but that was all. So, James was very surprised when he received a phone call from Eleanor inviting him to join the Rector, HB and the Duke of Messina for lunch after the ceremony.

The ceremony itself also reserved some surprises for James. The Duke greeted him with unusual warmth and referred in glowing terms to his contribution to European Union scholarship in his speech. Winstone was his usual pompous self but he seemed ill at ease, while Arbuthnot appeared to be simmering with rage. It was all very strange.

At the lunch which followed, the Duke spent most of the time discussing with James the institutional problems of the European Union. Unusually for an Italian, the Duke shared some of James' euroskepticism. Neither Winstone nor HB had anything to contribute and were left out of the conversation. When lunch ended, the Duke immediately prepared to leave. He wished James well and thanked Winstone, somewhat stiffly, for the Institute's hospitality. Winstone replied with fulsome thanks for the collection. The Duke perfunctorily shook HB's hand and was gone. HB also left, without a word to either of his two colleagues.

"James, I'd like to see you if you have time," Winstone asked in a friendly, almost sycophantic tone.

"Of course, Harold," James replied.

He was perplexed. What was going on? What was behind the Duke of Messina's privileged treatment of him, HB's bad humor and now Winstone's unctuousness? They arrived at Winstone's office and the Rector invited James to sit down. He offered him a brandy, which James accepted. If by now he was completely mystified by the turn of events, the Rector's next words only increased his bewilderment.

"I understand from Dr. Bromhoeffer that the young lady with whom you were…" Winstone hesitated, searching for a convenient euphemism. "…you were well acquainted, has now left the Institute. Consequently, there is no reason to pursue the matter. Your resignation will not be needed."

James stared at the Rector in disbelief. This made no sense. The fact that his faithless mistress had left the Institute—James felt a sharp stab of pain at the thought—hardly excused his breach of the Institute's Ethics Code. Sensing that James was not convinced by his logic, Winstone quickly put an end to the discussion.

"I want you to remain on the faculty, James," he said firmly. "The photos have been confiscated and the matter is closed. No-one is to know about it."

The obvious reaction was to thank Winstone for his unusual generosity, but James couldn't bring himself to do so. He was sure that the Rector was acting from his own selfish motives, whatever they may be. So, he just nodded his acquiescence and made for his office to relay the news to the lads. Thank God, he hadn't told Veronica about his impending resignation.

———

There was no abatement to Antonietta's suffering. During the day, she was consumed by a constant pain that sapped all her vitality. Unable to face her friends, she spent the days between crying alone in her room and the consoling presence of Anna in the kitchen. She would leave the house only to run errands for the maid, just as she had when she was a child. At night, the pain became intolerable agony. She was tortured by images of James with Carolina and, even worse, Annya. The blond silhouette pursued her into her dreams, and she would awake, gasping for breath, her soul wracked by grief.

———

James arrived at Danny's on Friday evening with a magnum of champagne and a large bottle of Scotch.

"I intend to get thoroughly pissed," he announced to his friends. "A good idea," Bill agreed. "You certainly have something to celebrate." James' only reply was a non-committal grunt.

"You know, James," said Danny, opening the bottle of champagne. The cork popped out with considerable velocity and nearly decapitated Piotr. Even James was forced to laugh. Encouraged by this change of mood, Danny unwisely continued. "I think there's a connection between Antonietta's departure and your reprieve. You should find her and ask her."

James exploded. "When are you assholes going to understand that I want nothing, absolutely *nothing* to do with that worthless whore," he shouted. "Of course she's not connected with my reprieve, as you call it. How the hell could she be?"

Somewhat pacified by his outburst, James downed his champagne and held out his glass to Danny for a refill. "She dropped me because it was all a game for her, and it wasn't fun any more once the shit hit the fan."

There was a silence. Feeling ashamed of his outburst, James tried to make amends. "I can tell you one thing," he said with a rather forced grin at his friends. "This reprieve, as you call it, was Winstone's decision alone. You should've seen HB's face. He was furious."

"That's interesting, very interesting," mused Danny. "I bet you this signals the end of the HB-Winstone tandem. HB doesn't like to be crossed, and he won't forgive Winstone. We're in for fascinating times."

James left around midnight and arrived home to find the house in darkness. Veronica and the children were asleep. He poured himself a Scotch and sat down, reluctant to go to bed where he knew he would be tortured by dreams of his lost happiness and images of Antonietta with other men, perhaps even the Marquesa. It was like this every night, and in the morning he had to force himself to despise and hate her before he could face the day.

It was the end of May. The weather was glorious but Antonietta was back in her bedroom trying to stem back persistent tears. She'd driven downtown in the vain hope of alleviating her anguish by a visit to the Uffizi gallery, but once she'd parked her car, she'd been beset by such despair that she'd returned in tears to her parents' villa. Am I condemned to this misery for the rest of my life, she was asking herself despondently when there was a tap on her bedroom door. It was her uncle, the Cardinal.

"May I come in?' he asked, opening the door.

"Of course, Uncle," Antonietta replied, wiping away her tears as surreptiously as possible.

The Cardinal sat down on a chair and surveyed the desolate spectacle of his niece sitting on the bed. "Don't you think it would be better to talk about it?" he asked gently.

"About what?"

The Cardinal sighed. "About why a vivacious and fun-loving young woman has turned into a sad recluse."

Antonietta looked hard at her uncle and replied simply, "Passion."

"Ah!" The Cardinal was silent for a few moments. "I have difficulty believing that it's an unrequieted passion," he said. "No man would be fool enough to refuse you."

"It was worse than that, Uncle." Antonietta turned her tear-filled eyes upon the Cardinal. "It was an adulterous passion."

"Do you want to tell me about it?" her uncle asked.

There was no censure, just sympathy in his voice, and between bouts of sobbing Antonietta recounted how she had seen James at Mass, the passion he'd evoked in her, her frenetic attempts to combat it, her surrender, the few months of bliss she'd spent with her lover and her sacrifice to save his career. When she'd finished, she collapsed on the bed and buried her face in a pillow.

The Cardinal put a hand on his niece's shoulder in a gesture of consolation. "My dear Antonietta, I can feel your pain, but, believe me, you have made the right decision. Such relationships can only bring great unhappiness, even worse than what you are now experiencing. Believe me."

Antonietta raised her head and turned round to face her uncle.

"Nothing could be worse than what I am now suffering. *Nothing!*" she cried. "It eats at me, all the time. I don't have a second of peace. It overwhelms me, makes me sick with nausea." She clutched her breast. "Here, where my heart is, there is a pain, a dreadful pain. It's constant." She paused to catch her breath. "So don't tell me there is a greater unhappiness."

Putting her head in her hands, she exclaimed with an emotion that vibrated throughout the room. "James Markham, I wish to God I'd never set eyes on you!"

"James Markham!" her uncle exclaimed, emerging in his surprise from the shock produced by Antonietta's graphic description of her inner torment. "Did you say 'James Markham'?"

Antonietta stared at her uncle in disbelief. "You *know* him?"

"He's British?" Antonietta nodded. "Catholic?" She nodded again. "Thirty-odd?" Antonietta couldn't contain herself any longer. "Uncle, for the love of God, tell me. *Do you know him?*"

Giovanni contemplated his niece. What a terrible irony that it should be the son of his closest friend who was responsible for this devastation. The Cardinal experienced a sudden feeling of guilt, remembering the oath that he and Philip had sworn in the Augustinerkeller. It was as if God, through Messina, had avenged their profanity on his innocent niece, as if she had been brought to swear an oath on the Holy Scriptures in order to thwart their pagan oath.

"Yes, I know him," he admitted in a low voice. "He's the son of my friend, Philip Markham, the Marquis of Derwent."

Antonietta started as if galvanized by an electric shock. "James is the son of a *marquis*?"

"Well, he's the younger son," her uncle replied, "which means, if my knowledge of the English peerage is correct, that he has the courtesy title[24] of Lord James Markham."

If the Cardinal had stopped there, Antonietta could perhaps have found a way to deal with her newfound knowledge. Unwisely, he added the information that would bring her close to death. "He's very wealthy. He has shares in the family bank."

Antonietta turned white. "His family owns a bank?"

"Yes. The Carlisle and District Bank. It's the third largest in the UK."

Antonietta stood up and kissed her uncle on both cheeks. "Please leave me," she requested. Her uncle attempted to talk to her again, but she cut him off in best Palmieri style. "I've heard enough, Uncle," she said. "I wish to be alone."

Once her uncle had left the room, Antonietta abandoned herself to the bitterness that was building up within her. She had sacrificed her happiness, the passion that fed her like manna, for nothing, *nothing*! The pain, the suffering was all in vain. James didn't need his job. He wasn't an academic who had to work for his living, he was a wealthy aristocrat. Now, she understood the expensive cars, the fabulous restaurants, the trips throughout Latin America. Why, oh why hadn't he told her? Why hadn't *she* told him?

All she wanted was to run back to James, to beg his forgiveness for leaving, to reclaim her happiness. But she was bound by that terrible oath, an oath she had sworn in ignorance of her lover's real identity. Many other a woman would have used this as an excuse to renounce the oath and follow her heart, but Antonietta, despite her harsh disillusion, was too superstitious, too bound by the ancient ties of her religion, to do so. God had tricked her, and she was caught in the hell He'd created for her.

Antonietta reached up and tore down the crucifix that her mother insisted should hang over the bed. A demented rage seized hold of her and she threw the cruxifix on the floor and stamped on it. "*Porco Dio,*" she screamed, unaware of the crucifix biting deeply into her bare feet. Soon it was covered in blood and Antonietta sank down, exhausted, on her bed. She lay there, barely conscious of the heat beginning to pervade her body.

That night, the fever started.

———

James arrived in Santiago on Sunday, June 2. After checking into the hotel, he walked down Avenida O'Higgins towards the Moneda Palace, but with every step he took, recollections of his last trip to the city with Antonietta became more insistent. Before even reaching the presidential palace, he fled back to the solitude of his hotel room. The evening was long and miserable. Even the food in the hotel's excellent restaurant had a sour taste.

James spent two days in Santiago. During the day, he was taken up by his discussions at the University of Santiago, and on Monday evening he dined with his Chilean counterpart at Coco's, one of Santiago's most famous restaurants. It was a very enjoyable meal. They drank rather too much Carmenere, but at least this enabled James to fall asleep before he was troubled by images of Antonietta's unfaithfulness.

Wednesday arrived, and James boarded a plane for Buenos Aires with enormous relief. He'd spent the previous evening on his own with a large bottle of Scotch as solace for the emptiness that encompassed him. Hopefully, this evening would be spent in the company of Carolina.

---

The della Chiesa family was gathered around Antonietta's bed. Her brother Paolo had come from Rome to join the others in their vigil for the young woman, who was consumed by a fever that defied diagnosis. As he watched his daughter slip into an ever deeper coma Paolo wept at his helplessness. His brother-in-law, the Cardinal, took him aside.

"I think I know the cause of this fever," he whispered, not wishing the others to hear.

He told Paolo about Antonietta's passion for James Markham, and her decision to leave him because he was married. He didn't mention the circumstances under which she'd left or the oath to Messina.

"Her heart is broken," he concluded sadly.

Paolo was overcome by remorse. "I was too caught up in my work to notice her suffering," he moaned, looking over at his daughter. "I'd prefer her married to a divorced man a thousand times than watch her die before my eyes." He walked to the bed, took hold of Antonietta's burning hand and covered it with his tears. Caterina put her arm around him. "All we can do is pray," she murmured.

---

James entered the Hotel Plaza San Martín amidst a welter of emotions. Uppermost were his hope of finding a willing Carolina and a tentative anticipation of the sexual delights to come, but lurking as always in the background was the vision of Antonietta. The last time he'd set foot in this hotel, it was with her.

He saw Carolina immediately. She was busy dealing with two irate Americans and didn't notice him. James marveled at her composure as she explained, politely but firmly, why their room was not yet ready. Won over by her charm, the couple agreed to take another room. Carolina turned towards James.

"Dr. Markham," she said with a slightly mocking smile. "What brings you back to Buenos Aires?" If she was surprised to see him, she gave no hint of it.

James had trouble collecting himself. He'd forgotten just how attractive Carolina was, with her long blond hair, her serene blue eyes, her inviting breasts beneath the tight blouse.

"I have some discussions with the University of Buenos Aires," he said awkwardly. "And, of course, I wanted to see you."

Carolina didn't react. Instead she took James' Visa for an imprint and handed him a registration form to sign. She prepared a keypad for his room but pushed it to one side.

"It's the same room as last time," she told him. "505."

Ignoring his hand outstretched to take the keypad, Carolina motioned towards the elevators and turned to the couple behind James.

"May I help you," she asked in her slightly accented English.

James walked slowly over to the elevators. It seemed clear what Carolina was up to, but he had difficulty believing it. After all, it was many months since their brief affair, and it was unlikely that such a pretty girl had just twiddled her thumbs waiting for a man she hardly knew. Not knowing quite what to do, he stopped by the elevators, but the strange looks from other guests drove him off to study the dinner menu for the hotel's restaurant. Within seconds, he heard Carolina's mellifluous voice behind him.

"Here's your keypad, James. I finish at eleven, so be in your room."

With that, she gave him a delightful smile, full of promise, and returned to the reception desk. Somewhat overcome by the rapidity of events, James made his way to his room, the vision of Antonietta now clouded by that of Carolina.

# CHAPTER 20
## Thursday, June 6 to Friday, August 23, 2002

Whether it was the fervent prayers of her family or merely the natural course of events, Antonietta emerged from her coma. It had been nearly a week since she fell ill, and she was weak and pale. But the hearty Florentine fare cooked by Anna, the splendid wines her father fetched from the cellar and the warmth of her family soon restored a semblance of her radiant beauty.

The doctors insisted that she remain in bed for a few days. She lay there, thinking as always of James and longing for him, but there were no more tears. Perhaps she had used up her allotted amount. Sometimes she regretted surviving, at other times the idea of dying without seeing James again was too horrible to contemplate. Yet, as she reminded herself, she had sworn to renounce him for ever.

On the second day of her convalescence, the Cardinal came to see her. He was contrite. "I feel responsible for what has happened," he told her, intending to disclose the oath he'd sworn with Philip Markham. At the last moment he thought better of it. "I should never have talked to you of passion. It was irresponsible and inappropriate," he said instead.

Antonietta smiled at her uncle and shook her head. "No, Uncle, it would have happened anway." She cocked her head to one side. "On the other hand, it wasn't a good idea to tell me how rich James is. It made me realize that my sacrifice was meaningless, and I wasn't able to bear that thought. That's why I fell ill."

"Your sacrifice isn't meaningless, Antonietta," the Cardinal responded. "I know the measure of your pain, but it's better than a marriage that would have cut you off from your family and your religion and probably, in the long run, lost you James Markham's love." He took his niece's hand. "Time is a great healer."

"Not for me, Uncle. Time may accustom me to the pain of my loss, but it will never heal my sorrow."

———

It was June 10 and James' 35th birthday. Carolina had taken the day off and they had traveled by hydrofoil to Montevideo. It was warm for the southern hemisphere's midwinter, and they were able to sit on the beach.

"I prefer Montevideo," James declared. "At least it has a decent beach." Carolina was put out. "How can you say that, James. Buenos Aires is so much more exciting and, if you want a beach, you can always come here."

Carolina pouted, and James had a sudden flash of Antonietta. It had been like this all week. However much he enjoyed Carolina's easy company and the pleasures of her voluptuous body, he had difficulty repressing images of his faithless mistress, particularly in the aftermath of sex. Antonietta had always been at her most gorgeous when she was newly sated.

They had dinner at the elegant Arcadia restaurant in the Plaza Independencia. The next day they returned to Buenos Aires where Carolina started work at three in the afternoon. James wandered aimlessly around the city, visiting a number of cafes, before returning to his room to read and wait for Carolina. She arrived a little after eleven. She slipped off her clothes, removed James' dressing gown and pressed her nude body against his. They kissed with James running his hands slowly down the smooth skin of Carolina's back. He laid her on the bed, caressed and kissed her breasts, her stomach, the inside of her thighs, before exciting her sex. This time, instead of penetration, he turned her over and kneaded her buttocks. She protested weakly when he ran his fingers and tongue between them, but she let him have his way with her.

"I shall miss you," he told her after she'd turned over and was cuddled against him.

Carolina looked up, and for once her eyes lacked their normal serenity. "I wish I could believe you," she whispered, putting her hand over James' mouth to silence his reply.

They slept until noon. James quickly packed and Carolina accompanied him to the airport.

"The next time, I'll meet you and you can stay at my place," she told him. "That's if you bother to tell me you're coming."

She had the same mocking smile with which she'd greeted him a week ago. James promised to tell her. Carolina gave him a last kiss and he passed through security.

———

June was nearly over, but the passage of time had done nothing to alleviate Antonietta's sorrow. Although she no longer secluded herself in her room to weep for her lost love, the pain was not the less intense and at times unbearable. At night, when she was beset by imaginings of James with another woman, Annya in particular, she was seared by jealousy.

As yet she hadn't found the courage to take up her social life in Florence, and today was no exception. After helping Anna with the evening meal, she was at home reading some poems by Leopardi. The phone rang. It was her friend, Gino della Rovere. He invited her to a party at his apartment on the following Saturday, July 6. Instinctively Antonietta refused.

"What's got into you, Netta?" Gino inquired. Antonietta hated her name being shortened, but for some reason she accepted it from Gino. "You've become a recluse."

He's right, Antonietta thought. Moping around her parents' villa was not achieving anything. The ache she still felt in her heart told her that.

"I've been ill," she said. "If I feel better next week, I'll come."

"You'd better," Gino admonished her.

———

James arrived in his office. He greeted his secretary, Sheila, who doted on him. She handed him the day's mail.

"There's a proposal from your friend, HB, for the July 15th meeting of the Governing Council," she informed him with a grin.

James studied the proposal. Arbuthnot was suggesting that all re-appointments to the positions of Section Head and Dean should be done by way of a new competition instead of an assessment by the members of the Section concerned, or the faculty at large in the case of Deans. It was a typical HB power grab. His proposal would take re-appointments out of the hands of the Section members and the faculty and place them in a committee that he doubtless hoped to control.

James had no stomach for another fight with HB. The loss of Antonietta had drained away his energy and, in any case, his own re-appointment was four years away, assuming that he would want it. He went mechanically through the rest of the mail and was about to fetch Bill for a liquid lunch when Hamid arrived in his office. He looked pale and worried.

"Have you seen Roy's proposal?" he asked. James nodded and pointed to the document lying on his desk.

"This is aimed at me because of that Hunt business," Hamid went on. "I'm the only officer up for re-appointment next year. I'd get in on an assessment but not with a committee stacked by Arbuthnot. He'd see to that."

James sighed. He knew what was coming.

"I need your help, James," pleaded Hamid. "People listen to you. I want you to canvass against the proposal. I can't do it. It would seem too self-serving."

"I'm a Section Head," James objected. "I could be seen as self-serving as well."

"No, James." Hamid replied wistfully. "You have a solid academic reputation. You'd be reappointed whatever system they use. People know that."

The Governing Council comprised the totality of the Institute's professors, and Hamid's request would entail going round all of them, except HB's buddies. It was not an enticing prospect but at least it would prove a distraction from the constant battle to eliminate the bittersweet memories of Antonietta.

James agreed to do it.

———

Antonietta mingled with the guests at Gino's party, trying hard to avoid Rudolfo Guardini and his crowd. Unfortunately, she didn't mix in the same artsy circles as Gino and found no-one enjoyable to talk to. If she'd come to take her mind off James, the evening was a complete failure. With every person she met, her longing for him became even greater. To console herself, she drank liberally and was a little tipsy when she was accosted by the Marquesa de Avila y de la Torre.

"I heard you had returned from Canada, Countess." The smooth voice was like honey and Antonietta fell immediately under its spell. She gazed at the Marquesa's provocative dress, which left little to the imagination.

"I've been back over two months, Marquesa," she replied, her eyes fixed on the Marquesa's décolleté. The Marquesa noticed and smiled seductively.

"I think we have the most inviting décolletés at this party," she remarked and, before Antonietta could stop her, she ran a finger along the deep cut in Antonietta's dress, almost touching her nipples. "Don't you?"

Antonietta drew back from the Marquesa with a gasp, not because of the shamelessness of the gesture but at the spasm of pleasure that had traversed her body under the Marquesa's touch. Unable to answer, she just stood there in confusion, intoxicated by the subtle scent of the Marquesa's perfume.

"Netta!" It was Gino, who whisked her away from the alluring Marquesa. He led her over to the bar and poured her another glass of wine. "Be careful of the Marquesa. She's a lesbian, and you're her type."

Antonietta blushed deeply. Luckily Gino misinterpreted her reaction. "Sorry, I didn't mean to shock you, but I thought you should be warned."

At that moment Gino's lover, Antonio, arrived, and the three of them were soon engaged in amusing chit-chat. For the first time since her flight from Canada, Antonietta was doubled up with laughter as Gino described Antonio's attempts at renovating their apartment.

"We bought it for three hundred million lira," Gino recounted, "and now Antonio's renovated it, it's worth about a hundred million less."

Antonietta looked fondly at Gino's smiling face. An aristocrat like her, he had nothing of the empty snobbery of their class. It's a pity he's gay, she thought with regret.

"That's unfair, Gino," Antonio protested, sipping his expresso. "It's only worth fifty million less."

They continued to laugh together, but Antonietta found herself seeking out the Marquesa with her eyes. She was nowhere to be seen. Antonietta felt relief tinged with disappointment. After Gino and Antonio had wandered off to join other guests, she left the party.

When she arrived at her car, she was infuriated to find that two of her tires had been slashed. Now she would have to call a taxi and arrange to have the car towed to a garage. She was taking the cell phone out of her purse when a Mercedes convertible with its roof down stopped beside the immobilized Alfa Romeo. It was the Marquesa.

"Countess," she called. Antonietta walked over to the Mercedes. "I see you have a problem. Allow me to give you a ride."

The Marquesa lent over and opened the passenger door. As she did so, Antonietta caught a glimpse of her fulsome breasts, naked under the dress. She knew what the Marquesa wanted, and she suspected that her sudden appearance was linked to the fate of her car's tires. A little drunk and entrapped by the overpowering sensuality of the Marquesa, Antonietta felt the powerful stirrings of sexual desire after two months of abstinence. She climbed into the Mercedes.

They arrived at the Marquesa's villa. The door was opened by a very attractive blond girl dressed only in a skimpy nightdress.

"This is Irena, my Albanian maid," the Marquesa explained.

Antonietta was not fooled. The girl's attire and the wanton manner in which she was leering at them made it very clear that her duties in the house had little to do with housework. To Antonietta's relief, the maid left them to return to her bed. For one dreadful moment, she'd thought that the Marquesa intended her to join them. Once she was gone, the Marquesa led Antonietta up the stairs to her bedroom.

She turned on the lights. They were dimmed and basked the room in a sensuous glow. Without further ado, she slipped off her clothes and stood opposite Antonietta, eyeing her with expectation. Her large breasts had lost some of the firmness of youth and dipped a little in a pear shape, but this rendered them all the more inviting. They cried out to be fondled. Her sex was denuded and the faint odor of her sexuality electrified Antonietta. The tautness of her small nipples betrayed the force of her desire. Her lithe and trim body was a golden color with no marks of modesty. Antonietta, in thrall to the sexual magnetism of the Marquesa, imagined her sunbathing in the nude, disrupted only by bouts of lesbian pleasure with her pretty Albanian maid. She could feel the arousal between her thighs and undressed, a little self-conscious at her nudity for she hadn't been waxed since returning to Italy. But the dark hair that partially hid her sex didn't seem to bother the Marquesa, who gazed lustfully at Antonietta's naked body, taking in the full splendor of her lubricious beauty and anticipating its enjoyment. Antonietta walked towards the Marquesa and, taking the yielding flesh of the older woman's breasts into her hands, flicked her tongue over the Marquesa's nipples.

"Turn around," the Marquesa ordered.

She pressed herself against Antonietta's back and began to fondle her hardening breasts from behind. She rubbed the erect nipples between thumb and finger and Antonietta's body shivered with excitement. The Marquesa kissed her in the neck and ran a finger down her spine, continuing on between her buttocks. She caressed her intimately with the lightest of touches. Antonietta squirmed, her sex wet and avid for gratification.

"You have to earn your pleasure," the Marquesa whispered and lay down on the bed, her legs opened.

Beside herself with lust, Antonietta devoured the Marquesa's voluptuous breasts and ran her tongue over the smooth skin of her stomach and belly before using it to savor and arouse her bare sex. Soon the Marquesa was writhing and crying out in ecstasy. Antonietta made her turn over and teased her, using both tongue and fingers, until her release finally came.

"Now it's your turn," the Marquesa told Antonietta, beginning to fondle the young woman's breasts and lick her nipples.

Antonietta abandoned her body to the Marquesa's licentious caresses with groans of sexual bliss, her longing for James temporarily stilled. She allowed the most indecent intimacies and reveled in the spasms of delight this gave her. Her desire mounted with every lascivious contact until she could contain herself no longer. A surge of pleasure ripped through her body that eclipsed all thoughts of her miserable plight and left her panting.

Physically sated, the two women lay together, naked, relishing the erogenous perfection of each other's body. When their lust was rekindled, the Marquesa introduced Antonietta to pratices she had never known before. They revolted her, but the revulsion only served to arouse her libido all the more and she became insatiable. Ultimately both women were overcome by exhaustion and fell asleep.

Antonietta woke first in the morning. She felt used and degraded. She looked across at the woman who had seduced her so completely. But the Marquesa was not to blame. Antonietta had known from the instant she stepped into the Marquesa's car what awaited her. She had wanted to be in the Marquesa's bed, partly out of sexual desire and partly in order to drown her grief in carnal rapture. She'd succeeded but now, after the perversions of the night, she felt not only the anguish of loss but also that of guilt. She no longer deserved James.

Resolving never to see the Marquesa again, Antonietta fled from the villa. Once she was well clear, she called for a taxi. She went straight to Mass, not at the Basilica but at Santa Maria Novella. She didn't want her family to see her face, which probably still bore the marks of her perverse enjoyment.

On Monday, the Marquesa called Antonietta at her parents' house. Antonietta was petrified and begged the Marquesa not to call her at home. She would never see her again, she told the Marquesa. She was not a lesbian, and she'd been drunk on Saturday night.

Yet, the Marquesa continued to exercise a powerful attraction for Antonietta, and by Friday she was thinking with regret of the sexual joys she'd renounced. She decided that she needed a man, otherwise she would succumb anew to the lure of the Marquesa. She called her old friends from university days, Alessa and Paulina, and arranged to meet them the next evening at Fiasco's[25].

———

James spent the week before the meeting of the Governing Council on July 15 discreetly canvassing against Arbuthnot's proposal. He had divided the faculty into three groups.

The first was those professors who could be relied upon to follow James' lead and oppose HB. Apart from Bill, Piotr and Danny, this comprised James' new ally Hamid Khan, Christine Desmoulins and Klaus Berger from his own Section, and Anne-Marie Legrand and Claudio Pettroni from LAC. This made nine certain votes, together with his own, out of a total of forty-seven.

The second group was made up of those professors allied to HB or Winstone. These were Len Flint, Ed Tocheniuk and Fred Gowling from FEB, Ed Williams and Nathan Golberg from James' Section, and Brian Wilkins, Georges Campeau and Emily Wright from LAC. Of these, only Gowling, Flint, Campeau and possibly Wilkins were sure allies of HB. The others were closer to Winstone. Counting HB, this group amounted to nine professors as well.

The rest of the faculty could be considered neutral, although James hoped for a positive response from Saleema Nadjani, Elliot Hunt, Ilse Bromhoeffer and perhaps also Pierre Forget. However, Danny had volunteered to canvas the last two.

After firming up the support of the first group, James turned his attention to the neutral members of the Council. It was a delicate business as he didn't want to appear vindictive against HB. This could prove counter-productive. Instead he would stress the more democratic nature of the present approach, which gave all interested professors a say in the appointment. As it turned out, his task was much easier than he'd feared. Danny had been right. The appointment of Flint to Bill's tenure committee had shocked and angered the silent majority, and there was a groundswell of opposition to any measure that would increase HB's power. There was also a simmering dissatisfaction with Winstone, partly because of his association with HB and partly because of lack of direction and erratic hiring practices. James reacted non-committally to these criticisms, Despite his present sense of futility, he still had vague thoughts of the Rectorship and it was not wise to be seen encouraging dissatisfaction with Winstone for his own ends.

By Thursday, James had secured enough votes to defeat HB's proposal handily, and Danny reported that both Ilse and Pierre Forget would also vote against it. On Friday, Ed Williams, whom James had not even bothered canvassing, stopped him in the Administration Building.

"I don't think we should let HB get too big for his boots," he remarked.

"Does that mean you're against his proposal," James asked.

Williams nodded and walked on. James watched him go and smiled. If this defection meant that Winstone's group had broken with HB, the Senior Dean was set for a humiliation. If only Antonietta were here to share in it, he couldn't help thinking, before chasing away the thought.

———

Antonietta arrived at Fiasco's. When she entered the smoke-filled interior, a tremor went through her. This was after all the bar James had frequented as a student, and doubtless in the company of his Spanish girlfriend. Jealousy and longing overcame her, and she was tempted to leave. Only the sight of Alessa waving madly from across the room and the merry circle of students around her changed Antonietta's mind. She forced herself to stay. After all, she'd come here to find an antidote to the lesbian enticements of the Marquesa.

Alessa and Paulina greeted her with much affection and heaped reproaches on her for not contacting them before. Luckily she didn't have to answer, as immediately she sat down, a tall, dark male student leaned over to her.

"So, you're the beautiful Countess della Chiesa," he said with evident admiration.

Antonietta started involuntarily at his accent. The student was obviously British. "I don't know about the 'beautiful'," she replied, returning the young man's smile. "And I'm plain Antonietta, not Countess della Chiesa."

"Fair enough," the student responded. He grinned at Antonietta. "I'm David Bannerman-Smith, but you can call me just plain David."

They drank and talked into the early hours. The infectious gaiety of the company and a rather too liberal indulgence in the bar's rather tart house wine distracted Antonietta from her heatbreak, and she flirted outrageously with David. He'd worked for an investment bank in London, and now he was studying for his doctorate in economics at the European University Institute. He had a typical British sense of humor and, together with his rugged dark looks, he reminded her of James.

He took her back to his small studio in Fiesole. She let him kiss her, but she had to fight back memories of James and she could feel herself trembling. It has to happen, she told herself, and almost in a trance she let him undress her. When he started to caress her breasts, she wanted to cry out for him to stop. He took off his clothes and led her to the bed. Her mind was full of the last time she and James had made love. She couldn't bring herself to take David into her mouth. Instead she caressed him until he was ready to take her. She feigned her climax.

It was so strange to sleep with a man other than James. She lay there, weighed down by nostalgia. Fortunately, David was already asleep. If she was with another man, she reflected, then James was probably with another woman. A vision of a triumphant Annya tortured her until, worn out by her suffering, she fell asleep in her turn.

The next morning David woke her with a cup of expresso. She contemplated the man who had now taken James' place, in bed if not in her heart. He was handsome enough, but Antonietta doubted he was a particularly good lover. Certainly if he didn't show any disappointment with her pitiful performance of last night, he didn't expect much. That was just as well. It would be a long time before she'd be able to abandon herself to a man again.

David wanted Antonietta to stay, but she had to meet her family for Mass and celebrate her 25th birthday with them afterwards. Her new lover wished her a happy birthday and kissed her before she left.

————

Once Winstone had effected his habitual royal entry, the Governing Council convened. The Rector called on Arbuthnot to present his proposal. The Senior Dean, who was unusually tense, went on about uniform standards and the good of the whole Institute. In his view, these essential factors in any re-appointment would be better safeguarded by a faculty committee than an assessment by individual professors. It was not a particularly convincing performance, but his allies, Fred Gowling and Georges Campeau, jumped in to give the proposal their enthusiastic support without, however, advancing any new arguments in favor of it. There was an ominous silence after they had finished.

"Any other comments?" Winstone inquired and immediately gave the floor to Klaus Berger, whom he must have known was opposed to the proposal. Klaus, a mild-mannered Austrian who had been passed over as Chair of LIR in favor of James, demolished HB's arguments.

"It boils down to trusting an impersonal committee, on which the Senior

Dean no doubt wishes to sit as an *ex officio* member, or trusting the judgment of those who actually serve under the Section Head or Dean in question," he concluded.

Berger was followed by an avalanche of criticism of the proposal. Brian Wilkins attempted in vain to defend it but was shot down by Ed Williams.

"HB's lost the Rector," Danny whispered to James.

He had indeed for, when the secret ballots were counted, only five professors were in favor.

That evening at Danny's, the discussion centered on the rift between Winstone and HB.

"As I told you," James was saying, "it's because Winstone stopped the ethics proceeding against me. He deprived HB of his vengeance, and HB hasn't forgiven him"

"I still think Antonietta had something to do with that," Danny insisted. "There has to be some explanation for her leaving."

"Yes, there goddam well is," James roared. "She's a faithless whore."

"OK, James." Bill placed his hand on his friend's shoulder. "You're probably right, but there's no need to yell at Danny."

James glowered and took a large gulp of whisky. The conversation turned to the mid-term review of the Rector, which was due in January of next year.

"How does it work?" enquired Piotr.

"There's a committee consisting of a representative elected by each Section and one by the faculty at large," Danny replied. "They prepare a report."

They were interrupted by the arrival of Bernadette, who was bursting with her news. "You know that football captain fellow," she told them. They all nodded except James. "Well, I saw him kissing some dark-haired girl."

Bill whistled. "That must be Françoise. If so, it means he's dumped Petra and gone back to her."

Danny and Piotr smiled at each other. James looked into space.

———

On the Wednesday after their first night together, David invited Antonietta to the cinema. She agreed to go, more out of resignation tinged with nervousness than enthusiasm. She needed a man, and David was as good a choice as any other. She resolved to put James out of her mind when they made love that night and try to find some pleasure in it.

Once the film was over and they were back in David's studio, Antonietta made him lie on the bed while she stripped in front of him. He drew her down onto the bed and began to caress her nude body. Trying desperately to suppress memories of James, Antonietta returned his kisses and began to undress him. Feeling like a whore, she took him into her mouth and willed herself to pleasure him. Afterwards he seemed at a loss what to do, so Antonietta pushed his head down her body for him to satisfy her. Her body ached for James but her sexual need was such that she came plentifully.

The next morning David suggested that Antonietta move in with him. She refused categorically. The studio was too small for two, and in any case she wished to keep her independence. David was disappointed but accepted her refusal with good humor. They agreed that Antonietta would spend Friday and Saturday nights at the studio, and perhaps other nights if an evening at Fiasco's left her unfit to drive.

Apart from their nights together, the two met frequently and gradually Antonietta accustomed herself to sex with David. It was rather pedestrian, but this suited her. She had no desire to repeat with him the extravagances of her sex life with James. However, though David calmed Antonietta's sexual frustration, he couldn't heal the ache in her heart. The worst time was after their lovemaking when David was asleep. Then, there was no rampart against the jealousy and pain that ravaged her.

———

It was a beautiful August day when James arrived in Buenos Aires. There was not a cloud in the sky, and it was a pleasant fifteen degrees Celsius. He had kept his word to Carolina and she would be waiting for him. He felt a thrill of expectation but also a little guilt. He should have stopped over in Mexico to settle some problems with ITAM[26] in Mexico City, but the pull of Carolina had been too strong. It wasn't only that he desired her. He found in her arms some way to fill the terrible void left by Antonietta.

James passed through customs. As always the Argentinean officials were charming, and he asked himself what evil genie had led their two countries into war. The question became even more pertinent when he glimpsed Carolina in the crowd greeting the flight. She was dressed in an elegant beige jacket and skirt, and she was smiling at him from a distance with that artless serenity that was so entrancing. She ran up and kissed him.

"I'm not working until Monday," she informed him.

They took a taxi to Carolina's apartment, which was situated in an upscale residential part of the Recoleta and decorated simply but with taste. James was surprised.

"How can you afford it?" he asked.

"It's difficult," Carolina admitted, "but I was brought up in a poor part of Buenos Aires, and I always swore that one day I would live in the best part of the Recoleta." She grinned at James. "Besides, it's near to work when I need some money at the end of the month."

James cringed and took Carolina into his arms. "Is that true, or are you just saying it to make me jealous."

"Both," Carolina replied, laughing at the shocked expression on James' face. "I told you before that I do that."

"I didn't really believe you."

Carolina laughed again and opened a bottle of wine. "Don't worry," she said, "it's not the end of the month yet."

James shook his head. "What am I going to do with you?"

Carolina pulled him to her and gazed up at him with her piercing blue eyes. "Drink some wine and then make love to me."

———

Antonietta was moving into her new apartment, which was near to her old one in the Borgo Ognissanti. She liked the Santa Maria Novella district with its boutiques and the eponymous Dominican basilica where she would go to hear Mass and occasionally to pray. The painters were still putting the final touches to the redecoration of the apartment. She should have waited for them to finish, but tomorrow was the Feast of the Assumption and she would be busy with her family.

It would be a relief to be on her own without having to make up stories to explain her nights with David. She had taken the precaution of not installing a phone line. She would rely on her cell so that her mother wouldn't know where she spent her nights. David was helping, and she sensed that he wanted to move in with her. There was plenty of room for the two of them, but she was not prepared to commit herself. She enjoyed his company but her heart still belonged to James. Although she knew it was impossible, she still cherished deep down a frail hope that one day she might be reunited with him.

———

After a weekend walking around the Recoleta with Carolina, making love

253

to her, spending tranquil moments in cafés under the charm of her radiant personality and demure beauty, James came rather brutally down to earth on Monday. So that they could spend the evenings together, Carolina had arranged to work from eight to four. This meant that James was left to his own devices for most of the day, and the black thoughts that Carolina was able to disperse came back with full force to haunt him. Try as he might to banish Antonietta from his mind, one thought kept pursuing him. If he was with Carolina, who was enjoying Anotonietta's gorgeous but faithless body?

If Carolina noticed James' bouts of introspection, she didn't allow them to disturb her. She had an inner serenity that fascinated but also frustrated James. She satisfied all his physical desires and her company was like silk, soft and yielding, but there was nothing to latch on to. It was not that she lacked substance, it was finding it that was difficult. James had the strong impression that she didn't want to reveal herself. Any time he became more serious, Carolina would divert the conversation with an enigmatic smile.

It was only when it came time to part that Carolina's façade—if that is what it was—slipped a little. She kissed James with unusual emotion.

"I'm spending the last two weeks of November in a cousin's apartment in Montevideo," she told him. "Do you want to join me?" Surprised by the invitation, James didn't answer at first, so Carolina added with a grin. "As you know, there's a beach in Montevideo."

James laughed, remembering her indignation at his preference for the Uruguayan capital. "Yes," he said. "I'm not teaching this term, and I'd love to come."

Antonietta arrived at David's studio for her Friday sleepover around five. He greeted her with a kiss and a broad grin. Before she could ask the reason, he held up two tickets.

"We're going to a Laura Pausini concert tonight," he told her proudly. Antonietta felt her body tense up and returned David's kiss longer than usual so she could hide her distress.

"I thought you'd be pleased," he said.

The concert was sheer agony for Antonietta. Every song reminded her of James, of the time she had longed for him in the cottage, of their moments of bliss together. David noticed that she was flushed. She assured him it was just the heat of the concert hall. The interval came and Antonietta restored her composure with a glass of wine. It didn't avail her as the next song was the one she'd always associated with the pain of losing James, even before she'd renounced him. No sooner had Laura Pausini intoned the first words of *come se non fosse stato mai amore* than Antonietta broke down. Bursting into tears, she rushed from the hall, followed by an anxious David.

"Just drive me home to my apartment," she implored.

Neither of them spoke on the way. Once they arrived at the apartment, Antonietta apologized and, although all she wanted was to be alone, asked David to come in. After all, he was entitled to an explanation. But he had already guessed. "Who was he?" he asked Antonietta.

"He was a man I met in Canada. I fell desperately in love with him, but he was married. So, we broke up." It all sounded so banal that Antonietta cried out, "I love him still, I'll *always* love him."

David put his arm around her. "You'll get over it in time," he said without any rancor.

Antonietta nodded, but she knew in her heart this was not so.

# CHAPTER 21

## Monday, September 9, 2002, to Friday, January 24, 2003

It was the beginning of term at NIIS. The students were milling around and the professors were putting the finishing touches to their lecture notes. James was busying himself with the administrative details that accompany every new academic year, but it was a half-hearted effort. Try as he might to put them aside, he was dominated by memories of last year.

On Tuesday, a notice came from the Rector's Office announcing that candidates for the Rector's midterm review committee had to be declared by Friday, September 27 and that the election would take place on Friday, October 18. James called Danny and they agreed there should be council of war at Danny's that evening. It was essential to prevent the committee falling under the control of faculty close to Winstone.

James welcomed the distraction provided by the upcoming campaign. The first step was to secure suitable candidates. Bill wanted to stand but Danny advised against it.

"Anyone would think I have the plague," Bill complained.

Danny gave him a pat on the back to console him. "None of us must stand," he explained. "The committee must be seen as completely neutral. We're too associated with James, who is perceived as a possible replacement for Winstone."

Over the next two weeks, Danny and James discreetly sought out professors who could be relied upon to produce an honest report, which both were sure would be damning for Winstone. By the time September 27 came along, they had found Claudio Pettroni to stand against the ubiquitous Brian Wilkins for LAC, Jason Levy against Ed Tocheniuk for FEB and Klaus Berger against Ed Williams for LIR. Christine Desmoulins had initially agreed to stand as candidate for the faculty at large but pulled out at the last moment. This wasn't a real problem as the other candidate was Bill Wachowitz, a genial

American who taught international business in FEB and who had no particular connection with Winstone or HB. However, on Danny's prompting, Saleema Nadjani took Christine's place.

Each of the candidates held a number of meetings to feel the pulse of the faculty and to explain their approach. All stressed the need for an objective and fair review, but Williams and Tocheniuk also argued against conducting a witchhunt. This was a sign that the Rector was nervous about the review. James and Danny were confident that, given the prevailing feeling in the Institute, their candidates would be elected, and this is what happened. A celebration was convened at Danny's for the Saturday after the election.

———

Antonietta started her doctorate in economics at the University of Florence on Monday, October 7. David had tried to persuade her to enroll at the European University, but the specter of James loomed too large. She also continued to resist his none too subtle hints that he should move in with her. She appreciated his sense of humor and intelligence, but there was only room in her heart for James. Besides, David was a mediocre lover and, in her sexual frustration, she now yearned for the carnal excesses of her time with James and was constantly tempted to return to the Marquesa's bed. There was a strong element of resignation in her relationship with David. He was not ideal, but what man, apart from James, would ever be?

———

"It's unlike Bill to be late," remarked Danny as they waited for him to celebrate their success at the elections. "He normally can't wait to get into the sauce."

Bill's car pulled up outside Danny's house. To everyone's surprise, Petra emerged from it with Bill. Once in the house, they were harassed by questions and admitted that they were, as students put it, "an item." While the others were eloquent in their congratulations for this happy development, James had mixed feelings. He was glad for Bill, but the radiant Petra both brought home the emptiness of his own life without Antonietta and stirred his jealousy. Proceeding from an image of Antonietta in bed with Petra, he conjured up her luscious body being enjoyed by the Marquesa. He left early.

———

Inevitably, Antonietta's mother came to hear of her liaison with David. One of her women friends had seen the two walking around Florence holding hands.

"Who is he?" Caterina inquired of her daughter.

"He's doing his doctorate in economics at the European University," Antonietta replied. "He's British."

"I suppose he's just another nobody," Caterina commented acidly.

It was unlike Antonietta to show anger towards her parents but now she snapped, worn out by the constant pain of missing James and the effort to find some meaning to her relationship with David.

"He may be a nobody to you, Mother," she shouted, "but he's the man I love and you will learn to mind your own business."

Outraged by Antonietta's defiance, Caterina slapped her. "How dare you speak to me like that," she cried furiously. Her face burning, Antonietta gave her mother a look of such ferocity that Caterina cringed. She then turned on her heels and stalked off without a further word.

Once she was back in her apartment, Antonietta wept from regret and shame. Why on earth had she behaved so badly? Was it really worth provoking a rift with her mother for a man she didn't love, whatever she may have said in anger? Would this nightmare, this kaleidoscope of despair and longing never end? She thought of breaking up with David, but what would that achieve? She even felt guilty at the thought. He was so considerate and she enjoyed his company. It was not his fault that she couldn't put her passion for James behind her, and perhaps not his fault either that she was sexually frustrated. As James had once told her, only partly in jest, she was oversexed.

———

James spent November 13 and 14 in Mexico City finally resolving the problems with ITAM. He arrived late afternoon on Saturday in Buenos Aires to be met by Carolina. The beginning of term with its reminiscences of last year and the anniversary of his first night with Antonietta had weighed upon him, and he was happy to find solace in Carolina's bed. She accommodated and often anticipated his desires and lent her body willingly to any immodest use he wished to make of it. Her conversation was light without being frivolous, her temper even without boring him, her disposition sunny but not without a concealed depth.

On Monday they traveled by boat to Montevideo. The apartment in which they stayed looked over the ocean—or more correctly, the estuary of the River Plate. They relaxed on the beach, swam in the warm sea, ate too much and laughed a lot. They made love until the early hours. Carolina might lack the passion of Antonietta but she knew how to satisfy a man. Once, after draining James expertly of all lust, she taunted him. "I'm a professional, you know," she whispered with her mocking smile.

Yet, despite the pleasures Carolina procured him, James was not free of Antonietta. As he lay on the beach, he thought of Punta del Este and Antonietta's Brazilian bikini. At times he found himself aching for the sultry volatility of his raven-haired former mistress. Watching Carolina twist and turn in bed as he serviced her, he was often beset by jealousy. To whose indecent touch was Antonietta now consigning her lubricious body?

November ended and it was time to return to Buenos Aires. James spent one last night with Carolina and left on Sunday, December 1 for Montreal. He arrived the next day to the habitual cool welcome from Veronica. On Tuesday, he spent the day catching up with administrative matters, apart from lunch with Bill.

"Well, did you roger her?" Bill asked with a prurient grin.

"We enjoyed ourselves," James replied, not wishing to go into detail. He winced as Bill slapped him on the back. He really didn't go for this North American bonhomie.

"Let's hope she's cured you of Antonietta."

"Don't mention that goddam woman." James raised his voice, but his anger was directed at himself not Bill. Two weeks with Carolina should have cured him, but it hadn't.

James returned home to find Veronica waiting for him with four boarding cards in her hands.

"Who is Carolina Sanchez," she demanded to know, "and what were you doing spending two weeks in Montevideo with her?"

James was caught. Stupidly, he had left all four boarding cards in his jacket and it was impossible to deny that he had traveled both to and from Montevideo with Carolina. He was tired and dispirited and incapable of dreaming up a story.

"I was having an affair with her," he replied, astonished by his own candor.

Veronica turned white with rage. She walked around the room in circles and then turned to face James. "I will *not* live with a sinner," she expostulated. "I am a Benedictine oblate[27], and I'm committed to living a Christian family life. How can I do that with a man who mocks the sacrament of marriage?"

James looked at his wife in amazement. This was the first he'd heard of her being an oblate, but it explained her excessive religiosity and disdain for sex.

He also felt repulsion. The pursed lips, the fanatic gleam in her eyes, the coldness of her whole bearing, how to God had he put up with her for so long? Without a word, he went upstairs and fetched his suitcases, which were still packed.

"I'm leaving," he told Veronica. "I expect to see the kids every other weekend. Any problems, and you'll hear from a lawyer."

He drove off to Bill's place.

———

David left Florence for England on Monday, December 16 to spend Christmas with his family. Depressed and vulnerable, Antonietta feared she would prove an easy victim for the Marquesa's erotic charms, so she decided to spend Christmas at her parents' villa in Fiesole. Despite the presence of Paolo and Monica for part of the time, it was a miserable experience. Her mother had not forgiven her for the episode over David or indeed for her relationship with him, and she was distant and cold. Her father tried to make up for her mother and plied her with good Italian wine, but Antonietta's heart was not in it. She longed for James and at times the pain was so unbearable that she considered taking a plane to Canada to see him. But the oath held her back. It was not so much religious conviction as a superstitious fear of divine wrath if she broke it.

———

On the Wednesday after the day he separated from Veronica, James came back to the house to pick up some things. Veronica greeted him with a look of cold disdain and didn't say a word, much to James' relief. Most of the time he was there, she spent praying. James wondered idly what she was praying about. That he would convert from his wicked ways? More likely that he would be struck down by lightning and consigned to hell for all eternity.

He established himself in one of the bedrooms of Bill's house. Bill was sympathetic about his break with Veronica, in fact he was enthusiastic. "You should've done it a long time ago," he told James.

He was more than willing to help James out, but Petra was now living with him and James felt awkward with their *ménage à trois*. He also had a lingering jealousy of Petra, and her presence recalled Antonietta's sexual promiscuity. What a whore, he told himself. The contempt didn't resist the night when he was assailed by images of Antonietta in all her loveliness. The next week he started to look for his own apartment. He found one in Ste. Adèle, not far from

Bill's. That would be convenient after an evening's over-indulgence.

The children spent the weekend of December 14 with him at Bill's. Susanna asked him when he was coming home and went very quiet when James gave an evasive reply. Peter said nothing. James wasn't sure what Veronica had told the children, and he was ill at ease with them. He felt relieved, and at the same time guilty, when the time came to drive them back to Prévost.

To take his mind off his unhappy personal situation, James spent much of the next week buying furniture and other paraphernalia for the apartment. He moved in on Friday, December 20 and left the next day to spend Christmas with his parents in England.

———

The Saturday after Christmas was the Lescia's party. Antonietta remembered how last year she had gone to take her mind off James. She would do the same this year, except that now he would not be waiting for her in Toronto on her return to Canada. Her parents were not going. Her mother was in Rome and her father was attending a conference somewhere in Germany.

Antonietta was apprehensive about meeting the Marquesa at the party, but once she saw her, a thrill of excitement ran through her. The Marquesa was dressed, as always, in such a way as to exhibit all the enticements of her body, and Antonietta felt a sexual attraction towards her that she couldn't suppress. Noticing her stare, the Marquesa came over to her. "Do you want to come back to the villa after the party?" she asked, her eyes undressing Antonietta as she spoke.

A feeling of revolt, mixed with carnal desire, came over Antonietta. She had renounced the man she loved, she suffered every day from this renunciation and the present man in her life didn't satisfy her. The promise of perverted bliss that would blot out her misery seduced her. She nodded and walked away, not wanting people to notice her talking so intimately with the Marquesa.

———

James was happy to be in England. Here at least was somewhere that didn't remind him of Antonietta, and the hurly-burly of sisters and their offspring and the joys of English country pubs provided ample distraction during the day. The night was a different matter, but by now James was becoming resigned to the torment of his nocturnal reminiscences. He went for walks with his father and they discussed sheep-rearing, which was his father's new hobby. It was far from the life of high finance and politics in which he had spent his whole adult life, and James envied him the calm and peace he'd found through his involvement with the family farm

His mother was a less restful experience. She was horrified at his separation and urged him constantly to reconcile with Veronica. "Think of your children," she kept telling him. It was difficult to explain to his mother that, if reconciliation with Veronica meant living up to his marriage vows, he wanted none of it. So, he just promised to think about it in the vain hope that his mother would drop the topic. She didn't, so James decided to take up his brother's invitation to spend New Year's Eve with him and his family in London.

———

Antonietta followed the Marquesa to her villa. There was, thankfully, no sign of the maid. Without even waiting until they were in the bedroom, the Marquesa pulled down Antonietta's dress, detached her bra and began to fondle her breasts. Antonietta abandoned herself, and soon she was naked on the sofa, luxuriating in the expert ministrations of the Marquesa's fingers and tongue. She let herself be turned over and satisfied in a way that obliterated all else but her sexual enjoyment. Still full of lust, she stripped the Marquesa in her turn and enjoyed and pleasured her voluptuous body. Afterwards, they mounted the stairs to continue their unbridled sexual activity in bed.

The next morning, Antonietta felt the usual pangs of guilt and disgust at the unnatural delights in which she had revelled, but she let herself be persuaded to stay for breakfast before leaving for Sunday Mass. Of course, she never went to Mass. She arrived back at her apartment in the early evening and showered, as if to purify herself. She looked at her naked body in the mirror and was ashamed at the use to which she had put it.

What am I becoming? she asked herself in alarm and resolved yet again to resist the tempting pleasures offered with such dissolute skill by the Marquesa. It was better to suffer pain and longing than allow herself to become so debauched. What would James say if he knew? This dreadful thought gave her a feeling of strength, and she went to Santa Maria Novella to pray that it would not desert her.

———

New Year's Eve was not particularly enjoyable for James. His brother was as pompous as ever and only talked about the bank and his success at running it. Worse still, he was on a diet and drank only Perrier water, while his wife had never drunk alcohol. James indulged his vice but found it difficult to enjoy himself in such circumstances. He was immensely relieved when the time came to return to Canada.

He arrived Thursday afternoon on January 2 and immediately went to pick up his children. They were happy to see him and show off all their Christmas presents. They spent an enjoyable few days in James' new apartment. On Friday and Saturday evening, Danny and Bernadette and Bill and Petra came round for drinks. On Saturday, Piotr managed to get away from home for a few hours as well. Their good-humored intemperance was a pleasant change from the austerity of his brother's house.

James took the children back to Prévost on Sunday evening. Before they arrived, they plucked up the courage to complain about their mother. She was becoming ever more religious and praying the rosary every day. This worried James and decided him to make an attempt at reconciliation with Veronica for their sakes. She refused. First, he had to confess his sins publicly and mend his ways.

"Perhaps you'd like some monks to whip me like they did with Henry II[28]?" he suggested sardonically.

Veronica glared at him. "You are a sinner and a blasphemer. I cannot live with you because I know you are incapable of changing. You are damned in my eyes."

As James left the house, he had the definite impression of a whiff of sulphur in the air.

———

Antonietta met David at the airport on December 31 and drove him back to her apartment. They made love very conventionally, but she was glad to feel a man's body next to her. It made her seem more normal. She got ready for the evening's celebration and drove David to his studio for him to prepare himself. They met Alessa and Paulina and other friends at Fiasco's and drank and danced until the early hours. For once, Antonietta enjoyed herself, exhilarated by the festive atmosphere.

The sense of exhilaration did not last. Within a few days, the suffering returned and also her sense of sexual frustration. For all his excellent qualities, David neither fulfilled the yearning in her heart nor her physical desires. She longed for James and was tempted again by the Marquesa. It didn't help that she kept calling.

———

James' life as a batchelor began in earnest once he returned from England and was living in his own apartment. Try as he might, he didn't enjoy it. He was alone too often and prey to jealousy and a love he was desperately trying to turn into hate. During the day, he was partly successful although his moodiness told of the inner struggle he was going through. To distract himself more than out of lust, he traveled some evenings to Montreal to enjoy callgirls in a hotel room. At least he forgot his pain temporarily in the spells of pleasure these hookers procured him.

On January 14, the midterm review of the Rector was released. It was very critical, citing in particular poor financial management and dubious appointments of friends with poor qualifications. The review singled out Ed Tocheniuk, Nathan Goldberg, Ed Williams and Emily Wright. The Rector was also criticized for lack of direction and a poor working relationship with the Section Heads. The appointment of a Senior Dean, which had not been necessary, contributed greatly to this poor working relationship. As he read the report, James felt a great sense of satisfaction. If he had written it himself, he couldn't have done a better job. Winstone was finished.

Two days later, a group of professors came to see him. Winstone had to go, they told him. James reacted cautiously. He couldn't afford to be seen as a prime mover in getting rid of Winstone if he wanted to replace him. He told the group that he was not prepared to act without consulting the Deans and other Section Heads. Once his colleagues had left, he called Danny, who agreed to play the role of front man.

Over the next few days Danny canvassed opinion in the faculty. With the obvious exception of Winstone's cronies, there was a strong feeling that the Rector should resign. At no time did Danny mention James as a possible replacement. "One thing at a time," he told an impatient Bill Leaman.

It was not clear where HB now stood, but he had at most four supporters, so this was not a problem. What was strange was Winstone's inertia. He seemed to be doing nothing to save his position.

The Deans and Section Heads met, at Danny's invitation, on Tuesday, January 21. All except HB agreed that Winstone should go. HB argued that he should be given a second chance but on very strict terms. He was obviously afraid that James might take over and doubtless wanted the strict terms to include more power for the Senior Dean. The others, including Forget who was normally inclined to compromise, were having none of it. "Enough is enough," he declared with uncharacteristic firmness.

All but HB signed a letter to Winstone inviting him to resign for the good of the Institute. As the meeting broke up, HB couldn't resist a last show of defiance. "Your letter will mean nothing without the Senior Dean's signature," he growled.

Danny took the letter to the Rectorate after the meeting. Eleanor told him that HB had already been there and booked an appointment to see the Rector first thing on the morrow. It was clearly a last minute attempt to stiffen Winstone's resolve. He might despise him, but HB knew that his influence would disappear if ever Winstone were replaced by James. No longer so confident that the letter would have the desired result, Danny joined the lads for a drink at James' apartment. The atmosphere was morose.

It needn't have been. Winstone had already made his decision and by the time HB arrived for his meeting, a letter was already circulating to the Deans and Section Heads to the effect that the Rector was resigning as from July 1, 2003. Very soon, a number of professors, including Hamid, Ilse and Forget, were urging James to stand for election as Rector. Even Elliot Hunt came to see him and offer his services in any campaign.

That Friday, there was an excited evening at Danny's. Victory now seemed so near. "It depends to some extent on whether it's an internal or external process," Danny commented. "If it's internal, James should be shoo-in."

There were many presumptious toasts to the new Rector, and James was quite drunk when he arrived at his apartment. Mercifully, he fell asleep immediately and was spared his usual nocturnal torments. However, when he woke up the next morning, he remonstrated with himself. You won't get to be Rector if you're picked up for drunk driving, he told himself. He resolved to restrict his nights of excess to those occasions when he was at home or could walk from Bill's. It was stupid to blow it now he was so near. But near what? Not happiness, that was certain, but at least power.

# CHAPTER 22
## Saturday, February 8 to Tuesday, March 11, 2003

The second week in February is a time when there are no classes at the European University. Many of the students take advantage of this respite to go skiing, and David was no exception. Antonietta didn't accompany him. She hated skiing and, in any case, she'd committed herself to attending Gino della Rovere's Valentine's Day party on the Friday of that week. She knew the Marquesa would be there and, sexually frustrated and emotionally distraught, she welcomed the prospect of the erotic delights of her bed.

The Marquesa was involved with other guests when Antonietta arrived. Deliberately, she drank a lot to drown any qualms about what she was planning. By the time the Marquesa noticed her, she was quite drunk and, with a provocative smile, the Marquesa offered her a ride. Antonietta was about to accept when she heard a familiar voice.

"Antonietta, how lovely to see you!" It was Philippe de Pothiers.

"Philippe! What are you doing here?"

In her surprise and pleasure at this unexpected reunion, Antonietta completely forgot about the Marquesa.

"I've spending some time at the Careggi clinic," he explained. "I'm studying some new techniques your father has introduced." Philippe couldn't suppress a wicked smile, which Antonietta returned.

"Antonietta, come on," the Marquesa interjected. "We have to go."

Philippe put his arm around Antonietta in a protective gesture. "The Countess and I are old friends," he told the Marquesa. "Please allow us the privilege of talking a little together."

With a heinous look at Philippe, the Marquesa stalked off. Antonietta watched her go. The spell was broken, and she realized with horror what she had been about to do.

"I'm drunk, Philippe," she said. "Please take me home." She turned the full force of her beautiful eyes on her one-time lover. "Or anywhere else you wish." Philippe drove to Antonietta's apartment. She asked him in and slipped off her dress. "I want you to make love to me," she said without ceremony.

Philippe removed the rest of Antonietta's clothing and caressed her nude body. She cried out in surprise when he picked her up and carried her into the bedroom. She lay on the bed, naked, watching him undress. What happened next both astonished and enchanted her. It was no longer the rather pedestrian lover of the Chateau Frontenac, but a dissolute rake who wrang from her screams of ecstasy.

Panting and bathed in perspiration, Antonietta broke off their embrace. "How you've changed, Philippe," she gasped.

Philippe laughed. "After our last bout, I realized my inadequacy, so I found a young mistress in Paris to give me some further education."

Antonietta was highly amused. "Well, she was a good teacher," she said. "I'm very impressed."

Philippe gazed into Antonietta's eyes and, behind the amusement, he detected her deep sadness. "Do you want to tell me about it," he asked. "And why you were about to abandon yourself to that lesbian slut."

Fighting back her tears, Antonietta recounted the whole sad story, including her brief encounters with the Marquesa.

"You need to find another man," Philippe declared. "One who is not married."

"I have," Antonietta wailed, "but I feel no passion for him. At times it's worse than having no-one. It just makes me long for James even more."

"And me?"

"With you, it's pure sex. You make no emotional demands on me. I can handle that." Antonietta looked away in embarrassment. "That's why I went with the Marquesa."

They spent the next day walking around Florence. Antonietta found a strange comfort in Philippe's presence, just as she had in Quebec City. She was sorry when the day ended and they parted.

———

On Monday, February 17, the Board of Governors of the Institute finally announced that there would be an internal choice for Rector. Their experience with Harold Winstone had obviously made them wary of outsiders. There would be an election by the faculty for Rector on May 1, but the Board reserved the right to appoint a person of its choice in place of the person winning the election. Candidates were to declare themselves by Friday, February 28. At their Wednesday evening get-together, the lads decided to keep James' candidacy under wraps until that date. There was no point in giving the opposition time to talk him down before campaigning began in earnest.

The breach between Winstone and HB was confirmed the following Friday when the Rector appointed Bill Leaman as one of the members of the committee to conduct the assessment of Hamid Khan for re-appointment as Head of the FEB Section. Bill was proud like a child of his appointment, and Petra was particularly happy.

"You see, Bill," she told him. "I'm changing your life."

Danny and Piotr agreed enthusiastically. James was silent, but he had to agree that the end of the Winstone-Arbuthnot axis boded well for his candidacy.

———

Over the next two weeks after David's return from his skiing weekend, Antonietta arranged a number of trysts with Philippe. She felt a little guilty when she made love to David after being with Philippe, but she needed him. Philippe satisfied her sexually and, as she had met him before James, she was more able to disassociate him from the man she still loved to distraction. Moreover, whereas James for David was an unknown menace hovering over their relationship, with Philippe she could talk openly about him. This brought her a measure of comfort.

———

Three candidates declared themselves by the deadline of February 28: Brian Wilkins, Bill Wachowitz and James. The following Sunday, there was a council of war at James' apartment. Elliot Hunt was also there. Bill had argued strenuously against including him. He thought him unreliable. "He was taken in by HB over that Annya business," he reminded James. Piotr was at best lukewarm. As a Pole, he had an ingrained distrust of men who didn't drink. Danny, however, supported James. "We're too much of a clique," he told Bill. "Hunt will bring a different perspective. I think we need that." So, Hunt was included.

First, they discussed the two other candidates. Wilkins had only managed 22% in the vote for a faculty member on Bill's tenure committee and might suffer from a perceived closeness to HB. Wachowitz worried James more.

"He's honest, pleasant, unlikely to rock the boat," he commented. "He'd make a good compromise choice. He could come up the middle."

Next, they turned to the substance of the campaign. It was essential to keep a momentum going and not peak too early. They agreed that there would be a couple of new proposals each week, and each week would have a different focus. The first week would be devoted to finance. It was an important issue but a little arcane. It was ideally suited to the first week of campaigning when interest was still relatively low. The two proposals were the formation of an elected finance committee to assist the Rector and the provision for monthly financial disclosure statements. The committee would have the right to refer matters on which it disagreed with the Rector to the Governing Council, which would have the last word. This would end the Rector's discretionary control over the Institute's finances, which had proved so disastrous under Winstone.

On Monday afternoon, as James was preparing to announce the first proposal to a meeting of professors, Bill burst into his office.

"Wilkins has pipped you to the post," he told James grimly. "He's suggested setting up a finance committee at a lunch with some professors from FEB just like the one you're planning."

James was shocked and dismayed. "Are you sure it's the same proposal?" he asked. Bill nodded. "Right down to giving the last word to the Governing Council."

James put his head in his hands. What was he going to do? He couldn't substitute the disclosure proposal as it was quite detailed and he didn't have it with him. Elliot had taken it to solve some accounting problems that James didn't understand. But he couldn't now make the committee proposal. He would appear to be just apeing Wilkins. The result was an inconsequential meeting in which James promised a more open administration in touch with the problems of professors. It didn't impress many people.

The presentation of the disclosure proposal was scheduled for Wednesday afternoon. Just before lunch, Elliot Hunt came to see James. He was furious.

"What's going on?" he bellowed at James. "Your apartment must be bugged. Wilkins has just told a meeting of LAC that he favors a monthly reporting system on the Institute's finances. It's not as detailed as our program, but it's very close."

"My God!" James was horrified. "What indeed is going on?"

He was pressing Elliot for more details when Bill arrived in the office. He glared at Hunt. "Are you the snitch?" he enquired aggressively. "It has to be you." He grasped Hunt by the collar and began to shake him.

James intervened. "Calm yourself, Bill," he said. "It's not Elliot. He's as upset as we are."

Bill was unconvinced but said no more.

Danny and Piotr joined them, and it was agreed that James would present his proposal as a supplement to Wilkins. It was no use trying to convince people that it had been drawn up before Wilkins talked to LAC. This was better than another empty meeting like Monday's. Or was it? Both Campeau and Gowling were at the meeting, and they took a gleeful delight in making hay out of James apparently following Wilkins' lead. Three days into the campaign, James was floundering. Luckily, it was only the first week.

The next campaign meeting had been set for the following Saturday, but Elliott was in Toronto and so it was postponed to Sunday. Left with nothing to do on Saturday evening, James accompanied Bill and Petra to the student bar. He didn't like fraternizing in this way with students, particularly as he was running for Rector, but he felt depressed and needed a distraction, both from thoughts of Antonietta and the problems with his campaign.

James was seated with Petra and Bill and a couple of Bill's colleagues from FEB when Annya joined them. She was looking particularly attractive, wearing a tight blue sweater that emphasized the curve of her breasts and the brilliant color of her eyes. Despite Petra's disapproving glances, James let himself be sequestered by her Polish beauty. They both drank too much.

"We're leaving," Petra told James pointedly. He waved airily at her and Bill and continued his conversation with Annya. After a few minutes, she asked him to drive her home. "Elliot doesn't like me driving when I drink," she explained.

"I never drink and drive," James assured her. "I drink first and drive afterwards." Annya went into peals of laughter and pressed herself against James. The scent of her perfume was intoxicating.

If he'd been a little less under the influence, James probably wouldn't have accepted Annya's invitation to take a last drink in her apartment. He did, without weighing the consequences. Once in the apartment, Annya disappeared and when she returned, she was wearing a very scanty bikini.

"Do you like it," she asked James. "I bought it for my next trip to Mexico."

The sight of Annya parading her well-proportioned and alluring body brought James quickly back to his senses. Elliot was a colleague and a valuable member of his election team. It was hardly a good idea to bed his girlfriend, however appetizing she was. When Annya came and knelt down in front of him, he pushed her hands away from his belt.

"No, Annya," he protested. "I can't do this to Elliot."

Annya threw back her head and laughed. "Really?" Her voice was full of irony. "James, you're a fool, a blind fool." She undid her bra and put her hands under her perfectly rounded breasts, offering them up to James. "You won't touch them because of Elliot?" she asked in the same bantering tone.

"For Christ's sake, Annya, get dressed." James looked away, remembering Oscar Wilde's line about being able to resist anything except temptation.

"Do you know why Wilkins made those proposals?" Annya asked.

James shook his head.

"Because Elliot gave them to him."

As she said this, Annya stood up and removed the bottom part of her bikini. James stared at her, taken aback as much by her lubricious nudity as Elliot's betrayal.

"Why?" he stammered.

Annya began to undo James' belt, and he no longer stopped her. "Do you remember the appraisal of Doefman's paper from that Dutch professor?" The belt was now off and Annya was undoing the zipper on James' pants. All he could manage was a nod.

"Well, you sent it to Elliot with a caustic comment that made him think you knew that he was lying."

James again pushed Annya's hand away. A few moments more and he would be incapable of rational thought. "Lying about what?" he asked.

"About him and I," Annya replied.

"You mean, you and he were together *before* the end of term?"

"Of course." Annya smiled up at him. "He's terrified that, if you become Rector, you'll re-open the process. That's why he's helping Wilkins."

James was torn between shame at his own lack of discernment, disgust at Hunt's duplicity, and desire. Annya had extricated his sex and was caressing it. "But, why would I have him on my election team if that were the case? It doesn't make…"

At that moment Annya took him into her mouth. She aroused him and then stopped. She straightenend herself and placed James's hand on her pert breasts. "Why don't you take your revenge?" she asked, her lips pursed in a promiscuous pout. She was irresistible.

Annya led James into the bedroom. She lay on the bed. "I've wanted you to fuck me for a long time." Her voice was hoarse with lust. James undressed. He caressed the soft inviting breasts, the smooth, sunburned skin of her body and enjoyed her trim and avid sex. "Come in me," she ordered, and, fighting back thoughts of his first night with Antonietta, James penetrated her.

"Why did you tell me all this?" James asked as they lay together afterwards. Annya gave him an enigmatic smile. "It was a way to get you to fuck me. But I also want you to win. HB's a shit, Wilkins is an asshole and Wachowitz is a wanker."

James burst out laughing, and they took their pleasure with each other again. This time more adventurously, much to Annya's delight.

———

Besides her two lovers, Antonietta was also pestered by the Marquesa's phone calls. She refused to meet her, but the Marquesa persisted time and again. "I know you want me," she insisted. "I know you want the pleasure I alone can give you." Finally, Antonietta lost her patience. It was Friday afternoon, March 7. "You're a perverted and immoral woman who has taken advantage of my vulnerability," she fumed. "I'm not a lesbian, and I want nothing more to do with you."

The following Sunday, Antonietta and David were woken up by a phone call from Gino della Rovere, informing them that the Marquesa had committed suicide. Antonietta felt at once saddened and relieved. There was also some guilt. Was it because of her that the Marquesa had killed herself? Had she really needed to be so harsh? After all, the Marquesa hadn't forced her. She'd been a willing participant in their lesbian escapades. But surely this didn't mean she'd been obliged to become the Marquesa's mistress?

———

It was past midday before James finally tore himself away from the carnal pleasures at which Annya proved herself so adept. "Do you make love like this with Elliot," he asked. Somehow Annya's sexual licentiousness sat ill with Hunt's austere Protestantism. Annya just smiled and James didn't press the point.

He dressed and returned to his apartment to wash and shave before picking up the children from Prévost. He drove them to Bill's, who was giving a party. Everyone was there including Ella and her two girls, Isabella aged eight and Natalya aged five. The children went off to play, although Peter's expression told of his reluctance to spend the afternoon with younger children who were, into the bargain, girls. The women chatted among themselves, and the men sat down to decide how to deal with Hunt's treachery.

"I told you not to trust him," Bill said smugly. "Now we're up shit creek." James was about to give a sharp retort but Danny got in first. "I don't agree. We could use this to James' advantage."

Bill was skeptical. "I'd like to know how."

Danny gave one of his crafty smiles. "First, we dream up some stupid proposal, let Hunt think tonight that we're going to use it and wait for Wilkins to make a fool of himself."

"He won't fall for that," James objected. "Wilkins is not that stupid."

"No, you're right," Danny admitted. "So we take a controversial proposal, instead. Let's say, we propose the abolition of the Sections. No-one wants that, but I think Hunt and Wilkins may just buy it."

James laughed and shook his head in admiration. "Are you sure you weren't brought up by Jesuits, Danny?"

"No, my good man, by pedophiles."

Once the hilarity had subsided, Danny continued. "If, perhaps that's a big if, but if Wilkins falls for it, James can confront him and threaten to expose his underhand tactics unless he withdraws."

"And Hunt?" Bill asked.

"I can't do anything about Hunt unless Wilkins uses the proposal," James said quickly. "Otherwise, he might suspect Annya."

Bill looked at James with suspicion. "I hope you're not getting yourself too involved with that lying bitch?"

"She may be a bitch," James replied with a smile, "and she's certainly a lier, but she's a real bombshell and damn good in bed."

As he said these words, James felt a pinch of remorse. What on earth would Antonietta say if she heard him? Then came his immediate reaction; what the hell did it matter? On the contrary, it served her right for her falseness and infidelity.

That evening, Hunt arrived and they decided on the proposal for abolishing the Sections. He didn't show any surprise. On the contrary, he pointed out that many places now were de-departmentalizing. After he left, the group decided on the real proposal, which was the creation of an executive committee consisting of the Section Heads and the Deans to advise the Rector. This would ensure better communication between the Sections, the administration and the Rectorate.

James deliberately delayed his presentation of the real proposal until Tuesday afternoon. This gave Wilkins enough time to present the fake proposal, which he did on Tuesday morning to a breakfast meeting of professors. It was greeted with derision. "After the problems we've had with Winstone, nobody wants a Rector calling all the shots," an irate member of FEB told the hapless Wilkins.

Piotr attended the meeting and reported back to James and the others. They were immensely pleased but, above all, relieved that their stratagem had worked.

"You've got him now," Danny told James.

James delivered his own proposal later on Tuesday, and it was enthusiastically received. Hunt was there and from his somber mien, it was clear that he understood that he'd been found out and tricked. He left before the end of the meeting, but James caught up with him in the quadrangle.

"I don't know what game you're playing, Hunt," he told him, taking care not to incriminate Annya. "I don't want to see you again at any of our meetings, and if I'm appointed Rector, you'd be advised to find another place to work."

With that, James carried on towards the LAC Building. Wilkins was surprised to see him and obviously nervous. James didn't waste time or words. He informed his rival candidate that he'd discovered his underhand tactics and would expose them if he didn't withdraw from the election.

"No-one would believe you," Wilkins blustered.

"I faxed myself a copy of the proposal you were stupid enough to present. The fax has Monday's date."

This was completely untrue, but it was a good ploy. It's a pity I didn't do it, James thought as he left Wilkins' office without exchanging any more words with him.

The next afternoon, Wilkins withdrew from the election, and James received Annya in his apartment. She made frenetic love to him. It seemed to excite her that she'd betrayed the man whom she was supposed to love. She offered her body without any modesty to all the exigencies of James' lust. It made him feel uneasy.

"I don't understand you," he told her.

"I don't want you to understand me," she replied. "I just want you to fuck me."

James surveyed the naked young woman lying next to him. Her self-assurance reminded him of Carolina as did her blue eyes and long, blond hair. But beneath Carolina's poise, there was lightness and an elusive warmth. Annya was darkness. Even when she made love, you could feel the malice below. Yet James was entrapped by her promiscuous sexuality and the delights of her wanton body. But once she left, he ached for the wholesome passion of his lost love.

# CHAPTER 23

## Wednesday, April 16 to Thursday, May 29, 2003

David left Florence for England on Wednesday, April 16, to spend Easter with his parents. The next evening was the annual party given by Princess Angelina Farnese. Knowing that Philippe would be there, Antonietta took extra care over her appearance. She wore the same cream-colored dress she'd worn to *Tosca* in Montreal. In fact, she re-created the same picture of sensuous perfection that had enthralled everyone at *Le Reine Elizabeth*. It wasn't a good idea. Looking at herself in the mirror, she was flooded by reminiscences of that evening with James and broke down. Once she had mastered her sobbing, she took off the dress and put on a jacket and skirt. She resurrected her make-up more demurely.

Antonietta arrived at the sumptuous Farnese palace with her parents. No sooner had they made their way up the imposing baroque staircase than they came face to face with Philippe.

"Ah, Count de Pothiers," Paolo exclaimed, delighted to meet his colleague. "May I present my wife, Caterina, and my daughter, Antonietta."

Philppe kissed Caterina's hand and did the same to Antonietta. "I am pleased to meet you, Countess," he said. "I have heard much about Count della Chiesa's beautiful daughter." Antonietta just managed to keep a straight face. "And I, Count," she replied, "have heard a lot about my father's charming new associate."

Caterina shot Antonietta a disapproving look. This was not the way to talk to a married man, it said. To allay any suspicions that her astute mother may entertain, Antonietta wandered off to join other guests. But she kept an eye on Philippe, and at the first opportunity buttonholed him.

"Come to my apartment after the party," she entreated him.

"À vos ordres, comtesse," he replied with a grin.

———

Once Wilkins had withdrawn from the election for Rector, it was plain sailing for James. Wachowitz's only chance had been to appear as a compromise candidate, but now that he was being compared directly with James, his pleasant geniality was not sufficient to garner much support. As a result, James slowed down the rythmn of his campaign and spent more time with his children.

This time was necessary because Veronica was becoming ever more obsessed by her religious devotions. The children complained that sometimes she was so taken up with her prayers that she forgot to prepare their supper or their sandwiches for school lunch. On the weekends when they stayed with her, they were left very much to their own devices.

"She doesn't seem to care about us any more," Susanna told her father sadly. Peter was more direct. "She's becoming really weird," he declared. James decided to take the children every weekend. Veronica didn't object, in fact she seemed relieved.

———

Antonietta spent Thursday night and all of Good Friday with Philippe. His easy-going charm soothed her troubled spirit, and his new sexual prowess satisfied her lustful sexuality. They had just finished making love on the floor of the living room when Philippe turned to Antonietta with a sad look on his face.

"I'm returning to France tomorrow," he told her. "My time here is finished, and I must spend Easter Sunday with the family."

"I shall miss you," Antonietta replied, her eyes filling with tears. "You're my only consolation." They spent one more night together and then Philippe departed for Paris on Saturday morning. Before leaving, he sat Antonietta down on the sofa.

"Why don't you go to Canada and talk to James?" he asked her. "Why do you let an oath that was sworn in ignorance, one can even say under false pretences, prevent you from going back to the man you love with all your being?" Looking at Antonietta with sympathetic sternness, Philippe added,. "If you don't, your passion for him will destroy you."

"I can't," Antonietta replied, her voice redolent with despair and sorrowful resignation. "If I break that oath, no good can come of it."

Philippe sighed, kissed Antonietta gently on the mouth and left. Once in his car, he called an old friend on the cell phone. It was André Pointet, who happened to be the President of the European University Institute in Florence. It was a long shot but worth a try, for Antonietta's sake.

With Philippe gone, Antonietta was left alone to the emptiness of her life. Unable to face the day before her, she drank a bottle of Scotch and slept. Luckily she'd arranged to go to the cinema with Alessa and Paulina that evening, otherwise she would have been consumed by her misery.

David arrived back on Tuesday. Antonietta was glad to see him and she let him spend the next few nights in her apartment. She was afraid of being on her own, but his presence didn't cure her. She was plagued by longing for James and regret at Philippe's departure. Still sexually underserved by her boyfriend, she even found herself wishing that the Marquesa were still alive. This cannot go on, she would tell herself, but life just continued in the same tormented way.

---

The results of the election for Rector were known by late afternoon on May 1. It was a clear victory for James with 76% of the votes to 24% for Wachowitz. Even James was surprised and, of course, that night was one of great celebration. Only Danny sounded a note of caution.

"It's not over till the fat lady sings," he warned. "The Board still has the last word. They could even appoint HB."

The others refused to let him dampen their spirits and they were all very much the worse for wear when the evening ended in the early hours. This included Danny, who called Bernadette to tell her that he was spending the night at James' apartment. Bill and Petra were able to walk to their house and only Piotr drove home. He was more wary of Ella than the police.

Nevertheless, despite the brave words, the next week was nerve-wracking for all of them. The Board members consulted the Deans including HB, the two other Section Heads and even Winstone himself. Danny had not been able to discern their thinking from his meeting with them. Finally, on Thursday, a week after the election, James was summoned to meet the Board. They offered him the post of Rector.

"Congratulations, Dr. Markham." The Chairman of the Board shook James' hand. "We can discuss salary in due course, but are there any particular requests or conditions you wish to raise?"

There were none and, after shaking hands with all the Board members, James left to join his friends. He informed them of the appointments he was going to make. Of course, the position of Senior Dean would be abolished, and

Wachowitz would also replace Arbuthnot as Chair of the Ethics Committee. Danny, as Dean of Administration, would regain both his position as the senior dean and his office, and Bill would become Assistant Dean of International Affairs in James' place.

"Does that mean I get to travel all over South America?" Bill asked with a prurient grin. He received a black look from Petra. "You're not going anywhere," she declared.

James also told the group that he was minded to appoint Klaus Berger to serve out his own term as Head of the LIR Section. Danny warned against it. "He's still bitter about being passed over last time in favor of you. I think you're taking a risk." James disagreed. "He's always been on our side, and everyone likes him. He'll be even more bitter if he's passed over again."

Once the excitement over James' appointment died down, Bill piped up. "I've got two pieces of news myself," he announced. "First, the assessment committee will recommend re-appointment for Hamid."

Bill paused to let this news sink in. They all raised their glasses in a toast to the absent Hamid, and then everyone, except Petra, looked expectantly at Bill. He took a large gulp of whisky to keep them on tenterhooks and announced that he and Petra were getting married in Edmonton on August 16.

"You're all invited and James is going to be best man." Bill turned to James with a broad grin. "That means you have to look after the bridesmaids, including Petra's hot sister, Mila."

There was a second round of toasts to the prospective bride and bridegroom. James was as happy as anyone at the news, but he felt a jolt as he thought of his own forlorn plans to marry Antonietta. For her they had meant nothing. He turned away so the others couldn't see the tears in his eyes.

After an exhausting week, James was relieved to spend a quiet weekend with his children. Their wide-eyed admiration touched him, and he entertained briefly the idea of seeking a reconciliation with Veronica for their sakes before realizing that it was out of the question. At the end of the month, he was spending two weeks with Carolina at Puerta Vallarta in Mexico.

He drove the children to school on Monday morning and arrived in his office just as a phone call came through for him. It was his old friend from Spain, Rodrigo de Fuentes y Muñoz, with news that the Marquesa de Avila y de la Torre had committed suicide.

"They say it's because she was deserted by her beautiful young mistress,"

Rodrigo told James, who was assailed by a twinge of jealousy. Was that beautiful young mistress Antonietta?

———

May 1 is a holiday in Italy called the *Festa del Lavoro*. For Caterina della Chiesa, it was a travesty that the day was taken over by trade-unionists and other communists. So, she always insisted that the family attend Mass in honor of St. Joseph in order to endow the day with its proper religious significance.

Antonietta had spent the previous night at David's. She was preparing to join her family at the Basilica when David sat her down. His manner was unusually serious.

"Antonietta, I love you," he said, betraying a certain nervousness. "I know you still think of that man in Canada, but it's over now. Forget him and marry me."

Antonietta had no idea what to say. She still longed for James and could never quite abandon the dream that they might somehow, through a miracle, come together again. She knew it was a dream, and miracles rarely happen. Besides, she was bound by her oath and was too afraid of divine retribution to break it. She and David had been together now for almost a year. If she couldn't have James, why not David? She promised him she would think about his proposal and went off to meet her family.

Antonietta paid little attention to the service in the Basilica. Her mind was dominated by the question of her answer to David. Strangely, she didn't pray for guidance, perhaps because the considerations that moved her were of a very secular nature. The truth was that David didn't satisfy her either sexually or emotionally. Far from marrying him, it was more logical to end the relationship. Yet she shied away from this decision as well. She preferred the comfort of his company to the bleakness of her own solitude. Certainly she could find someone else, but would he be any better?

Antonietta made an excuse not to have lunch with the family. Her mother was still distant with her, and she didn't feel like fencing with Giovanni and his insipid wife. She drove back to David's studio and told him that she needed more time. Relieved not to receive a blunt refusal, David was only too happy to oblige her.

———

On the Tuesday after James' appointment as Rector, he and Winstone had lunch together at the *Le chat botté* in Saint-Sauveur. Winstone seemed happy that James was taking over and was unstinting in his congratulations. They discussed the various problems facing the Institute, most of which Winstone conveniently laid at HB's doorstep.

"He misled me," he told James with an air of self-pity.

James was non-commital. He disliked HB but the real cause of the problems had been Winstone's own incompetence and weakness. However, there was little point in spoiling a pleasant, collegial lunch and, besides, there was some information that James really wanted from Winstone.

"Tell me, Harold, why didn't you kick me out over that business with Antonietta della Chiesa," he asked, feeling a twinge of misery at mentioning her name.

Winstone hesitated but James insisted. Finally he came up with the explanation. "The Italian Ambassdor made it clear that the European collection would only remain at the Institute if you were still here. So, I chose to hush up the affair."

"What about HB? What did he think?"

Winstone gave a ruefule smile. "He was furious. HB was more interested in getting rid of you than having the collection. He called me every name under the sun, and that was the end of our friendship."

"Why didn't he at least spread rumors to hurt me during the campaign for Rector?"

"He didn't dare." Winstone smiled again, this time with self-satisfaction. "After he insulted me, I told him that if he ever breathed a word about you and that Italian girl, I'd call for an investigation into Flint's submissions. That shut him up."

"What about the photos?"

"I had the student come to my office and give me the negatives. Luckily it wasn't a digital camera, and he hadn't made any other copies. I destroyed everything, and that was that."

"Why didn't the student talk?"

"I warned him not to. I told him that what he did was close to blackmail. It wasn't, of course, but he believed me."

Winstone's account called forth conflicting feelings in James. He was curious why the Duke of Messina had gone out on a limb for him. Were his friends right? After all, both the Duke and Antonietta were Italian. But why would an ambassador put his career at risk at the behest of an inconsequential student, no matter how beautiful she was? He dismissed the idea of any connection. As for Winstone, James couldn't help admiring how he'd handled both HB and young Wrangel, but that was only to be expected from a former government official. They weren't much good at doing anything constructive, but they were past masters at protecting their asses.

The following Thursday, Annya came to James' apartment. They made love even more indecently than usual. Annya was desperate to be taken in every possible way and to give pleasure using all the considerable expertise she possessed. After three hours of indulgence, James found out the reason. While still playing with his sex, Annya told him that this was their last time.

"I'm getting too attached to you, and I hate that," she explained. "I can't control you, and I want my freedom. I can do what I like with Elliott and, besides, he's going to Florida now you're Rector. I don't want to miss out on the Florida sun, and perhaps I'll find a rich older man whom I can milk."

Although he was shocked by Annya's amorality, James had to admit that at least she was honest. She wasn't playing a game, like Antonietta. There was no tenderness between them, but their last kiss before Annya left was not devoid of emotion.

"I have a horrible feeling that I won't be able to forget you," Annya confessed, "but I'll damn well try." James watched her leave with a mixture of regret and relief.

The following week James went to see the colleagues affected by his initial appointments. The first was HB. When James entered his office, HB looked at his nemesis with undisguised hatred.

"So, Markham," he sneered. "You've come to vent your aristocratic spite."

James surveyed his beaten enemy without pity, not even deigning to rise to Arbuthnot's taunt. His voice was calm but the contempt beneath the surface was unmistakable.

"I am abolishing the post of Senior Dean," he said, "which you have used to subvert the Rector and serve your own contemptible ends. You will vacate this office by July 1 so that Dr. Redfern may re-occupy it."

HB stared glassily at James as if he couldn't believe that his reign was really over. James reserved one further humiliation for him.

"You will also be replaced as Chair of the Ethics Committee. Here too, you have used your position for your own ends without regard for truth or justice." This was undoubtedly true but, unknown to HB, he had in fact been right about

Elliott Hunt. However, in James' view, this didn't excuse his unethical behavior.

The two glared at each other. At last, HB collected himself. "I'll be watching you, Markham," he snarled. "I'll be watching every day, and I'll crucify you when the time comes. There are lots of pretty girls in the Institute."

James lifted his fist but contained his anger just in time. It was fortunate for both of them that HB hadn't mentioned the name of Antonietta della Chiesa.

James' next visit was with Bill Wachowitz, to whom he offered the Chair of the Ethics Committee. "You're perfect for the job, Bill,' he told his former rival. "You'll be fair, you have no axes to grind and everyone likes you." Wachowitz was surprised but obviously delighted. "I accept, James," he said. "I look forward to working with you."

The meeting with Klaus Berger was less satisfying. He seemed to treat the appointment as his due and hardly thanked James. Unlike Wachowitz, he offered no declaration of support for the new Rector. James was disappointed and uneasy. Perhaps Danny had been right after all. Unfortunately, it was too late to backtrack. He made his way back to his office and sat down, immersed in his apprehension.

"James!" It was Sheila, his secretary. "There's a phone call from some foreigner."

James picked up the phone.

"Dr. Markham?" a voice enquired.

"Yes."

"André Pointet, President of the European University Institute in Florence."

The President's Italian had such a heavy French accent that James continued the conversation in that language. The President appeared relieved. He came to the reason for his call.

"We would like you to be the invitee of the Students' Visiting Speakers Committee on November 21$^{st}$. We want you to give a talk on the future of the European Union."

The European University Institute! Florence! Antonietta's home town! James' stomach churned under the avalanche of emotions that gripped him. Was she in Florence? How would he manage to be in the same city? Instinctively, he prevaricated.

"We're counting on you, Dr. Markham," the President insisted. "We want to hear a British perspective."

James let himself be persuaded to give the lecture. The President was very pleased. "Excellent. The Secretary of the Visiting Speakers' Committee will send you the tickets and inform you of all the arrangements. His name is David Bannerman-Smith."

As usual, James took the children for the weekend of May 24 and 25, particularly as he would be with Carolina in a week's time. Peter informed him that his mother had cut herself badly on a piece of glass underneath the fridge. He seemed concerned that she hadn't sought medical attention. James reassured him. "I'm sure she'd see a doctor if it were really serious," he told his son.

———

Antonietta and David left Florence for a touring holiday on Monday, May 26. Antonietta loved Verona with its grandiose plaza and remarkably preserved arena, but she was disappointed with Milan. The Cathedral was impressive from the outside, but the interior was drab and uninteresting. The La Scala opera house was swathed in scaffolding, and in any case the season was over. Monte Carlo also didn't impress her. It had come to ressemble a concrete jungle. She enjoyed Nice but was happy to be on their way to Avignon. She had never visited the papal palace there. Suddenly, David took the motorway to Marseilles.

"I've always wanted to see that city," he told Antonietta.

The motorway took them through Toulon and then on to Marseilles. On the way Antonietta noticed an exit to Les Lecques. It was too much. Memories of her idyllic days there with James descended upon her, and she dissolved in tears. David stopped at the next *aire*[29].

"I'm sorry, Antonietta. I had no idea," he told her, wiping away the tears.

"It's not your fault," Antonietta replied. "I have to deal with it, and I will."

David took heart and smiled. They continued towards Marseilles. He seemed to believe her, but Antonietta knew better. She was no further getting over James than the day she'd boarded the Alitalia flight in Toronto for Italy, half demented with grief.

# CHAPTER 24
## Friday, May 30 to Monday, July 14, 2003

James met Carolina at the airport in Mexico City. It was the end of May. They spent an enjoyable night in the airport hotel and left the next day for Puerto Vallarta. It was the hottest season of the year, and they spent most of their time either in the swimming pool or making love in the air-conditioned hotel room. On June 10, James' 36th birthday, they had dinner in one of the finest restaurants in Puerto Vallarta, *Le Café des Artistes*. It was then that James learned that Carolina would be 24 exactly a week later.

"We're both Gemini's," she said with a grin.

James grinned back, but it was a little forced. He was thinking of Antonietta, who would be 26 on July 14.

Carolina's cell phone rang. She excused herself and took the call. While she was talking, James scrutinized her face to find some indication of her feelings. The clear blue eyes betrayed nothing. For over a week they'd made love, laughed together, had long conversations, but unlike Antonietta, whom James had felt he knew intimately after just one night together—a dreadful miscalculation, it now appeared—Carolina remained an impervious mystery.

"Why were you looking at me so intently," Carolina asked, putting away her cell phone.

"I was trying to decipher what you're really thinking," James replied.

"What you mean is whether I've fallen in love with you like most of the other women you've had affairs with," she countered with an enigmatic smile.

James reddened with embarrassment. That was exactly what he meant but, put so bluntly, it sounded unforgivably arrogant and egoistical. He hastened to redeem himself. "Let's drop it Carolina, I've no right to pry like that."

"No, James, it's a fair question," she assured him. "The answer is that I won't allow myself to fall in love with you, because there are at least three good reasons why our relationship can't go anywhere."

"Tell me," James asked, intrigued by Carolina's sudden openness.

"Well, in the first place, you're married with two young children, and I can't see you divorcing." Carolina stopped and looked questioningly at James.

"Perhaps not," he said guardedly, not wishing to disclose his separation from Veronica. "But go on."

"Secondly, I can't see a man like you marrying a hooker like me."

"You're not a hooker," James responded vehemently, "You may occasionally have sex for money to round off the month, but that doesn't make you a hooker. At one time, it was quite common for respectable French women to do the same, and no-one would've dreamed of calling them hookers."

Carolina put on a delightful smile. "Perhaps I'd better move to Paris then," she said. "Still, I can't see myself as the wife of a British lord."

James stared at her in amazement. "How on earth do you know I'm a lord?"

"Partly by chance." she replied. "I looked you up on the internet and saw you went to a school called Ampleforth. I went to the school's website and they have a short biography of some former pupils. I couldn't find your name but I clicked on Charles Markham. When I found out he was a viscount, I looked up his family in Debret's Peerage and, lo and behold, I found Lord James Markham."

James' amazement turned to admiration. "That's quite some detective work," he commented. "But you're wrong. I don't give a damn about your month ends. It certainly wouldn't stop me marrying you."

"Perhaps not, as you would say." Carolina smiled sweetly at James before delivering the *coup de grace*. "However, there is the third and main reason. You would never marry me because you're not in love with me, and you're not in love with me because you're in love with someone else."

James was stunned "That's not true," he protested.

"Yes, it is," Carolina replied calmly. "You told me that you hadn't contacted me because you weren't ever in Buenos Aires. I appreciate you wanting to spare my feelings, but it was a lie nonetheless. I saw you in the Recoleta with a very beautiful, dark-haired woman who was clearly not your wife. It was in La Biela."

"Yes, I lied," James admitted. "I was in La Biela with a woman and I was in love with her, but she proved to be a faithless hussy and I've almost forgotten her."

"I wish it were true," said Carolina, "but it isn't."

The clear blue eyes seemed less serene. James took Carolina's hand in his. This short conversation had turned his image of her upside down. She wasn't a good time girl intent only on indulging her senses without any commitment. She had feelings but was sensible enough to control them when they couldn't lead her anywhere. And she was extraordinarily perceptive.

"Let's go to a night club," he suggested. "I'm a lousy dancer, but it's time we had a little romance."

James paid the bill and they went to *El Gato Tonto*, a new and very expensive nightclub. They found seats in the corner and ordered some wine. They listened to the music without speaking. James was trying to come to terms with a young woman who suddenly meant more to him than just a fling far from home. The band started to play "Feelings" and a woman sang it in Portuguese.

"Whenever I hear Portuguese sung, I've the impression of being in a bordello," James remarked.

Carolina burst out laughing and the tension between them eased. They got up to dance. James held Carolina very close.

"Of course, I'm in love with you," she whispered. James was about to reply, but Carolina put her hand over his mouth. "Don't lie, James," she told him.

Without a word he led her out of the nightclub. She made no protest and they were soon back at the hotel in bed. This night, there was passion in their love-making. Afterwards, James gazed at Carolina as she lay next to him. Perhaps she didn't have Antonietta's stunning beauty, but she was exceptionally pretty and her body yielded nothing in voluptuousness to his perfidious Italian mistress. He had no desire to patch up his marriage with Veronica, so why not marry Carolina? He asked her whether she would consider marrying him despite her three reasons. "I'll think about it," she replied.

The phone rang. It was Bill Leaman. James was about to ask, rather irritably, what on earth he was doing phoning in the middle of the night but stopped himself. There was an urgency about Bill's voice that silenced him.

"Veronica's been taken to hospital," he told James. "She's unconscious and suffering from acute septicaemia."

James was stunned. "Good God," he gasped. "Is it serious?"

There was a short silence. "She may die, James," Bill said quietly.

In a daze, James told Bill he would come home immediately. He felt a dreadful sense of guilt. Here he was frolicking with his Argentinean mistress while his wife perhaps lay dying in hospital. He told a shaken Carolina what was happening, and they made plans for the next morning. She would return to Buenos Aires and he would return to Montreal. There was no more talk of marriage.

———

It was the evening of June 10. This was James' 36th birthday and Antonietta's thoughts were centered on him. Where was he? With whom was he celebrating this day? Carolina? Annya? Some other woman who had taken her place? She took out of a drawer the watch she had bought in Bandol to give him on his 35th birthday. Sadness and longing overcame her and she covered it with her tears.

Antonietta was alone. David was in the library working on his thesis, but Antonietta had no interest in her's. After a few unsuccessful attempts at writing the outline for her supervisor, she gave up. She went into the bedroom, threw herself on the bed and abandoned herself to the sorrow that was ravaging her. She was hauled from her misery by a ring on the apartment door. It was Irena, the late Marquesa's so-called maid.

Antonietta gazed in astonishment at the pretty Albanian. She was dressed in a very provocative summer dress that was cut low enough to show off the soft roundness of her breasts.

"What do you want?" Antonietta asked.

"I want you to help me," Irena replied. "I've nowhere else to go. I have no money, but I have this."

She thrust a document into Antonietta's hands. It was the Marquesa's will, which had been drawn up in Spain. Antonietta read it, not understanding much of the legal jargon but enough to know that the Marquesa had left her entire fortune to Irena.

"You should take this to a lawyer," she told the young woman.

"I'm afraid," Irena replied. "I'm an illegal immigrant, and I don't want to be sent back to Albania." She lifted slightly the hem of her short dress. "If you help me, I'll do anything you want."

The meaning was clear, but Antonietta put the temptation of sexual indulgence aside. The situation was already complicated enough. The only person she could use to help Irena was her brother, Giovanni, but if she did, he would want to know why the Marquesa's maid had come to her. Worse still, he might guess why. Briefly, she entertained the idea of sending Irena away, but she balked at such cowardice.

"I'll show this will to my brother," she told Irena. "He'll deal with it without denouncing you. In the meantime, you'd better stay here."

Irena's eyes undressed Antonietta. Uneasy and aware of her own desires, Antonietta showed Irena into the guestroom. "You can sleep here," she said and shut the door steadfastly after the Albanian.

Back in her own room, she was beset by images of her lubricious guest. She imagined caressing and pleasuring her nude body, and she wanted to go to her. With great effort she resisted the temptation and, after much tossing and turning, fell asleep.

———

James arrived in Montreal late afternoon on Wednesday, June 11. He was met at the airport by Bill and his children. They were crying, and James took them in his arms and tried to comfort them. "I'm sure everything will be alright," he said without conviction. The expression on Bill's face told him that the truth was otherwise. He held them tightly against him in the back of the car while Bill drove to the hospital.

"Did she go by herself to the hospital?" James asked of no-one in particular.

"I called an ambulance," Peter replied. "Then I called Dr. Leaman."

James looked at his son and closed his eyes. Never had he felt himself so insignificant, so worthless. It had been up to his eleven year-old son to succor his wife while he was gallivanting in Mexico.

"I'm sorry, Peter," he muttered.

In a gesture that took James quite by surprise and brought him close to tears, Peter kissed him on the cheek. "It's alright, Dad," he said. "You weren't to know."

They arrived at the hospital and made their way immediately to the intensive care unit. They met Petra, who was in tears. She was with a doctor and the expression on his face portended the worst. He took James aside.

"I'm sorry, Lord Markham," he said with a British accent. "Lady Markham died an hour ago. There was nothing we could do. She left it too late."

James had a sense of the unreal. Just a few days ago, June 7, was his twelfth wedding anniversary. Now his wife, the mother of his children, was dead, and all he could think of was how strange it was to be called by his title in a Canadian hospital.

"Can I see her?" he asked, wishing to make amends for his insensitivity. The doctor led him to the room where Veronica still lay. James gazed at the woman he'd once cared for. He knelt by the bed with his head bowed. "Forgive me, Veronica, if it's because of me that this happened," he murmured.

He looked up and noticed the serenity of his dead wife's features. Now you're where you've always wanted to be, he thought. He kissed her lifeless cheeks and stood up. With one last glimpse at the woman who was supposed to have been his life's companion, he crossed himself and left the room.

———

The next day after Irena's arrival, Antonietta went to see her brother, Giovanni. She told him about Irena and the will without offering any explanation as to why the Marquesa's maid had come to her for help. Giovanni promised to deal with the matter without any cost and made no further comment. However, Antonietta has the unpleasant impression that he'd guessed why Irena had sought her out. Acutely embarrassed, she took her leave and drove to David's studio. He wasn't there and she returned to her apartment. She cooked a meal for herself and Irena. Their conversation was stilted, and Antonietta was relieved when it was time to go to bed.

Fighting the same temptation as the previous night, Antonietta was unable to fall asleep. The door of her bedroom opened and Irena appeared, completely naked. Helpless before the attraction of the Albanian's appetizing body, Antonietta abandoned herself to her intrusive caresses. Excited beyond endurance, she threw herself at the young woman and enjoyed her whole body, bringing her to a noisy climax. Afterwards she let herself be satisfied by Irena without any modesty, drowning herself in the ecstasy of their excesses. When it was over, she asked Irena to leave.

"Don't ever come into my bedroom again," she told her.

But she was aware of her own weakness, and the next day she left Irena in the apartment and went to stay with David, out of temptation's way. Not suspecting the reason, David was delighted to welcome her. Antonietta left her cell phone with Irena.

On Friday, Giovanni phoned his sister with the news that the will was a fake. Antonietta was horrified. It was not because Irena had lied to her, it was because she now realized that she'd nearly fallen victim to a honeypot trap. Clearly, the Albanian had assumed she could buy Antonietta's acquiescence in her duplicitous scheme by offering her body. It made Antonietta feel cheap and immoral. Oh, James, what have I become without you? she bewailed. Immediately, she called Irena and ordered her to leave the apartment.

"Are you sure?" Irena asked with mocking irony. "You enjoyed me that night. I'm still available."

Antonietta erupted. "If you're in my apartment when I arrive, I will denounce you to the immigration authorities," she shouted and put down the phone.

When she reached the apartment, there was no sign of Irena. Her cell phone was there, but some jewels and a small amount of cash were missing. This was a small price to pay. Much heavier was the knowledge that Giovanni had acquired. She just hoped that, for once, he would show her some loyalty.

———

James moved back into the house the day after Veronica's death. He kept the children out of school and tried his best to bring them comfort. Susanna was very tearful, but Peter was more stoical. It was from him that James learned how mystical and detached from life Veronica had become just before the accident. He told his father that, despite all his pleas, his mother had refused to seek treatment. He recounted how, on Tuesday, Susanna and he had wanted to have a cake to celebrate their father's birthday even though he was far away. He'd gone in search of his mother and found her unconscious in bed. He'd phoned an ambulance and Bill Leaman. Bill had accompanied the ambulance to the hospital and Petra had driven them there.

As he pieced together the last weeks and days of his wife's existence on this earth, James became more and more convinced that her death was a form of suicide. A very Catholic form, as befitted her. The wound, which he'd seen on viewing her inert body, was deep and serious, but it had been easily treatable. The only explanation James could find for her refusal to seek medical attention was a desire to quit this life. His sense of guilt lessened. In a way, he and even the children had been an obstacle to Veronica's religious vocation. She had forced her asceticism on them all. There had been no warmth in her religion, just a dry love of God and a selfish longing for paradise. I may be a sinner, James thought to himself, but I'm damn well going to give these kids the affection their saintly mother couldn't—or wouldn't—give them.

———

The episode with Irena finally persuaded Antonietta to let David move in with her.

"Let's see how it works," she told him. "I'm not rushing into anything, but I want to give us a chance. Keep your studio, though, just in case."

Overjoyed, David agreed to her terms. Over the next two weeks, he gradually moved his things.

On the next visit to her parents, Antonietta plucked up the courage to tell them. Her mother was about to make an unpleasant scene but her father, still mindful of the pain of nearly losing Antonietta, put his wife firmly in her place. "It's Antonietta's decision," he declared. "She's old enough to make it, and we have to respect it."

Her mother acquiesced but her manner towards Antonietta became even colder. This contributed to Antonietta's pervasive sadness.

———

During the week after their mother's death, James stayed at home with the children. He called some of his colleagues to garnish their views, aspirations and complaints. Tom Buchanan told him that, now the Institue was in safe hands, he wanted to retire. James didn't attempt to dissuade him. At sixty-eight, Tom deserved some rest. Although he knew that Bill would expect to take over from Tom, he appointed Anne-Marie Legrand instead. Bill was put out.

"I wanted that job, James," he complained.

"Listen, Bill," James explained, trying to be patient. "I need another woman and a francophone in the administration. Besides, Anne-Marie speaks Spanish, French and Italian, and you barely speak English." He grinned at Bill, but the pleasantry didn't go down well.

"Fuck you, Markham," was Bill's response.

"For Christ's sake, Bill," James pleaded. "I can't give you this job. I've already made Danny the senior dean again and you Assistant Dean of International Affairs. If I were to make you a Dean, people would say the same about me as they did about HB. Jobs for the boys. Be reasonable."

Bill said nothing for a moment. "OK, Jimmy," he conceded. "I was out of line. I'm sorry." Now he returned James' grin. "Anyway, Petra wouldn't let me take the job if it meant travelling abroad. For some reason, she doesn't trust me."

"I can't think why not." James laughed, immensely relieved at having pacified his friend.

That Saturday, everyone except Ella and her girls, met at James' house. Bill brought an extra large bottle of Scotch as a peace offering. James told his friends belatedly about Winstone's explanation for why he hadn't required

James' resignation. The general consensus, which James still persisted in refuting, was that Antonietta had something to do with the Italian Ambassador's quite undiplomatic interference in the Institute's affairs. "He had no right to say what he did," Danny insisted.

"What am I going to do with Winstone's and HB's merry men," James asked, brusquely changing the conversation. "I don't think generosity will cut any ice with HB's lot, but I'm not sure about Winstone's bunch."

"I would offer them an olive branch," Danny suggested. "It won't cost you anything. I would do the same with Flint. He's not a bad sort, unlike those assholes, Campeau and Gowling, and that snake, Wilkins."

On Monday, Susanna and Peter returned to school. The shock of their mother's death had worn off, and it was better for them to be entertained by the end-of-year games than moping at home. James himself went to the office. Eleanor, the Rector's secretary, came to congratulate him and express her condolences on his loss. She was followed by Winstone, who appeared genuinely affected by Veronica's sudden demise. James accompanied Winstone back to the Rectorate and dictated a memorandum to Eleanor, setting out the new appointments as well as Tom's resignation and the abolition of the post of Senior Dean. He asked Eleanor to arrange a dinner for Tom.

James spent the rest of the week planning the changes he wanted to make to the Institute's administration. He met privately with Winstone's supporters, Tocheniuk, Williams, Goldberg and Wright. He assured them that there would be no witchhunt, and their futures in the Institute would be up to them. There would be no more presents but also no unnecessary obstacles. James also talked with Flint, more or less in the same vein. All except Goldberg, who seemed distrustful, promised James their support. Flint, in particular, was relieved and grateful.

James spent all his evenings with the children. They talked about Veronica, and James became more and more convinced that her death was a suicide in disguise. The glass on which she'd cut her arm was probably from the wineglass Antonietta had let fall on that fateful day when he'd succumbed to her incandescent beauty. The bitter irony was that Antonietta had indirectly freed him to marry her when she no longer wanted him. He felt a great sadness, which Susanna interpreted as sorrow for her mother's death.

"You've got us, Daddy," she told him. James put an arm around his daughter and kissed her. He glanced across at Peter and was surprised by the skeptical look on his face. It was as if he'd guessed his father's real thoughts.

July 1 arrived and with it James' installation as Rector. He made a speech promising reforms to make the administration more efficient and transparent and to recapture the drive of the Buchanan years. It was well received, although HB and his cronies didn't join in the applause. Afterwards he took possession of his new office, only to be confronted by a large, ugly woman who introduced herself as the Provincial sexual harassment officer.

"What are you going to do about sexual harassment in the Institute?" she asked belligerently, sitting down without being asked.

James was tempted by a facetious reply but controlled himself.

"There is an established complaint procedure. If the complaint appears justified, the matter comes before the Ethics Committee. Any professor found guilty of sexual harassment is disciplined. He may be fined, suspended or dismissed depending on the gravity of the offence."

The woman leaned over, her voluminous and ill-formed breasts spilling onto James' desk. "What about women who don't *know* they've been sexually harassed?"

James looked at the phenomenon before him with incomprehension. "If *they* don't know, how the hell am *I* supposed to know?" he asked, his voice rising in irritation. "And, by the way, men can also be sexually harassed, or isn't that in your credo?"

The woman stood up. "People like you are the problem," she declared and stalked out of the office.

Eleanor, who'd heard the whole episode, came to apologize. "She snuck through without me seeing her," she told James, who laughed. "Well, at least she won't be back. I don't think she liked me."

All the activity since his return from Mexico had taken James' mind off Antonietta to some extent without eradicating the jealousy and emptiness that plagued him. He awoke on July 14 realizing that it was her 26th birthday. He wondered who she was celebrating it with. He wandered downstairs to make himself a coffee and collected the mail from the outdoor mailbox. There was a letter from Carolina. He opened and read it.

*My dear James. I cannot pretend to you or myself that I have not fallen in love with you, but I cannot marry you. My life is here in Buenos Aires.*

*It is not perhaps the perfect or even the most respectable life, but it is the one I am comfortable with. Please leave me to live it. I would not be strong enough to resist if you came to see me, but our marriage would be a catastrophe for both of us. I shall never forget you. Carolina.*

# CHAPTER 25
## Tuesday, July 15 to Tuesday, November 18, 2003

It was the hottest summer for years and Antonietta decided to spend mid-July to mid-August at her family's villa on the Versilia Riviera. Her mother allowed her to invite Alessa and Paulina but no men, particularly not David. This didn't bother Antonietta. David was taken up with his thesis, and she didn't care for Alessa's and Paulina's boyfriends. In fact, she was glad to be on her own. There was a discotheque near the villa, and plenty of men to indulge her dissatisfied lust. To allay David's suspicions and assuage a little her conscience, she agreed that he would spend two weekends at the villa. Alessa and Paulina also arranged for their boyfriends to visit them.

The girls spent the first three days sunbathing, swimming in the sea, cooking and dancing away the evenings in the discotheque. They all flirted outrageously, but it went no further. Alessa's and Paulina's boyfriends came for the weekend, and on the Saturday evening Antonietta was left to her own devices. The sun and the skimpy bikini she'd been wearing all day served to stir her libido, and after an hour or so in the discotheque she left with a man whose name she didn't even know. They made love on a deserted beach. The man was younger than Antonietta and very virile. She was exhausted when she arrived back at the villa. The sex hadn't been particularly exciting, but there had been plenty of it.

The next week Antonietta brushed off the young man's renewed advances in favor of an older man. He had an apartment on the Riviera and took Antonietta back there. This time Antonietta couldn't complain, and both her thighs and buttocks were sore from their excesses. It was nearly midday when she returned to the villa. Both her friends were outraged at her infidelity.

"What ever would David say?' Paulina asked, quite beside herself at Antonietta's behavior.

"I don't know and I don't care," Antonietta replied coolly. "I'm not in love with him, and that man at least knew how to satisfy me."

"If you're not in love with David, why don't you leave him?" Alessa asked, confounded by Antonietta's indifference.

Antonietta didn't reply, but her friends pressed her. Both of them liked David and were dumbfounded by Antonietta's casual attitude. Eventually, she told them about James. "He's the only man I love, the only man I'll ever love," she exclaimed, her eyes brimming with tears. "Neither David nor any other man can ever mean anything to me."

After this confession, her friends left Antonietta in peace. She spent two more nights with her new lover. At the end of the week, she told him that her boyfriend was coming for the weekend. He shrugged and wished her good luck. She never saw him again.

The weekend with David passed pleasantly enough, but after his departure Antonietta returned to her promiscuous ways. What she wanted was anonymous sex, and she managed to find a different man for almost every night of the week. She continued the week afterwards, albeit at a slightly lesser pace, and by the time David arrived on August 9 for the last weekend at the villa, Antonietta's surfeit of carnal pleasure meant that she had little enthusiasm for more sex with David. He noticed her apathy and tackled her. Never a very good liar, Antonietta was forced to confess her infidelities. David was very upset but too deeply in love with her to make the break. He pleaded with her not to cheat on him again. The sight of his distress moved Antonietta and she promised. After he left, she didn't accompany Paulian and Alessa to the discotheque for the final three nights of their stay on the Riviera.

———

James spent the last half of July preparing his reforms of the Institute. He intended to present them to the September 15 meeting of the Governing Council. His proposal for a finance committee involved each Section electing a representative, and the elections would be held on October 1. The Executive Committee, which did not need the approval of the Governing Council as it was purely advisory, would have its first meeting on Monday, September 19. James decided to advance the tenure procedure to the first semester. This way, a person denied tenure would have more chance of finding another job as most universities hired in the first few months of the year. Danny would take HB's place on tenure committees. James also hired an accounting firm to prepare the first monthly statement of the Institute's finances for the initial meeting of the new Finance Committee on October 8.

On Saturday, July 26, James left for Mazatlan with the children. He preferred Puerto Vallarta but there were too many memories of Carolina to pursue him. He regretted her decision, but he accepted that she was right.

The weather was very warm with some rain. The children enjoyed the break. James talked to them about their mother and how she must now be very happy in Heaven. This made an impression on Susanna, who seemed to come to terms at last with her mother's death. Peter was more taciturn, but he showed no signs of grief. He and James ventured once to swim in the sea, nearly drowned and stuck to the swimming pool after that. James had been quite scared, but Peter treated it more like an adventure.

James was content to spend this time with his children, in fact he owed it to them, but he was also frustrated. They were too young to be left alone in their room in the evenings, and so he was condemned to watch TV with them. This prevented him from approaching a pretty brunette who appeared to be on her own. She had long dark hair that reminded him of Antonietta. It was now over a year since she'd left him, and he was no nearer getting over her. He was still convincing himself that he hated her, but the façade was wearing thin.

They arrived back in Quebec on Saturday, August 9. The following week was very boring for James. He had to drive Peter to his soccer games and Susanna to her swimming classes. Danny and Bernadette came round on two evenings, but Piotr was away in Poland with his family and Bill and Petra were in Edmonton preparing their wedding. Life had never been so meaningless for James and he became very depressed. His spirits improved a little when it was time to put the children on a plane for England to stay with his parents. The next day, August 14, he was leaving for Edmonton with Danny, Bernadette and Piotr, who had just returned from Poland the evening before. Ella was staying behind to look after the girls.

James was unimpressed by Edmonton. It was a typical modern North American city, lots of concrete and little charm. He went for a walk with the others along the river bank, which was quite pleasant, and they had lunch in an English-style pub downtown. In the afternoon, Bernadette wanted to see West Edmonton Mall, reputed to be the largest shopping mall in North America, but James stayed back at the hotel. Bored, he watched a couple of films.

The wedding rehearsal was that evening. One of the bridesmaids was a school friend of Petra's, a pleasant looking brunette of no particular distinction.

The other was Petra's eighteen year-old sister, Mila. She was blond like her sister but had none of Petra's poise. From the way she looked at him, James suspected immediately what was afoot. She was pretty in a teenage way, but she inspired resignation more than desire in James. Here was another meaningless encounter, like Annya and, in a way, Carolina. He was relieved when the rehearsal ended and he could spend a boozy evening with his friends.

The next day was the wedding, and both Bill and James were in poor shape. "I can't get married like this," Bill groaned. James hauled him off for a brisk walk around a park that rejoiced in the rather ugly name of Hawrelak Park. As they walked, it began to snow. "Good God," James exclaimed. "It even snows in August in this Godforsaken hole." However, despite their ire at the Edmonton climate, the cold air did them good. By the time they were back at the hotel, they'd both recovered.

The wedding went off without a hitch. Petra was extremely beautiful and James had never seen Bill looking so elegant, decked out as he was in a rented tuxedo. After the ceremony in an Orthodox Church, which went on far too long in James' view, there was afternoon tea at the Hotel MacDonald, where everyone from Quebec was staying. Mila flirted with James, which made him feel awkward. She was, after all, Petra's sister and he wasn't at all sure she would approve of him bedding her.

The reception was held at the Faculty Club of the University of Alberta in a large dining room that overlooked the Saskatchewan River. In the distance was the Edmonton skyline. The snow had stopped and it was now a warm sunny evening. James danced with both bridesmaids, but gradually Mila came to monopolize him. Almost against his own volition, he found himself dancing very closely with her as the evening ended.

"Take me back to your hotel," she whispered once Petra and Bill had left.

Despite her tender years, Mila was an expert in the sexual arts. She reminded James of Annya with her complete lack of inhibition and dispassionate pursuit of pleasure. James found her somewhat over-demanding. He was still exhausted when he awoke to find her, fresh as a daisy, wandering around in the nude gathering up her clothes.

"Hi," she called over to him and began to dress. She went into the bathroom.

"Have you money for a taxi?" she asked upon re-appearing.

"There's my wallet in the jacket," James replied, taken aback by the young woman's cavalier attitude.

Mila took two $20 notes out of the wallet.

"This should do," she said, adding nonchalantly. "It was a great night. Thanks." With that she departed, leaving James completely flummoxed. He shook his head. "Today's youth," he muttered to himself.

Around midday, James, Danny, Bernadette and Piotr caught a plane for Montreal. Petra and Bill were off on their short honeymoon in Hawaii. "I want to go somewhere where they speak a normal language," Bill had told Petra when she suggested Costa Rica.

"How did you find Petra's sister?" Danny asked James. Her flirting had escaped no-one's notice. James was non-committal. For some reason he was ashamed to admit that he'd slept with her. In any case, he told himself, gentlemen don't tell. Danny didn't pursue the matter, but the sly grin on Bernadette's face told James that she'd guessed the truth.

———

Antonietta arrived back on Thursday, August 14 from the Versilia Riviera to a reserved welcome from David. He asked no questions but was clearly suspicious.

"I behaved myself," Antonietta assured him. "I never went to the discotheque again after you left on Monday."

David didn't appear convinced.

"You can ask Alessa and Paulina," Antonietta added crossly and then dropped the subject. If he didn't want to believe her, that was his problem.

Antonietta was glad to leave the apartment the next day to meet her family for Mass. It was the Feast of the Assumption. The greeting she received from her mother quickly changed her mind.

"I hope that boy didn't come to the villa," she said

Antonietta lied but her mother remained skeptical. Antonietta's father intervened. Aware of the torment that his daughter had been through, and perhaps was still going through, he came to her defense, rebuking his wife sharply.

"If Antonietta says he wasn't there, that's the end of the matter, Caterina."

Caterina said no more and they entered the Basilica. Lunch afterwards was quite enjoyable, despite a few digs at Antonietta from Renata. David wasn't mentioned again.

The relationship between David and Antonietta remained strained. Antonietta was outwardly contrite for her infidelities but inwardly defiant. She wasn't engaged to David and didn't owe him anything. If he were a better lover, perhaps she'd be more faithful. She regretted asking him to move in with her. While trying her best to convince him that it was not the end of their relationship, she persuaded him to return to his studio in Fiesole. It would be more convenient, she argued, as he needed to be near the library to finish his thesis. With great reluctance, David agreed.

She did feel guilt but it was towards James not David, and it was not because of Philippe or the men from the discotheque but because of the Marquesa and Irena. She comforted herself with the excuse that her lesbian diversions, like all her sexual flings, were just an attempt to escape from her obsessive longing for James. She came to repent of her sacrifice. How could she have believed that she could live without him? Why had she thought that his career was so important that it was worth sacrificing her love for it? What would it have mattered if he were disgraced and impoverished as long as they were together? It was worse now that she knew who he was. She contemplated the sterility and misery of her life and played with the idea of suicide. There was nothing to live for, but suicide was a mortal sin and she was afraid of the act.

August melted into September, and on the first day of that month David moved back to Fiesole. Absorbed by his thesis, he spent most of his time in the library. He and Antonietta saw each other much less, which suited Antonietta even though she feared solitude. Then, out of the blue, Philippe called her on Wednesday, September 24.

"Philippe!" she cried, overjoyed to hear his voice. "Where are you?"

"In Paris," he replied, "but I shall be in Florence tomorrow and I plan to stay until the following Monday. Can you get away?"

"Of course. I have a party with David on Thursday evening, but I'll tell him I have to go somewhere after that. I'll be free Friday and all weekend."

---

Antonietta spent a comforting weekend with Philippe. He satisfied her sexually while acting as the confidant of her love for James. He asked her whether she'd seen him.

"No," she replied, mystified by the question. "How could I have seen him?"

Philippe said nothing but just hoped that his friend André had done his bidding. Before leaving Antonietta on Monday morning, he made her sit down and listen to him.

"If you won't go back to James, then make something of your relationship with David or find someone else," he told her.

"Why?" Antonietta replied. "No man can mean anything to me but James. David's considerate and intelligent, but he's a lousy lover. I can't force myself to love him, or any man other than James."

Philippe sighed and left. He called André Pointet and was thankful to know that James would soon be coming to Florence.

———

At first all went well for James at the Institute. His proposed reforms were well received at the September 15 meeting of the Governing Council. The candidates announced themselves for the election to the Finance Committee. Saleema Nadjani and André Boisseu were unopposed in FEB and LIR, respectively. In LAC, James' friend Claudio Pettroni was opposed by the ubiquitous Wilkins, but James was not concerned. He was confident Claudio would be elected.

The first meeting of the Executive Committee took place on September 19. The initial discussions were collegial, but then Ilse Bromhoeffer came up with her perennial idea of replacing the nine-point grading system with A to D. Forget objected mildly to the idea but Berger raged against it, and the discussion degenerated into a slanging match.

"Whatever got into Berger?" James asked Danny after the meeting. "I've never seen him so worked up."

"I told you not appoint him," Danny reminded James. "You thought he was a nice guy. I've always thought him mealy-mouthed, and now he's got some authority, he'll throw it around and make your life difficult."

Following closely on this unfortunate meeting was the report from the accountants on the Institute's finances. It declared that the Institute was badly in need of funds, so James charged Danny with setting up a committee to direct a fund-raising drive. This provoked murmurs within the faculty, no doubt stirred up by HB and his cronies, that Danny was being given too much power. A consequence of this disaffection was the surprise election of Brian Wilkins as the LAC representative on the Finance Committee. James was dismayed. Running the Institute was not going to be as easy as he'd thought.

James' dismay was justified by Wilkins' performance at the first meeting of the Finance Committee. He tore into the financial report and practically accused James of conniving with the accountants to undervalue the Institute's assets. Unfortunately, the accountants had failed to include land owned by the

Institute in Montreal, where it was originally to have been located. James protested that he hadn't known about it, to which Wilkins replied, unkindly but perhaps with some justification, that his ignorance was no excuse. Luckily Saleema intervened and offered to prepare the next report. This offer seemed to placate Wilkins, who said no more. Relieved, James agreed.

It is said that bad luck comes in three's. This was certainly the case for James when he received Nathan Goldberg's file from Klaus Berger with a note that he was going to propose him for early tenure. James was flabbergasted. Goldberg had only been in the Institute for three years and published nothing of any note. He immediately went to see Berger, who remained adamant.

"He's got good references," he said curtly. "Check the file and you'll see."

James did just that and saw to his disgust that the referees were from NUC. Danny had been right. Berger was getting his own back for having been passed over as Section Head in favor of James by allying himself with HB. Proposing Goldberg for tenure was a clever ploy. The only hope was that the committee would vote against. The worst scenario was a split vote, which would leave James with the impossible choice of supporting Berger or defying convention and voting against a Section Head's proposal for tenure. In the first case, Berger would win an important victory, endearing him to Winstone's former supporters and perhaps reconciling them with HB, and the Institute would be saddled with a mediocrity; in the second, James would set the Winstone crowd against him. He was the loser whatever happened.

By Wednesday, October 25, Saleema had finished preparing the next month's financial report, and she and James arranged to meet at the Institute the following evening to go over it. She arrived, wearing as always the Islamic scarf that so irritated James. The report was quite complicated and James was no accountant. It was well past eleven when Saleema finished taking him through it. She looked at her watch and groaned.

"I've missed the last bus. I'll have to take a taxi."

"Nonsense," James told her. "I'll drive you home."

Saleema shook her head. "I'm not supposed to be alone in a car with a man."

James laughed. "Well, you will anyway if you take a taxi." As Saleema didn't react, he added with a smile. "At least you know you can trust me."

Saleema gave James a strange look. "Can I?"

There was something in the tone of her voice that puzzled James. "Of course," he replied, and they departed the building together.

Saleema lived in Ste. Adèle, quite near to James. He stopped the car, expecting her to rush off. Instead she hesitated and looked up at James, treating him to the full force of her dark eyes. They reminded him of Antonietta and, involuntarily, he bent to kiss Saleema but checked himself in time. He was shocked by his own behavior and half expected Saleema to slap his face. Her reaction was quite different and completely unexpected.

"You could always convert," she said, without looking away.

"Convert to what?"

"Islam."

James could hardly believe what he was hearing. Was this an oblique admission of an attraction, perhaps even something more? Not knowing how to react, he took refuge in facetiousness.

"I have enough problems with Christianity," he replied, "without taking on a religion that would deprive me of one of my few pleasures in life."

"Which is?"

"Drinking. To excess."

"That's a pity." Saleema got out of the car and whipped off the scarf covering her head, releasing her long dark hair. She was the nearest any woman could come to Antonietta's beauty and James stared at her, open-mouthed.

"Enjoy your whisky," she called out mockingly and walked towards her apartment building.

The next day, James recounted the scene to Bill. "I don't know what to make of it," he confessed.

Bill roared with laughter. "You really are naïve, Jimmy. It would seem to me quite obvious. You convert and you can have her. I've always said she had the hots for you."

James sighed. "I don't know what it is about me, but women either dump me, leave me because they love me too much or want me to convert to Islam."

"Perhaps you should stick to teenage girls," Bill suggested with a smirk. The illusion to Mila Markovic was obvious.

"Damn girl," James growled. "I told her not to tell anyone. What the hell does Petra think of it?"

"She was amused. Mila's a scalphunter, and she was hardly going to keep quiet about getting your's. It was quite a coup for her."

"My God," James groaned. "Once I was married with a mistress on the side, and now I'm just a scalp."

"Don't complain. She must have been a good lay. She's had enough practice according to Petra."

"Yes," James admitted with another sigh. "They're all good lays. But that's all. It's depressing."

Bill leaned forward to James. "Now, I don't want you shouting at me, but I'm going to tell you something. You'll never get over Antonietta, so you'd better go and find her and discover why she left and persuade her to come back. I've never believed she dumped you. She was head over heels in love. There *has* to be an explanation."

Bill paused, expecting a violent reaction from James, but none came. "I'm going to Florence late next month," James said quietly. "Perhaps I'll see her."

This was the nearest James had come to admitting to his friends that he was still in love with Antonietta.

———

Antonietta was pleased when the university term started on October 6. She still had some courses to take, and the work would occupy her mind. It also gave her an excuse to delay starting on her thesis. As yet she hadn't even submitted the topic to her supervisor. David was still working hard on his thesis and hoped to finish it by Christmas. Antonietta wondered whether he would then return to England. They hadn't talked about it.

The weeks passed. Sooner or later Antonietta knew that she would have to give David a definite answer to his proposal for marriage. As she was thinking about him, he called her on the cell phone. They agreed to meet at Fiasco's that Friday evening and Antonietta would spend the night in the studio. David was not in a particularly good mood when he joined her. He'd been planning a skiing weekend in November, but now he was saddled with babysitting some law professor who was coming to give a talk at the Institute.

"I though you were pleased to be elected Secretary of the Visiting Speakers Committee," Antonietta remarked dryly.

"Not when it interferes with my skiing."

They went to the studio and made love. David was unusually active, perhaps to soothe Antonietta's irritation with his inordinate love of skiing. He fell asleep afterwards and Antonietta, more assuaged than usual, did likewise, but not before wondering idly who that law professor was. After all, James was a law professor.

———

The election for the faculty member on Goldberg's tenure committee on November 3 was between Jason Levy and Ed Williams. James was due for another shock, for it was Williams who was elected. That evening he gave vent to his bitterness.

"I don't understand people," he grumbled to his friends. "They elected me in opposition to HB's and Winstone's crew, and now they're electing them back on to committees. I always thought academics were assholes, and now I know."

"It's irritating, I know," Danny said, trying to placate him. "They probably see it as a way of counter-balancing my and Bill's influence. They don't want to exchange one clique for another."

"Well, whom do you think I should appoint to the committee?" James asked. "I can't pick someone who's obviously on my side. Those idiots are likely to see it as the same trick Winstone pulled with Larry Flint on Bill's committee."

"I played tennis once this summer with François Vian," Piotr told them. "He's a nice guy and not connected to any of us."

Bill wanted to know whether he was trustworthy. He was skeptical about francophones.

"I think so," James interjected. "I never had any problem with him when I was Chair of LIR."

Vian was duly appointed and the committee met on Tuesday, November 18. James was confident it would vote against awarding Goldberg his tenure, but he was to suffer another disappointment. When the vote was taken, Forget unexpectedly voted for tenure, together with Berger and Williams, while Danny, Hamid and Vian voted against. It was the worst possible outcome. Reluctantly James used his casting vote in favor of tenure.

That evening Bill hosted a get-together. Still furious with what had transpired, James was soon well into his cups.

"Bloody people," he kept repeating. "Thank God I'm off to Florence tomorrow."

"Well, don't get too drunk," Bill told him. "You know Antonietta doesn't like you drinking too much."

Piotr and Danny cringed, fearing an explosion from James. Instead, he just smiled wistfully.

# CHAPTER 26
## Friday, November 21 to Saturday, November 22, 2003

Antonietta had spent Thursday night at David's studio. It was now the morning of Friday, November 21, a day that Antonietta would never forget. It had been a very late night, and they were sleeping in.

"Christ!" exclaimed David. "It's already eleven and I've got to meet that law professor at the Hotel Imperial at twelve."

He quickly shaved and washed, and dressed in a rush.

"I've got to drive him back to the hotel for seven," he told Antonietta. "Do you want to meet at Fiasco's later on?"

Antonietta shook her head. "After last night, I want to go to bed early. I'll come over tomorrow afternoon."

Disappointed, David said no more and left. Antonietta prepared herself leisurely and drove back to her apartment. She tried to do some reading for her courses but found it difficult to concentrate. She was beset by a terrible longing for James and, for once, permitted herself to daydream about meeting him again. It was on a beach in France.

———

James was waiting for David in the hotel lobby. He felt queasy about being in Florence. He couldn't stop himself wondering whether Antonietta was in the city, and what she was doing. He'd been tempted last night to look for her telephone number on the offchance that she was in Florence, but the memory of her letter stopped him. Whatever the others wanted to believe, she'd dumped him. So what was the point of seeking her out?

David arrived and drove them to the European University Institute. It was strange for James to be back after so many years. Nothing had changed much. They arrived at the building where lunch was to be served. James was greeted by André Pointet. It was an excellent meal accompanied by a vintage Amarone, but it didn't quieten James' nervousness. He half expected to see

Antonietta any second. It was most unsettling.

After lunch, David took James to the lecture theater where he was to give his talk. As they entered the building, James heard David swear.

"What's the matter?" he asked.

"I've forgotten my wallet," David replied. "I'll have to phone my girlfriend and get her to bring it to me."

As he had no change to make the call, James lent him his Visa. David went off and came back looking rather crestfallen.

"Problems?" James enquired.

"She wasn't very pleased. She has to go over to my place to pick it up. I thought she was still there."

"That's a woman for you," James commented, unaware of the profound irony of the situation.

———

Not suspecting that David's phone call was being made with James' Visa, Antonietta was not very pleased to be hauled out of her sweet daydreams. She agreed reluctantly to fetch David's wallet and bring it to him after the lecture. He told her to come around 4.30. This didn't leave much time, so she went immediately to the studio in Fiesole. She stopped off at her parents' house for a frosty expresso with her mother and arrived at the EUI promptly at 4.30.

Antonietta entered the lecture theater. The talk was already over and David was talking to a tall man who had his back to her. She gasped and felt her heart constrict. From the back the man looked exactly like James. She hesitated but David had already seen her and was waving her over. He said something to the man while pointing in her direction. The man turned round. It *was* James.

Antonietta felt dizzy and grasped at a table to steady herself. Engulfed by an indescribable emotion, she slowly walked, trembling, towards the man she loved with all her being. Mechanically she handed David his wallet, not daring to look at James. She was forced to when David introduced them.

"Hello," she stammered.

James merely nodded in reply, ignoring her outstretched hand. Antonietta was transfixed by the coldness of his manner and the disdain in his eyes.

David was quite ignorant of the drama being played out before him. Someone had nabbed him and he was deeply engaged in conversation with that person. James started to walk away. Antonietta stared at his disappearing back in panic. He couldn't go away like that, he couldn't! She strived for something to say that would retain him and uttered the first thing that came into her mind.

"How is your wife, Lord Markham?" she asked, immediately cursing herself for having said something so stupid. James wheeled round and fixed Antonietta with a look that made her wilt. "I cannot see how that's any business of your's, Miss della Chiesa," he replied and walked off. Antonietta was mortified. She felt faint with grief and collapsed into a chair to collect herself. Then she rushed off without a word to David.

She drove back to her apartment and threw herself on to the bed, convulsed by sobbing. She had a dreadful pain in her heart and her head felt as if it was going to explode. Her whole being revolted at the appalling idea that James hated her. This, added to the dreadful price she was already paying, was too much. She couldn't bear it. Once she was capable of thinking straight, she resolved to go and see James. She would explain why she'd left him. It was true that she'd sworn not to do so, but as long she didn't recommence her adulterous liaison, where was the harm? It was an unnecessary accretion to her other promises. By now, she hated Messina for the oath he'd made her swear.

Such at least was Antonietta's conscious intention. Yet, she took care to make herself up so as to bring out all her beauty, and she changed into the most erotic lingerie she possessed. She chose a tight-fitting sweater with a V-neck that displayed and accentuated her bosom, and a short skirt that showed off her long, graceful legs. She was a picture of irresistible lubricity, as she had to admit when she surveyed herself in the bathroom mirror. And all this just to stop James hating her? Antonietta discounted her ulterior motives and left the apartment. David was bringing James back to the hotel at seven, and she wanted to catch him before he went anywhere for the evening.

———

A deluge of emotions gripped James as he walked away from Antonietta. Meeting her with another man had stirred him to a raging jealousy. She was faithless, a whore, an unfeeling bitch. And that mocking comment about his wife. How he hated her!

Yet he couldn't stop himself looking back. He watched Antonietta leave the lecture theater with a sinking feeling in his stomach. He had the impression that his heart was leaping out of its enclosure. Seeing his former love in all her radiant beauty had brought back just how much she'd meant to him, and he wanted to run after her. Remembering the letter, he stopped himself. Antonietta's eyes may have shimmered with passion, but it was for that twit David Bannerman-Smith, not for him.

James attended the reception given in his honor after the talk. André Pointet was a gracious host, but James found it difficult to reciprocate. He was too immersed in his own dark thoughts and regrets. Strangely, Pointet didn't seem to mind. On the way back to the hotel with David, James was cold and distant. He barely thanked him when they parted. Once in his hotel room, he sat down in a daze on the bed, unable to sort out the conflict within himself between love and desire for Antonietta and despair and jealousy at her betrayal.

There was a knock on the door. Surprised at the intrusion, James went to open it. He stared in utter amazement at the sublime vision before him. It was Antonietta.

"James, I must speak to you."

Antonietta turned the full force of her pleading eyes upon James, who tried with all his strength to maintain his composure and resist an overwhelming desire to take her into his arms. He willed himself to remain cold and unyielding.

"I cannot see why," he replied.

He made to shut the door, to remove the temptation of those exquisite eyes. Never had Antonietta appeared so lovely, so desirable.

"James," Antonietta implored, preventing him from closing the door in her face. "You loved me once. For the sake of that love, please listen to me. *Please.*"

James could feel his resistance crumble and he sought frantically for words that would drive this faithless beauty away.

"So, when I was a disgraced academic, you dumped me," he said, simulating a contempt he was no longer capable of feeling. "Now you've found out that I'm a wealthy lord, you're trying to creep back."

He expected Antonietta to be indignant, to march off, but instead she gave him a pallid smile.

"So, if I can prove to you that I'm not after your title or your money, you'll listen to me?"

"I don't see how you can," James replied but, as he said the words, he knew how much he wished she could.

"I know who you are because my uncle told me." Instinctively Antonietta drew herself up and her voice acquired a slightly imperious tone.

"Your uncle?" James looked at Antonietta, quite baffled. "What's your uncle got to do with me?"

"He's your father's closest friend." Antonietta paused, enjoying the sight of James staring at her openmouthed. "My uncle is Cardinal Palmieri. His sister is my mother."

By now James was shaking his head in disbelief. Antonietta smiled at his discomfort and delivered the *coup de grace*.

"I should perhaps have introduced myself before," she said with deliberate nonchalance. "I am the Countess Antonietta della Chiesa. Like you, I come from a family that owns a bank. It's the *Banco Regionale*. Perhaps you've heard of it?"

James slumped down into a chair, incapable of saying anything. He put his head in his hands, assailed by a deluge of emotions: shame at the arrogant assumption of his own superiority, incredulity and amazement that Antonietta was an aristocrat and the niece of his father's closest friend and, above all, relief that her reappearance was not due to opportunism. She was his equal both in birth and wealth. But there was still the letter, the fact that she had left him. Confused, beset by a dreadful longing for her, he looked up with tears in his eyes, and at that moment Antonietta realized what deep down she'd known from the start. She hadn't come here just to stop James hating her. She'd come to reclaim her love and her happiness, and she would do so, despite Messina, despite her religion, despite her family.

"Have you never wondered why you were not dismissed from the Institute?" she asked, kneeling down in front of James.

"Evidently the Italian Ambassador told Winstone that the European collection would only stay at the Institute as long as I was there. He wanted it so badly that he decided to hush up the whole business." There was bitterness in these last words.

"Do you know why the Italian Ambassador told Winstone that? After all, it was a very undiplomatic interference in the Institute's affairs;"

"No, I don't."

Antonietta took James' hands and gazed into his eyes. "I couldn't bear the thought of you being disgraced and humiliated," she told him, her voice breaking with emotion. "So I went to Messina and asked him to save you by threatening to remove the collection if you were no longer a member of the

Institute. I knew Winstone would do anything to keep it."

"Why would Messina agree to that?" James asked dubiously. "Just because you're an Italian countess?"

"No, my darling." Antonietta kissed James' hand, and involuntarily he stroked her hair with the other. "He agreed because he's my godfather."

"Mother of God!" James stared at Antonietta, the remnants of his manufactured rage and contempt swept away. He let himself be inundated by the passion he'd tried in vain to deny and destroy during the last endless, horrific months.

"And the price?" he asked, placing his hand under Antonietta's chin.

Her eyes filled with tears and the emotion stifled her words. James answered for her. "You had to give me up. Was that the price?"

Antonietta nodded, the tears now flowing copiously down her cheeks. "It was a terrible, terrible price. Messina made me swear an oath on the Holy Scriptures, and ever since my life has been a constant torment. At times the pain of losing you was so great that I felt I was going to die." Antonietta let James wipe away her tears, and her eyes suddenly burned with fury. "I renounce that inhuman oath," she cried. "I love you and I cannot and I *will not* live without you."

"I have been a blind fool." As he spoke, James' voice was at times submerged by the intensity of his feelings. "All the others told me that you'd left for a reason, they even suspected your departure was connected with my reprieve. I refused to believe them. It would have meant that you *had* loved me, and I couldn't live with that. The only way I could survive your departure was to tell myself that you'd played me for a fool. My anger was the only rampart against the insanity of living without you."

He took hold of Antonietta's hands. "Forgive me."

"There's nothing to forgive, my darling." Now it was Antonietta's turn to wipe away James' tears. "After that horrible letter I forced myself to write, it was easy to fool yourself." Antonietta smiled at James. "To be honest, I'm happy you reacted like that. It tells me how much you love me."

James drew Antonietta's face towards him. "I do love you. I have never stopped loving you. I had to manufacture my anger anew every day. It was like a clown putting on his make-up in order to perform."

Antonietta' eyes glowed with happiness. She bent forward to kiss James but drew back.

"On second thoughts, James, I will only forgive you if you make me two promisess."

"Anything, my love."

"First, you must promise that we will never be separated again, not for a day, not for a night."

"Of course." James drew Antonietta's pursed lips towards him and kissed them. "And the second promise?"

"That tonight you'll make up for all the nights I spent without you."

"Only if you promise the same."

Antonietta smiled seductively and their mouths moved together. In a frenzy of passion, they drank each other's kisses. Antonietta stood up, her lips swollen, and led James towards the bed. She made him sit down while, slowly, she undressed before him. She paused before stripping completely to tantalize him with her sensual lingerie. She succeeded and by the time she was naked, James was unable to control himself any more. He pulled her down on the bed and devoured her breasts and proceeded with his lips down the smooth flesh to her sex. He slipped off her string and began to excite her with his tongue and fingers. Antonietta groaned and her body twisted in ecstasy from side to side. Before she began to rise to her climax, she pulled James up towards her, rolled him over on his back and took off his remaining clothes. She ran her breasts down his body and rubbed her nipples along his shaft. She took it into her mouth. Soon, neither could contain themselves any longer. Antonietta lay down on her back and James penetrated her. She dug her nails deep into his back, feeling his warmth within her as she reached orgasm.

When it was over, Antonietta still clung to James. Her eyes were filled with tears.

"What's the matter?"

"Tell me it's over," she begged. "Tell me the nightmare is over."

"Yes, Antonietta, it's over. This is not a dream. I have another wound to prove it."

Antonietta kissed the deep scratch she'd given James and, placing her arms around his chest, held him closely to her so that he could feel the soft flesh of her breasts pressed against his back.

"I've learned a dreadful lesson," she murmured in his ear. "I thought I could live without you. Now I know all that matters to me is my love for you. I *will* marry you, oath or no oath, and no matter what my religion or my family says."

The last words were said with vehemence.

James turned round and smiled at Antonietta. "My darling, you don't have to renounce your oath to Messina or your religion or your family." He paused to enjoy the perplexed look on Antonietta's face. Now it was his turn to surprise her. "Veronica died in June from septicemia. I am now a widower."

Antonietta was aghast. "That's awful, James. The poor woman. Whatever happened?"

James explained how Veronica had cut herself badly on the arm and had refused to seek medical care until it was too late. He didn't mention that the offending fragment of glass was probably from the wineglass Antonietta had once dropped on the kitchen floor.

"Why didn't you insist on her seeing a doctor?" Antonietta asked. However much she may have wanted Veronica to disappear from James' life, the idea that James might in a way be responsible for his wife's death disturbed her.

"I wasn't living with her at the time," James replied, aware that he was opening a can of worms.

"Why?" Antonietta's voice was redolent with suspicion and jealousy.

James drew a breath. He explained as briefly as possible how he'd spent some time with Carolina in Montevideo and Veronica had found out. As a result they had separated.

"You mean she found out that you were having an affair with Carolina?" Antonietta's eyes were blazing. "When was this?"

"Early December."

"Were you in love with her?"

James tried to take Antonietta into his arms. After a struggle he succeeded.

"We've both had other people, Antonietta. You can't hold Carolina against me. I love you, I've never stopped loving you and I've never been in love with anyone else."

He stared into Antonietta's eyes where passion mixed with resentment. "Were you in love with David?"

Antonietta shook her head. "Who were those 'other people'?" she asked, furrowing her brow.

"Carolina and a few whores in Montreal."

"No-one else?"

There was little point in lying as his guilty expression had already betrayed him. "Annya," he admitted, "but only for a brief period."

Antonietta erupted. "I *knew* it. I knew she'd get you. I'll never forgive you. Now I'm glad I gave myself to the Marquesa."

Antonietta immediately regretted what she'd said. She turned away, fearful of James' reaction. He turned her face back towards him. "Did she commit suicide because of you?"

"Perhaps," Antonietta admitted. "But I was not her mistress, James. I swear it. It only happened twice. Please forgive me," she pleaded.

James was silent as he fought to master his jealousy. "Of course I forgive you," he said at last, much to Antonietta's relief, "as long as you promise to behave from now on and to tell me the truth about the others."

"I promise, I promise, I promise," Antonietta cried, pushing James down on the bed and smothering him with kisses. She recounted her relationship with David, her flings on the Versilia Riviera and her affair with Philippe de Pothiers. James questioned her closely about Philippe.

"I'm very jealous of him. He seems to have meant something to you."

Antonietta drew back and surveyed James with a contented air. "I'm glad you're jealous, but there's no cause. Philippe was a friend; you are the love of my life."

"Anyone else?" James asked, only partly reassured about Philippe de Pothiers.

Antonietta shook her head. She was too ashamed to admit her sexual encounter with Irena. James suspected she was concealing something but let it go. He wasn't particularly keen on owning up to his night with Mila, particularly as it was possible that Antonietta might meet her.

Suddenly Antonietta propped herself up. James grinned. It had been a long time since he'd been faced by an inquisitorial Antonietta.

"When are we getting married?" she demanded to know.

"How long does it take to get married in Italy?' he asked.

"Ages."

"Well, perhaps your uncle can help. What's the good of being an archbishop if you can't cut a few corners?"

They agreed that they would ask Uncle Giovanni, as Antonietta called the Cardinal much to James' amusement, to marry them next Saturday. After that they'd leave for Canada. If he couldn't, they'd leave straightaway and get married in a civil ceremony in Quebec. A religious ceremony in Italy would have to wait until later. Once that was decided, Antonietta came on top of

James and pressed her breasts against his chest.

"Make love to me again, James. Make love to me without any decency, any modesty."

James obliged. Once Antonietta's screams had died down, he turned her over on to her back instead of taking her anally. Watching her naked body squirm under his touch, he continued to draw moans of pleasure from her. When she was finished, he moved up her moist body and feasted on the dazzling beauty of her face. Antonietta pulled herself up and kissed James passionately. She pushed him down and came on top of him so he could enjoy her splendid buttocks while she fellated him. Afterwards Antonietta lay in James' arms, her face glowing with gratification.

"When I see you like this," James told her, "it's inconceivable to me that I was ever able to live without you."

"I didn't live," Antonietta replied, burying her face in his neck. "I just existed."

"Even with the Marquesa?" James couldn't resist the question. Antonietta looked at him in surprise. "Why are you so jealous of her?" she asked. "After all, you had Carolina and Annya."

"It's not the same," James replied. "They could never give me anything you can't give me, and more. But I can't give you all the pleasures of the Marquesa. I'm not a woman."

"That would be true of most men, but not you. You satisfy all my sexual needs." Antonietta looked up at James. "After I left you, I suffered unbearable pain. I would have slept with the Devil to have a few moments of respite. That's why I went with the Marquesa. I was frustrated and I was desperately unhappy. The Marquesa took advantage of that. But I didn't have an affair with her, like you did with Carolina."

Antonietta's dark expressive eyes suddenly became moist with tears. "I'm sure you thought of marrying her."

"I admit the idea crossed my mind, but I never asked her and I don't think I ever would have," James replied, aware that he was not telling the whole truth. It was not a good enough answer to ward off Antonietta's attack.

"I hate you, I hate you," she cried, setting about him with a pillow. "If the Marquesa were still alive, I'd cheat on you with her."

James finally managed to raise himself up and seize hold of Antonietta's flailing arms. Tears were streaming down her face. "Listen to me, Antonietta."

He held her down as he spoke . "Were it not for Carolina and that travesty of you I concocted in my own mind, I couldn't have survived your departure. I never would have believed until then that it was possible to suffer such mental agony."

"Tell me you forgive me for the Marquesa."

James nodded. "But I'm jealous of anyone who's held you, enjoyed your body, given you pleasure," he told her. "So jealous, it makes me sick to my stomach."

Antonietta put her hands around James face, drew him to her and kissed him. "So now you know how I feel about Carolina and Annya. But you have no need to be jealous. I want no-one but you and I never have. Tell me it's the same for you."

Antonietta's eyes implored James. "You know it is," he replied.

They made love again with unquenchable ardor amidst protestations of love, storms of jealousy, bitter reminiscences of their separation until dawn began to break. It heralded the beginning of their life together and the fulfillment of that profane oath sworn years ago in the Augustinerkeller by two frivolous students. Such is the force of destiny.

# EPILOGUE
## July 2009

Carolina was bored. She'd known from the beginning what was expected of her during this cruise with Giorgio, but a constant diet of sex and sunbathing was proving very tedious. She stood up from the deck of the yacht and draped a silk dress over her skimpy bikini.

They were anchored very close to the shore of Nice, and Carolina could see the people walking along the *Promenade des Anglais*. Idly, she picked up the binoculars and scrutinized the strolling mass. Suddenly, her body stiffened. It *couldn't be*. She went to the telescope at the front of the yacht and trained it on the man she'd seen. He was with two adolescents and they were looking towards a beautiful dark-haired women who was coming up to them with two small children hanging on to each hand. The older children took care of what were presumably their younger siblings and, oblivious of all the people around them, the man and woman embraced each other. Carolina grasped the ramp of the yacht. If I hadn't written that stupid letter, that could be me, she thought bitterly.

"Carolina!" It was Giorgio. Carolina turned to look at him. He was handsome, virile—and rich. What else could a girl want, she told herself, chasing away her regrets. One day she would find out.

# ENDNOTES

[1] *Calcio* is the familiar Italian word for soccer, but Antonietta is referring to a peculiar Florentine version of the game, which mixes soccer and rugby and is played by four teams dressed in medieval costumes from the oldest sections of Florence: Santa Croce, Santa Maria Novella, Santo Spirito and San Giovanni. The final game of the tournament takes place on June 24.

[2] The *Academia dell Crusca* (literally, the Academy of the Bran), is a literary academy that was founded in 1582 for the purpose of purifying the Italian language in its Tuscan form

[3] In England, only the holder of the title and his wife (not the other way round) are considered nobility. In continental Europe all the family of a noble are covered by the patent of nobility. Hence Antonietta has the right to the title of countess.

[4] The system at NIIS is similar to that in most North American universities. A beginning academic is appointed as an Assistant Professor. An Assistant Professor must apply for tenure within five years, which is granted if the person shows genuine research potential and he or she then becomes an Associate Professor. Otherwise, they must leave the institution. Some time thereafter, normally a minimum of five years, an Associate Professor may apply to become a Full Professor. This is referred to as "promotion" and is only granted to someone who has, at the very least, a national academic reputation.

[5]

[6] The English nobility is made up of barons, viscounts, earls, marquises and dukes. Their female equivalents are baronesses, viscountesses, countesses, marchionesses and duchesses. All except dukes and duchesses are normally referred as just Lord or Lady So and So.

[7] As the younger son of a marquis, James is entitled to call himself Lord Markham.

[8] In Europe, the second floor is what North Americans would call the third floor.

319

[9] This prayer was conceived by St. Bernard. The words are: "Remember, O most loving Virgin Mary, that it is a thing unheard of that anyone ever had recourse to thy protection, implored thy help and sought thy intercession and was left forsaken. Filled, therefore, with confidence in thy goodness, I fly to thee, O Mother, Virgin of virgins; to thee I come, before thee I stand a sorrowful sinner. Despise not my words, O Mother of the Word, but graciously hear and grant my prayer."

[10] Like many other languages, but unlike English, French has a familiar "you" (*tu*) and a formal you (*vous*). In Belgium and Canada, the *tu* form is used extensively, but in France it is reserved for young people and close friends.

[11] The Carmenere grape variety was once very popular in Bordeaux but was wiped out during the phylloxera plague in 1867. Fortunately, it had been imported into Chile in 1850 and has survived. It is similar to Merlot but richer and sturdier.

[12] In Argentina and some other countries in South America, Spanish is referred to as Castilian (*castellano* in Spanish).

[13] Carolina, which is the girl's name, is telling the truth. The British invaded what is now Argentina twice in 1806 and 1807. They were beaten back on both occasions.

[14] La Barra is a trendy café just off the Plaza San Martín, where James' hotel is located.

[15] Giacomo Leopardi (1798-1837) is one of the greatest lyric poets in Italian literature. His collection of poems, *I Conti*, are full of introspection and longing.

[16] There are many versions of the tale of Tristan and Isolde. Perhaps the most well-known is that told in Wagner's eponymous opera. Attempting to poison Tristan for killing her fiancé and then to kill herself, Isolde is fooled by her maid into offering him instead a love potion from which she also drinks. The overwhelming passion for each other that ensues leads the pair to become lovers despite Isolde's marriage to Tristan's uncle, King Mark. Banished and wounded, Tristan dies just as Isolde arrives to heal him and she herself dies from her passion after singing one of Wagner's greatest arias, *Isoldes Liebestod.*

[17] A whore's sauce. The name comes from the fact that this is supposed to be the favorite dish of Rome's ladies of the night.

[18] Laura Pausini is not well known in North America, but she is the most popular Latin singer in Europe and Latin America. She sings mainly in Italian but also

in Spanish and Portuguese and, occasionally, in French and English.
[19] When you are absent
[20] *Il Piacere* ("Pleasure") is a novel by Gabriele d'Annunzio (1863-1938) that tells of a passionate love affair between Count Andrea Sperelli-Fieschi d'Ugenta and Elena Muti, the Duchess of Scerni. When the Duchess suddenly and without explanation deserts Sperelli, he reacts with self-destructive bitterness and vilifies his former mistress in his own mind by perverting his recollections of their affair.
[21] The official name of the airport in Montreal is Pierre Trudeau International Airport, but its former name is still more commonly used
[22] A looney is a one-dollar Canadian coin.
[23] As if we had never been lovers.
[24] A courtesy title is one that has no legal validity. They are bestowed as a matter of courtesy on the children of British nobles.
[25] This is the best-known of the bars at the European University Institute.
[26] *Instituto Técnologico Autónomo de México.* It is perhaps the most distinguished business school in Mexico.
[27] A Benedictine oblate does not take any vows or enter a convent. Instead she is associated with a Benedictine convent and promises to lead an enriched Christian life according to the gospel as reflected in the rule of St. Benedict (450-547). To become an oblate, a time of preparation is necessary. This starts with a solemn enrolment as an oblate novice of St. Benedict. The novice is presented with a medal of St. Benedict and a copy of his Rule. A year later she makes the Final Oblation and becomes an oblate of St. Benedict for life. She offers herself to God through:
 —regular worship;
 —support for her local parish
 —the practice of moderation in the use of the goods of this world
 —the perception of sin and any attachment to it as wrong;
 —seeing no other reason for living except to love and be loved by God;
 —working to promote family living.
[28] King Henry II of England did public penance for the murder of Thomas Becket. This included being whipped on his bare back by monks.
[29] French motorways are expensive, but there are studded with pleasant stopovers, replete with restaurants that even serve wine! These are called *aires.*